DESTINY ARISING

Jan Foster

SO SIMPLE PUBLISHED MEDIA

OTHER BOOKS BY THE AUTHOR

The Naturae Series by Jan Foster

Risking Destiny

Discover a villain's creation in this Viking Age tragic romance Prequel.

www.books2read.com/riskingdestiny

Destiny Awaiting

The enemies to lovers Prequel. Escape to Agincourt, wherein averting a war between their races and their countries, Aioffe and Tarl's battles of the heart are destined to fight with faith and hope itself.

www.books2read.com/destinyawaiting

Disrupting Destiny

Book 1 –Tudor reformation tears a country and fae lovers apart. Can a secret destiny bring them together?

www.books2read.com/disruptingdestiny

Anarchic Destiny

Book 2 – A forgotten heir, a queendom in crisis... chaos will reign as Bloody Mary makes her move for power.

www.books2read.com/anarchicdestiny

Destiny Arising

Book 3 – Five crowns will fall in a deadly prediction. Can Aioffe catch the killer of queens before she's next to die?

www.books2read.com/destinyarising

<u>Fables from Naturae</u>

Historical Fantasy short stories featuring characters you love from the Naturae Series in pacy adventures in a magical past.

Myth, Mist and Madness

www.books2read.com/mythmistmadness

Blind Bill

www.books2read.com/blindbill

A Rose in Midwinter

www.books2read.com/arim

As Above, So Below

www.books2read.com/asabove

<u>Rebels and Resistance Series by J.H. Foster</u>

Gripping WW2 historical suspense novels – parallel stories to share

<u>**The Rebellious Maus and the Pogrom**</u> – A YA Prequel Novella to Sewing Resistance set in 1930's Germany

A young Hannah and Kat decide to ignore their guardian's advice and go shopping. Can they escape danger when a Pogrom leads to a riot and will Hannah risk everything to impress a handsome saviour?

BUY NOW www.books2read.com/rmatp

or **READ FOR FREE by subscribing to my mailing list with a historical focus – www.escapeintoatale.com/rebels**

<u>**Sewing Resistance**</u> – Seamstress. Spy. Survivor?

As Nazi forces tighten their grip on Paris, two women are drawn into the heart of the Resistance. Bound by friendship, a silent son, and driven by survival, they risk everything in a dangerous fight for freedom. *Sewing Resistance* is an unforgettable tale of love, loyalty, and courage under fire.

BUY NOW www.books2read.com/sewingresistance

<u>**Boy, Resisting**</u> – Silenced. Steadfast. Saviour?

A middle-grade, illustrated novel **co-authored with James Warwood**

Silence was supposed to keep me — and my secrets — safe. So I accidentally became a spy...

BUY NOW www.books2read.com/boyresisting

Find out more about works authored by Jan Foster/J.H. Foster at **ww w.escapeintoatale.com/books**

Join the Escape Into A Tale Newsletter and receive a free gift of a book and much more!

www.escapeintoatale.com/subscribe

CONTENT WARNING:

Some scenes in this book, while historically accurate, may be distressing to some readers. For more information, please visit

www.escapeintoatale.com/books/triggers

Published by So Simple Published Media

First edition April 2024

Cover Design – getcovers.com

Paperback ISBN – 978-1-917062-00-8

E-Book ISBN – 978-1-917062-01-5

Hardback ISBN - 978-1-917062-06-0

www.escapeintoatale.com

CHAPTER 1

STARS FROM BEHIND BARS

May 1556, Yorkshire Moors

Crowns would fall, many of them. Women's thrones - vacant for the taking. The future Nemis fore-saw in her visions was not safe for Queens. Locked away, jolted from side to side in a closed cart trundling across the moorland, there was nothing a mere witch like she could do to save them. A captive with no-one she could trust to tell or warn of what could happen. Few humans would believe her anyway, for although everyone knew magic and witchcraft existed, those who could truly control it were often shunned or forced into hiding, lest their true nature frighten. Creaturekind - witches, vampires, fae and daemon - were bound by a Treaty to avoid exposure or interference in human affairs. It did not specify protecting them, but surely it should?

Nemis shivered, despite the warmth of the orange sunset sky glimpsed through the tiny window bars. A debilitating chill, heralding another bout of visions, threatened to overtake her, to drown her in darkness and confusion. The visions began at the same time as strange starlights in the night, two days ago, while she'd been imprisoned in Beesworth gaol. It had to be the star's fault, Nemis reasoned as her teeth chattered in her jaw, for nothing else unusual had happened during her months of captivity.

When the display was first sighted, the other prisoners had clanged on their doors to be freed, crying with fear at the awesome sight glimpsed through their tiny windows, while she had jittered, fitted and screamed until dawn. The following morning, Nemis - accused of murder by witchcraft - and Sarah Fell, a drunken, unrepentant thief and doxy, had been bundled into the mobile prison without explanation or warning. There had been no time to tell her son or his guardian of her movement to York, or of the Queens' deaths she predicted. Telling almost anyone about the peculiarities of being a se'er witch wouldn't help free her anyway.

Nemis huddled into herself on the rough wooden seat, knocking knees to shaking jaw. Foetid straw scattered over the filthy wood floor, so damp it barely rolled when the cart lumbered over a dip in the track. Her shivering caused the links in her chains to quiver and chink together. The fruity, hay-like smell of droppings caught in her throat as the carthorse dragged its load towards York. In the darkening enclosure, her senses heightened, a sure sign of change within her about to strike.

Her skin crawled, no matter how much she scratched. Wrapped around her head, her scabby arms were streaked with the blood her nails had drawn, disguising the crawlie bites which marred her entire body, testament to months of captivity. Before long, the writhing would start, like a snake twisting inside her belly which she could not scratch out. Her wounds would re-open.

Sarah Fell snored opposite; her duckies heaved plump over a too tight corset and quivered with each snort. Her sound slumber was no surprise as Nemis had kept her awake with shrieks and cries both nights since the stars first displayed their glittering streaks. Poor Sarah had told her as much, in no uncertain terms, and complained nobody wanted to hear her unholy screams. That it wasn't natural - her eyes rolling back, body quaking, barely breathing. 'Near fit to die', as Sarah put it, before spitting at her. They had spoken little on the journey since, as the woman was too frightened of Nemis's strangeness.

Across the moor, evening squawks of pheasants called and the occasional owl hooted. As darkness deepened, Nemis stared through the bars of the narrow aperture at the back of the closed cart. When the starlight streaked across the sky, no doubt her torture would begin once more. Dread tightened her chest as she tried not to think about crowns falling off at the moment of their bearers' last breath. The impressions are more than her usual, dispassionately observed images which flicked before her eyes. In these new visions, Nemis experiences the agony as if her own. Over and over, she has died in her dream-like state, and fears each time she will never awaken again.

The first is a watery demise - buffeted in the tide, the water flashing pink and frothy but the pain stabs her chest. She splutters, arms flailing, her fingers reaching for something but she knows not what. Her ribcage hurts, the pain binding her as tightly as the cold prison of the waves. A crown drifts away from her as she sinks.

The next is in darkness, pungent with spice. All she can hear are the whispers between wails. She catches a glimpse of a crown, tumbling from her fingers.

For the third, her body convulses, agony streaking through her being. She screams, her voice echoing, over and over. Just out of reach, the same crown, but she is exhausted by the effort of straining for it.

The next is the strangest, for she looks down at her own body and it is bathed in red light. The hunger she feels gnaws through her bones and she wrestles, fighting the arms which hold her down.

Then, somehow, she is the same person but distracted by the flash of blades, arcing through the air, over and over like a silver blizzard.

But the worst is yet to follow. The one which leaves Nemis shredded on the floor and unable to move. It is the absence of anything other than her insides being wrenched from her very skin. Her soul peeling away in agonising strips until she is nothing but a husk. Her head drops, and the weight of her crown tumbles off.

Each time, in the hazy, twilight moments as she rouses, Nemis knows without any doubt, what she sees - experiences - in the shadows is the death of Queens. Their treasured crowns will fall, doubtless leaving chaos in their wake. She cannot forget the sensations of vision, yet cannot recall the detail. Fear of recurrence has plagued her waking hours, and the closed cart with all its smells, darkness and jolts doesn't assuage her terror.

The last light of the sunset disappeared and the chill clamped in the pit of her stomach. She clutched the rough wooden seat, drawing her hands up and down its length, ignoring the splinters which caught in her fingertips.

Please, not again, she prayed.

The cart slowed to a stop and, for a moment, she could breathe easier. Wood smoke, and the welcome smell of food. Pottage maybe, or the remnants of a roast, lingered in the air. Had they arrived in York yet?

Perhaps tonight would be different, if she could only be outside again. Maybe under the moonlight the prickling to her skin would cease.

She nudged Sarah with her foot to wake her. As the old woman stirred, Nemis's shaking intensified. She fought to remain conscious, to listen to the muttered negotiations between the cart driver, the accompanying official, Alf Cooper, Assistant Sheriff, and another man with a different accent.

"She'll stay put. T'other one won't be a bother if we keep her fettered," Alf said.

"Tha's welcome, then. I've a room out back 'fer the thief, a small one mind, wi' a lock on't door. The witch'll have to stay in the cart. And there's a chamber 'fer you pair and the best stew this side of Rosedale." He chuckled. "If tha'd been here twenty years earlier, I'd have sent yer witch to the old Abbey 'fer the nuns ter pray over."

A grimace flashed over Sarah's face as she glanced through the tiny window. Then she sneered. "Pretty, pretty. Here's my pretty."

Nemis's arms, heavy with shackles, slid down from her knees and the chain dropped to the floor with a thud. Another night locked in this stinking cart. She didn't dare look at the sky - what was the point? She knew the starlights were there again because the sensations in her body told her so.

A key rattled in the lock, then the wooden door swung open. "Mistress Fell, you're to come with me," ordered Mr Cooper.

Sarah shuffled forwards, her tattered skirt catching on the rough planks as she pushed herself out. "She made me," she muttered, as her hand inched her skirts higher. Then she cackled, "Would yer like to sample me secrets? A warm meal and a drink is all I ask."

As she spread her bare legs, Mr Cooper responded with, "Foul doxy," and slapped her thighs.

Sarah screeched. "Fie upon thee!"

Nemis's head lolled against the cart's wall. The small space seemed to widen, as if the presence of another person had held the darkness in check. She squinted at the doorway, the change in light hurting her eyes.

Behind the Assistant Sheriff, the innkeeper held his hand over his brow as he peered inside. His nose wrinkled. "She looks like a witch an' all." He sniffed. "Bit young, like. Still, I'll not 'ave 'er causing upset in my place."

Alf nodded. "Understandable."

The door slammed shut. As the lock clicked, Nemis collapsed.

CHAPTER 2

ILL PORTENDS

May 1556, Hanley House, Beesworth

The child's face flushed as he stirred and glanced up. "Look, it's there again," he squealed, and pointed at the yellow streak cleaving the dark sky. Mark tugged on his guardian's sleeve to wake her. "See? I told you there was a pecul'r star last night and the night before. It's come back, and everyone in Beesworth will be afeared again." He thrust his best stone into the inky night. The iron pyrite glittered under the light of the fiery ball, half the size of the moon, as it burned a gash across the blackness. Tiny orange-white sparks sparkled in its celestial tail. "'Tis like a star has fallen from the heavens. Or an angel."

"Maybe it is both. Maybe neither," Lady Hanley said and rolled her shoulders back to release her stiffness. "Either way, there's no need to be frightened. I've seen many starlights over the centuries, and nothing has come of it, no matter what the scriptures and doom-mongers say such heavenly things portend. Although," she sniffed, "I doubt it will stop them trying. Queen Mary'll no doubt use it as further justification for her actions against the heretics."

Mark blinked, such concerns beyond his comprehension. His shoulders rose, then dropped. "Tis pretty. A fire show in the sky."

Her thin lips stretched into an indulgent smile. There was a joy to be found in a child's wonder she now understood, and at her age and situation, it was rare to find joy in much.

She took the young daemon's hand and pulled him onto her lap. Her wing bumps twitched, still sensitive even though the appendages had been docked many decades ago. Her eyes narrowed as her sharp fae night-sight caught movement in the sky below the streak. Her eyebrows tensed together, wrinkling her paper-thin skin. "But, perhaps tonight is different." She pointed. "Look to the trees yonder."

He slid down from her warm skirts and peered into the darkness. Seeing nothing remiss, he scanned down the steep slope and down the path which wound around the hillock. "What am I looking for? A wolf? A badger?"

"In the sky?" She shook her head and laughed softly. At nearly ten years of age, Mark was still naïve, despite having a foot in both human and creature worlds. "Have you ever seen a wolf fly before? Foolish imp."

As she looked over the Northumbrian fields spread beneath them, a shiver ran through her. "Mark, fetch Uffer out of bed. Quickly now."

He frowned up at her. "But he'll be grumpy."

"Rouse him, boy, and bring blankets as well." Her petticoats rustled as she stood, knocking the stool over. "Make haste!"

Mark pinched his lips. "But..." He stared at her for a moment, then thought the better of answering back. After a glance at the skies, he stuffed his stone in a pocket, then darted around the corner of Hanley House, to the back door.

Lady Hanley gripped her embroidered bodice, wizened knuckles whitening as she gazed into the night. "Perhaps I'm too quick to make judgement," she whispered to herself.

A shimmer, tempered orange by the falling star's light, approached. She recognised the outline of Joshua's enormous wings, black translucent panes flashing as they fluttered closer. In his grasp, a bundle of legs and arms laboured his flight and he appeared unsteady as a dragonfly might, pummelled by unseen winds as he traversed uneven land below.

Distinctive rainbow-like wings, which she had not laid eyes upon for over a century, flapped steadily beside him. She gasped. "Princess Aioffe!" She shook her head as if muddled. "Queen Aioffe, now of course." Her chin towards the heavens as she brought her hands together. "Praise the Lord, for they have returned."

Joshua stumbled as he landed some feet away, at the corner of the house. "Mary," he panted, long legs wobbling as they found solid ground. "Where's Nemis?"

But Lady Hanley had dropped to a deep curtsey, head bowed.

Aioffe alighted serenely beside Joshua. Her arm shot out to help steady her husband, her attention immediately on the body he carried. "Is Spenser still with us?" She frowned.

"He's alive," Joshua mumbled. "I hear his heartbeat."

She cupped the base of the bundle strapped to her chest. "We made it."

Long blonde hair rose wild about her heart-shaped face, her azure blue eyes widened as she glanced up at the three-storey manor house jutting into the sky. Her hand rose to her head, fingers reaching to adjust a crown which was no longer there. Instead, she tucked a strand of hair behind her ear then tugged her dark blue gown straight. The flowing design hung loosely over her slim frame, but the hemline was muddied shreds above her bare feet. Around her waist, a large purse dangled from a rope, equally splattered with muck, and a dagger hung on her hip.

Dressed in a peasant-like rough cotton shirt and trousers, Joshua tossed his head to dislodge strands of his shoulder-length blond hair from his lips. Dried mud cracked across his face as he grimaced. "What's another few yards? I'll take him upstairs," he panted. He clutched their friend to his chest and staggered towards the front door.

Spenser's head lolled over the crook of his elbow, slack jawed, eyes rolled back into his skull. A skinny arm dangled and twitched; the only movement in his inert, near lifeless body.

Lady Hanley's head rose, although she still crouched in front of Aioffe. "Your Highness. The honour…" Although they had met before, under vastly different circumstances, she had not been Queen then. Her elevated position demanded a certain respect, ingrained into her by millennia of serving royalty.

Aioffe's gaze snapped to the old fae. "Please, Mark's father needs assistance. I need no honouring."

The front door squeaked as it banged open. Uffer, still in his nightgown, stood in the doorway with a candle. His grey, weary face brightened as soon as he glanced across the narrow grassy patch. "Oh, your Highness!" His eyes moistened.

"Lord Anaxis! Uffer, it's so good to see you but…" She ran to him, "Please help. Ambassador Spenser - he's badly hurt."

Uffer's mouth dropped open as, emerging from the hallway, Mark pushed past them all and barrelled across the grass. "Papa!" He skidded to a halt a foot away from the fae, blinking rapidly as he saw the limp body Joshua held. "What's wrong with him?"

Aioffe knelt so she was his height and bowed her head. Her voice came soft and comforting. "Mark, he's going to be all right. He had a difficult time in Europe." Gently, her fingers reached to touch his, but he jerked away.

Spenser groaned and he tried to raise his head. "Mark?" His fingertips flicked, then fell limp. His skull lolled back into Joshua's chest.

"He just needs some rest, and some of your mother's medicine," Joshua said, with as much conviction as he could manage.

Mark's dark eyes darted between them. "But Mama isn't here." His lip trembled and his hand reached for his father's skeletal fingers peeping through the filthy frilled cuff. "He's so cold. Too cold."

Lady Hanley stood, her jaw clenched. "Nemis is close by, but not here." She shot Joshua a warning glance, jerking her head towards Mark. Then her gaze landed on the bundle strapped to Aioffe's chest. "The babe is healthy still?"

Aioffe's lips lifted in a weary smile. "Well, thank you. Exhausted but fine." Her hand caressed a small head bulge through the cotton sling.

"Little One is with you?" Mark turned back to Aioffe, relief colouring his cheeks.

"She has a name now. We called her Hope," Joshua said, grinning as he watched the boy's face flush with happiness as Aioffe pulled aside the sling.

As she showed him a peep of the sleeping baby's gingery-blond hair, lit faintly by the moonlight, the bundle stirred. Aioffe drew the fabric down further and dropped a kiss on a deep red stain, the shape of a butterfly's wing, on her cheek. "She can fly too, although not very far."

Aioffe's gaze flicked to Mary and Uffer. "Do you think there's room here for us all?"

Uffer drew himself tall. "Of course. Ambassador Spenser should rest in the Golden Room. Unless his Lordship's room should be prepared?"

Lady Hanley bristled. "The Golden Room should house our most prestigious guest." She unfurled her fingers towards Aioffe. "Mark's father would recuperate better in his Lordship's room." She glanced at Joshua. "I have, of course, had the window locks removed since your last visit."

Joshua stepped towards the door. "Good. The last thing Spenser needs is to feel like he's a prisoner again. He's suffered enough this past year while he was in Europe with Aioffe."

Aioffe met Lady Hanley's enquiring eyes. "The fae there, and their Queen, have very different ways of handling guests."

"Come, come." Uffer beckoned them across the threshold and held his candle aloft inside. "Waste no more time dawdling. My Prince, you know the way I believe? I will fetch fresh linens and water."

Joshua shot him a grateful look and followed. Lady Hanley swept after them, her chin jutting forward. "I shall see the Golden Room is made ready."

Left alone in the garden with Mark, Aioffe took a last glance at the fiery ball in the sky and stroked Hope's head. His face fell as he retrieved his stone from his pocket then studied it. Her wings caught in the moonlight as they dropped. As she turned to enter the house, he said quietly, "Pretty things." He shrugged. "They always seem to cause trouble."

"Yet you had a star of your very own in your pocket." Aioffe's voice caught. "To hold dear and guide you with earthly concerns. It is a rare treasure indeed, young man. And, did the stars above not guide us in our flight back here? To bring your father and baby Hope home to you."

Mark's tense expression eased. "I suppose."

"And you were here waiting for us," she said. "Because of this strange falling star." She dropped her hand onto his shoulder. Tendrils of her magic oozed unseen into him, calming the child. "Whatever is destined for us all now has less to do with the stars, though, and more to do with love and hope. For it is love which kept your father alive, to return to you."

The boy nodded. "Maybe you can bring Mama back, too."

"That's what we intend to do," she replied. For hundreds of miles, the burden of freeing their friend from her imprisonment, and saving her life, hung like a weighty cloak over both her and Joshua's shoulders. In many European states, to be accused of witchcraft was almost a death sentence in itself; in England, Aioffe hoped calmer minds might prevail.

She guided Mark towards the door. It didn't matter to the boy that Nemis was a powerful witch; to him, she was more importantly his mother. Nemis's children, her husband Spenser, and her friends needed her as much as she, no doubt, needed their help.

Chapter 3

LIMITATIONS

King Henry Fitzroy strode into the High Hall, at the very centre of the citadel in Naturae, with purpose. A third, awestruck night of watching the spectacle of the enormous fireball streaking across the sky had inspired him. He was alone in his optimism, for Fairfax, his daemon lover, had suffered with pangs of fear the first night it had appeared. Henry had reassured him the best way he knew how: with distraction in bed, followed by subsequent star-gazing to reassert that the other stars, especially those which Fairfax used for nautical navigation, remained in their usual places. Apparently, Henry was the only person on the island to view the celestial occurrence as a sign of joy. Of hope.

The Fae Elders, informed by their wisdom of centuries, were jittery but steadfast in their assurances: humans would be more concerned about ill portends than creatures who lived so much longer generally were. It was all a matter of perspective, and Henry, being young for a vampire, should prepare himself for the hysteria which would befall humankind. Henry had yet to decide if this was tacit encouragement of his eternal rule over the Fae of Naturae, or if they meant for him to seize the opportunity such widespread fear might present. A vampire presiding over a fae nation may be a break from tradition, but the timing of the starlight, months after he had assumed the throne, didn't mean his rule was doomed, did it?

So spectacular were the lights, still faintly visible in daytime, work rebuilding his dominion fell behind as the fae workers became distracted. Unrest threatened. Thus, it fell to him to quash the rumours which the stars' continued presence caused, circulated by the younger fae who knew no better. Uneducated whispers about ill omens overheard from their trading partners on the mainland. Henry meant to gather the whole population from across the island of Naturae, this afternoon, in some form of celebration to reassure his subjects.

Several worker fae sat clustered around the vast, soaring supportive trunks in the High Hall, gossiping instead of performing their tasks in the communal area. Above the white stained branches, wings hummed as more workers twittered while they cleaned the vaulted ceiling, polishing the inlaid silver swirls until it seemed they shone as brightly as the stars. Henry had ordered a deep clean in readiness for his impromptu celebration, but it was taking far longer than promised.

Mindful of the need to demonstrate his calm management of the unsettling situation, he nodded to every fae who paused their conversations and turned to acknowledge him as he progressed to the dais. He noted, with some pleasure, their response to his neutral expression had not scared them into meek submission. Or grovelling, as he had seen some humans do in the presence of greatness. Rather, it showed their respect for his authority as de facto, self-proclaimed King of Naturae, he told himself. A good start to what could potentially be a defining day.

Assembled at the far end of the Hall, the Council of Elders and worker representatives. His throne awaited at the head of a highly polished oval table. Their muttering ceased at the slap of his shoes up the dais stairs. Henry stood taller than most fae and men; a new golden crown adding even more height sat atop his red-golden hair. When all eyes were upon him, Henry flashed the Council a grin, just enough to remind them of his unusually long incisors. His difference to them. His superiority.

As Thane, the unofficial worker-fae leader, stood ready with his pre-amble to open the session, it did not seem so strange to Henry that a vampire should rule over Fae. Rather, with all the accommodations they had made to keep him as their king, their protector, this was the natural order of things. He had ample food, clothing, and workers at his beck and call to bring him anything he so desired. He was, after all, born to rule. And rule he did, as wisely and kindly as he had been taught to. And, with more consideration than his father, Henry VIII, had shown his people.

"My liege," Thane said, using the term which Henry had deemed appropriate to address him by. It inspired loyalty to Henry's mind, a far more effective a tool to rule with than terror. Above all, he wanted to be seen as a just monarch, as well as a powerful one. The title sounded particularly pleasing in the deep, rolling tones of Henry's most respected ally on the Council.

Without his usual preamble, Thane continued. "It has come to our attention that European Fae, led by Queen Illania, are on the move." The expression on Thane's face was grave, as if this was of significance. "Closer to Naturae."

Henry frowned, then gestured for Thane to continue.

"Our spy network is concerned they have moved to the shores of France and that," Thane paused to glance at Issam, the co-ordinator of Naturae's spies, "they intend to cross into our Naturae realm, first crossing England and then up into Scotland, close to this island's shores."

"Is their movement unusual? Is it an army or just a few fae?" Henry asked, ignoring the implied scepticism in Thane's voice. His mind ran through the various implications such a show of force would have, were it humans he was dealing with. Any hint of troops approaching these island territories would have sent his father, and indeed, his half sister and current Queen of England, Mary, into a tailspin with worry. The fae were an entirely different breed, however, and, given their wings, movement across countries and continents might not be considered cause for concern.

"It is," Issam said. "Aside from their Ambassador, Lord Spenser, we have little interaction with them. They are," he glowered through busy grey eyebrows, "quite different in how they operate."

"Different how?"

Issam and Thane's heads dropped to stare at the polished tabletop. The elder responsible for areas of Scotland, whose name was so complicated to pronounce Henry hadn't bothered to remember it, growled, "As different as you are from us."

Ignoring the slight, Henry tapped his index finger on his short, neat beard. "How much do we know of them? Are they armed? Do we know their numbers?"

Issam squirmed. "My people have not indicated such information. It was always Ambassador Spenser who represented European interests, sharing what was pertinent knowledge only."

"And where is he?"

Thane's mouth twitched. "No-one knows. He was last seen accompanying our late Queen to his - their - court. At least, we believe that was their intention, but Prince Joshua was unclear on the matter of her disappearance. Then he left as well. The last word we had from him was delivered by yourself. The letter from him stating Queen Aioffe had died."

The Council fell silent, no doubt considering the implications further now mention of their dear Aioffe's last known location had been made. The evidence they had was, at best, flimsy, because unbeknownst to the fae, Henry had forged the letter himself just before taking the throne. Before the subject of how they came to believe she had died could be re-examined, Henry slapped his hand on the table. "So, not only am I missing a crucial diplomat who could tell us whether this movement poses a threat to our lands, we have scant information from our own people. We do not know this Queen Illania's intentions at all."

He pursed his lips. "Captain, what's the status of our troops?"

The Captain's jaw clenched. "Ready as ever to serve, my liege. But, if I may remind, you assured us of your personal protection when you took the throne." His beady eyes bored into Henry.

"At your invitation, I remind you all. And protect the fae of Naturae, I will," Henry said smoothly. "From my kind. Have I not provided training for your soldiers on how to strike at vampires?" He looked around the table. "Although I will, as necessary, be the bridge between fae and vampire. But, it is not vampires who concern us now. I believed you yourselves would be the experts in how to defend yourselves from attack by fae. Should it come to that," he added. "Will it?" He raised an eyebrow.

"One never knows with the foreign sort," the Captain replied. He looked at his hands and muttered, "If Queen Aioffe had not died, she would have known the best approach."

"Would she indeed." Henry cursed inside, vowing to correct the leader of the Fae army of his continual insolence sometime soon. The Council had a way of putting that indecisive, weak-minded female on a pedestal which wore on him. His good humour vanished. He had no idea if Aioffe was alive or dead, but she had not returned to Naturae to challenge his rule, and that was what mattered. Why couldn't they see she had abandoned them? No matter what he did, how much he did for the fae, sometimes it seemed he would never replace their beloved Queen in their affections.

Today was not the time for admonishments or re-education. He dropped his hand to his lap and drummed his fingers on his thigh. The potential for this European Queen to interfere with his usurping deception about Aioffe's death ran foremost through his mind. He had a hunch Aioffe had failed to find the Europeans at all, and instead, fled her responsibilities and marriage. Henry had little faith in female rulers; it wasn't their fault, but women hadn't the temperament to reign. His theory was currently re-enforced by the disastrous decisions his half sister Mary had made, both in her marriage to Philip of Spain and his conquering ambitions, and her decision to take England back to Catholicism. Would this Queen Illania be any different, he wondered? Perhaps, if she were publicly questioned about the disappearance of Aioffe, it might put the fae's lamentations to rest and allow him to rule without their constant whining.

From what little he knew of Aioffe, she had been a peaceable sort. He supposed she too would seek what he now suggested as a solution: "A diplomatic approach must be made." Henry addressed the table in a clear, authoritative voice. "Since we are not, to my knowledge, at war, it would be prudent to extend an offer of our most gracious hospitality to Queen Illania. As she is so close to our shores, this might also afford us an opportunity to see what her intentions are through the very making of the invitation."

He raised a hand and held his palm flat, as if weighing up the options. "If she ignores our request, then we can make ready to defend ourselves. And if she accepts," his other hand rose to balance the statement. "We can hope this is a visit to explain what happened to your late Queen Aioffe when she left these shores."

And find out what he needed to do to secure his throne, permanently. The fact Aioffe hadn't made a reappearance supported his assertion that she was dead. If she did return, which seemed more doubtful as time went on, he'd have to deal with her, but for now, he must maintain the façade of innocence.

Henry's gaze roamed down the table, meeting the fearful eyes of the Council. "I shall pen the note myself. King to Queen. In the meantime, I want this Ambassador Spenser found." He glared at Issam. "Wherever he is. What say you?" He closed his fists and watched.

The Council nodded to each other, their expressions still mournful.

"As you wish, my liege," Issam said. "I'll instruct them as soon as we conclude business here."

Thane glanced around the table, his jaw firm. "There is another matter we wish to discuss."

"Ah, yes," Henry said. "The celestial celebration. I was thinking…"

Before he could continue outlining his plans, the Captain interrupted. "No, my liege. It is about creation. Of succession."

"Surely you joke?" Henry forced a laugh. "I promised you a stable and eternal rule. Forever."

"My liege," Thane said. "Your own immortality is not in dispute. Yet, there are duties which only those with royal bloodlines can perform."

Henry was all too aware of human requirements for royal bloodlines as a requirement to rule. As Henry VIII's bastard son, he had bloodline credentials. His problem, when he was human, had been legitimacy in the eyes of the Church, not in the opinions of his peers. The same Church who then made him a vampire with a plan to place him on the throne when his father died, except Edward had been born a few years after this turning.

A few council members shifted in their seats. Henry's lips pursed in the pregnant pause which followed. "What duties?"

"Blessings," Thane said. His cheeks flushed. "It is a royal task."

Henry's eyebrows gathered, wrinkling his smooth forehead. Blessings. How very religious, not at all what he had expected.

"In the Pupaetory." Thane pointed towards the window. Past the sacred twin trees, a slim building nestled high in the treetops. A balcony ran the length of its long sides, an atrium of sorts sat beneath a glass roof, with housing cells lining the walls. Henry had visited once before, when he first came into power. It was where the young fae lived and were educated until they were old enough to join a worker family group. A nursemaid informed him pupae, baby fae, were grown on vines, from some sort of chrysalis, rather like butterflies. The impression he had was the fae were some kind of living fruit which matured over a number of years before 'pupaetion', but he had not tarried long enough to see the vines themselves as they were kept locked away in a separate chamber of the Pupaetory.

Thane's head hung, and he muttered, "No new pupae have grown since the last pupaetion. The vines need Blessings."

"Are the plants sickly?" Henry asked. "Perhaps they only need more light. Or water." This was about the extent of his botanical knowledge. "Trim the surrounding trees. Don't you have some gardeners to take care of it?"

The fae Elders shook their heads. "Royal Blessings are needed," one of them whispered.

"What do you mean?" Henry asked, deciding to ignore the niggle in his head, which whispered he had made a faux pas. "Do you need me to bless some water for them?"

Perhaps there was a greater link between religion and the fae than he had supposed. The vampires who worked closely with the Catholic church performed such duties to appease the faithful. Henry considered he might know enough of the ritual to attempt to make water holy, if it came to it. He had been raised in the faith and spoke fluent Latin.

"It is not water, my liege," the Elder from Scotland said. "The creation of fae can only be done by a Queen. It is their ability, unique to royalty. We must have a royal. A Queen."

Henry's teeth clenched together as the realisation dawned on him. That royal lineage might be a physical necessity for the survival of faekind had not occurred to him. Until now.

Chapter 4

THE SEARCH

1 **st June 1556 Beesworth**

It was barely an hour past dawn and a line of do-gooders marched their way towards Hanley House. Joshua's stomach sank as, hidden by the drapes of the library window, he watched the procession of dark-robed men, clutching papers with sombre faces. As they ascended the steep hillock, the village elders and officials puffed and panted, pausing to catch breath and casting nervous glances above. "What do they want?"

Aioffe swept Hope into her arms, pinning down the delicate red wings beneath her blousy petticoat, then peered around his shoulder to see. The toddler wriggled, chubby hands reaching for the wooden toys strewn by the fireside. "Perhaps it's to do with Nemis," Aioffe said, bouncing their daughter on her hip. "A date for the Assize?"

He shrugged. Why send so many people just to confirm the arrival of the circuit judges who would try his friend's case? A messenger would have sufficed, if gossip didn't reach them first. "Maybe. The Sheriff told Mary yesterday, she's already been moved to York." He glanced at Aioffe, then brushed a loose strand of hair from Hope's cheeks.

Aioffe's heart fluttered as his caress revealed the large, butterfly-shaped red mark which marred the toddler's otherwise pretty face. "We should hide in the attic. We haven't aged since we left, amidst the upset of 1536. Someone might remember us."

She glanced at the pair of chairs facing the fireplace as Spenser stirred. Although it had been only a few days since their arrival, he spent most of the time dozing. The journey had taken much out of him in his weakened state, a result of months of his Lifeforce being drained by his mistress, Queen Illania. His appetite had not returned, despite Aioffe's insistence he needed more than the Lifeforce from the supply of rabbits Lady Hanley kept around. She suspected his weakness had more to do with his mind; Nemis's fate concerned them all, but Spenser had barely spoken since hearing they had so narrowly missed her. All his energy was saved for interactions with his son; his nightly rest was punctuated by screams which echoed through the halls. Even awake, he stared vacantly into the fire, refusing to unburden himself about his recent torture, as if the act of sharing would cause him to re-live the experience.

Aioffe said in a low voice, "You'll have to carry Spenser, though. I don't think he's quite up to the climb yet. Perhaps if no-one is here to let them in, they'll leave."

"I want to face these wantwits myself," Spenser growled. "They don't know me, although they should." He leaned forward, grabbed the poker and waved it like a sword. "Nemis is my wife. 'Tis absurd they have locked her away from us on such ridiculous notions of witchery. Even though she actually is one, she could never harm anyone."

Joshua strode over and removed the iron from Spenser's fingers before he could drop it on Lady Hanley's rug. Given the room was lined with peculiar papers, scrolls and books, waving around the hot implement was hazardous when his balance was still wobbly. After replacing it in the stand, Joshua cursed under his breath. A daytime aerial escape was near impossible when so many men had emerged from the forests surrounding their isolated sanctuary.

"We should have left days ago." He shook his head. "I should never have led us back here. Our history in Beesworth keeps a target on our backs, and Hope was one of the causes of Nemis's detainment. I can't be seen, as t'was me they sought for Alice's murder twenty years ago. Someone will remember. Aioffe had merely disappeared at the same time as Mistress Tunn's daughter died, but still, someone might recall her face and the name of Mistress Meadows, too."

He sighed, then reached over to stroke Hope's tiny, bare feet. "Maybe she shouldn't be here at all?" His eyes gazed into Aioffe's bright blue ones. "We all shouldn't. Just in case..."

Aioffe stiffened, clutching Hope tighter to her. "She's just a babe. An innocent."

Although Nemis was Hope's birth mother, she insisted the unusual fae child, with her mixture of witch, vampire and daemon Lifeforce, belonged to Aioffe and Joshua. Having wings meant she was destined to be their baby and heir to Naturae. The fates of the four parents were thus intertwined, which was scant comfort while one of their member was locked away.

Joshua said, "But the birthmark? They'll say it's the Devil's Mark again. Just like before."

Aioffe shook her head. "We're jumping to conclusions, my love. They could be here to see Mary, or on other business."

"Lady Hanley would sort them out," Spenser called from the armchair in front of the fireplace. "Except she's at market, with Mark." His pale hand clutched the red fabric, knuckles white with tension as he tried to sit up and peer around the wingback.

"A curse and a blessing," Joshua replied. If anyone could muddy the waters with peculiar behaviour in the presence of officials, it was Spenser's son. Ever since his mother had taken the blame for him stealing trinkets at the May Day, even Lady Hanley, who had a special bond with the daemon, struggled to keep his outbursts and erratic nature under control.

"Uffer's occupied, tucked away down the hill, so he can't answer. The only way," Spenser said, attempting to rise, "is for me to handle this, and you all to stay hidden. I don't have to hide from officials. I'm a respected gentleman in some circles."

Joshua helped Spenser stand, then re-tied his robe so it covered his wings. "We'll take Hope to the attic, and Spenser, do your utmost to send them away. Tell them..."

A loud banging on the front door interrupted him.

"Fly," Spenser growled.

Hope squealed as Aioffe bundled her close and followed Joshua, darting through the hall, up the stairs, and into the jumbled space in the eaves. They crouched behind trunks and waited. Repeated pounds on the door thudded through the old house. They froze at the creak of the entrance opening; fae hearing enabled them to listen as clearly as if they were in the next room.

"We are here, sir, to search the premises," an officious voice announced in broad Yorkshire tones. "We are led to believe this was the primary residence of an accused witch. Nemis Claybourne."

"Where is your paperwork?" Spenser snapped.

"Art tha' the owner of the property, sir? A Lord Hanley?"

"No," Spenser replied. "The mistress of the house is out. I cannot allow you in without her presence."

"We have come a long way," the first voice grumbled. "From York."

Joshua recognised the next voice - the pompous tone of the Beesworth Sherrif's assistant. The very man who had detained Nemis that fateful Midsummer night of her arrest. "Then we will wait until Lady Hanley returns. A peculiar boy, who also lives here, is implicated anyway. He'll need questioning. He's usually around and about, causing trouble."

Spenser said, "He is with Lady Hanley."

Aioffe and Joshua shared an anxious glance. In their haste to hide, they had left their belongings, including the toys made for Hope, all over the house.

"And the babe the witch bore will need pricking, as well," the official added. "Is it here?"

Hope was clutched even closer. Joshua's heart threatened to pulse from his chest.

"We discussed this, Sargent," the man from Beesworth said. "And agreed the babe could be pricked here, with Lady Hanley as witness. Tis the only way to know if she has been marked by the Devil himself, or no."

"Where is the babe?"

Joshua squeezed his eyes shut, his lips moving in silent prayer.

"She has been taken into the care of..." Spenser paused.

Joshua's mind raced. "Did I tell him...?" He muttered to Aioffe. "He's been so ill, how much can he remember?

"Tell him what?" Aioffe said. "I told him of our past here, in Beesworth. How Alice Tunn was murdered by Lyrus before he kidnapped me, but at the time, you were accused of Alice's murder. Lady Hanley rescued you and then you found me on Naturae. While we were flying back from Europe, you told him all about your return, nearly twenty years later, with Nemis. That's when Hope was born."

"Yes, but then Alice's father, William died, which mattered little to us at the time. The Midsummer celebrations were soon after, and that's when Mistress Tunn accused Nemis of killing her husband, of being a witch. Fairfax stepped in to defend her and Mark. He promised to get baby Hope and Mark baptised, but... did I tell Spenser the moniker he used to convince Alf Cooper?"

Aioffe shrugged. "Spenser has survived many centuries already, he'll charm them if he can't remember."

"The care of whom, sir?" The Beesworth man pressed loudly.

Spenser's voice rang with certainty. "Sir Thomas, yes, Sir Thomas Fairfax, I believe. He lives near Harrogate."

Joshua let out a sigh of relief and glanced at Aioffe. Thank goodness fae memories were long. Living near eternal lives also meant one had to remember details. Shame his own recollection, especially of being human, was not reliable.

"Oh yes, the one who was getting the children baptised, again? Of Denton Hall?" Assistant Sherriff Cooper grunted.

"The same."

"Well, that settles it. We'll search this house now, then the babe, with her papers, can be examined before trial in York."

"I'm not letting you enter without Lady Hanley's approval," Spenser said. "Tell me, how fares the accused?"

"And you are?"

"A close family friend, visiting my distant relative, the mistress of this house, in the hope of some respite. I know her Ladyship is keen to be kept abreast of the case, as it involves her former servant. Please, how is she?"

"She's arrived in York, but already causing a disturbance."

"What sort of disturbance? Is she well?"

Hope wriggled in Aioffe's arms and was offered a knuckle to chew upon. Aioffe winced as small, sharp teeth bit but at least the toddler stayed quiet.

"Say's she's seein' things. Things which she oughtn't talk about."

"She's a strange one. When we took her there, t'was around the time as those lights were in the sky," the Beesworth man said. "Even in the closed cart, they affected her. Those screams, I'll never forget. Like a banshee, she was."

Joshua's throat tightened. They had been so close! Just a day or two earlier and his friend might have been saved from a far easier prison to get her out of.

"Tis certain the upsetting of other prisoners alone will be enough to condemn her. I witnessed it myself and I'll be telling the Assize as much, 'fer sure."

Spenser said, "Plenty of people were frightened. It means nothing."

"Well, she's locked up tight now, in the cells below York Castle, so she won't be seein' no starry nights for a while." The man from Yorkshire huffed. "It'll all go in my report as sorcery."

With a grunt of disgust, Spenser said, "Nothing in this house will be going into your report. Not without her Ladyship's say so." The hinges squeaked once again.

A thump of fist against the thick wood of the door frame.

"We have the paperwork, sir. Now let us in."

"Gentlemen," Spenser's voice rose. "Do you wish me to report to the judges that you have improperly obtained evidence upon which your case might hang? Without her Ladyship to witness your search, it would be called into question. For all I know, you might seek to plant something incriminating here. I do not know you, or your men, and, my eyesight fails so I cannot read these papers you proffer. I am not a lawyer, nor learned enough to know whether these deeds are correctly signed by the proper authorities."

Silence.

"I suggest you return tomorrow."

"You could get rid of something important by then!" The Assistant Sherrif cried out.

"If I was so minded, I would have done so long ago. You will find nothing here except the displeasure of your superiors." Weariness crept into Spenser's tone. "Now, for the love of God, leave the afflicted alone. I would not desire you to suffer my maladies as well. You see," he coughed weakly, "I have recently returned from Europe, where pestilence is prevalent. It's not certain... but I fear I may succumb."

Joshua and Aioffe listened to the muttered grumblings between men for a moment, imagining Spenser was perhaps showing them the marks upon his wrists as further proof of his contagion.

"We pack and fly away tonight," Aioffe whispered to Joshua. "Our presence puts everyone here in danger."

Below, the door creaked to a close.

He nodded. "And the spy network. What if Uffer had been the one to answer the door? There's no disguising the strangeness of him and he'd have never stood up to the barrage of questions. Not at his age."

"He'd have tried his hardest to protect us all, though, as always."

Heavy footsteps on the stairs halted their whispers. "It is clear," Spenser said from below, labouring for breath, "we need to be in York."

Hope perked up and looked around at the sound of his voice, "Spense. Spense," she lisped. Her pudgy fingers reached out as if to grab him.

Joshua flung open the attic trapdoor and trotted downstairs. "You should rest, my friend. We will pack." He helped Spenser into his bedroom, concerned by the paleness of his skin.

Aioffe followed, her face distraught. "They said naught about how she was," Spenser bemoaned as he laid back on the bed. He blinked away tears. "In the darkness, she'll be so frightened."

"We'll pay whatever we must to alleviate her conditions." Joshua gave his shoulder a brief reassuring squeeze, knowing what little consolation it was.

"These humans. They wouldn't know a real witch," Spenser said. "I've seen it on the continent. It's not even the Church to blame, for all the vampire's meddling. It's foolish human superstition. Nemis could never hurt anyone." He swallowed his hurt. "She should never have tried to help a human."

"We know," Aioffe said. She placed Hope on the bed next to Spenser, who immediately crawled over and snuggled into him. "We'll go as soon as it's dark." She ran over to help Joshua, who was emptying the drawer's contents into his travel sack with as much haste as possible.

"Travelling at night won't make a difference," Joshua said, glancing at Spenser. "We cannot fly all that way. I'll pack Mark's belongings too," Joshua said. "We cannot leave him here."

Their dilemma hit him afresh and his throat tightened. "There has to be a way out of this. An escape. A way to make them realise Nemis has done nothing wrong."

"All our powers are useless here," Aioffe's fists clenched. "If it's writ, that's all they see."

"Bureaucrats!" Spenser spat. "The curse of humanity."

She sighed. "I'll send kestrels to find Fairfax. We will need those papers to prove Hope's baptism, or they could come after him as well and goodness knows where he is right now."

"I could forge them?" Joshua offered. Much as though he loved his friend, the element of chaos which trailed in Fairfax's wake concerned him. With so much else at stake, was it wise to involve the daemon? "More reliable than depending on him?"

She shook her head. "From what you said about the night this all happened, surely it would be better if he can also be available as a witness? I'll ask him to meet us in York."

Spenser groaned. "Relying on a daemon to save a witch." His hands trembled as he pulled a blanket over himself. "What is the world coming to?"

CHAPTER 5

YORK

Near constant drizzle, despite midsummer approaching, made passage cross the moors difficult. There was no alternative but land travel for Mary, Mark and Spenser, and no-one else able to drive a cart but Joshua. Leaving Uffer at Hanley House, Lady Hanley insisted her status would help their relocation, but it was Mark she was reluctant to be parted from. Given they had no coin of their own, Aioffe and Joshua had little choice but to agree to her coming.

Joshua sat up front, swathed in a woollen blanket, blinking against the wind driving over the tops, whilst the others huddled together in the belly of an old hay cart. The old destrier plodded past the heather-lined banks with stoic resolve. Despite it being customary for the highest-ranking member of the party to lead the way, Mary lagged behind them on her own horse, occasionally disrupting the quiet with curt directions and grumbles about the pace. Progress along the deep-rutted track was slow, punctuated by potholes masquerading as puddles. As the days passed, criss-crossing the rugged landscape, miserable weather and apprehension about what awaited them in York stifled much other conversation.

Eventually, the moorland trail joined a wider thoroughfare, busy with other carts and riders, and the dismal weather finally lifted. As the cart approached the high stone borders of the old St Mary's Abbey of York, its passengers were pale with exhaustion and numb from the chill and bumps. Joshua called back in a cheerful voice, "Not far now." He pointed to the twin spires of York Minster which jutted above towering, blackened city walls. Numerous other church steeples peppered the township, but none as tall or beautiful as the Minster's.

He pulled on the reins and slowed to navigate around a stray sheep's bottom, poking into the track as it grazed and oblivious to the nuisance it caused. Aioffe took advantage of the delay and, with Hope still drowsy in her arms, clambered over their belongings to join Joshua on the bench seat so she could see the city better.

As they passed low-built wooden houses close to the crenellated wall, little signs of civilisation perked them all up. A few pot-bellied pigs rooted in the yellow stubs of the recent harvest. Peasants toiled in the fields surrounding the Kings Manor, which lay on the outskirts of the city.

"I recall the Abbot House was rather fine," Mary said, drawing alongside the cart. "Until they renamed it in honour of and to house Henry VIII, on his Great Progress to the North." She sniffed and nudged her mare on. "What a spectacle it was. I've not been back to York ever since." Her back straightened as they passed the Abbey Gatehouse and continued towards Fulford Gate.

Passing through the enclosed barbican, hooves echoing as they struck the cobbles, sent a shiver through Aioffe. Fae usually avoided large cities, because they housed a greater concentration of creatures, similarly hiding among the human population. Most vampires, witches and daemons looked like humans, but not fae. Even though their wings were bound and hidden beneath layers of clothing, there was still a chance the strange lumps between the shoulder blades could be noticed. A fear of discovery, of her otherness, especially in jostling crowds, constricted Aioffe's throat.

The danger pressed closer than ever, now she had a child to protect. She clutched Hope tighter to her chest as the cart emerged into a narrow street.

Hearing a muffled squeal, she checked over her shoulder, back at the chests and sacks they had brought with them, and noticed Spenser had also drawn Mark into his arms. The embrace was awkward, and more for Spenser's comfort than his son's. At least Mark physically appeared human, she thought, with no features which might draw unwelcome attention, except for his erratic behaviour and obsession with shiny objects and stones. Spenser's skin was still grey, his face skeletal, which lent him an otherworldly look.

Underneath overhanging eaves, hawkers and traders sat on wooden blocks, touting, shouting for business. Leading from the thoroughfare, narrow and low snickleways separated the buildings, too narrow for a cart to go through but just wide enough for barrels and handcarts. People from all levels of society, from the colourful guild capes of merchants to the drab poverty of the lower classes, milled in front of their horses with little care for who had entered their city. Liveried watchmen with the city's arms emblazoned on their jupons cast bored eyes over the cart, then idled on Lady Hanley's imperious figure trotting ahead of them. Dressed well and in accordance with the sumptuary laws like all nobility and titled persons, she stood out and was of interest, although the guards did little more than straighten their stance.

Lady Hanley pulled up after they entered a large flagstoned square, lined with shops and barrow stalls. The marketplace bustled with the noise of haggling and the smell of freshly baked pies reached their noses. She slid from the saddle and tied the reins to an iron ring on the wall.

Almost immediately, a small boy clopped across to them. The patches to his shirt were frayed and his battered clogs far too large for his feet, but he grinned up at Lady Hanley with no shame or guile. "Watch tha's horse fer a pennie?"

Her lips pursed and she glanced at Spenser and Mark. "A pennie. No more, no less. But, here's thruppence as well, for the pie you'll fetch for my young ward while we gather ourselves."

Joshua clambered from his bench seat and secured the brown destrier alongside her mare. He nodded to the scamp, then helped Aioffe and Hope down.

Lady Hanley dropped a few coins in the awaiting grubby hand, then turned to Joshua. "We'll meet back here once you've found her, and I've secured suitable accommodation for a few nights." There was no need to mention the particular requirements for privacy the fae shared. Staying inside the town walls, which would close upon night curfew, would only suffice for a short while. They had agreed on the journey: if they couldn't get Nemis out of prison quickly, renting a large enough house for them all was a necessity. It had to have access to open countryside for hunting under cover of darkness. They were all committed to staying in York until Nemis could be freed, however long it took. Rooms in an inn were too temporary a solution.

Mary slipped Joshua a small drawstring purse, fat with money. "Thank you," he replied, understanding why she had not elaborated or explained her gift. The last thing they needed was to announce they were here to visit a prisoner. He glanced at Spenser as Aioffe passed their child into his waiting arms. "We'll be as fast as we can."

Spenser's lips pressed together and he blinked rapidly. "Bear her my heart," he said in a strangled voice. It had also been agreed Mark and Hope were not to see Nemis yet, and since Spenser could only manage a short walk before collapsing, he was best to keep an eye on his son and Hope until they knew more about Nemis's circumstance.

"We will," Aioffe said, knowing any other platitudes or reassurances were meaningless without evidence.

Joshua and Aioffe entered the castle via a long drawbridge over the King's fishpond, a wide swell enclosing the inner bailey and tower mount and filled by the River Foss. The soldier manning the gatehouse to York Castle directed them across the huge courtyard, to one of the towers. Enclosed by high yellowed limestone walls with sentries patrolling above, they clutched each other's hands tight, aware their every move across the quiet space was watched by sentries from the tower looming over York. The old castle, with pockmarked, shit stained walls was surrounded by another moat, stinking and buzzing with low water, which isolated the steep-sided mound. The inner bailey, containing the court and prison, was near desolate and shabby, as if forgotten about. Only the stables, detectable by the smell of droppings and straw piled and steaming, showed any sign of activity.

But, as they neared the turnkey's abode and office, Aioffe realised the impression of abandonment was misleading. From the very ground underneath, her extraordinary hearing picked up the wails and sobs of captives. "The gaol," she whispered to Joshua, "is beneath."

Her eyes flared at him, her choice of words deliberate. In Naturae, prior to becoming Queen, she had been held captive in The Beneath. She had always had a fear of being enclosed, which had only increased since her stay in the darkness underneath the trees of the citadel. He grimaced, wishing for an alternative, while silently prayed she would be able to cope with what lay ahead of them, for it was sure to bring back unwelcome memories for them both.

A peeling sign outside the third tower along said simply, Keeper. Upon their knock to the closed door, a turnkey answered. He peered out, watery grey eyes wandering over the arrivals and a sneer on his mouth. Thin lips smacked together as soon as Joshua mentioned Nemis's name. "The witch?" He shook his head. "Isolated now. Not supposed to have visitors."

"None?" She glanced at Joshua.

"At all. She's disturbed, see. Upsets the others."

The thought of entering a gaol in the first place was bad enough to cause Aioffe's chest to constrict, but to be refused entry made her palms sweat. She withdrew her hand from Joshua's and moved onto the next stage of their plan to gain them entry. "Can an exception be made? For family." She batted her eyelashes at him. "We have travelled so far."

The turnkey shook his head, greasy strands of his hair barely moving with the motion. "No exceptions wi'out High Sherrif's say so."

"Then perhaps," Joshua interjected, as Aioffe seemed to waver in the non-existent wind, "you could permit my wife a drink? A sip of water, or ale?"

Aioffe raised a hand to her forehead and made to swoon.

"Please, it would be a kindness I could pay handsomely for?" Joshua said as he thrust an arm around her waist as if she were about to fall.

With a snarl, the turnkey opened the door wider and stepped back. Joshua half dragged Aioffe inside. A faint groan escaped her lips as he sat her down on a stool.

The gaoler poured something from a flagon into a wooden cup and passed it to her. Her fingers came up quickly, circling his wrist in a caress. With clear eyes, she gazed at his mousy features and pushed her will through his skin. "What a saviour you are," she whispered. "A credit to your master."

A hint of a smile appeared on her victim's face. Less of a snarl, at least.

Her eyes flicked to Joshua, aware he hadn't seen her affect a human's will in many a year. He swallowed and nodded. His eyes willed her to continue her touch hypnosis, an ability unique amongst fae.

Gradually, the turnkey's features relaxed as she silently calmed him using her mind. She said, "There is no reason why Nemis Claybourne shouldn't have visitors. No reason to refuse them entry at any time. She knows these people and won't cause any upset."

The gaoler chopped his lips as if tasting something, then said, "Still, there'll be questions. Of recompense."

Joshua withdrew the purse Mary had given him, just within Aioffe's line of sight.

"We'll pay a fair fee," she reassured. "More than enough for your trouble to take us to her. Now."

"Sixpence per person," the turnkey murmured. "'Tis the usual amount, an' fair."

Joshua's eyebrow rose but Aioffe didn't want to push her luck. "We thank you," she said in the gentlest of voices and released him.

The man straightened, bewildered. He turned towards the door, his hand dropping to the bunch of keys hanging from his belt. Aioffe stood, not entirely steady as subjugation without pulling Lifeforce in return momentarily weakened her, but there was no time to waste. As soon as her touch was withdrawn, her influence would be short-lived.

Joshua pressed some coins into the man's hand. "I'll take you down now," the turnkey said as he shuffled towards the yard.

They entered another tower, embedded within the walls, through an arched doorway. Inside the cool entry chamber, another door revealed stone steps, circling up and down. To the stairwell above, shafts of sunlight lit the way, but leading down, the torches on the walls had not been lit. The gaoler shot them a wry glance. "Mind y'step, pretty Mistress. There's many have fallen through want of care."

Or been shoved, Joshua thought as he peered down the dark stairwell and wondered how far underground they led. Aioffe gripped Joshua's hand again. He squeezed it gently as they descended.

The turnkey led them down a dank corridor, into a maze lined with domed cells, which was surprisingly warm and humid. A few torches holstered on the walls smoked, providing scant light to see the listless residents. No daylight brightened the horror. As they walked past, their presence was either ignored entirely, or, hands shot out, between the iron rails, beseeching them for food or a cup of drink.

Aioffe kept close to Joshua, head down, unable to look at their dirty, gaunt faces. The inhumanity of the prison ached deepest for her and she curled her fingers against the miserable strands of Lifeforce, shaded grey with disease and despair, which swirled around the floor. With heightened senses, the rank stench which lingered about the airless dungeon nearly overwhelmed them both and tears sprang to their eyes.

After a walk which seemed like miles, the gaoler stopped in front of a small wooden door. His eyes seemed to gleam in the darkness as he twisted his ring of keys. Clink, clink, clink, each sounded like a tiny bell tolling down time. Around and around until he found the right one. He grunted as he thrust a key into the lock. "Five minutes."

Aioffe gasped as the door swung open.

Nemis sat, legs splayed on the stone floor with her back to the wall opposite the door, staring straight at them. Or, she would be, if her eyes weren't rolled back and her hands jerking.

The turnkey sniffed. "She's at it again, then."

Aioffe rushed towards her. Joshua had to duck his head to enter the tiny room, then found he couldn't stand straight next to the slim pallet bed. Dread trembled his fingers as he crouched over his friend.

Nemis moaned, a long drawn out heartbreak.

"We are here," Joshua said, kneeling to gather her into his arms. "Nemis? Come back to us, dear friend."

His entreaties were not working, so Aioffe fumbled in their satchel while he perched on the bed and cradled Nemis in his lap. She retrieved the medicine they had found amongst her belongings in Hanley House and pulled out the cork. As the heady vapours replaced the stench of damp straw and defecation in the room, Aioffe tipped all that remained of the only draught known to work on Nemis's fits between her pale lips. Maister

Jeffries would have to be found, and fast, if they were to get hold of any more, for it was a secret recipe known only to healer witches like he.

Her body felt cold to Joshua, so he rubbed her arms as they waited for the potion to take effect.

"Nemis," Aioffe whispered. "All will be well. Please, come back to us. Please!" Just as she shared a worried glance with Joshua, Nemis stirred.

"Spenser?" She groaned.

"Alive," Aioffe said. "But he suffered in Europe. He's here in York with us, and will visit as soon as he's able. He said to tell you, you have his heart."

"Mark and Hope are with him, and Lady Hanley," Joshua added. "We're doing everything we can to get you out of here."

Nemis blinked and drew in a choked breath. "Oh Aioffe, you must go. Hide somewhere." She gazed at her friend. "I see death."

"I'm fine," Aioffe said. "Don't worry about me."

"No!" Nemis said and sat up. She clutched Aioffe's forearm and said earnestly, "I saw the death of a queen." She shook her head. "At least, I think it was a queen. Queens, perhaps."

"What do you mean?" Joshua said. Nemis's visions were often ambiguous, but always true. They had brought him to Aioffe's side, led him to Naturae, right when he thought his love was dead. They had also foretold the arrival of Henry Fitzroy to its shores.

Nemis's head dropped. "I'm there. In the room where it happens." Her shoulders trembled. "But sometimes, it's a different place. Over and over, I see five crowns tumbling. Queen's crowns. Some stained by blood, some tainted by something else." Her eyes rose to stare at Aioffe. "All queens."

"I'm not a queen anymore," Aioffe said.

"They all die. Unnatural deaths."

A shiver which ran down Aioffe's spine. "Naturae is ruled by Henry now," she said in a quiet voice. "So I'm no longer a queen, don't worry. The spies told Mary. It is just as you foretold. A dark heir has taken my throne."

"But you will always be the Queen of Naturae," Joshua said, his stomach clenched painfully, as if squeezed by pliers. "Even if you aren't there now, you are the rightful queen."

Nemis drew in a ragged breath just as the turnkey rapped on the door and called, "Say your goodbyes."

She lifted her head, fingers clutched tightly around Aioffe's arm. "You must be careful. Promise me."

"We promise to get you out of here as soon as we can," Joshua said, his mouth dry.

"We'll return with news and food," Aioffe insisted. "Is there anything else you need? Clothes, a blanket?"

"I need herbs," Nemis said. "Not only for myself, but there's another prisoner whose joints cause her pain in this place. They'll only worsen if they aren't treated. Henbane, some hemlock and coriander for her fever." She looked mournfully at the vial of her medicine. "I don't suppose there's any more?"

"We will send out kestrels for Jeffries. He must be somewhere, but no-one has seen him for years. He can make some," Joshua said with gritted teeth. At a time like this, they needed all the wisdom he might provide as well, even if he couldn't be trusted.

Nemis's bottom lip tightened over her front teeth, holding back a sob. "I can't live like this," she said hoarsely. "It's constant. The visions. They all think I'm crazed. Everyone's frightened of me."

Joshua glanced over Nemis's head to Aioffe. Like hers, his eyes glistened with fear and tears. "We came to get you out. We will."

The door swung open. "Time to go," the turnkey said, his mouth twisted into a snarl. "She's going nowhere for months."

"What do you mean?" Aioffe asked.

"The Assize won't be held 'til next year. And the docket's already full." He jerked his head towards the passage. "Or didn't you notice?"

Nemis wept. "Tell Mark... tell him I think of him every day, and to shine his stones for me. And Spenser... ask him to rest. He never rests enough. My heart aches for his."

As Aioffe hugged Nemis goodbye, she tried to push what little Lifeforce she could give into her friend, to provide some comfort. But Nemis's aura was tinged with the blackness of terror, absorbing all she gave with no effect, which concerned her more than the sorry state of her friend.

CHAPTER 6

FRIEND OR FOE?

Autumn 1556, Naturae

"It's not good enough!" Henry slammed his fist on the desk in his chambers. A jug of fresh blood wobbled, splashing some over the many papers which littered the surface. He wheeled around to face Fairfax. "The Elders are keeping things from me. I know it. Illania will be at Naturae's shores any day and I'm ill-prepared for what to expect." He scowled down at the stained desktop and sighed. "The spies, the ones you trained, have sent no word. We have no idea about what they want, or if my invitation has even been accepted. Or, if the Europeans come for war."

Fairfax shrugged and munched the last of his jam and bread before pushing himself off their bed. He'd not been present at the Council session which Henry had just returned from, because he was not permitted too close to fae. He brushed the crumbs from his beard and said, "I'm sure it will be fine. You've attended enough royal audiences in your human life. Queen Illania should be flattered by all the arrangements you've made for either eventuality. Although," he glanced through the russet curls which fell over his face, "you know I'll have to leave soon."

Henry huffed and dabbed ineffectually at the red spilled mess. Parting was always awkward and not knowing when Fairfax would return, a constant frustration. His leaving Naturae was the safest option, even though Henry would far rather have had his constant company and support. But daemon blood, in particular it's Lifeforce, as the fae called it, was too alluring for his lover to stay long on Naturae, especially with unknown fae approaching. It was a natural, toxic defence against vampires which put daemons only just above humans in the superiority chain, and the fae were attracted to it like wasps to Fairfax's jam. Daemon blood was also highly valuable to witches for their potions and spells, which made any encounters with creaturekind a risk Henry felt uncomfortable about taking.

Waiting until Henry poured himself a replacement cup of deer's blood, Fairfax said, "The ways of faekind are as mysterious and mystical to me as well. You should not expect to be aware of every nuance and variation between creatures without experience."

After draining the cup, Henry refilled it, then growled, "Vampires are the same the world over. Our needs, our wants, they vary only in intensity and personality of the humans we were before. I thought the fae would be similar, if not the same. They all look alike." Except Aioffe and Joshua, they had different wings.

And yet, the Council would only say the Europeans were not like the Naturae fae, without explaining why or how. In the privacy of his chambers, Henry could be honest with Fairfax. He sank onto the bed and dropped his head. "You'd think it would make it easier. That they all want the same thing. Stability. Calm. Decisive, tolerant and equitable leadership. But no, it's not enough. I'm not enough."

Henry thought to the other problem the Council had pressed him on earlier, the declining population issue, and sighed. All fae were pupaeted on vines, which still hadn't any new pupae despite Henry walking amongst them for hours a day, like a royal apparently did. He'd tried talking to the stalks, cleaning their leaves, peeing on the roots, bleeding on them even, to no avail. Without a Queen to impart Blessings, no-one knew what else to suggest; the vines grew bushy but devoid of cocoons.

"At least the fae can live together peaceably," Fairfax said, injecting a note of levity into his tone. He wafted his long fingers around, pointing through the window at the treetop dwellings the worker fae lived in. "Can you imagine what would happen if daemons congregated in one place? Mayhem." He pulled on his deep pocketed trousers and fastened the lace of his over shirt. "Daemons aren't alike at all. Just look at your half sister, the Princess Elizabeth. You told me she was touched with, 'tainted by' you called it, the afflictions of my kind. And Mark, Spenser's son. He's not at all like I or any other daemon. Even witches vary in abilities. Why wouldn't you expect the same to be true of fae?"

Henry snorted. "The fae call your kind halfling's." He met Fairfax's eyes. "As if you were less." He gulped down the remains of the deer's essence, which had been provided fresh from its slaughter this morning. He felt himself ease as the sustenance spread through him, although he longed to hunt himself. Animal blood sustained him, but human blood would satisfy him far more. How long had it been since he'd properly fed? Henry's pale cheeks twitched. Too long.

Fairfax put a comforting hand on Henry's arm. "I'm sure the Council's obfuscation has less to do with respect for you as King, and more about... misunderstanding."

Henry gazed into his lover's green eyes and softened. "Then why can't they tell me anything about these European fae?" He sighed. "Why is it they place so much emphasis on the differences, rather than what brings them together?"

Lord knows, there was enough misunderstanding as it was. Enough to drive a wedge between fae and the rest of creaturekind, despite the tenuous progress he had made to smooth matters. The scores of letters he had written to the vampire leadership assuring them of his desire to stay true to the Treaty and remain behind his own borders was testament to his diplomatic abilities, after all. And no vampires had dared to rise against him, thus far, in complaint at his rule. Henry had done his duty, and built a paperwork and promises bridge between the dominant creatures, just as he had sworn to do. But these fae of Naturae, still they defied him. Glossing over how their kind operated as if it was common knowledge to all. Perhaps they knew nothing?

Fairfax's grin stretched wide across his cheeks, dimpling their freckles. "Only you, a complete outsider, not even a fae, who has brought this community together again, given them purpose, direction and meaning under your tempered rule, could worry about petty politics. You dolt."

Henry glanced at his lover, the familiar, teasing tone as ever a balm to his hot temper. "When do you have to sail?" He reached out and pulled Fairfax closer, down beside him on the bed.

Fairfax's fingers stroked the auburn hair from Henry's forehead as their eyes met. "The tide turns in a few hours."

A sharp rap on the door prevented any further tenderness. "What is it?" Henry called out.

"The sky, my liege. Tis full of fae!"

Henry's eyes shot up. Above, through the circular star-gazing aperture in the ceiling, a mist of grey darkened like rain clouds. His fingers clenched over Fairfax's. "Hide," he whispered, then he grabbed his crown from the bedside table. "Please, stay here. You cannot leave now, and I cannot risk... you."

After dashing outside, Henry scowled as he stopped in the middle of the landing platform and glanced up again. The atmosphere above was thick with throbbing wings. Now a green, brown, grey blanket, the blue of the summer sky was obscured by a mottled moss colour over the entirety of his island. Henry's fists clenched.

Far more fae than he could have imagined had descended on his shores, and still, he did not know their intent.

Filing onto the platform in orderly lines, as instructed, were the finest of his soldiers. They had guarded the citadel vigilantly for weeks, and now, their moment arrived. With Henry's appearance, they circled closer to protect him. Within moments, he was surrounded by shining silver armour. Only his head, topped by his crown, stood proud of their helmeted heads. His feet planted firmly on the wood, as he had suggested that to be airborne if - when - the Europeans appeared might be seen as aggression. It was an order Henry now questioned to himself, but did not voice.

Although he had observed it before whilst overseeing their training, his breath still caught at the sight of Joshua's clever yet delicate design for Naturae's armour. Ripples of steel which adorned the close-fitting tunics were designed to flex with flight, and gleamed despite the cloud of fae blanketing out the autumn sunbeams. Ankle and wrist bands, studded with curved spikes, had been coated with poison, ready to slash and subdue. Stubby brown wings fluttered between their shoulder blades in readiness. In their hands, Henry's addition to the army's weaponry: miniature cross-bows capable of firing multiple silver-tipped arrows with one shot. Along the railings, an arc of small cannon had been mounted, loaded with spiked silver pellets and tipped skyward; a hinge alternatively enabled them to spray the forest floor with deadly projectiles. Pre-measured sacks of gunpowder were piled neatly in crates nearby, and torches blazed in holders the length of the railing.

Without looking behind himself, he knew the rooftops would be lined with soldiers, more hidden in the structures nearer the roots beneath, armed with daggers to hurl. Even the worker fae were now proficient at spinning silver-coated blades at targets, although the aerial acrobatics of Naturae soldiers were beyond their capabilities.

As he tilted his head to study the swarm, the canopy of wings peeled apart. The split bathed his troops in sunshine once again. A golden vessel swooped down, held aloft by poles attached to the chests of muscular bearers. The chariot - an ovoid-shaped tub - approached without fanfare, drawing close enough for him to hear rustling from inside the closed capsule, but not see what was within. Alongside the flying egg, a tall, slim fae, dressed in a long velvet gown with a pale face, glared at him. Long black hair streamed behind her in the wind, catching in her huge dark wings, which reminded Henry of Joshua's appendages. He noticed she didn't bother with a cape to hide her differences when on land.

"Queen Illania?" Henry called up.

The female fae jerked her head towards the tub, then curled her lip. "Who the hell are you?" She frowned, her nose twitching with distaste. "Vampire?"

At her words, the muscle-fae abruptly drew up short. They looked to each other as they hovered a furlong away, uncertainty souring their expressions.

A bang on the lid of the tub jolted them to attention. The dark-haired fae cackled. "Mother. One vampire, that is all."

With an unspoken command, the fae cloud fell into rank, forming an arrowhead in the sky. The hum of wings intensified. The leaves on the nearby branches quivered with the force of their wing beats.

Henry drew himself up, his chin jutting forward as he responded, "One vampire. One King. One nation of Naturae stands with me. Now, state your intentions, or leave."

There was a certain satisfaction in knowing behind him, a hundred armour-piercing arrows were pointed directly at the golden tub and its companion.

CHAPTER 7

STANDOFF

The tub vibrated with dull thuds, as if feet drummed against it. A mottled green-winged fae swooped over, grabbed a tiny handle at the front, then flung the lid back. Once the cover had fully rotated on a hidden hinge, a small head, topped with a golden crown, peered down at Henry. Pinched rosebud lips parted and a shrill voice hurled "*Stultissime!*" towards the bearer fae.

Henry flicked his fingers out to hold his guard from attacking. It was but a Latin insult which loosely translated as calling them incompetent fools, but the venom in the voice could easily have been mistaken for an aggression. The four chariot bearer's wings pivoted, beat rapidly, then the transport shot towards the landing platform.

The tub, the thin companion, followed by the looming arrowhead of airborne fae covered the distance in a flash. Naturae's fae flipped their weapons ready into a firing stance and hovered a foot above the wooden floor. As the chariot swooped to a standstill several feet from the railing, a soldier trained his cannon's nose to point directly at the vessel.

For a moment, only the hum of wings could be heard as both sides stared at each other. Unable himself to see much more than a flash of airborne spears through the flank of guards circling him, Henry balanced on his tiptoes ready to dart forward and jump.

Then, hearing what sounded like a chuckle coming from the chariot, he gestured with his hands for the protective circle of soldiers to part and allow him through. He held his head high, jaw set, and thought of the regal posture his father, the imposing Henry VIII, assumed when approaching an unknown dignitary. He stepped across the planks with a sedate pace befitting the hundreds of eyes upon him. Although his own heart did not beat as it had when he was human, Henry was certain he heard blood rushing in his ears. Perhaps it was the wind.

He reached the platform edge and stood next to a cannon-wielding guard. His chest filled with pride. His Naturae fae had been unwavering in their defence thus far, especially with what might be considered overwhelming numbers in front of them. Strange, green clad worker fae and soldiers formed a wall of eyes and wings, aiming spears at him.

With his shoulders rolled back, he stared straight into the deep-set, dark eyes of tubs' occupant, which wrinkled in shrewd appraisal of him.

"I present her Majesty, the High Queen Illania. Revered ruler of the five tribes of faekind in the dominions of Middle Europa, Southern Europa and Eastern Europa and all subjects within," a squeaky voice proclaimed. "Accompanied by her daughter, the esteemed Princess Caesaria."

Henry glanced underneath the tub and spotted a figure dressed in what he supposed was dusty ornamental robes hovering beneath the Queen. He bowed his head briefly and placed his arm across his chest. "You are welcome to Naturae, your Majesty. I am Henry Fitzroy, King of Naturae."

Illania scoffed. "No such thing, boy. A male can never rule the fae. Nor a vampire." She spoke in heavily accented Latin.

Again, Henry felt a flush, this time of anger. Responding in Latin as well, he said, "The fae of Naturae have accepted me as their ruler. This matter, this realm, is not of your concern or jurisdiction." He didn't want to start this meeting with hostility, especially when they were obviously outnumbered. His hands and arms splayed open in the universal gesture of welcome. "However, since you are here now, you and your people are guests on our lands and in our skies. We offer you our hospitality - I take it you received our messages?"

As the several kestrels bearing his formal invitation had not returned while Illania had progressed closer to Naturae's shores, Henry pursed his lips and waited, but she did not acknowledge his invite or question at all.

It was the height of rudeness in human diplomatic circles, not to mention a threat, to ignore an invitation. He frowned and wondered whether there had been a problem with the kestral system all creaturekind used.

The arrowhead rippled mid-air yet Illania still said nothing. Her gaze swept lazily over himself and the ranks of Naturae troops.

Henry asked tightly, "Or do you seek provocation instead?"

"This isn't provocation," Illania chortled, revealing slightly pointed teeth, white against her red face and the abundance of blonde hair which coiled over her golden robe. "It's fact. A man cannot rule faekind."

Henry raised an eyebrow. "It is deliberate provocation to strike such a formation with your people upon your arrival." He gestured to the armed arrowhead. "As much as it is to question my leadership. I ask again: please state your intentions and business in this realm."

The slim companion, Caesaria, cackled and shared a glance with her mother.

"Where is Queen Aioffe?" Illania asked, sitting up in the chariot and looking over the amassed Naturae fae. "Why is she not here with her handsome Prince to greet us?"

Henry's lips pressed together briefly, noticing a catch to her question. With deliberate slowness, just in case any of his own populous could speak Latin, he said, "Questions which we also seek answers to. In short, she has not been on Naturae or seen for some years."

Illania frowned, which lent her face a petulant cast. "That puts a rather different complexion on matters."

Caesaria flew closer until her long black skirt draped over the railing. "And where is our Ambassador?"

There was something peculiar to her tone Henry could not place. "Absent without my consent." She was so close, he caught the tang of iron wafting in her breath. Revealed in her sneer, the points of her teeth. Almost vampiric, Henry considered with some bemusement. One leap and he could bring her down though; she had made the deadly mistake of approaching a vampire with the advantage of speed.

The Queen's frown deepened as he turned to look at her again. A well-placed arrow to her chest would pierce the rolls of flesh covered only by a silk gown, and this would be over. Her fae would become his, and he could rule over Europe...

She shook her head as if confused. "Ambassador Spenser. He is very dear to us. He left my lands in poor health, yet, the loss of an esteemed member of my court will have grave consequences."

But before Illania could elaborate, Henry interrupted with a glower. "If you came in search of answers, we are short on them."

This conversation about Spenser's whereabouts could take a dangerous turn if he did not hasten the arrivals to somewhere more private before continuing it. Knowledge was power, and he fought to keep his frustration at his spies' failure showing upon his face. If she did know something of what happened to Aioffe, Joshua, and Spenser, he would prefer to control the narrative.

Diplomacy, Henry reminded himself. He had promised the Council. Or, at least, the appearance of cordial relationships. He forced his lips into a smile and attempted sincerity. "However, we will share what we know, and are honoured by your visit. You must be tired from your flight. Naturae, in the spirit of friendship and peace, would be happy to accommodate you until you recover."

The Queen's eyes glittered as she flicked them towards Caesaria, then back to Henry. "Our arrival is most timely. You, 'King' Henry, have a problem, and I have the solution."

Caesaria said, "We accept your invitation." As her face turned to Henry, her thin smile seemed as genuine as his own.

With a waft of her fingers, Illania commanded, "Only royals and our personal guards need accommodation. Our people will reside on the south side of your island."

Henry glanced at the sky full of fae, noticing then the vast quantity of chests, barrels and baskets held by workers hovering in the distance. The sight of all their baggage reminded him of when his father had gone on a Progress around the kingdom, or indeed, when he had travelled as a child. The court brought everything necessary for its comfort, including beds, cooking equipment, wardrobes of clothes, not to mention all the troops, weapons and armour, needed to accompany a ruler. Illania was presumably no different.

He nodded, opting not to ask for how long they might stay, and mindful of the discourteous nature of such a request. His Council could no doubt discuss this with her people and inform him. Maybe then he would be able to determine whether he had just invited an enemy or an ally across his threshold.

CHAPTER 8

TWO PROPOSALS

As soon as the Queen, the Princess Caesaria, their personal guards and bearers had been shown to the renovated Ambassadorial quarters, Henry called his closest advisers into his chambers.

Restraining himself from pacing, he addressed the room. "There are far more of them than us, and my strategy of diplomacy appears to have curtailed any violence, for now. I invited you here to discuss our next step, in privacy, so the workers aren't alarmed. Clearly, the messages we had from our spies failed to convey the scale of what has arrived in our skies. We need to understand what they know. What they want. And, what this proposed solution to what they consider our problem is." His gaze lifted towards Fairfax, sat on his packed chest in the corner and his jaw tensed.

"He should not be here," Thane said, jerking a thumb at Fairfax before his face softened. "I'm sorry, friend, but it's true."

Fairfax shrugged, his freckled face the picture of innocence. "I'm packed, but I'll do what Henry wants."

"Your disruptive presence has been tolerated by us, daemon," the Elder for Scotland said gruffly, "but it breaks the Treaty just as much as having a vampire on our shores does. My liege," he added, as if his moniker would soften the blow. "The Queen could report him and all your work undone."

"Thomas will leave as soon as there's an opportunity, don't worry," Henry said. "We have more pressing matters, though. Not least," he glanced at Thane, "their numbers. Our guests will deplete our resources if they stay here long. We should put aside our original plans for a ceremonial event and meet with them quickly. Where would you advise?"

The Elders, after some discussion between themselves, considered the High Hall was not neutral ground nor with enough spiritual significance to faekind. Eventually, they proposed the standing stones of Stenness or its pair, the Ring of Brodgar, as ideal locations for the two sides to meet. These ancient sites of worship, used by Aioffe's mother and her mother before her, for Lifeforce ceremonies, lay on the mainland, only a short flight away.

Henry dismissed this idea. "A sky filled with fae would be noticed by humans."

"We could meet at night, unseen," an Elder proposed. Like vampires, the fae had nightsight.

Henry shook his head. Darkness was not the issue, indeed, he considered it a friend. But, as he was unable to fly, he would have to travel there by ship, a voyage of at least a few hours. This impediment would only serve to highlight his different capabilities, placing him at a strategic disadvantage. Although, the more he considered how the fat queen travelled, an idea formed in his mind.

Publicly though, he reminded his Council, "The nights are too short at this time of year. Midsummer approaches. We must demonstrate our adherence to the Treaty and remain hidden to human sight."

Thane re-iterated the advantages of the Great Hall, although his expression indicated his reluctance. "It may not fit everyone in, so be as public as we'd intended, but it is the heart of our home and all could hear what they have to say."

And therein lies the problem, Henry thought. He glanced towards the Captain. "Filling the rafters with both populations would be a squash. Aggravating. Given we remain uncertain about their intentions, it might be prudent to meet with fewer numbers, in less ceremonial circumstances first. Maybe something less formal - my father used to share a meal sometimes, so perhaps a cup of fresh blood enjoyed in the sunshine?" Shame a hunting party was out of the question.

The Captain nodded, understanding Henry's voiced concerns. "Outside is easier to defend, my liege." He stroked his grey moustache. "There are the twin trees of Naturae, of course?"

"Ash and Elm?" Thane perked up. "The origin trees, yes. And staying on Naturae means the mist will conceal our activities."

Nodding to himself, the Captain extrapolated. "The balconies of the Pupaetory are close; the woodland nearby is still dense and defensible. Many people could gather in the sky, but if you held a meeting on the ground, your conversation wouldn't carry far without deliberately raising your voices."

An ancient Elder, responsible for the southwest territories of England, although he had not been there in many decades, slapped his hand to the table. "The very trees Queen Aioffe demonstrated her royal abilities on." He pushed his chair back and stood, wings quivering with emotion. "What a fitting way to honour her as well. How I miss the Blessing Gatherings we had in the small clearing there." He shook his head. "So much harmony, much more than under her mother's rule."

Although Henry disliked the Aioffe-reminiscing direction the session took, sentimentality appeared to sway the Council. And, being on the ground was infinitely preferable. More than ever, he wanted himself and the Council to appear united before Queen Illania. He announced, "Then it's decided. Captain, I trust you will take all precautions you feel necessary for our security. Thane, I know I can count on you to make the appropriate logistical arrangements and, with the Elder's advice, I will issue a formal approach, making it clear only the Queen and Princess and her closest advisors are invited to attend." He beamed at his advisers. "Naturae will show these Europeans we are one people, under one eternal ruler, and we will not be cowed."

Once the gathering dissembled, Henry strode across his chamber to a downcast Fairfax. Their eyes met. "You must leave while Illania meets with us," Henry said, blinking as his chest tightened. "They will be distracted then, and you might be able to slip away unnoticed." He gripped his lover's shoulders. "I beg you, do what you can to find Ambassador Spenser. If he lives, he will no doubt have left a trail. If he is in this realm, someone, somewhere, must know. I cannot risk her retaliating if we cannot explain his whereabouts. For all the diplomacy I can muster, he seems of great value to our 'guests'. More so than Aioffe, it appears."

"What of her?" Fairfax asked. "Do you think the note was real? True?"

Henry turned away. "If she is alive, she has not returned to her people. That says it all." He poured himself a cup of blood. It wouldn't do to be low on energy, not with so much at stake today.

"Then," Fairfax stood and straightened his habitually dishevelled clothes. "I take my leave of Naturae, for now. Please, my love, decide nothing permanent until we know more. I'll start in Beesworth, for I know people dear to him there, and, well, I suspect Prince Joshua has gone back if he's anywhere." He glanced away. "For he has not returned here and I don't know where else he would have gone if Aioffe is..."

"A wise plan," Henry nodded. As long as his love was away from these people. Safe in England, he could handle himself against most foe, especially now he had mastered knife throwing. He opened the desk drawer and pulled out the bundle of blades he kept there. "Please, take these. You need the practise! I'll write a note ordering Spenser to return."

Fairfax chuckled. "I always had the sense Aioffe trusted Spenser, but there were others who never did. Do you know, Uffer once mentioned to me Spenser's family were among those who murdered Aioffe's grandmother. Stabbed her. There, in the High Hall, probably in the same spot Queen Lana... died in."

There was no need to remind Henry that his lover had accidentally killed Aioffe's mother. Unpredictability was one of the traits he most enjoyed about Fairfax, even if it did cause upset on occasion. He brushed his thumb across Thomas's cheek with tender strokes.

His lover whispered as they shared a lingering look into each other's eyes. "I cannot help but worry for you. Those lights in the sky - they mean something, even if you don't believe it. Change is coming."

Henry suppressed a shudder. Foolish. Whimsical. He mustn't let this invasion distract him. He reached to grasp Fairfax's hand. "I told you," he said. "Such a human concept, assigning meaning to the movement of stars. These matters are outside of anyone's control. You are more than that. Better than that." He pulled him closer. "And you are everything to me."

"Then marry me," Fairfax said, with sparkling eyes. "Well, not in a Church, I know, but commit to me. In public, if you like. Before your people. Pledge to be with only each other. Let us make a positive change."

"Do you mean it?"

Fairfax nodded, joy widening his smile. "If I am to have a shorter life than you, then the very least you can do as king is make it a happy one. Choose me and only me. Choose love."

Henry laughed gently. "I had never considered it before." He shook his head in wonder. "A marriage between men. A promise between lovers. The Church - humans - would never approve, but there is no such authority here. I will think about it."

"I'll return with answers, for your answer." Fairfax giggled.

Along the branches of the vast ash and elm trees, wish ribbons fluttered and wild roses and other blossoms, gathered from around the island, infused the small clearing with heady perfume. Beneath the vibrant green leaves, Henry and his Council stood to attention as Queen Illania's tub sedately flew down the path towards them. In his head, Henry calculated how long it would take for Fairfax to row out to the Wanderer, make ready the sails and be gone. The slowness of the procession improved the odds of his lover's escape with every wing flap.

As the assemblage glided closer, Henry noticed Caesaria's scornful glances at their elaborate, colourful decorations. True, there was less formality than perhaps a ruler might expect, less pageantry than he himself was used to as far as royal audiences went, but the Naturae fae were unconcerned about ornaments and gold. Within a few hours, Thane and his workers had created a representation of their history which illustrated their deep understanding and bond with their habitat. It might, at very least, soothe away tension with its aromatic scent.

When the chariot stopped, the bearer fae pulled their spear-staff's out and held them vertically to their sides. Several female fae flew up from behind and swooped down to assist the Queen. Without much dignity, she half rolled, half stepped out of the contraption and faced Henry and only a few of his Council representatives.

Of diminutive, rotund stature and now swathed in a golden robe, she reminded him of his father's coronation orb, with a crown perched on top instead of a cross. Her pudgy fingers glittered with bejewelled rings. Her face boasted cherubic rosy cheeks, a pouted mouth and an expression of serenity, which Henry suspected was entirely cast for his benefit. She pursed her lips and stared him up and down. "A thorn amongst the roses, aren't you?"

She chuckled as Henry, in his plain gold crown and a simple, informal jacket, frowned.

"Never mind," she said, thin green wings fluttering up from behind her. "I bring you, bring Naturae, the salve you need."

As she waddled towards the table, handmaidens darted forward, across the clearing with an enormous long cushion. Naturae workers hurried to pull away the heavy chairs, and confusion flashed across the Council's faces. But the handmaidens weren't finished; they tugged the bolster around on the grass in front of the table, wrestling with its weight and puffiness as if wrangling a snake, until the padding formed an incomplete circle. With a sigh, Illania flopped down in the middle.

Henry stood, tall and momentarily uncertain. If he sat at the table as planned, he would only address the back of her head. He selected a location several feet from her but still close enough to converse without raising his voice.

She patted the cushion next to her. "There's no need for distance, my boy. I don't bite!" Again, she chortled at her own wit. As he shuffled his bottom nearer, she said, "We'll soon be family."

He froze, the gasps of the Council members like off-key singing in his ears.

Caesaria inched closer, spiderish in a wispy black gown with trailing sleeves. His head shot around as her hand landed on his shoulder. She leaned in and whispered, "I might bite though," then tittered.

Henry was lost for words, left gaping like a fish as the Princess drifted over the cushion and elegantly perched between her mother and he.

"A solution, you see?" Illania cackled. "Or do you deny you need a Queen to rule, vampire?"

He swallowed. "Naturae has no need of any other ruler." His gaze flicked to the assembled Council who lurked about the edge of the table. They stared at the ground, refusing to meet his eyes but their rigid stance betrayed their unease. Diplomacy be damned. "We do have need of answers, though. Given you were expecting to see Queen Aioffe here, I do not suppose you have travelled this far without some other purpose to your visit?"

Illania sniffed, her gaze sliding around the clearing as a hush fell.

"What happened to Queen Aioffe," Henry pressed. "Her people want to know."

Dark, angry eyes flashed at him. "She, her Princeling, and my Ambassador left us nearly a year ago. They aren't in my realm." She huffed. "I would know."

But she didn't seem so certain, Henry noticed. Some of his advisors began whispering between themselves. He had to call them back to order. "Queen Illania, Princess Caesaria, why did you come here?"

"We were in the vicinity." Illania wafted her fingers around. "And, with all upset that priest-loving Philip of Spain is causing in the Netherlands, I thought it best to..." Her lips smacked together, a little tut escaped as if she chewed on something disgusting. "Best to make sure we fae stand united. That the Treaty remains intact." She glared at Henry. "But now I see, there is an opportunity to ensure the vampires are kept in check."

"King Philip is no vampire," Henry said. "No threat as long as we all abide by the Treaty."

If anything, having observed Philip's marriage to his half sister Queen Mary, Henry knew the Spaniard was partly daemon, but it was true: vampires surrounded him from dawn to dusk.

"His policies and warmongering suggest otherwise. And now, as his wife, the zealot Queen Mary of England - part of Naturae's realm - allows him dominion. It's only a matter of time before the Catholic Church regains the stranglehold." She sneered. "She has already begun burning the new faith's most ardent supporters, I hear. Do you want the Inquisition to search your shores? In Europe, they pursue the different, the creatures, with as much passion as they do the heretic."

Henry shrugged. "Human matters, religious differences, are not fae concerns. The Treaty states as much. I do what I can to bridge the gap between creatures. Besides, the Vampire Courts are aware of my rule here, and have no quarrel with it."

Not that they had acted upon, anyway.

"I have no quarrel with vampires either." She chortled. "Some of my best 'friends' are vampires." She cast a knowing glance at Caesaria. "We have much more in common than one might assume. It is religion to blame for the upset, for humans at least."

"Religion itself isn't evil," Henry replied, having been brought up a good Catholic. Upon his conversion to vampire, he had realised the truth of the deception the Bible claimed about life after death. "Nor is any belief system. Only when religious teachings are misinterpreted. Prompting people to commit evil acts in the name of their version of good versus evil."

Illania snorted. "There is no good and evil. Only power. I assumed, Henry Fitzroy - ill-begotten son of Henry the confused - you of all people would understand." She half smiled. "Just like I assume you now see the problem your father faced, with succession."

Like a glittering ball, her bejewelled hand waved in the direction of Caesaria, who tilted her head demurely. "My solution to your concerns. Take a bride who will deliver the blessings Naturae needs and unite faekind, forever."

Henry's stomach sank. Caesaria's thin lips stretched into a flat line.

"Or, you can simply be a caretaker king. Until Aioffe and her husband return. With their spawn."

CHAPTER 9

ON THE EDGE OF TRUTH

Naturae

The Captain stood awkwardly to attention as Henry sat down on his throne. "My liege, we request permission to enter the wider realm, find and recover Queen Aioffe. Queen Illania has confirmed they were alive when they left her realm."

Henry had been expecting revolt and had his answer ready. "Denied." He glanced around the table; startled expressions prevailed but he had to be blunt and put the harsh truth before them. Only then might the matter of Aioffe be laid to rest for once and for all.

"There is little point in discussing it. This is my final answer and there's no need for continued debate." He held his hand up as the Council protested. With a glare, they fell silent.

"If we believe what Illania reported, that your queen was alive and well, then why has she not returned to you?" He held up his hands, shoulders brushing the tips of his hair. "Years ago, she left you to travel to Europe, with no explanation. No care for your well-being. Just flew off, and was

never heard from again. She. Abandoned. You. And not for the first time."
His eyes widened. "Obviously, if - IF - what we are now being told is
true, the note Fairfax received and read to you must have been intended
to deceive. Written to persuade you of her death. I don't know why else
Prince Joshua would say it."

Henry swallowed, because, of course, he did know. Regret for ever having forged the damned letter seeped into his mind and he shoved it away.
He allowed the Council a moment to process the possibility they were
being lied to, before pressing on with his persuasion. "Unless... the note
was written under instruction from Aioffe herself."

"Are you suggesting she planned this?" The Captain tugged his beard,
then said through gritted teeth, "That she falsified her death so we would
not look for her?"

Henry swallowed, his shoulders dropped as if this was a revelation. "I am
saying, even if we believe Illania's version of events, Aioffe clearly does not
wish to return or she would have by now. There are those among you now
who will remember the 'Great Search' which was undertaken when she
disappeared the first time. It produced no results, she wasn't found, and
cost many lives."

Several heads dropped, and Henry knew he had them then. "I will not
unnecessarily risk fae lives. There was no-one better at hiding than Aioffe.
No-one found her before, except by chance, and no-one will again."

He shrugged. "If I were to be in her position... lying to you. Misleading
you." His crown glinted as he shook his head solemnly. "I would not
consider myself worthy of the title."

Henry glanced down the line of disappointed faces; his jaw clenched
firm with resolve. "It can only be that she doesn't want to return to you.
I can say, it is a weighty task to rule, and not everyone is cut from cloth
strong enough to withstand it. We all saw how much reigning took from
her. How unhappy she was."

Thumping his hand on the tabletop, certainty ringing through his voice, he ordered, "This is why there can be no debate. No discourse about the past. No search. Dead or alive, your queen has left you. And I'm the one who's picked up the crown, with your blessing, to guide our people into a new future. A stable one."

"But not an everlasting one," Thane said. "A Queen is necessary for the creation of our kind. While I appreciate what stability you bring to Naturae, I speak for the workers. The people you preside over."

Henry's jaw clenched. He had a suspicion he knew what the respected advisor would raise next.

Thane gestured around the table. "And we need more people. More workers. More soldiers. More fae of all creeds and abilities. You may well be right, my liege. Perhaps we should accept that Aioffe isn't returning. Which means, the European proposal to marry Caesaria isn't the worst idea,".

Henry presumed Thane adorned himself with what was supposed to be an encouraging smile, but it resembled more of a grimace.

The Captain said stiffly, "Marriage with Illania's daughter could, as Illania herself said, be the solution we need."

"It's a terrible plan," Henry replied, looking around the Council. "We can find another way to solve Naturae's issues." Although, at this moment, he couldn't fathom how.

The Scottish Elder leaned forward, arms on the tabletop and glared at him. "Sometimes it is necessary to sacrifice personal preference, for the good of the realm. Your father knew it. Your half sister knows it. And no doubt, Elizabeth will marry for political gain as well, if Queen Mary hasn't promised her to another already. Trouble only arises when a ruler tries to bring feelings into the equation. I've seen it many times."

Henry frowned. "Human rulers are not the same as us. Creatures are different."

Vampires didn't need a mate to reproduce, or blessings magic. Another reason why they were superior. He sighed as if the weight of the world sat on his shoulders, then shook his head.

"I promised you an eternal, stable rule. I cannot see why we should ally ourselves with another tribe of fae - who you have already said are very different to you - when we have stability and status already."

The Scottish Elder's eyebrow rose. "Humans marry for continuity. Security. Alliances. All of which we need."

Henry noticed the Captain nodding his head.

"They marry to build an empire," another Elder said, then his lips tightened. "Or go to war for it. This is not the fae way. Unnecessary. Our kind pre-dates such trivial matters as territory and borders. We are tribal and have had such lines in the land imposed upon us."

"I agree," Henry said. "Those humans and creaturekind with shorter lifespans have the tendency to only look at borderlines and expansion of them. Which is why we must be better."

"That's all well and good, but it doesn't solve our problems, my liege." Thane fumed. "I urge you to consider the proposal, at least."

Henry nodded. "I will, but my decision will be final." His lips tightened as he gazed down the table with a stern look. To his mild surprise, the Council seemed to accept this. Pride in his victory flushed through him, along with no small amount of leniency. "Now, let us turn to practical matters. We must plan how best to accommodate the needs of our guests on the island."

CHAPTER 10

A FAMILIAR FATHER

1 **558 York**

Lady Hanley had secured the rental of a narrow and sparsely furnished accommodation on Blossom Street, on the road from York to London. Its location outside the city walls was ideal for the fae, offering an easier night time route to the countryside, even if it sat on a thoroughfare which was noisy and busy with carts and horses during daylight. Despite officially citing three bedrooms upstairs, these transpired to be two chambers barely fitting a bed and a large cupboard. With only a kitchen and a dwelling space on the ground floor, after a long winter cooped together, the household felt decidedly cramped. Used to the larger Hanley House, Mary dictated their daily routine and running of the house. But, in spite of the expense of city living, Mary, Spenser and Mark unanimously agreed the view of the fields to the back of the property was remarkable and afforded the illusion of space. The condition set was that above all else, the fae were only to fly in the dead of night, and not unnecessarily expose themselves by frequenting the town too often. When Aioffe was too happy, her skin had an unfortunate and highly visible tendency of glowing, which was too eye-catching for safety, Mary said.

She didn't need to worry. Aioffe and Joshua were too preoccupied with what to do about Nemis to pay Blossom Street's aspect or the illuminating skin much heed. From their arrival in York, and after their visit to the gaol, they decided not to mention her visions to anyone outside of Spenser and Lady Hanley, yet the secret sat uncomfortably with both. The prevalence of other creatures they had both smelled and sensed on subsequent visits, guarding the castle and prison, complicated any thought of springing their friend from the depths of captivity. The sheer number of soldiers around, even with Aioffe's ability to sway their minds, rendered their chance of a successful, unnoticed escape improbable. Impossible. Another solution had yet to present itself, and until it did, Nemis's fate weighed on their minds like a ticking clock about to chime. A date for her trial had not yet been given.

While the household waited for any return of kestrel, with a message from Maister Jeffries or Fairfax, or any news from the fae spy network, Spenser, Mark and Mary argued. Their mutual desire to visit Nemis was a common subject of disagreement, as well as their inability to change her situation. Her frailty and foul, frightening confinement was, Spenser acquiesced, too much for the sensitive boy to see. Too much also for his heart-sick mind to cope with so soon after the horrors he had endured. "It is," he said hollowly, "easier to imagine my wife as just away, since there is little I can do to ease her suffering. I cannot cause her more distress by letting her see me thus. It is better she remembers me whole," his voice broke, "than have her bear witness to this shadow of a husband."

"If you would only feed more," Aioffe said, concerned about his ongoing weakness. "I'm certain I could lull a human for you."

But Spenser just shook his head. "I will not ever take Lifeforce from a human again. Not now I know how it feels to be fed upon."

As the days and weeks passed into months with no certainty of a date for the Assizes arrival, the household grew fractious. Simply to visit Nemis required money, along with the very necessary purchase of food and clothing for their ever-growing and hungry children. Aioffe could only repurpose and let out so many garments, and summer was coming.

The issue was forced one morning when Mark bemoaned his small, watered down portion of porridge. Lady Hanley clomped down the stairs and announced: "I've nothing left, I'm bled dry," she ranted. "My coin near all spent on the extortionate rent for this place." Her lips pursed and she turned to Joshua. "You'll have to find work if we are to stay. Support your family like a man would."

Granted 'permission' to have a little more freedom, Aioffe and Joshua had familiarised themselves with York's bustling streets and traders. With their priority shifted to securing steady income to the household, within a few days of asking around, Joshua found regular work at a blacksmith near the Minster. Aioffe had less success with finding a position in one of the several dressmakers and could only find piecemeal work. At night, they nestled close together by the cold fireplace, mourning the loss of the tools of their trade and the freedom having just a little capital meant. Resuming their old identities as Master and Mistress Meadows, silversmith and seamstress, at least made them feel established in the city, even if they had no reputation. Yet.

After a morning wandering the market in search of cheap, warm cloth to make Nemis some clothes, Aioffe suggested Joshua and Hope toddle home to rest. On an uneven, cobbled street known only as the Shambles, she walked carefully, trying to avoid the splashes from the overflowing central gully. A cacophony of knives, squeals and traders cries competed with the stench of rotten offal and rank effluence, all threatening to overwhelm her senses. Hanging in the shop windows, sheep and pig carcasses buzzed with flies. Twisty, and dark even in daylight from many overhanging floors, the

Shambles was ripe with the smells of butchery which lent it the name. Aioffe clamped her mouth shut and wished she could hold her nose.

Towards the top of the street, she found the apothecary, which she hoped would have the herbs Nemis requested for some other prisoners on their last visit. Outside the tiny shop, a steady passage of people and animals being taken to the open air slaughterhouses meandered up the narrow road.

Herbs procured, as Aioffe came out of the door, she started. Walking towards her, a vampire she remembered only too well. Her heart faltered and she froze. The question of if he would recognise her was soon answered.

His face twisted with consternation as his gaze fell on her. "I never forget a face," Father McTavish said, neatly sidestepping a loose chicken.

A chill ran down Aioffe's spine. "Neither do I."

His beady eyes roamed over her. "But I did not expect to set eyes upon you again."

McTavish had been the first vampire she had encountered after escaping Naturae, over two centuries ago. The ancient, half blind priest had shamed her, revealed her wings to Joshua, or Tarl as he was known by then, back when he had been no more than a human thief. An innocent. And, before she had saved her husband's life by making him a fae in a wood near Agincourt, over a century ago. An unintended side effect of the transformation was the loss of his memory - Joshua had no recollection of the incident or the priest, as far as she knew.

"The fact you can see clearly at all is a surprise to me," Aioffe replied, thinking fast. Something, or someone, had healed the cloudiness in his eyes which had prevented him from being able to mesmerise Tarl when he had interrupted them at that first encounter on Wrye. She frowned as she tried to push all thoughts of Joshua and Hope away. With as much subtlety as she could, Aioffe turned her left hand so her ring was less visible.

"The passing of time," McTavish said, "has made many things clear to me, and I have lost as much as I have gained." He inclined his head. "Misjudgement has a price for my kind."

The grimace which followed could have been ominous, but for the intent to show her how he'd been punished. His fangs had been removed! There was no sign of them now, only gaps where they ought to be. Their absence made him infinitely less of a threat. But still, she remembered how fast he could move. How ruthless he had been.

"Your judgement then and now is irrelevant," she said. She jutted her chin forward, her fingers falling to the blade she carried upon her belt.

His eyes flicked around, assessing the street as he said in a low voice, "On the contrary, there is much I now know, former Queen Aioffe, of Naturae."

Aioffe gasped.

"I won't tell of our reunion, if you won't? A favour from me for a favour from you?" His lips curled into a sneer as Aioffe recalled he had offered her such a bargain once before.

"Although, I hear one of ours rules your realm, in your stead," he continued.

The heat of anger flushed through Aioffe, but she focused on calculating how to escape without being noticed in this busy street. Her wings were bound inside her corset, and it was too narrow and slippery to dart down the cobbles without colliding into someone or an animal. Vampires were fast; she couldn't outrun him.

"Perhaps, we never met?" McTavish continued. His look turned sly. "I see no benefit to either of us revealing what we know. That you should be here, in York. That I am. Do you agree?"

She drew in a breath. Nothing was without price for vampires. "What do you want in return?"

"Oh my dear," McTavish said, in a simpering tone which was at odds with what little she knew of him. "Simply your forgiveness will suffice."

"For what?"

"For my past sins, of course. What else?" The priest shrugged. "As I said, many things have now become clearer to me. I have recently found new purpose in life. A revived faith, if you will." He paused and wet his lips, then sought her eyes again. "To justify the means by which I received my cure, I must atone for previous transgressions and seek forgiveness from those who survived them. You included. My penance, if you will."

As he gripped her arm with intense strength, Aioffe studied his face. She watched the black Lifeforce dance around him, which suggested he told the truth, even if he was choosing his words very carefully. Every wrinkle in his wizened face spoke of the many transgressions which he had borne, and of the many victims he would have to ask for absolution.

As the only other creaturekind who lived a near eternal life, they were both aware of the need to be able to live with one's actions against the less powerful beings. It appeared Father McTavish had indeed found a way to reconcile his sins with religious service, for he still wore a priest's robe. The black vestments, of course, were welcomed under Queen Mary's rule. A cross pendant hung from his neck, which he fondled with spindly fingers.

She had no idea how his faith could have restored his sight. Such matters were beyond her abilities, but perhaps a witch like Jeffries had been able to cure him. Her eyes narrowed. A witch of such power who could perform such miracles might be of use to them, but she dared not reveal anything of their circumstance by bargaining or trying to elicit such information.

Once more, an innate preference to avoid confrontation and escape leapt into her mind. The longer she spent here, not returned from shopping, the greater chance Joshua would seek her out. She sighed. It served no purpose to cling onto the past, nor did she want the Father to find out he still lived. Better to give him what he wanted and leave. So much time had passed, so many other adversities had happened and been forgiven, she couldn't see any reason not to grant him what he asked.

"I forgive you."

The Father dipped his head. "For that, I owe you my gratitude." He met her eyes and seemed sincere. "I am here and everywhere in York. You can usually find me around the almshouses, dispersing comfort to those in need, or the leper hospital of St. Nicholas." He put his nose in the air and sniffed. "But necessity brings me here as well. Perhaps we shall meet again sometime."

The thought of bumping into him again made her skin crawl. Since she had no need of a ready supply of blood because she could hunt for it, Aioffe resolved to never visit this apothecary again. "I bid you farewell, Father."

As she scurried away, Aioffe didn't look back. The past was best left there, for no good could come of re-opening old wounds. She twisted her silver wedding band around her finger and wondered, had she done the right thing by not telling Joshua the full truth of their first meeting?

CHAPTER 11

THE WANDERER RETURNS

To reach Blossom Street from the Shambles, Aioffe had to cross the river before she could exit the walled city. She chose to go south, past the castle, on the assumption Father McTavish would return to the almshouses. A circuitous route would be a wise precaution, she decided. She walked along the city walls and stood on the river bank for a moment. The rushing of water downstream, where the Foss met the larger Ouse, should have calmed her mind before she returned home. Yet, a niggle fidgeted on the fringes of her consciousness.

Upstream, towards the centre of the city, a cluster of boats were being loaded at the docks. Watching the buzz of activity, the barrels and chests being hauled onto the decks, reminded her of Southampton, when Henry V had amassed thousands upon thousands to voyage to war with France. Her disquiet grew, although she could not place why. Perhaps it was simply seeing McTavish again which kept bringing to mind the past. She looked downriver, where, in the distance, something else familiar caught her eye.

A few hurried paces later, Aioffe reached the pebbled beach at the mouth of the Foss. She paused next to a clump of trees, laden with ripening fruit which occupied the triangle of land between the two rivers, and stared down the wider river course of the Ouse. Her heartbeat quickened at the sight of patchwork sails. Whilst not uncommon for repairs to the sheets to be made in whatever fabric was to hand, the sheer colourfulness and pattern of them was unmistakable. The Wanderer!

Aioffe beamed. Her arm shot into the air, waving as the sleek sailing vessel drew nearer. There was no mistaking the man at the tiller, although, she had spotted him probably long before he could even see her tiny form on the riverbank. While she waited for the breeze to bring their friend to York's shores, she reached out with her mind to Joshua, reassured that he was close enough for her to sense his presence. Her heart eased as she felt the warmth of his mental touch in response. She wished he was by her side right now. Although they had hoped for a message in response to the kestrel Lady Hanley sent out about baptism papers for Hope, Fairfax's arrival was unexpected. How welcome he would be as a guest was a matter yet to be established.

Fairfax's grin, full of white teeth and freckles flashed at her as he leaned on the tiller arm, guiding his pride and joy towards the sandy embankment. But then, he blinked, and his face fell.

She frowned, watching the usually agile daemon slow down as he paced across his deck. The anchor stone dropped, as heavy as the weight which seemed to fall on his shoulders with every move. Because the Wanderer was still deep in the river, he untied the rowing boat which trailed behind, lead it around to the ship side closest to her, then clambered down a rope ladder to alight.

"What's wrong?" she called over, as he rowed with his head bowed. But he did not reply. His lips muttered silently together.

As soon as the hull scraped on the pebbles, she ran towards him. "Fairfax! Are you well?"

He sat motionless in the boat, gazing back at the Wanderer.

She put her hand on his shoulder, mindful of the daemon Lifeforce strands which encircled his body. Although only she could see them, to any fae, daemon energy was alluring. Addictive.

After years of absence from her presence, his strands today vibrated with confusion, far more than the usual chaos he embodied, and lurid yellow with contrition. Or was it guilt? She frowned. The jumble of energy reminded her of his state after he accidentally killed her mother, over two decades ago. Since then, Fairfax had matured into his middle ages, helped them re-build the fae spy network, then fallen in love with Henry, the usurper. His loyalty had always been questionable, but Joshua and Mark were closely bonded to him in friendship.

She sighed. "What's happened? Please, let me help."

He turned to her, vivid green eyes meeting her bright blue ones; his expression guarded and sorrowful. "I didn't quite believe you lived. But when I went to Hanley House to find Joshua, Uffer told me you were here, in York. I thought, doddering in his years as he is, that he was confused. Mistaking the past for the present. So I came. I was in such a hurry, I never thought about what to say when I saw you."

He swallowed as if it pained him, but his speech jumbled out, disjointed and as confused as his Lifeforce. "But... with Henry, you see? As he is. *Where* he is." He shook his head. "Although I am heart-warmed to see you alive after all, I can't call you Queen anymore, can I?"

A lump rose in Aioffe's throat and she found herself speechless. His words made a sort of sense, and explained the disharmony she saw in his Lifeforce.

His shoulders heaved as he let out a sigh. "I don't know how to be when... when it is my lover who has cost you the throne." He looked down, staring at his colourful square-toed shoes. "I am so sorry. Until I saw you before me, it somehow never occurred to my foolish mind, that what Henry does *was* - is - wrong."

True, Henry ruling over her Queendom went against every precedent, but, she had never wanted to be Queen anyway. And now there was Hope, and Joshua, and Nemis to free. What happened before, and after she went to Europe to find an heir... who ruled the realm and people of Naturae, felt like a whole other world. Another time, one which had nothing to do with where she now lived and what the future held for her. She hadn't forgotten Naturae. Just... put its fate to one side.

She glanced up the river, taking in the walled city, the throb of human activity, the simplicity of it. Here, all she had to do was stay hidden. Her only responsibility was to her family and to her friends. Guilt was behind the lump in her throat, she realised, not sympathy for Fairfax. Once again, she turned her back on her destiny, and her past, without dwelling on the consequence.

But, did it matter? Her people would be taken care of by Henry, she knew. He was not a cruel man, and she deserved some happiness. Some simplicity for a while. To be normal. Raise a child. Love her husband. Free her friend. Didn't she?

Aioffe swallowed the lump. Guilt did no-one any good; it was an entirely redundant emotion which would not solve anything.

"Do not worry. Here, I'm simply Aioffe, Mistress Meadows. Wife and mother." Her fingers squeezed his shoulder. "And I am grateful you have returned to us all." It seemed to be a day for love and forgiveness, she thought wryly. First, the old priest who had inadvertently brought her together with Joshua; now Fairfax, for falling in love with Henry and bringing him to Naturae's shores.

His hand covered hers, warm to her cool skin.

"I am ready to be whomever you need me to, Mistress Meadows. But I don't arrive with good news."

"Then you had better come home with me and tell us all," she said.

"I have much to explain," Fairfax replied, gathering his bag. She stood as he clambered out of the boat. He glanced at the trees behind her and said mournfully. "It is the season for plums, I believe. I shall make us some jam. I am in sore need of it, and you will be too when you learn what I know."

"Look who's here!" Aioffe called, as soon as she opened the door. Inside the warm kitchen, Spenser and Mark sat at the table. Their faces lit up when Fairfax poked his head around.

"Tommy!" Mark dropped his piece of bread on the table, ran over and flung himself at his friend, who hugged him back then ruffled the boys' hair.

Joshua's face split into a huge grin, although Hope looked wary of the relative stranger. Greetings over, Fairfax commented on how big Hope had grown since he last saw her as a baby, then eyed the loaf of bread on the dresser.

"Hungry as ever?" Joshua laughed.

"He did mention something about making jam," Aioffe said. She dropped the bag of herbs and plums on the table and took off her cloak.

Fairfax grinned. "I've not eaten 'proper' food for weeks. Naturae isn't very accommodating in that regard."

"What news of from there?" The deliberate casualness of Aioffe's tone fooled no-one. She pulled out her knife, which hung, holstered, from her belt, and sawed away at the loaf.

After pulling out a chair, Fairfax collapsed onto the seat and opened his bag. He glanced at Spenser. "Henry tasked me with finding you, Ambassador. And I am mighty glad I finally have." He extracted a wrapped bundle and began unravelling the strings which held it closed. "Your Queen has arrived on Naturae island, and is asking questions about your whereabouts."

Aioffe spun around. "Illania is in Naturae?" She dashed to Joshua's side and picked Hope from his lap. Cradling her, she buried her head in the toddler's hair. The last time they had encountered Illania, she, Joshua, Spenser and Hope had barely escaped with their lives. The news of their foe on home shores made her heart pound with fear.

Joshua's face darkened and he caught Spenser's eye. The older fae froze, terror whitening his already pale face. He had been the one who suffered the most at Illania's hands. "And what is Henry doing about it?"

Fairfax said, "She's making quite the impression, and somewhat aggressive about finding you, Ambassador. Territorial, I would say." His fingers ran over the knife blades, snug in little pockets, then he frowned. "I'm sure the letter from Henry, requesting your return if I found you was in here."

With a shrug of his shoulders, Fairfax seemed completely ignorant of the tension his announcement brought. "Henry bade me depart before they could find out why she came. We knew of her approach through the spy network, of course. I'm surprised you didn't. Henry chose diplomacy even in the face of her apparent aggression. There were thousands of them! So, given the allure of my blood to fae, I left while they were distracted by a formal meeting of monarchs."

He glanced down at the bundle and began fiddling with the throwing knives. "Hmm."

There were five of the curved blades and a slot in the leather pouch for a sixth, which Fairfax's fingers lingered over. The knives were quite beautiful, with neatly wrapped cords around the handles and deadly, sharpened curved blades. At the end of each handle, a circle for spinning on a finger. The set was ancient in style, as the fashion these days for the old-fashioned art was for straighter, dagger-like knives, but to Aioffe they seemed like a cherished collection. An heirloom, she wondered?

"Thomas, answer the question," Joshua snapped. They were never quite sure if the daemon deliberately obfuscated or whether his attention span was simply terrible. "What is Henry doing about Illania? What does she want?"

With a shrug, his eyes flicked to Aioffe. "I don't know what occurred after I left, but Illania told Henry, in front of all the fae of Naturae, you and Joshua left her realm. Alive and with a baby."

Aioffe's mouth dropped open as her head swivelled towards Joshua. "Oh no!"

Fairfax gestured towards Hope. "Is she well? And Nemis?"

Joshua said through gritted teeth, "What happened when the fae found out Aioffe was last seen alive?"

"I would respond, if I knew. I had to go though. Henry told the Council you clearly didn't want to come back, and that was that." He scratched his head. "I'm missing a knife and the letter."

"Maybe you left them on the ship?" Mark said. "I could go and get them? Did you sail the Wanderer?"

"It will be dark soon," Spenser growled, clutching his son's arm. "Curfew. There'll be no wandering around now."

"Do you know," Fairfax continued, "Nothing's been right since that falling star." He shook his head and frowned. "It's as if something's looming. A spectre of doom." He chuckled, then stopped abruptly. "I could have sworn someone else was on board with me. Seems silly, now I think of it. I've probably just been away for too long. But...a shadow, hiding in the night. I couldn't check as I was too busy actually sailing to look below deck."

Spenser rose from his chair. "There'll be no more talk of shadows, spectres, doom, or missing things. We have more important matters to concern us."

"Nemis, of course," Fairfax said. His face filled with remorse. "What do you need me to do?"

Spenser sighed deeply. "I cannot return to Naturae knowing my wife remains in captivity. Nor do I want to face Illania."

Aioffe handed Hope back to Joshua and went to Spenser, consternation tightening her face. "We planned to visit her tomorrow. Let's see what she wants. You don't need to go back and face Illania. Your family is here. There's always a home for you with us."

Fairfax grimaced. "Your Queen was quite distressed you weren't on Naturae."

Spenser paled. "Being Naturae's Ambassador is my calling. A role my family have performed for generations. If I don't return, then doubtless my mistress will come after me. Find me, and therefore find you all. I cannot risk her discovering our situation; I've worked too hard to keep my lives separate, but loyalty is everything. She expects me to put her first, forever." His lips trembled at the prospect, then he said, "Answering the summons protects you all. Besides, I'm useless to anyone here."

Joshua looked at Mark. "A father is always needed."

"And a husband," Aioffe said.

"I must return as she has summoned me," Spenser replied with a shake of his head. "It's more than a matter of honour, it is who I was born to be. A servant to my Mistress, even though I would rather serve another Queen and people instead. Perhaps if I go, see what she wants, she'll leave Naturae."

Aioffe and Joshua looked at each other. They had both witnessed the draining effect Illania had on fae, and there was nothing to suggest she would only feed from her own people to build up her powers. "Won't she..."

"Feed from me again?" Spenser's lips clamped tight and he ruminated for a moment. "No. I don't think so. I was punished thus before, toyed with as a means to keep you with us, Aioffe. I'm not leverage for anything, if I go alone. I'm just an Ambassador, a diplomat. As long as I do my job and report between the courts, she has no reason to doubt my loyalty, or capture me. That is my purpose, the job I have done for centuries.

My vine-family - all the other Ambassadors across the world - we're too important for her to risk displeasing. And fae do not kill fae."

"They'd better not," Joshua said darkly.

Aioffe huffed. "I doubt Nemis will be convinced either. You must see her, to explain, before you go if you are so set upon this action."

Spenser hung his head. "I know."

CHAPTER 12

UNWELCOME NEWS

Once again, Aioffe worked her magic to convince the turnkey to take herself, Joshua and Spenser into Nemis's cell. After embracing her mostly healed husband, Nemis chastised him in a loving manner for his gaunt frame. He glossed over his experiences, and she knew him well enough not to push.

In the darkness, Nemis's skin tone looked paler, greyer, than usual, which was to be expected after such a long captivity. Aioffe and Joshua were delighted she was alert, and hungry for the food they brought, especially Fairfax's fresh honey and plum jam.

"Don't they feed you anything?" Joshua asked. "Surely they can't allow prisoners to starve."

She shrugged. "Tasteless porridge, daily. Dirty water. Barely enough to keep anyone alive, and certainly not well. And all of which adds to the bill I must pay when I leave."

"Then we will pay, and for better treatment while you are here," Joshua said. He sliced off a hunk of bread and passed it to her.

"I brought more herbs," Aioffe added as Nemis crammed the crust into her mouth. "Fairfax visits and sends his regards, but no reply from Jeffries yet as to when he'll arrive with more of your tonic. How have you been?"

Nemis stopped chewing. "Most days, I'm inside the visions, so I don't see this." Her lips trembled as her eyes cast around the dank walls, then she shivered. "It doesn't matter. I know what's coming. Soon. All the queens..."

Aioffe placed her hand on Nemis's shoulder. "I told you, I'm not a queen. There's no need to fear."

"All queens. You must warn them, every one."

Joshua glanced at Spenser, then Aioffe. At home, they had all tried hard to forget Nemis's prediction, and half convinced themselves it was nothing but a side effect of her captivity. Yet, she brought her visions up with every visit. Joshua said, "Without specifics, any warning would be useless. Can't you tell us anything about what happens?"

Nemis shook her head and resumed chewing. "It is too much. Too much. The wailing. The upset. I can hardly bear the observers' grief. The shock of it. Queens taken before their time. The pain of it is too much and I can't think straight."

"Are they human or fae?" Spenser asked.

"They are women in a man's world. That's all I can ascertain."

"How can you know?" Joshua asked.

"The weight of the mantles they wear - 'tis armour to protect themselves. And, when they die, the women who surround them do not pick up the crown, yet grieve with the sadness of losing a sister."

Much as though they wanted to believe her, even Nemis would admit her visions were unreliable. Some visits, grew so frustrated by the lack of detail she could recall, she persuaded herself they were only a living nightmare.

Aioffe asked, "Where do they die? Can you tell?"

"Too dark to say. One is in a bedroom, though, richly decorated with many other people around. Incense, I think, burns. Although it's hard to tell amongst the smell of other herbs."

"Is it day or night?" Aioffe asked, reining in her frustration and using a deliberate, impassive tone. "Can you hear anything?"

"If I could only remember," Nemis said. "But, all I awaken with is the heaviness of grief." She gazed at her husband. "When I'm there, it feels familiar, almost like when I lost my babies, but I can't fathom why. Oh, to be home again, to rest peacefully."

In the silence which followed, Spenser sighed. "I must tell you something." He dithered as Nemis tensed as if bracing for a punch.

"The children?"

"Mark is well, and Hope. They grow strong and sturdy, but they miss their mother." Mark in particular had retreated into himself as the time passed, but no-one could bear to tell Nemis.

Nemis gripped her husband's arm. "You must never let them see me here. Like this. Tis bad enough I suffer, but for them to see what comes of being different will only make them fearful of themselves." She smacked her lips together like a crone. She paced away from them, wringing her hands. "No, I stay. However long it takes, I will prove I am innocent of their charges so my son can be proud of me."

"We thought about... about freeing you from this place before then," Joshua whispered. A plan to spring her out had not yet been fully fleshed out, but was very much a matter discussed amongst the adults.

Nemis lashed out. "What sort of example would I set? No, I will not go until I'm brought before a judge who can see what kind of person - a woman - I am. I have hidden what I am before, and it bought us nothing but pain."

Aioffe sighed. "But surely..."

"I said no!" Nemis span around and glared at them. "Mark must see me defend myself, so he knows what is true and right. I did not kill Master Tunn. I am no murderer."

"Witchcraft itself is not a crime, only causing death by it," Aioffe said. "I don't know how they can possibly prove your responsibility for his passing."

"All I did was ease Master Tunn's pain. He was going to die anyway," Nemis said. "But, I'm warned by others here, I'll be pricked until I confess."

"The Assize might be some time, next year even," Joshua said. The circuit judges travelled the country hearing cases and passing their judgement, but bad weather and illness frequently caused disruptions to the schedule. They had heard nothing of when the next sessions might be, and all the while, the prison swelled with captives accused of a variety of violent crimes.

"We must consider how we can ensure the truth is revealed in a manner which does not confirm you are even a witch. Innocent of the charges they will levy against you thoroughly established." He glanced at Aioffe. "It might take some persuasion, but we have to put an end to this."

Spenser crossed the cell to her. "And, my dear, in the meantime, I must return to Naturae. I cannot fly that far so Fairfax will take me there and back. A week, two at the most. My mistress in Europe demands my presence, for she is on the island."

"The Fae Queen is there? So close? She should be told." Nemis's dreadlocks shook as she wrung her hands. "Warned, although I know you do not speak of me at all to her. Just, do not say it is I who told you so."

"I hardly think she is in any danger," Joshua interrupted. "She is very powerful and ancient, and has thousands to protect her."

"She is a woman in a man's world," Nemis echoed, "if Henry is ruling Naturae. The dark heir. Any queen is at risk. Five crowns, falling." Her eyes flared at them all, daring them to challenge the information she had imparted at their peril.

They fell silent for a moment, each considering who Nemis might have seen dying. Aside from the two fae queens, there were many more in the human realm, including the closest: Mary I of England, and her cousin, Mary, Queen of Scotland and France. Across Europe, numerous female regents or wives of Kings.

The turnkey's rap on the door startled them all. "Time's up."

Nemis flung her arms around Spenser and buried her head in his chest. He winced slightly as she squeezed, but grasped her just as tightly. "Go, alone but with my love as strength, and come back to me soon," she whispered.

"Always in my heart," he replied.

CHAPTER 13

THE FIRST TO FALL

York, November 1558

The Church of the Holy Trinity welcomed the apparently wealthy Lady Hanley and her household into its needy embrace, as any charitably inclined, religious entity would. Both parishioners and clerics always paid deference to those who might bestow their financial benevolence upon them, however peculiar her Ladyship's ensemble of blacksmith, his wife and two children of mysterious parentage may be. As they filed into the second-from-front pew, Aioffe straightened Hope's new bonnet. Once seated, she gently smiled in polite acknowledgement of the welcome nods of neighbours and merchants nearby. Hope gazed around the half restored paintings to the walls, some still smudged with the whitewash which had covered them for so many years.

Although the Priory had long been dissolved, gathered in a recess on the opposite side of the aisle, Benedictine monks had their heads already bowed in prayers for the poor. They reminded Joshua of Maister Jeffries; he couldn't help but wonder at why their kestrels seeking the ex-monk with their entreaties for Nemis's medicine had gone unanswered. His disgruntlement with the old healer - duplicitous yet always with a care for his fellow creaturekind - had niggled at him for decades. The longer the delay, any reminder of his continued absence rose Joshua's ire. What could be more important than helping Nemis with managing her distressing visions? He knew the witch, an ardent Protestant, occasionally worked with members of royalty in London, but it had been months since their arrival in York. More than enough time for Jeffries to travel from anywhere in the country to their aid.

Lady Hanley shushed Mark, who fidgeted as they waited for the Mass to begin. The smell of incense, wafted by a small boy in robes which had seen better days, drifted towards them and the congregation stood. The processional through the nave was swift and sombre-faced.

Aioffe flinched as Joshua then sat; the barely noticeable wing bumps on her shoulders rippled beneath her clothes. She huffed, then gracefully lowered herself to join him on the bench. Unable to ask about the tendril of fear which reached his mind from hers, for silence fell. Joshua glanced around the church to see what had upset her as Reverend Gippes approached the altar to venerate it.

As everyone made the sign of the cross and the Reverend turned to face the assembled and begin the Mass, Joshua's eye caught one of the other priests. He stood among the usual clerks and curates, and stank of vampire.

The old priest stared directly at him with a curious look. In the back of his mind, Joshua's unease grew. It was not unusual for vampires to be clergymen in the service of the church, he told himself, especially now Catholicism was the national religion again, by Queen Mary's dictate. The face seemed somehow known to him, although, as he searched his memories, he couldn't place where he had seen him before.

Aioffe dropped a hand on his thigh, jolting him out of his reverie. With her eyes, she gestured to the pulpit, where the Reverend was imparting the introductory rites in monotonous, impassive tones. Pudgy fingers fiddled with his ecclesiastical vestments, stroking them as if the fabric would provide him with divine guidance.

Joshua frowned. They had been to this church many times, to ensure their presence was noticed just enough to suggest compliance to the law. Usually, Gippes officiated with all the confidence and passion of a true believer, even in the face of adversity. He had been forced to leave his marriage and publicly paid penance for it some months earlier, after Mary's royal proclamation repealed the right of clergymen to marry. The Reverend, like many others retaining their employment delivering spiritual salvation to their parishioners, had been faced with the choice of losing his position or yielding a family life. His sacrifice had been much lamented in the pulpit, but delivered as news in the form of inspiration: the power of the Lord's affections and approval of the Queen could replace the love of his family. Yet today, the man's hunched demeanour spoke of deep sorrow.

After dispatching with the familiar Latin greeting to the service, the Reverend sagged against the pulpit. His audience waited patiently for him to move into the Penitential Act. Minutes passed before his head rose as if dragged up by a string. "It is with the greatest of sorrow that I bring you the news," he said in English, then drew a laboured breath in before continuing. "Our beloved Queen Mary has passed into the arms of our loving Lord. She joins our Saviour, Jesus Christ, in heaven."

A collective gasp erupted.

Once again, Joshua felt Aioffe stiffen at his side. They shared a glance, and he noticed fear pinched her oval face. "A queen," she mouthed, then looked about with wide eyes.

The congregation rustled with emotion, and it seemed too much for the priest in the pulpit. He leaned forward, resting his head on the note ledge as his hands gripped the carved wood.

Hope nestled into her mother's side. "Mama, what happens now? Do we still have to do Mass?"

Absently, Aioffe shushed her. Her face had drained, and she was as pale as many others in the room. But, Joshua understood, it was not only shock which caused his wife's terror. Was this the start of Nemis's prediction?

"We received notification just recently of her sudden death," Gippes said, having gathered himself. "In addition, I have been informed by other sources the prince we celebrated her carrying not many months ago has not been born, after all."

A woman behind them burst noisily into tears, which set off quite a few others. Even Lady Hanley purported to join in, extracting a lace-edged handkerchief and dabbing at her clear eyes.

The monks began to sing, a low, melodic lament which echoed the sorrowful sentiment of most of the congregation. Joshua dropped his head, moved by the music.

Hope and Aioffe, however, stared straight ahead, their fingers twitching as they drew in an unexpected surge of Lifeforce. Such an event, lacking since the rise of Protestantism in places of worship, was an opportunity to gather strength and power which Aioffe had lacked lately. She could only pull this essence from strongly held beliefs or a crowd's emotions, or directly from still beating human blood. Sustenance to keep her alive came from animals like all fae did, but a blood diet alone weakened her abilities.

Joshua noticed Hope's hands curl and wriggle with some surprise. That Hope would have the same needs and gifts as her mother wasn't unexpected, only that she should do it so young, as this was the first time he witnessed her drawing the Lifeforce in the same way. Was his daughter even aware of what she was doing, he wondered? Even though they were not related by birth, nor was she a fae pupaeted from a vine, the near five-year-old was a unique combination of all creaturekind. Conceived during a Blessing Ceremony in Naturae with a fae father, Joshua had helped when Nemis birthed her. Somehow, in her Lifeforce, Aioffe said she saw daemon and vampire as well, which they attributed to Henry and Fairfax's presence at Hope's conception. But, Nemis had always maintained the fae baby was destined to be the child of Joshua and Aioffe, binding them together in a family unit.

As the monks' voices soared into a final note, Gippes straightened and stared at his audience with a steely glare. Barely pausing for a moment's reflection after the hymn, he launched into the Penitential Act.

"I confess to almighty God and to you, my brothers and sisters, I have greatly sinned, in my thoughts and in my words, in what I have done and in what I have failed to do." The priest's voice cracked as he deviated from the established script. "I am indeed a sinner, Lord."

Falling to his knees behind the pulpit, all they could see was his fingers reach up. He entreated in a loud, impassioned voice, "It is my fault, my most grievous fault, for I have failed to bring to the light of your wisdom, Lord, those heretics who reside within."

Aioffe shuffled in her seat as the sounds of sobbing cut through the silent shock of the audience. Mark seemed affected by the change in atmosphere and began to mutter under his breath. His head moved from side to side as if trying to shake out the daemon. Lady Hanley patted his arm, pre-emptively restraining him while staring ahead with a stony face.

"In spite of your decree, our great departed Lady, we did not weed out enough of those sinners."

Mark squealed, an unearthly noise which echoed around the high ceiling.

But the priest carried on. "The heretics to the true faith. The vile witches," he spat, "who desecrate and defile the name of our Lord with their necromancy, their devil-loving rites and their wanton behaviour." The priest's voice then rang clear with zeal. "As you directed, they should have burned for their sins, that they might be absolved of their many sins against our Lord and our Queen."

At this, Mark's squirming and squeaking erupted. Hands balled as his arms waved by his sides. It looked as though he was possessed, but Joshua knew what was about to happen. He had witnessed the same buildup of uncontrollable emotion in the boy when Nemis had been arrested. He stood, quivering with rage, and screeched like an animal.

Suddenly, all eyes were on Mark. In the absence of Spenser as a calming influence, Lady Hanley tried to pull him onto to the bench beside her, but his back jerked. Mark began making loud grunting noises. His strange behaviour could not be easily ignored, especially in such a public place. To save further embarrassment, or possible accusations, Joshua knew there was no alternative but to remove him before he started screaming.

Joshua stood, grabbed the edge of his cape, and leaned towards the boy. With a swoosh, he wrapped Mark in the heavy material, gathering him into his arms. Aioffe and Hope shuffled quickly from pew to aisle as Mark jerked and wrestled against Joshua's chest. His muffled squeals continued as they dashed past a stunned audience.

Lady Hanley scuttled behind them, loudly excusing his behaviour in a tone which stifled any immediate contradiction to her version of events. "He is overcome, poor boy. The Queen... he is just too distressed at the news." She half bobbed a bow as they reached the doorway, which the Reverend Gippes didn't see, then trotted ahead of them to Blossom street.

CHAPTER 14

BLEED

Mark's recovery after his commotion in the Church took longer than anyone thought it would. When Reverend Gippes came calling to Blossom Street on Monday, Mark refused to come downstairs to talk to him and remained in his cupboard for the next two days.

Quieter than usual but driven by hunger, the sullen-faced child eventually rejoined the household for meals. Mary demanded he tell them why he had reacted so strongly, but he simply shook his head and tightened his lips. Privately, Joshua thought it might have been Gippe's vitriol against heretics and calling witches vile. The boy could not be cheered by Hope or any efforts to restore his spirits. Aioffe suggested sending a kestrel to request Spenser's return from Naturae, but Lady Hanley was adamant she could manage Mark, nor had the spy network informed them of their arrival on Naturae. He and Fairfax could be anywhere, and his son acting strangely was, in truth, nothing unusual.

Yet Queen Mary's demise hung like a pall over the household. Every time they had to pay for something with a coin with the monarch's head stamped upon it, they were reminded of Nemis's prediction and dread pounded through Aioffe and Joshua's hearts. It took a lot of restraint by

Joshua to keep their occasional hunting trips at night to the local area, and Aioffe frequently thought of flying away with Hope and her husband, just to escape the tense atmosphere of York. A peculiar yearning for her own bed in Naturae kept her tossing and turning when she should have been resting. Their pallet bed in the corner of Blossom Street's living area was a poor substitute.

A few days later, Gippes reappeared, catching them at their break of fast. Joshua had already left for work. The priest took one look at Mark and declared he would not be welcome at the special Mass to be said for the Queen, unless he was bled to have his humours restored to a correct balance.

"On such an occasion," Gippes pulled the gloves from his hands, "to miss the service would be viewed in a very dim light. Every loyal Englishman should attend this most sacred of moments while our beloved monarch is laid to rest in London. It is our duty to gather and pray for her devoted soul to find deliverance."

Meaning their absence would be noticed. Aioffe rested her hand on Mark's shoulder, sensing his agitation. "Would you perform a bleed yourself, Reverend?" Many times she had seen the leech gatherers knee deep in the Ouse, so there was surely no shortage of the critters most often used for medicinal purposes.

Gippes shook his head. "I would have recommended a visit to the Priory, the monks there were most experienced, but alas, it has not been functional for years. No, I cannot assist, for such a procedure cannot be done except by those more specialised in the technique."

"An apothecary perhaps?" Lady Hanley said. "There are many. I'm sure we can find one suitably equipped."

Gippes gazed at her steadily; in the absence of the man of the house, she was the most senior member of the household. "I recommend he's taken to Father McTavish, a visiting cleric in our parish. He witnessed the incident last week and offered his services."

It was fortunate he chose to glare at Mark at that moment because Aioffe paled.

"He usually travels around the country in an official capacity, deciding whether misdemeanours should be scheduled for the ecclesiastical courts or dealt with under common law. While the fate of these unfortunates accused of the crimes is decided and relevant parties notified, he offers dispensation of specialist spiritual services. We are lucky - he has agreed to assist those poor souls at the St Nicholas leper hospital while he is in York. He is widely acknowledged within the diocese as someone who treats..." His eyebrow rose as he turned to Lady Hanley. "Special cases. By going to him, it will be clear your intention is to seek the Church's help in the matter, rather than fall foul of the aforementioned ecclesiastical courts' judgement. Put simply, the boy has been noticed; Father McTavish can either help or will mark him as a heretic."

With the impending accession to the throne of Princess Elizabeth, a Protestant, a reversion to the system of fining people for their absence from church was on the horizon, if she chose to be as intolerant to Catholics as her sister had been to Protestants. Troubling times lay ahead. Accounting for their precarious household finances, a friend in gaol, a child marked of face and a boy whose behaviour could not be guaranteed, avoiding additional attention seemed the wisest course of action, irrespective of the personal risk.

"I shall take him," Aioffe said, being sure to sound convincing even though she dreaded another encounter with McTavish. She flicked her eyes to Mary, seeking her agreement. "This afternoon."

Lady Hanley lips pursed as if she wanted to object, but Aioffe added, "At the leper hospital," knowing full well Mary held a deep-rooted, and common, fear of the afflicted.

She strode to the door and opened for the priest. "See you at Mass, Father."

Gippes tipped his head at Lady Hanley and left.

"I should take the boy," Mary said, as soon as Gippes had gone.

Aioffe replied, "Mark shall come to no harm if I am there. It would be better for your standing if you weren't involved. Besides, I have a history with this particular vampire." Her eyes darkened.

"What kind of history, Mama?" Hope piped up.

"Nothing for you to worry about." Aioffe ruffled her daughter's hair, then glanced at Mark. His face looked pensive and his fists balled on the table. She added, "He isn't the first vampire you've met, and this one cannot bite. Remember how Henry helped you before? A drop of vampire blood will heal any cut. There is nothing to worry any of us," she said, a little too lightly. Convincing herself would not be so easy.

She glanced through the small window. "It's not too cold outside. How about we all walk to the riverside on the way and find a lovely stone for courage? Hope, you and Mary can then come back to make supper for when we return."

Hope beamed. "Yes!" She tottered over to Mark and tugged on his arm. "You're the best at stone hunting. Can you find me one while you're gone? Otherwise I'll miss you so."

It was hard for anyone to resist Hope when she was being charming, and Mark was no exception. His lips finally lifted in a slight smile and she flung her arms around his thin waist.

The Church of St Nicholas hospital lay outside the walls some miles west of York city. There were others, equally a distance away from where people lived and worked. To the casual observer, the church, set back from the well-trodden track of Lawrence street, looked like any other. But here, the afflicted lived side by side with those who came to worship. The chancel chapel housed the patients, that they might be healed by the Lord, while the nave was reserved for parishioners. Not everyone in residence was a leper; sometimes a colony was a useful, although costly, hiding place for other undesirables, like bastards.

Spinning the smooth stone chosen by Hope from the river's edges in one hand, Mark's other gripped Aioffe's as the church door creaked open. Shaded by the ornate stone porch, a veiled leper kept to the shadows as he grunted, "Who comes?"

Fearful, Mark shrank back, tugging her arm behind in his desperation to avoid proximity to the man.

"We are looking for Father McTavish," Aioffe said. "We were told he attends those here."

The leper jerked a bandaged fist. He shook his head and the grey rags covering his hair flapped, revealing the sores on his face. "Around back."

"Thank you," Aioffe said.

She led Mark around the white square tower and through a small, well-maintained garden allotment. Herb bushes and lines of vegetables were being tended to by another leper. As they pushed between an over-grown yew tree and the side of the church, she paused in her hoeing and stared at them.

Mark turned his face to meet Aioffe's eyes. "Don't be frightened," she whispered. "They deserve your sympathy. No harm will come to you." She deliberately dropped her glance to the knife on her belt.

Mark didn't look convinced and scuttled ahead.

As they rounded the corner of the church, a series of outbuildings and thatched barns came into view around a small courtyard. Since the doors were closed and the yard deserted, Aioffe paused and listened. Her heart pounded as she identified the Scottish accent of McTavish in the lean-to at the end. They crossed the flagstones, Mark's sweaty palm hot in hers.

Before she could knock, the door wrenched open. McTavish, although not a tall or large person, filled the low doorway. He nodded curtly, then stepped out into the afternoon light. His lips chopped together while he sized Mark up and down, pinching and prodding as if appraising a horse.

Never having seen him in full daylight before, the vampire appeared akin to any other non-threatening old man to Aioffe, aside from their unique smell. Noticing Mark's Lifeforce grow orange with alarm, she pushed a tendril of reassurance into the child.

"Good teeth?" McTavish barked.

Mark looked at Aioffe in confusion.

"Very," she replied. "Smile for the Father, Mark."

Hesitantly, Mark's lips stretched back. A closed-toothed grimace appeared on McTavish's face and he sniffed. "A good eater? The right things?"

"Yes."

"Sleeps well?"

"Yes." Aioffe wondered when the questions would turn to Mark's behaviour, but they didn't. McTavish sniffed. "Bring him in."

Aioffe followed the priest into the dim room. McTavish busied himself in a corner cupboard. "Sit. Sit," he muttered and waved his arm at the two chairs wedged into a small desk. He plucked off a dark green stole draped over the back of one chair and rolled it up. The gold thread of the embroidered cross, with a Celtic knot to the centre, shimmered in the low light of the dung fire.

Aioffe dragged out the other chair and pushed Mark into it. Sensing his nerves rising again, she stroked the nape of his neck and crooned, "This won't take long."

In truth, she had no idea, having never needed to be healed by a physic. What she did know was humans believed illness resulted from an imbalance of the four humours. It was common practice for them to be bled, most often by leeches, or purged, to rebalance the body. She put no stock in their medicine, as she could heal animals and trusted a witch's knowledge and magic more than a human's. But what Mark suffered from was being a daemon, and both she and McTavish knew this. His scent alone announced it to creaturekind, so what McTavish proposed to do to 'cure' him, in name at least, mystified her.

McTavish approached with an empty stone bowl with a spout and sharp knife. As he placed them down on the waxed surface, she noticed he'd arranged a line of small, empty bottles. The sight reminded her of the medicines Nemis had once made for her, to strengthen her when her reserves were depleted after blessing the vines in Naturae, and the tonic Maister Jeffries concocted for her visions. She sniffed, surreptitiously, inhaling the scents of the distillations - rosemary, mint, nightshade, and willow bark. Somehow, their presence alone reassured her McTavish knew what he was doing.

Mark squealed as the knife approached his neck, but the priest gripped his wrist. "Be still," he said. His eyes flicked to Aioffe, dark and serious. "I must be precise, and cannot use my usual methods on such a thing."

She nodded, and through her fingertips, pushed another tendril of Lifeforce into Mark. To hide what she was doing, she whispered, "Hush now," into Mark's ear.

McTavish frowned, then slowly advanced his knife again. A vein in Mark's neck pulsed and the priest licked his lips.

"The bowl," he said, in a slow, mesmerising voice.

Aioffe passed him the vessel as the blade sank in deep.

As Mark's blood spurted out, her touch kept him calm. The scent of iron and the tangerine scented strands of his Lifeforce filled the room. She felt her heartbeat pound at the intoxicating smell; she inadvertently leaned forward as if to ingest the alluring essence. Realising her mistake, this was Mark, she told herself. The danger was too great for her to have any of his blood.

"Such a shame it is toxic," McTavish said, turning his face to grin at her wolfishly. "Yet it has other useful qualities."

Mark flinched as the vampire dropped the knife on the desk and then nicked his own finger with his teeth. "You'll feel better now," McTavish said in his same pseudo-calming voice. The bowl full, he rubbed the cut on his finger to the nick, then placed the vessel down.

Mark's eyes rolled back into his head as the wound knitted together.

"Rest now," McTavish said. He placed the bowl of blood next to the line of bottles then turned to Aioffe. "He will need regular bleeds, if I am to report to the parish he is being properly treated." There was a gleam in his eyes which made Aioffe frown.

"I'll bring him."

"And, what about your... husband?" McTavish's lips drew back as he glanced at Aioffe's wedding band. "I may have been half blind when we first met, but he does seem remarkably.... young. For someone last seen in 1415. How is that, I wonder? For he is not vampire, I would have sensed it."

Joshua's rebirth had paused his aging over a century ago. Like her, he still appeared, in human age, to be in his late teens, the age he had been when he went to France with her. Aioffe drew in a breath whilst she listened to the slow beats of Mark's heart, sure he was asleep. "He remembers nothing of you, or the incident." She glared at him. "But I do. I may have forgiven you, but I will never forget."

McTavish nodded slowly. "Those of us with long memories never do." His gaze met hers. "But, a past can always rear its head. Often when you least expect it."

"He does not need to know what happened. If he did, he would not be as forgiving."

Mark's hand twitched; he would soon be free of the deep sleep the vampire's blood had induced.

Aioffe said, "Since we can neither keep to the agreement to have forgotten we met and meet the requirements Gippes has set for Mark's return to church, I will trouble you as little as possible save for bleedings when necessary. In return, I ask that you do not approach my husband or any member of my family. As you know who I am, you will also know I have certain connections who would not approve of your behaviour with regards to breaking the Treaty. Selling daemon blood is forbidden, so I trust you to dispose of it properly."

McTavish scowled, then his lip curled. "The past indeed haunts both of us." He nodded. "So it shall be."

In the hope he would stick to his word, she shook Mark's shoulder. "Mark, wake up. We need to go home."

The boy mumbled, then roused with a further shake. "Aioffe?" He blinked. "I had the strangest dream."

"You can tell me about it on the way," she said, helping him up. "Until next time, Father."

"Be sure to tread carefully out there," McTavish said. "Darkness falls."

Aioffe had the uneasy feeling he was not referring to the worn state of Lawrence Street or the cold winter which approached.

CHAPTER 15

REGENCY

December 1558, Naturae

"She went in the night," Thane said as soon as Henry opened the door. His eyebrows crossed as he waved a scroll at Henry. "The household staff just informed me. I checked the Ambassadorial quarters myself, and it's true. Illania has gone. Caesaria remains. I was passed this."

Henry strode across his chambers, glowering as he dragged on his robe. "How did we not notice her disappear?" He would have words with the Captain about this.

Thane shook his head. "It's only Illania and her guards. The majority of the European workers and army are still encamped on the other side of Naturae." He rolled his eyes. "Feasting on our beasts."

Henry raised an eyebrow. He reached for the scroll, broke the seal with more force than was required for the wax, and unrolled it.

'Given the fortunate circumstances,' he read the beautiful copperplate Latin, then translated aloud for Thane, *'I will replenish myself in England. An empty throne, perhaps for the taking? After all, it was due to you, and done for you. Nothing would make me happier than to return to good news of*

an impending alliance between our people and an expansion of our mutual interests.'

He frowned as he looked at Thane over the top of the parchment. "Find me Issam."

His advisor nodded. "There is one other matter, my liege."

"What?" Henry snapped.

"The Wanderer's sails were spotted entering the mist this morning."

Henry's heart leapt. "Send word for the Council to convene this afternoon to discuss this 'development' and I will not be visiting the Pupaetory today. Ask Issam to meet me at the dock."

Thane nodded and left. Henry grabbed his crown, tucked the scroll under his arm and marched down the corridor. After a brisk rap on the Ambassadorial quarters, he gritted his teeth.

When a guard opened the door, he said, "Where is she? Princess Caesaria."

The soldier glanced over his shoulder, then back to Henry. "Her Highness is expecting you." He stood back to allow entry.

Reclining on a cushioned seat at the foot of the bed, Caesaria's lips stretched into what he presumed she thought was a seductive smile. It was wasted on him.

"Explain this?" He thrust the scroll at her.

She arched a thin, black eyebrow. "No preamble? How bold."

"Where has the Queen gone and why?"

Caesaria's smile turned into a sneer. "There is so much you do not understand about royal fae. Do not worry," she stretched out a gaunt hand. "I will show you." As her lips parted, he noticed her prominent fangs. "We have much common ground to discover about one another."

"There is little point in moving towards any sort of alliance with you unless you can provide what apparently only a royal can." Henry pointed at the window. The Pupaetory walls shone grey and silver in the morning sunlight. "Show me you can bless the vines, or this entire charade is pointless."

Caesaria sighed. "Once again, dear Henry, you demonstrate your lack of suitability for the task of ruling faekind. Perhaps you would, as mother suggested, be better off among humans." She angled her head towards the bed, long hair sliding over her bare shoulder. "Only a queen can impart royal blessings." Then her dark eyes shone as she faced him. "A true queen, in every sense of the word."

"And as King, I am supposed to bestow the title upon you?"

"Yes. It must be a marriage in every sense of the word." Her eyes slid back to the turned down covers of the bed. "Every."

Henry thought for a moment. "Then we are at an impasse," he said. "Without proof of what powers you bring to Naturae, I cannot bind myself to you." He shrugged and strode towards the door. "I suppose it will mean disappointing your mother."

Caesaria growled. "She has bigger plans than you could conceive of for us both. I suggest you re-think." She jerked herself upright, fists balled, and stood. "Before you make a fatal mistake."

"What plans?" Henry stared at her, lips pressed together.

Neither spoke until she finally dipped her head. With a tone which dripped in sweetness and light, Caesaria said, "But of course, I should acquaint myself of the citadel which will soon become home."

"That would be wise," he said. "I do not take kindly to threats to myself or my throne." He stormed out.

The Wanderer pulled into the dock just as Issam dashed up to Henry. While he waited for Fairfax to drop the anchor stone, Henry asked his spy, "What is happening in England which might have caused Queen Illania to visit so suddenly?"

"My liege." The spymaster bowed. "News reached us yesterday. I was going to tell you when I had more information, but it's now been confirmed by several sources." His hands shook. "These humans, it's hard to separate rumour from fact sometimes."

Henry glanced as the shadowed wrinkles deepened on the old spymaster's face. What could Illania have done in only one night? He swallowed, braced for the report.

Issam lowered his head. "I regret to inform you, my liege, your sister, Queen Mary of England, has died."

"Died?" He frowned. She would have been only fourth-two, Henry thought. He felt little sorrow at the news, for his half sister had always refused to acknowledge his existence, despite the closeness in their human ages. "How?"

"Unclear, my liege. Some say a canker; some say grief at not bearing the Spaniard a son and heir."

"Foul play?"

"It's possible." Issam studied the rough dock planks. "She had been sequestered, lying in, for some months. And, of course, there was the previous pregnancy which bore naught."

"Witchcraft?"

"Again, I could not say for certain." He glanced warily at Henry and muttered, "She named Princess Elizabeth as her successor."

Henry's mind turned to his beloved little sister. Although half daemon, she was much beloved to him. And now destined to fill the vacant throne of England. The throne he once thought would be his. A slip of a girl, he'd last seen her when she was held prisoner at the Tower, by Mary on suspicion of treason. He could not help but feel relieved she had survived and, presumably kept her nose clean enough so she could succeed legitimately. Elizabeth was tenacious and clever, there was no doubt, but Henry's father had always abhorred the idea of a female ruler. Even Henry himself, a bastard, was preferable to succeed, until his half brother, Edward, had been born of course.

Queen Elizabeth. The very thought of it tore him in two. He swallowed, both pride and ire filling his chest. The English throne. The very seat he'd been promised.

Gazing straight at the Wanderer's painted sides, peeling and patched, Henry remembered how Fairfax had entered his life just after young King Edward's death. The daemon had done all he could to support Henry's quest for England's throne then. Would he follow him into battle once again?

A sea breeze whipped a chill through Henry's hair and Fairfax's thick cape swirled around him as he climbed down the rope ladder to the dock. While he waited for his lover to disembark, he fiddled with the edges of Illania's scroll. 'It was done to you and for you,' he recalled. Was England's the empty throne Illania meant? "Why else would Illania go to England after the death of a queen?" He mused aloud, tapping the paper to his chin. Does she want it? Or am I supposed to take it?

Issam looked at him curiously, then said, "Another passenger!"

Fairfax had reached solid ground and turned to hold the ropes steady. "Safe for you to come down now," he called up. A figure appeared on deck.

Henry's eyes widened as he recognised Ambassador Spenser. Thin, but still alive. His clothes sat bedraggled upon his once robust frame, and his skin a peculiar shade of grey-green.

Spenser met Henry's gaze with steady eyes. "Is she really here?" He called as he clambered down.

"After a fashion," Henry replied. As he walked to his lover, he noticed Spenser's grip on the ropes was firm, but movement an effort. A shadow of himself, Henry thought; what dreadful fate had befallen him?

He folded Fairfax's lanky frame into an embrace and muttered into his curls, "Oh, but I am glad to see your freckles again." He pulled back and planted a kiss on his lips.

"What do you mean, 'after a fashion'" Spenser interrupted.

Henry stood apart from his love. "Illania was here, until last night, when she disappeared with only her personal guard." He shrugged. "Her people remain. I know not when she will return, but she indicated she would." He waved the scroll. "However, England is without a crowned queen right now, and the timing cannot be coincidental."

Spenser pursed his lips. "She'll have gone to feed upon the grief of a nation, then." He looked relieved for a moment, then his face darkened again. "A female monarch dying, though. Is it coincidence?" He glanced at Fairfax.

"The prediction?" The daemon's eyebrow rose. "'Tis just one queen. An ailing one as well, if the rumours were true."

Spenser drew in a deep breath, then exhaled long. "Perhaps you are right, Thomas. One death does not a prediction make real."

"What are you talking about?" Henry asked, sensing a conflict within the fae. "A prediction?"

"My wife is lately plagued by visions," Spenser said. "Of queens dying."

Henry's brows furrowed. "Queens?" He glanced at the scroll, then the Wanderer. "How quickly can you make ready to go to London?"

Spenser groaned. "I don't suppose you could spare a rabbit or two before we sail again? I haven't the strength to endure the waves without sustenance."

Henry said, "I must warn my sister of the risk. I'll leave with Thomas as soon as I have informed the Council of these developments."

Spenser met Henry's eyes with an expression suggesting respect. "You could surely send a kestrel?"

Henry grimaced. "She was ever mistrustful of such messages. Of prophesies as well, but perhaps this one she might take seriously if the news of it is delivered in person."

Fairfax put his hand on Henry's arm and said, "Henry, if you are in England, then maybe you can also help Nemis? At her trial."

"Why would I help a witch?"

Spenser glowered. "It is her prediction which forewarns your sister."

Henry pondered his options. Dear as Elizabeth was to him, and warn her of the threat he undoubtedly would, there was more to his haste than he was prepared to speak of. If she didn't become Queen, or if she were to die, there were no other candidates for England's throne than himself... And, Elizabeth's successor would need to be in place to seize the moment, should such a thing come to pass.

His eyes flicked up the beach, glossing over the wind-waving treetops of Naturae. Should he do as Illania implied? What was the cost to his current situation? He reminded himself, if Aioffe intended to return, she would have done so by now. The only real risk to his throne here was Caesaria. Unpopular. Unproven. Naturae would never allow her to rule while he or Aioffe still lived. On this much, he was confident.

He cast his gaze along the dock, settling on the shabby shoes of the one person who seemed to hold sway with the Europeans stood before him. Henry smiled. A fae trusted by many, as Aioffe had trusted him as well. One who could not lay claim to his throne, but offered reassurance to Illania that all was well. A sensible man who could be relied upon to manage Naturae in his absence. Better yet, one whose loyalty to himself could be secured with relative ease.

"I offer you this," he turned to Spenser, looking him full in the face. "I'll influence any court it takes to free your wife if, in return, you act as my Regent in Naturae until I am back. It is not easy for a King to trust, but you have proven yourself worthy many times over. Your return will appease

Illania, when she comes back, and, if you fail to protect my throne and Naturae, I will fail to protect what is yours."

The Ambassador straightened, his eyes narrowed.

Issam grinned. "The Council would accept Lord Spenser as Regent, I am sure."

But Henry hadn't finished. It was only fair to give the fae a more complete picture of what lay ahead for him. "You should know, Illania has proposed I marry the Princess Caesaria, which I won't do unless she proves herself of use to Naturae."

Spenser's jaw dropped as Fairfax gasped, "But..."

Henry placed his hand over Fairfax's in reassurance, then stared at the citadel in the distance. "I do not believe she can perform though, not as a fae queen must. Nor are her ways liked much by my people. Yet," he tilted his head to one side and looked at his lover, "for diplomatic reasons, I must appear to give the proposition fair consideration." One side of his mouth tilted up. "For how long I consider is my prerogative. The passage of time is different for immortals."

"You do not know what it is you ask of me," Spenser said. He blinked then stared across the expanse of sea. "But, I fear without assistance, my wife is doomed to hang."

"Once in England, it will be easy for me to find out when her trial is to be held, so fear not. You should also know," Henry said, "Princess Caesaria remains here, tasked by me with blessing the vines."

Spenser inhaled, nostrils flaring. "She's as like to poison them." He exhaled noisily, then looked to the forest. "I'll definitely need more than rabbits."

CHAPTER 16

THE LETTER

York, January 1558

Joshua rubbed his hands together, warming them on the forge fire before he stepped outside the sheltering walls. The chill of a northern January winter bit, and blacksmith Coop's knuckles swelled. His aged joints ached so much he could barely grip a hammer, so Joshua had taken over all the wielding and welding lately to spare his employer the pain. Today, the freeze was accompanied by a howling gale whistling past the open workshop. The old man shivered, so Joshua turned back inside, gave Coop the woollen gloves Aioffe had knitted, poured him a warm cup of ale and urged him to bed. Coop grunted as Joshua bade him farewell.

The walk from the forge to Blossom Street was not far, but enough for tiny ice droplets to form in his whiskers. As he traipsed along the city wall buffeted by the wind, Joshua fancied he had never known such a squall as this, but in his heart, he knew it could not be true. Before rounding the corner, he stopped for a moment to gaze across the river, to the wetlands which were dark grey with white mounds where snow caught on the reed beds. He shivered, for the desolate plain clouded by snowflakes dancing in the breeze triggered some memory he couldn't put his finger on. Another place, he thought, too long past to accurately recall. Perhaps Aioffe would remember.

Just as he walked down the pathway to his front door, a kestrel landed on his shoulder. It shook itself free of the snow then nudged him with a cold beak. He glanced down, spying a note tied around its leg. With numb fingers, he unwrapped the little scroll, then gave the kestrel's neck a stroke and scratch. He pointed it towards the shelter built into a tree for just such messengers, in the back garden. The bird bobbed its head, then flew off.

They were expecting word from Spenser of his arrival in Naturae, so Joshua unravelled the wisp of parchment and read:

One queen downed by unclean hand, but wytch queen is next?

For the devil is an angel fallen, so sayeth a learned text.

Perhaps she lye close by?

With a jolt, his heart leapt into his throat. He re-read the note, frozen on the doorstep. It was not Spenser's handwriting, but scrawled by someone else, unfamiliar to his practised eye.

Much as though he tried to tell himself 'one queen downed' could simply be a reference to Mary's death, a crawling dread swept over him. He could not help but think of Nemis. Her visions. Her certainty about crowns tumbling which he and Aioffe had tried to ignore the threat of these last few years. But now a Queen had most certainly died, and prophecies didn't seem quite so easily put aside.

And yet, no-one else but Spenser and Lady Hanley knew of the visions though. Which could only mean, there was a killer. With a plan. He drew in a breath. Logically then, if indeed Queen Mary had died by foul means, did the writer threaten the next royal death? Or was the reference to a witch pertaining to Nemis? And, did it mean a witch, or which? Lye... did that mean lie as in on a bed, or lie as in hiding the truth? The play on words made little sense to him, although the note was clearly sent by a creature for none other would use a kestrel, and intended for someone in this, his, household.

The mention of angels feared him the most, for on occasion, when seen, he and Aioffe would suggest they were angels to reassure any human who saw their wings. His breath billowed out into the cold evening air, clouds which tugged away the scales from his eyes.

Why warn someone in this household if not to prevent a death, or threaten Aioffe? Or was it some sort of clue to who was behind the killings? He focused again on the words, determined to decipher them before he could plan what to do about the note.

He swallowed hard, hearing Aioffe comment on his late return through the wooden door. Mentally, he pushed a thought of his proximity as re-assurance into her mind, then shoved the note into his pocket. Until he could make sense of it, no-one could see its contents. No-one need know it had arrived. He opened the door.

Inside, Aioffe's blue eyes twinkled as she grinned a welcome from a chair by the hearth. Lady Hanley sat at the head of the table, reading a booklet with a frown on her face. Mark perched by her side, spooning dinner into his mouth with barely an acknowledgement of his arrival. Hope slid down from a stool and ran over, arms up. "Papa! Lift me!"

He swung his daughter into his arms and spun around and around, his heart swelling with each spin. He met Aioffe's dancing eyes and his mouth dried. Despite his smile back at her, a furrow touched her brow. Joshua knew then: he could not tell her of what lay in the folds of the clothes she had so lovingly made for him. Couldn't tell her of his fear her death was next. At all costs, he had to protect his family and spare them from the torment of daily dread and glimpsing into the shadows to see what danger lurked. He pushed all thought of the note from his mind, lest Aioffe enquire in her unique way.

"Stop, stop!" Hope cried, half giggling.

"Have you finished all your lessons for today, then?" He lifted her until her covered wing bumps almost touched the rafters.

"Yes!"

"She has. Some very nice letters," Lady Hanley said, putting the pamphlet in her lap and waving her fingers at the pile of wax tablets. She peered across the table at the wooden bowls. "But she has yet to finish her pottage and clean her plate."

"I'm not hungry," Hope whined. "I want to hunt."

"Not today," Aioffe said. "It is too cold. You must take sustenance as Mark does." Her eye flicked to meet Joshua's. "Your father has had a long day, and will soon be time for rest."

He dropped a kiss on Aioffe's forehead, then plonked Hope down on the stool. With a semi-stern look, he pushed the plate towards his daughter. "Eat, then to bed with you. Maybe tomorrow the weather will have lifted and we can go out to the forest."

Mary grunted and picked up the leaflet again, then, as if seized with rage, crumpled it up and threw it across the room, into the fire.

"What was it that irked you so?" Joshua asked.

"I could swear the Knox man is behind a plot of some kind," Mary replied. "Just the way he writes! For a learned man, he twists words so. Sedition! Perhaps our new monarch will finally hang him now he is returned to the country. Elizabeth, at least, is a Protestant like him, although he uses the pulpit of paper to damn all female rule."

"You've not been reading that rubbish again?" Aioffe said, lightly. "I would have thought it a waste of your pennies."

Lady Hanley's nose stuck in the air. "It's important one stays abreast of matters which pertain to who rules the country. Though," she added darkly, "Knox called for Queen Mary's removal and yet, I can find nothing in the pamphlet to suppose he was responsible. He'll doubtless continue to rail against Elizabeth as well, despite sharing a faith. His opinions on gynarchy have less to do with religion and more to do with hatred of all womenfolk. Of women who rule, he calls them monstrous and unnatural. Pah!"

Joshua's fingers tapped the note in his pocket while he thought. "If we are to give credence to the prophecy, we might be wise to consider all options."

Aioffe shot him a glance, then stood. She kissed her daughter then led her to the stairs. "Come, Mark, you must rest also."

The boy stared dully at her and said, "And what if I don't want to?"

"Mark!" Lady Hanley snapped. "In this house, my house, you will do what you are told."

"Won't!"

Before Mary could say something which would aggravate the situation, Joshua intervened. "Mark, if you get a good night's rest, then I'll take you to see the frozen river tomorrow at dawn. Snow is falling and it will freeze o'ernight and glisten at the edges as the sun comes up."

Mark's expression lifted.

"Now, go and tuck yourself into bed, lad," Joshua said in a stern tone. "For I do not want to have to tell your mother you misbehave. It'll only cause her concern."

Chastised, Mark followed Hope up to the bedchamber as the adults gathered around the table.

Mary said in a low voice, "The notices have been posted at the Town Hall. The assize is scheduled to arrive in a few months."

"I shall go this week and tell Nemis," Aioffe said.

Joshua sighed. "And no word yet from her husband." He shook his head sadly. "Without Jeffries' medicine, I fear the news will only increase her peculiar behaviour."

"Perhaps she would know what elements or herbs goes into it?" Aioffe asked. "Then we could seek another to prepare it? Or bring her the herbs needed if she could fashion it herself."

Even as she said it, Joshua knew it unlikely. Bashing a poultice together and applying it on joints was a simple enough matter with pestle and mortar, performed by many a cunning woman. Distilling liquids down, often for hours, required a more appropriate environment and equipment than the gaoler could ever be convinced to overlook; Nemis could hardly set up an apothecary in prison.

Mary said, "I have made extensive enquiries after the Maister through the spy network, to no avail. We still do not know if the visions have merit, either."

Joshua chewed his lower lip for a moment and forced his expression to appear neutral. "If we supposed they were true, and one queen has fallen, we ought to consider others who might suffer the same fate." He glanced at Aioffe, who was staring at him with a peculiar look.

"What do you know?" She asked.

He shrugged and looked towards the fireplace to watch the flames dance. "Only that Nemis has never been wrong, just obscure. We have lost one female ruler, and another is about to rise to her throne." He held up two fingers. "And now you say John Knox writes what many already believe: queens - women should not hold power. He has quite the following, especially in Scotland. The Protestants, the so-called Lords of Congregation, have been problematic for Mary of Guise since last year." A third finger joined the pair.

"As regent there, she is effectively a queen," Lady Hanley pointed out. "Or her daughter Mary, in France, the annotated Queen of Scotland and about to be Queen of France?"

Joshua glanced at Aioffe, raising a fourth finger, then said, "They are all queens, or acting as, in a man's world, are they not?"

Aioffe's jaw tightened. "Enough of this talk. All three Marys we speak of are, or were, Catholics. Knox is a follower of Calvin, and thus indisposed towards those who believe in popery. To hold any strong opinion in matters of faith is always dangerous. We fae have seen it change before, and it shall happen again. Do not be so quick to assume their deaths are part of something bigger, should they happen at all." She shrugged. "Visions aside, death is inevitable for humans. We should not get involved, in either their ruling or their choice of faith."

Joshua swallowed, fingertips burning somewhat where they touched the note. "And if it's not about religion? Even though you are no longer Queen of Naturae," he said stiffly. Warning his wife of danger had never particularly made her choose the safe route before, but he persisted. "You are still a queen. As is Illania. Nemis's vision was not specific to humans."

After a moment, Aioffe offered, "There are other fae queens, of course, around the world. Other tribes. But for now, should we only be concerned with those who are in our immediate vicinity? This realm?"

"Given it's Nemis's vision," Joshua said, "It's reasonable to presume the queens in danger are the ones she knows of, rather than any female ruler, anywhere. I don't think we can ignore what she has foreseen. Shouldn't we warn them of the threat?" His heart thudded against his chest and he could not look at Aioffe.

"Pah!" Mary exclaimed. "We have no evidence of anything. It is all supposition."

Aioffe stood and paced to the fireplace. "At this moment, Queen Mary's death, one death we know of, could be mere circumstance. It's more important for us to protect Hope, and Nemis and Mark, than to worry about what may pass for humans and their monarchy. Human rulers will rise and they will fall."

She turned to glare at Joshua. "Unless you know otherwise, we remain hidden. Tis the only way. To stay here, together, and raise our family. Find a way to save our friend. I will not cause undue attention to ourselves by getting involved in human matters. A treaty forbids it. What will be, will be."

"But what if you are next?" He said.

Aioffe poked the fire with uncharacteristic aggression. "Then they mess with the wrong Queen. Fae are not so easily disposed of." She stared at the poker tip embedded in glowing embers.

Joshua stood and crossed to her. He put his hands on her shoulders. "My love, if there is another death, by foul means, will you reconsider? I don't want to leave Nemis either, but for your safety, we'd be better off either returning to Naturae or starting over somewhere where we are not known. At least on Naturae, we have resources. Weapons. Spies. An army."

"Going back puts Hope's life at risk. There, she will be seen only as an heir. A peculiarity to be guarded at all times, like I was," she said. "She'll never be free to have a childhood, already she grows too fast. In time, her own destiny will become clearer. I want her to be able to decide how to live her life, but she'll not be able to if the choice is taken from her. If we return to Naturae, that's all she'll be - a precious commodity to be cocooned and kept safe until she's needed, not a person who has her own mind." She pulled away from Joshua and placed the poker against the stone wall. "And, do you forget, Henry is on Naturae, with Illania."

Seeing concern tighten his face, she swallowed then said, "My love, I know you would protect me, protect us, until you turn to dust. But, contrary to my usual instinct to run, this time we should stay. For Nemis, and for our family. Don't you see?"

"And what does your instinct tell you about the death of Mary of England?" He caught her hand in his and gazed into her eyes. Tenderness softened the tense lines about his mouth.

"That this is just the start." She said quietly, covering his fingers with her own. "We must be patient to see how the next months, years possibly, unfold before we act. And, we should treasure what we have, here and now, as the humans do. When we know more, then we can do more."

"But for now?"

"We bide our time."

Mary grunted. "It may yet prove to be nothing."

Joshua nodded. When he had time to decipher the note, then he would tell them. No point worrying anyone if he wasn't sure. They fought on enough fronts for survival, perhaps Aioffe was right and they shouldn't get involved with human matters. Chasing queens with vague concerns would only draw attention to themselves. Given the choice between scaring his family or exposing them unnecessarily, every time he would choose to protect them and their freedom.

CHAPTER 17

CROWNING

1 **4th January 1559, London**

The spectacle of his half sisters' Coronation Parade fed Henry's senses as well as lifting his dark mood. Returning to London and obscurity after so many years, the crowds which lined the streets looked like easy pickings. Dressed like a commoner, his hungry eyes drank in the sight unnoticed; his stomach ached, starved as it was of fresh human blood. Cities and celebration made it too simple to snatch someone down a side alleyway, he thought, resisting the urge which pulsed through him. Although the noise of trumpets and drums as the procession of Queen and nobles approached would camouflage any shrieks of surprise, there would be plenty of time later for sustenance. Henry's task took priority.

With Fairfax close by, they pushed between the well-dressed bodies towards a stage which had been erected, spanning the entirety of Gracehurst street. Elaborately painted backdrops billowed, stretched across three tiered platforms, dampened only by a flurry of snow. The January chill went unnoticed by the crowd in the heat of their anticipation.

A palpable buzz of excitement and a surge of claps greeted soon-to-be Queen Elizabeth's arrival. Despite his height, Henry had to rise to his tiptoes to see the golden canopy of the horse-drawn litter. Unfortunately, the covering and the sea of bonnets obscured all view of her, bar the glimpse of a pale bejewelled hand, waving gracefully in acknowledgement of the crowd's devotion.

The play started with a loud blast of coronets, then the players entered. On the lowest tier, they performed a short scene depicting the union of Henry VII and Elizabeth of York. Huge red and white roses framed the striking visual representation of Elizabeth's proud lineage. On the second tier, Henry's father and Anne Boleyn sat, and above them, a slight boy wearing a wig of bright ginger hair shimmered in the centre, representing Elizabeth herself, enthroned and crowned.

"Where does she parade next?" Henry asked Fairfax. His brow furrowed, and his temper short from restraining his hunger pangs.

"Cornhill," Thomas said, "for the virtues and vices, then Soper Lane."

"We go to Soper then, and hope."

Fairfax shook his curls. "I think it probable the crowd will only swell, the closer she draws to Westminster Hall." He gazed around. "I did not expect such numbers, I confess."

Today and tomorrow, anyone causing the slightest nuisance was likely to be thrown behind bars to wait out the events with the drunkards and troublemakers. His father decreed this measure for Anne Boleyn's coronation, and Elizabeth's was far more elaborate, welcomed and well-populated. He had misjudged the situation entirely, for in his absence, the English seemed keen to take Elizabeth the moderate into their hearts. Mary's good favour with the people burned along with the Protestants, a lesson he could have forewarned her about, had he been able to get near her.

He grit his teeth as he cast his gaze around. With the flank of soldiers, not to mention the armed members of the nobility who trailed in the litter's wake, there was scant opportunity to approach his sister without causing a scene, even by posing as a well-wisher.

The play finished with a roar of approval. As the crowds were directed to move aside, they jostled together, necks still craned for a glimpse of the golden saviour. Backs pushed to dirty bricks to create space on the gravelled road so the litter could turn and progress onward.

As the drums took up again, Fairfax grinned. "Elizabeth must be happy with all this pageantry."

Henry glanced over the hats and through the fine feathers poking up. Although not looking his way, he caught the radiance of her pale skin, the slender nose tilted up in mirth. Despite the years between them, at twenty-five, she had endured so much to reach this unlikely point.

And so had he.

The bitterness at his wasted sacrifice of his soul rose in his throat. "Let us leave her to it," he growled. "I have no desire to follow the crowd when a better moment may yet present itself."

One which only a vampire could engineer, perhaps. He searched his memory for a moment when a monarch might be alone on a day which was all about being presented to the people.

Henry prepared for his new task with the churning of jealousy in his belly. During the drunken revelry of the previous night, by a fountain which was soon emptied of wine, he found suitable prey. Once the cleric was mesmerised, Henry had his fill of blood as well as relieving the man of his vestments.

The day of the coronation dawned frosted and clear. As soon as the sun rose, Henry, disguised in his new costume, and dozens of other priests milled around Westminster Abbey. While he straightened flowers, put out orders of service and pads on the seats and swept the floor, the menial labour afforded him ample opportunity to re-familiarise himself with the layout of the vast cathedral. He found it strange that he couldn't find even a stone marking the final resting place of his half-brother, Edward VI, yet Mary was encased in a huge stone sarcophagus adorned with fresh flowers.

Old Sir Richard Sackville intermittently appeared, back bent with the responsibility of organising the entire coronation, of which today's ceremony was the most sacred. He hobbled about the cavernous room, his sharp voice fussing and snapping orders for perfect arrangement of the décor and the precious items to be used in the service. Just before the doors were flung open, the advisor rubbed the orb and sceptre with his sleeve to add a final shine as if dust could have settled on it since its placement on the altar.

Henry ducked his head whenever Sackville came near, for the member of parliament had also been present at Boleyn's coronation and could recognise him. A priestly disguise could only shroud Henry's body, not his hardly aged face. Henry remembered that Coronation in 1533 clearly, as he'd been only sixteen years old at the time and the heir apparent. He had stood next to his father for the whole ceremony, and been promised his own such event if Anne's swollen womb did not produce a boy. Neither event occurred, but the daemon temptress had borne Elizabeth. Henry's presence here was not just fortuitous, he thought, but prophetic; few others had witnessed both coronations. The wily organiser, if faced with a ghost from the past, might have him ejected on suspicion of trouble-making right when Henry needed to remain inconspicuous.... for now.

As guests began to file into the nave and take their seats, Henry slipped into a darkened corner behind the traverse to await his opportunity. Armed with his knowledge of the Abbey's recesses, Henry's mind quietened. From this vantage point, he could see only the long altar at the entrance to Henry VII's chapel, laid out with the basin and chalice, and hear only the rustles and quiet conversations of the attendees. His sister would arrive soon enough, and he could impart his warning as she changed robes mid ceremony.

Or... he could take her crown. The crown which sat just a few feet away, glittering like the beacon of power it embodied.

There would be challenges, but nothing which could not be overcome with the backing of any vampires in the congregation. After all, the Church had made him thus for precisely the purpose of ruling England. Temptation burned still for the throne he was promised, and yet, his black heart battled against his conscience. Sweet Elizabeth, the sister he adored. Even with Anne Boleyn's daemon blood running in her veins, could he really steal this moment of crowning glory from her?

As the hours ticked past with indecision plaguing him, a peculiar scent troubled his nose. It wasn't the pomades hanging from the wardrobe which held the clothes she would change into after the anointment. Not the spicy notes of incense, which lingered still despite Elizabeth's attempts to merge both Catholic Mass and Protestant ceremony, but something else. Something which caught in the back of his throat as medicine might. It tickled forth a memory, of a time when he had been a poorly human, and in need of respite. A peaceful journey to heaven was expected, if he ingested enough of a foul tasting tonic to ease his passage there. His eyebrows drew together as he placed the subtle floral scent.

Belladonna. The deadliest of nightshades used by healers as a curative or, he knew now, for a far deadlier purpose than sleep or cure.

His gaze landed upon the chalice. No-one else would drink from it this day but Elizabeth. The strong, blessed wine would camouflage the bitter taste easily - for that was also how he had been offered its relief. Had someone added a dose, perhaps too hefty a measure, to the cup which Elizabeth would publicly sip from after receiving the Eucharist? To what purpose? For her ease, or with a darker intent? And in this most visible of places?

A sweat dampened his palms. The Abbey was near full; any minute, the trumpets would sound with her arrival up the deep blue cloth. Every eye would be upon her as she entered. He could intervene and save her. Or, he could allow what was likely to happen if she drank from the cup to occur. In a divine moment, which seemed too perfect to be true, he could be crowned in her place. The people would accept him, not least because of the fortuitous happenstance of his presence right at the very site of her death, and beyond reproach as he was dressed as a simple priest. Why, even John Dee, Elizabeth's astrologer, had predicted this day, the 15th of January, as being the very day of coronation of a new monarch, despite it being a Sunday. Dr Dee had not specified which monarch.

A slow smile spread across this face as he imagined the weight of the bejewelled golden crown of England finally being placed upon his head. How his strong will would bear the responsibility well. Heavier and with more power than Naturae's, such a throne could only be held secure by a man such as Henry Fitzroy, firstborn son of Henry VIII and destined to rule...

A trumpeted proclamation sounded from the balconies above, echoing around the pendant and fan vaulted ceiling. Henry jumped. He wiped his hands on the priest's gown and slicked back his hair. Hardly ceremonial garb, but his regal bearing would compensate for the lack of ostentation he wore. Perhaps he would be seen as humbled by the honour of stepping in to the role. Inch by inch, he crept forward and peered around the screen to see Elizabeth's progress.

His breath caught. At that moment, sunlight seared through the coloured panes, bestowing an angelic glow over white silk skirts. Sunbeams lit her pale ginger hair, draped loose over her shoulders, and cast upon her face innocence, serenity and calm. Elizabeth gazed straight ahead, arms supported on either side by noblemen as she progressed down the aisle. Henry could scarce breathe at the sight of her as she stole the attention of the congregation. Tiny and yet huge. So like his father in countenance and composure, he felt humbled, shamed even, in her presence. Her brightness shone the light of truth into his heart, stabbing back the aspirations he thought of moments earlier. He could no more allow her to be killed than he could take the throne she too had waited for.

His last remaining kin.

His little playmate no more, but still the dearest of children to him.

Henry's feet ran swift across the cathedral. Hands grabbed the chalice and, with barely a sound made, he dashed straight past the altar. Reaching the wooden panels of St Nicholas's chapel, he tipped the contents of the chalice into a nearby flower arrangement. Then he pivoted and darted back.

In a human heartbeat, the ceremonial cup was back in position on the altar cloth. Void of all poison, and with it, his soul, in absentia, brightened just a fraction.

Safe once again behind the traverse, Henry clambered inside the wardrobe and shook his head at himself. Almost immediately, he considered his actions - had every last drop been drained? What if the cups surface still retained enough to cause the hallucinations or sleep? His stomach clenched; he should have wiped it down thoroughly rather than fear being seen. Why had he not done that?

Distracted by his ruminations, Henry missed the fractionally open wardrobe door closing shut. Only when his breathing grew laboured, trapped with the suffocating smell of pomade which clung to the garments, did he blink and listen. A rustle of skirts, a murmur of voices became audible through the wood. He forced himself to still. Any movement might invoke discovery.

What had he been thinking? What darkness had stolen into him that he should contemplate watching his sister die, by a fouler hand than his, just to take a crown? He lifted his gaze up, as if to the heavens, and for the first time in a very long time, prayed to something, someone, for forgiveness. Since his turning, he had wrestled with his own black nature, and the absence of his soul in many ways had been liberating. Yet the evil yearnings which possessed his mind of late were unfamiliar to him.

His eyes narrowed. Such hungry thoughts of power had not entered his head for years, until Illania's note had tempted him with the offer of more.

Henry started as the door creaked. He glanced through the folds of fabric and recognised the wizened face of Kat Ashley as she thrust her arm into the wardrobe. As she reached for the mantel of golden cloth hanging there, with quick reflexes, he grabbed her wrist. "Tell Elizabeth the chalice is poisoned," he whispered, pulling the lady deeper inside, towards his gaze. He stared into the wise eyes of his sister's long-time nurse and friend. With all the force he could muster through his quietened voice, he said, "With all the love of her brother, he commands her not to drink from it if she wishes to bear the crown beyond the end of the nave."

Then he released the wrist and waited. The lady's fingers wavered, then closed on the hanger.

"That oil," he heard Elizabeth say, "was naught but grease. Look, see how it sticks and ruins my complexion. And rank of smell."

"My Queen," Kat said, with some hesitancy.

"Wipe it off before it sickens me," Elizabeth ordered. "I must have the most virginal forehead ere been seen when I go out. People ought look to at the crown, not the stain of anointment on my face."

"I am bade tell you: do not drink from the chalice. There's poison in it."

"Don't be ridiculous, Kat!" Elizabeth gave a little stamp of her foot. Henry could not prevent a smirk in the darkness, for his sister had always been precocious. "I cannot placate everyone. You know this. The balance between rituals must be right for me to be accepted by the people."

"Your Highness - Lizzie - I am commanded to tell you this message, with love from your brother. Your life depends upon it."

Henry heard Elizabeth's loud exhalation. "Fine." Then there was a long pause. The rustle of silk and the slap of a sword being hung over her hip. "Where is he?" Elizabeth asked.

"In the wardrobe," Kat replied.

"He'd best keep silent in the shadows," Elizabeth said, in a slightly louder voice, which was entirely unnecessary for Henry's vampire ears. "But his presence fills me with joy, such joy as I would have named him my Champion had I but known he was here. Perchance, we could converse awhile then."

In the darkness, Henry grinned. Oh, but she was smart indeed.

CHAPTER 18

THROWING THE GAUNTLET

Later that day, Sir Edward Dymoke, the Queen's appointed Champion, readied his steed in the stables. Subduing him proved easy: at the mere suggestion of a nap from Henry, exhausted Edward removed his armour, then laid down in the hay like a babe in his undergarments. He now snored softly, entirely ignorant of losing his second moment of glory at the Coronation Banquet, which, Fairfax commented, was probably going to be a far more joyous and sweet occasion than her sister Mary's austere event had been. Henry's jaw clenched but he said nothing.

Fitting into Edward's small suit of armour was not as easy as its removal. For centuries, the hereditary role had been performed by the head of the Dymoke family, whose males were stocky and tall, like Henry. However, the breast-plate when strapped on was distinctly short and the plackart covering his stomach barely reached the top of his hips.

"This won't do," he hissed. Fairfax snorted with suppressed laughter, then yanked on the buckle. Henry glanced at the pauldron plates which were supposed to cover his broad shoulders. "Did I grow or did the metal shrink?"

"I heard the original suit was stolen, then worn by one of the leaders of the Lincolnshire Rebellion," Thomas said, reaching for the skirted fauld. "I suppose a replacement had to be made, and fit, for a smaller man. If we'd known this disguise was the plan, you could have brought one from Naturae. Joshua always did make a fine, flexible suit of armour."

Henry grunted, although he had a point. He winced as Fairfax dropped the steel shoulder protection over and proceeded to strap it into place. Despite having worn armour before on many occasions, Henry suddenly felt a kinship with the horse, which patiently stood, tied to the stalls, trussed up with a shaffron over its face, crinet and crupper strapped over neck and rear. The thought of jousting in this getup was ridiculous. Just walking would be an uncomfortable chore, let alone leaning forward in the saddle and aiming a lance.

He decided not to pull the right gauntlet on; fumbling with its tight fit to extract his hand would only cause mirth among the esteemed guests.

Fairfax handed Henry the helmet. "Don't worry, I'll make up some excuse if Sir Edward wakes before you're back," he said and blew him a kiss.

Henry grinned, slammed the visor down and galloped around to the Banqueting Hall. Reining up on the cobbles outside, he waited until the soldiers opened both the vestibule and inner doors. Animated conversation and polite tittering wafted out, along with the scent of roasted meat. He salivated, momentarily missing the taste of human food which would cause him much illness, were he to eat it now. Instead, he fixed his eye upon the tallest chair back in the room and nudged the horse forward. He cantered in, waving the gauntlet around his head. His entrance, although expected, caused forks to drop and many a guffaw. Probably because his armour was too small, he hoped, and not because a vampire had just stormed into the Queen's first official repast.

"As Queen's Champion," Henry pronounced, as clearly as he could through the visor, "I challenge anyone who doubts her right to rule. Speak now and face me in combat."

Silence fell as Henry's horse panted. All eyes were upon him, and for a heartbeat, it felt glorious. He drank their attention in, noting with some disconcertion a surprising number of vampires amongst the guests. Officials, noblemen, and, lining the walls, more than a handful of clergymen, some still adorned with popish accessories. Hot metal pushed against his forehead, preventing him from frowning. Was this how ruling England would be for Elizabeth? The two doctrines vying from the start? Mary had chosen to surround herself with creatures, for protection, but he had credited his sister with greater intelligence.

Henry puffed out his chest and trotted over to Elizabeth's chair, then, with a dramatic flourish, dropped the gauntlet to the floor. "Does no-one seek to assert a better claim on her throne? I vow vengeance upon anyone who would harm but a hair on her head. Personally."

The irony of his question, given the dark thoughts he had harboured only hours earlier, flushed his cheeks. He was consequently very grateful for the helmet. With deliberation, he swivelled his head this way and that, yet did not meet any eyes. As was the custom, people ignored him, picked up their forks once again and turned their heads to talk with their neighbour. Before long, conversation - slightly louder than it had been before - filled the candle-lit room.

Somewhat deflated, for it might have been fun or at least a challenge had anyone actually dared to take him up on the offer of single combat, Henry slid from the horse. On bended knee, he inclined his helmet to his half sister. She peered down her slim nose at him. "I thank you for your service, kind sir. It appears there is no challenger today."

"But there was earlier," Henry whispered. "And may yet be more to come."

She tilted her head back and laughed. "Oh, there always will be."

"You do not take me seriously, Lizzie. I have reason to believe an attempt was already made upon your life. The chalice held deadly poison within."

"T'was empty. Besides, I did not intend to drink from it anyway."

Her sass grated on him. Immature imp. "You took the sacrament. Good job I emptied the cup," he growled.

She drew back, pressing slim, elegant fingers to her throat as her piercing stare met his. "You're serious?" Her gaze then swept the room, cheeks flushed with anger. "Who would dare?" Then back to him. "How did you know?"

It had always been his preference to be honest with her, and the afternoon's attempt on her life had convinced him. "My abilities enable me to smell better than.... some. I do not know who or why, but I will find out. A proven se'er witch has foretold the death of queens and our sister then..." His pauldron clanked as he shrugged his shoulder. "I came to warn you. It may yet be discovered Mary fell a-foul of a killer's hand as well."

Elizabeth sniffed and picked up a sweetmeat. "Consider me warned."

"Eat or drink nothing which has not been first tasted by another!"

She froze, blinked twice then popped the morsel into her mouth. "Kat had one earlier," was her response to his glare. "I thank you though, brother. I shall tell Cecil of your cares, and set him to investigate also. Know this," she drew herself tall, her neck elongated as she rolled her shoulders back. "I may be a mere woman, but a king of heart and stomach. The English throne is well protected." She glanced at him and, switching expressions from haughty to her usual sweet smile, batted her eyelashes. "There, how did that sound? Manly enough to rule? Human enough?"

"You would do better look a man in the eye, and have a care for what goes into your stomach," he said, then stood, gathered the reins of his horse and stalked out.

CHAPTER 19

TO FACE A MONSTER

Gossip about the Assize's imminent arrival had reached Nemis by the time Aioffe next visited. After she confirmed the rumour, Aioffe asked how she felt now the dreaded day was approaching. There was still time to try and help her escape, but the witch was resolute.

Nemis sighed, then bowed her head. "The guards warned me I'll face certain 'tests' before I even reach the dock."

"What do you mean?" Aioffe thought back to the conversation they'd overheard in Hanley House's attic. Pricking had been mentioned, but surely, poking someone until they bled was a ridiculous way to prove a person was a witch.

Nemis shrugged. "That much I do not know. Confession is good for the soul, is all they say. Repent. Not that it would save me." She shook her head, the rat's tails of her dreadlocked hair dangled around her uncovered head. "How could I admit to something I have not done, and yet I cannot confess to what I know will pass."

"Lady Hanley has already established herself in the town as a person of good standing," Aioffe said. She bustled about the little, low space, straightening the ragged blanket on the pallet bed. "I will find out what they plan to do before the trial and when, and ensure she is a witness. Mary would not permit any physical harm to come to you." She could not bring herself to repeat what Mary had learned from the spy network. Of the trials across the continent, especially the hunts led by the Spanish Inquisition, which identified those who had supposedly made a pact with the Devil and punished them. Spenser had warned them all of the growing frequency of such persecution for years now, but there was no need to remind Nemis of the wider threat.

Aioffe's heart pounded, knowing what she had to say next would likely worry Nemis even more.

"We heard from Thomas." Her throat dried, yet she pressed on. "He will come for the trial."

"He brings the documents needed to prove Mark and Hope's baptism?"

Aioffe didn't want to extinguish the flare of relief in her friend's eyes, but knew she must. "He also brings Henry Fitzroy."

Nemis pulled back, shaking her head.

"Henry will defend you, Thomas says."

"No, no... not him." Her head shot up, grey eyes glinting with tears in the darkness. "He is the dark heir. He stole your throne."

With a shrug, Aioffe gazed at the floor. Facing him would be difficult for her as well, but she saw little other choice if Nemis was to be saved from the gallows on Knavesmire hill. "I don't know why he offers this service, but I think you should consider accepting his help."

"Why would I trust him?" Nemis's fist balled at her side, her arm shook with tension. "After everything he has done. Tell me, why should I entrust my life to his words?"

"We know no-one else with better knowledge of the systems at court. No-one more well read. And because he is a vampire. He can influence the judges in ways I cannot."

"I will not use trickery to prove myself innocent. I cannot."

"You must. We must."

"Then it will be unjust." She hugged herself, rocking, shaking her head. "I cannot, I cannot. I will lose myself again at just the sight of him." Her fingers unfurled. "Don't you see? I am weakened with these visions. What if seeing him makes them worse? Oh, I will be undone, and in public."

"That was then. Years have passed. This time, you can prepare yourself to see him. Fight for your life. Dispute the accusation and live to come back to us." Aioffe approached, her brows drawn with concern. "My friend, what choice do you have? We have not the funds for anyone else to represent your interests, nor are we learned enough in the law to make your case. We're told others so accused are rarely released. Or, you confess, and the judge will have no other recourse but to find you guilty of the charges and put you to the noose. Unless you agree to escape, there is no hope for your release without a lawyer disputing what they accuse you of. Too many have witnessed what they'll call maleficence with your visions."

She put her arms around Nemis's shaking, sobbing body. "My dearest friend, it pains me to say, but without help, we fear you would hang." There was no hiding the brutal truth; Nemis had to be made to see the consequences. "If you will not let us get you out of here before the Assize, and insist on facing the judges all on your own, Mark could be left motherless, and Spenser missing a wife."

Nemis howled, fear coursing through her. Aioffe held her close, pushing comfort down through her fingertips into her until she felt her friend ease. She closed her eyes, envisaging the smoothness of unblemished petals. With all her heart, she hoped that the healing boost she provided would force away any blemishes which might mar her friend's skin. The pock marks, the tick bites, anything which would show her as impure.

"I know what you're doing," Nemis snivelled.

Aioffe laughed softly, hoping she didn't really. "Of course you do. Do you blame me?" She pulled her friend apart from the embrace and looked into her eyes. "I know how hard a decision this is for you. If I could give you all my strength to endure, I would. If I could take the pain, or change the way things are, there's nothing I wouldn't do."

Nemis nodded. "I know. You risk enough to bring me this news. It is enough." She stared at the locked door and clamped her lips for a moment. "I will face him. And face my accusers. I cannot deny what I am, but I can defend my innocence. I choose to have a chance at life."

"With Henry's help?"

Briefly, Nemis's brows pressed together as she swallowed. "Yes."

CHAPTER 20

PRICKING

The people of York lined the streets and gawked at the procession of judges and their aides. The arrival of the circuit judges for the Assize was an event akin to royalty visiting, with much hope placed upon their imminent verdicts. Dressed in black legal robes, four men sat astride enormous horses, waving at the crowd and ignoring shouted entreaties for leniency as they passed. Hundreds of servants, staff, witnesses, claimants, and families trailed in their wake. A celebratory springtime air overtook the city; from snickleways to squares, hawkers, market traders, and entertainment vied for York's coin. The business which the retinue of lawyers, clerks, gentry and officials from far across the county brought was much welcomed, especially after so long an absence.

Joshua stood silent as they trotted by the open front of the forge. Instead of cheering, he prayed. Doubtless, the number of horses would earn the blacksmith extra coin, but most of all the judges heralded imminent closure for his friend's ordeal. One way or another, over the next few weeks or possibly months, the Assize sessions would change the path of their future. As he searched the faces processing past, his heart sank. Henry and Fairfax were not among their number, as promised.

But it was not so cheerful an occasion for Nemis. The night before, she had been moved to a different tower and locked in an isolated, windowless and unlit cell. She could not hear the crowds outside cheering the judges arrival, did not understand what hope it brought. All she could focus on was walking - up and down, around and around the circular room, endlessly. All day, for hours and without respite. Back and forth, to and fro, no break for her cramping legs or salve for her bare soles. If she flagged, a soldier yanked her arm until she walked again. If she stopped, a cat o'nine tails whipped her ankles. Then, as the chill told her night fell, she was bade stop, and rest on a stool.

At least she had been allowed to drink then, whilst being 'encouraged' by harsh voices in the darkness. Confess. Confess now and this stops.

Yet she had not yielded. Not spoken.

Then they left her be.

All sense of time passing ceased within the quiet of the stone walls. No-one visited, or brought her relief. She sat, cross-legged with hands bound to a stool, trying to remember happier days for comfort and to pass the time. The colours of Mark's soft hair, the warmth of Spenser's embrace, anything to ground herself and not fall into the visions which hovered, elusive, in the corners of her mind.

At some point, the door creaked open. She flinched at the intrusion. Malnourished, weakened and exhausted by the enforced exercise, Nemis closed her eyes again and hung her head. Strangely, she yearned to escape into the familiarity of her foresight, for they could not punish her further if she was possessed by fits, but all around her was black and her mind refused to co-operate.

"This is absurd," Lady Hanley's strident voice called through the darkness. "Fetch her some water, food, and unbind her at once."

"I cannot. She must fast," an unfamiliar, nasal voice said. "I remind you, you are here to bear witness to the next test. That is all."

"How long has she been kept like this?"

The rasp of a flint being struck. Nemis forced her eyelids to open. A yellowish hue bathed the flagstones, increasing in brightness as more candles were lit.

"She's been here for long enough," the male voice said, now behind her.

Nemis's numb wrists were tugged, jerked, then fell free of the rope. Her hands tingled as sensation returned.

"Stand!" the man ordered.

"Is that really necessary?" Mary asked.

Nemis's eyes flared but she bore down upon her blistered feet. She would do anything required of her, but confess. She stood, weaving and discombobulated, in the cold cell. Cool, soothing fingers landed on the nape of her neck. She blinked back the tears which sprung to her eyes. The scent the old fae carried about her, of hemlock and hay, comforted her.

"You are to remove her clothes."

"But it is freezing in here," Mary argued. "See how she shivers."

"How else are we to see the devil's marking? Strip her."

Nemis turned towards the sound of his voice, hidden in the shadows. The man was lanky, long of face and nose, with a shaved head. She croaked, "Who are you?"

He opened a leather bag on the floor. "I am the one who will examine you."

As he rummaged around, then drew out a small blade, Mary leaned close to her ear. "I am sorry for this. Comply or the test will not be deemed sufficient for the Judge. Master Godfrey has been paid to be thorough, and I'm assured his testimony as Examiner will stand uncontested."

Nemis nodded. Anything to get this ordeal over with so she could return to the relative comfort of the silent darkness.

As another two men entered the cell, Mary lifted the hem of her woollen dress, then withdrew its scant warmth, over her head. Underneath, Nemis wore only a plain linen petticoat, which then was also removed.

She blinked and looked around. A gaoler she recognised held a portable desk for a black-robed clerk she did not know. Their gaze wandered over her, mouths ajar. Perhaps they had never seen a naked woman before? She screwed her eyes shut, as if it would somehow prevent them staring.

"The accused is female, of middling years," Godfrey stated in a matter-of-fact tone.

Nemis heard the scratch of a quill and rustle of parchment in response. She sensed him step closer, and she could smell the beer upon his breath.

"Bears the marks of childbirth across her girth. There are children, yes? Are they implicated in the accusation?"

"Yes, sir," the gaoler answered. "And yet she still has not confessed. She has been walked but narry a grunt of contrition for what she has done."

"This examination will be thorough, for there can be no doubts if you wish her to hang for her crime," Godfrey snapped. "And what of the husband? Is he the father of the children?"

"She is widowed," Mary Hanley said, sticking to the story first circulated in Beesworth for cover. "Nothing sinister, just the sweating sickness. Most definitely the father. There ought be no contemplation of otherwise. He was a godly man, a close family associate of mine. As for the children, we have not heard all the charges yet."

Godfrey's nose wrinkled on his rat-like face as he said, "They will be detailed in due course after I have completed my examination. There could be more than maleficence to answer to, which I may yet discover about her person."

Nemis's head swam, the ever lurking visions clouding her judgement. Something inside their haziness begged her to succumb, retreat inside their terrors. Their reality was more real to her lately than this present horror. She shook and groaned; the darkness threatened her resolve. For her family's sake, she would not stain herself with a false confession.

She must not.

Nemis felt Mary's fingers wrap around her wrist; her thumb rubbed the inside, along the vein, as if the gesture would soothe. All it did was send the creeping crawlies of her visions scooting up her arm. Then, the warmth of a candle was held close to her, like burning judgement fire.

"Hold her arms up, away from the body," Godfrey ordered.

Mary squeezed her wrist tighter, tugging her back into the room again as she stretched Nemis's arms wide.

Her skin twitched as Godfrey poked and prodded over every inch, twisting her elbows and reaching them into the air so he could examine underneath them. Then, she felt the prick of something sharp on the tender skin beneath her breasts. A chill of steel as a blade lifted their weight.

He pinched the skin at the top of her breasts as he peered closer. He snuffled to himself, then muttered, "Nothing out of the ordinary here." His fingers nipped the skin about her waist, her hip bones, and the fold of skin of her armpits, then he huffed again.

"No witches teat or rake of claw. No warts, pustules or pocks. Her skin is as pure as a newborn's." Godfrey sniffed.

With relief, Nemis opened her eyes to see his nose wriggling underneath furrowed brows, as if he could scarce believe it.

"She must sit before I might properly examine lower." He paused, stood back and cast his eyes over her nakedness in entirety. "There is, however, a mark here," he pinched hard on her breastbone. His gaze flicked to hers, as if questioning her.

Nemis trembled. "It is but a mole," she whispered. Her last remaining shred of defiance kept her standing before him.

He nodded, beady eyes narrowing. "It is small, but will require a prick. There are remarkably few other scars, such as one might expect from a woman of your years." He tugged a dreadlock, grimaced, then gestured to Lady Hanley. "Her hair must be shaven to assess the skin underneath."

Mary sighed, exasperated, but withdrew a small knife from her pocket. "Sit down," she said, bringing the stool nearer Nemis's shaking legs.

The dreadlocks made the process easier, and, as Lady Hanley cut each one off, Nemis's mood lightened. The pile of hair grew like a nest of dead snakes on the stone floor, each more liberating than the last, until she was entirely bald. A smile rose on her face, which caused Godfrey to frown.

"Why does this please you, mistress? Do you cast off the Devil with the loss of your coiffure?"

"No, sir. The devil does not reside within me, so there is nothing of him to remove."

He advanced. "Then why?"

"I'm reminded of my time at the monastery," Nemis replied, staring steadily ahead the wall where she noticed a cross had been hung. She had not seen it before, in the darkness, but with the flickering candlelight lighting the edges of the wood to a warm brown, her smile broadened. It might have appeared to the men that she was entranced, but truth spilled from her lips. "The simplicity of a life of prayer. A virtuous life, helping others."

"You were a nun?" Godfrey seemed incredulous.

"A novitiate, for a while." Nemis bit her lip. To say any more about why she, so ill at the time with her fits and visions, had been placed in the care of the monastery's healers would not endear her to this man.

"And yet you stand accused of murder, fallen to the allure of the Devil's unholy practises."

Lady Hanley snapped, "Accused is not the same as admitted, or condemned."

Godfrey's fingernails raked over Nemis's scalp with more gentleness than she expected of him. His nails flicked up the scabs of lice bites. As warm blood welled, he signalled approval with little grunting noises. All of a sudden, he stepped away.

"Let the record reflect: she bleeds from the scalp, but no suspicious marks have been found." He pointed at Nemis's pubis, his expression apologetic. "She must be shewn there, as well."

Mary's lips tightened. "As you wish." She crouched in front of Nemis, to afford her any privacy which her body might bring. Her fingers parted her legs so they splayed, revealing her intimate areas. With a steady hand, her little knife cut away little tufts.

Nemis's head hung, her chin almost touching her naked chest. There was little left on her to defile. This much she could endure; as a midwife and mother, such intimacy with private parts was routine. It was the presence of the men in the room which made her uncomfortable.

Her job complete, Mary stood, twisting so her wide skirt slit covered Nemis's shame. "This exam only I and Master Godfrey need witness. Turn your backs."

Nemis heard the shuffle of their footsteps. Only then did Mary step aside to allow Godfrey to crouch between her thighs. He placed a candle on the floor and peered closer. His fingers probed the folds of her inner sanctum. All she could see was the top of his head, spiky haired with a deep wrinkle to the back of his neck. A tightness clenched her stomach, a revulsion unlike anything she had known. That this stranger should feel himself allowed to pinch and poke in places without her consent! She ground her teeth together and prayed the ordeal would end soon.

His fingers traced the ghosts of stretch marks upon her thighs, silver-grey and sunken, then scratched at them with his nail. She let out a sob, recalling suddenly the loss of her malformed babes. The pain of labour followed by the sorrow of seeing tiny fingernails which would never grasp hers. She blinked away tears and rose her gaze to Lady Hanley in a silent plea.

"That's enough!" Mary snapped. "I will testify there is nothing there if you cannot by now, Master Godfrey."

His fingers retracted their cursory, almost clinical examination, and he nodded. "I must be satisfied for my name to go on the statement, Mistress. But I conclude, there is nothing of any wonder down there."

Nemis had the distinct impression the man's familiarity with a woman's parts was somehow only driven by duty, or a curiosity, rather than an intimate knowledge of their workings. She met Lady Hanley's eyes, a question within.

Mary stared back at her with a hint of a smile and a slight nod.

Nemis understood then why she had paid for Godfrey's particular services: men who were not inclined to the matrimonial act with a woman would be less susceptible to wily maidens charms, nor driven by lustful thoughts from such intimate examinations.

"There is only the matter of the mark on her chest." He stood, drawing a pocket blade from his jacket. At his full height, he loomed over her, low on the stool. She pressed her lips tight as his knife approached; her head shied away from the glint. Mary bustled closer and peered over her shoulder. Nemis shut her eyes, with an expectation of pain. The blade tip poked, pulling on the skin just above her breast.

But no pain nor blood came. Her eyelids flicked wide and she turned her head to see Mary glowering at Godfrey. Her Ladyship's hand shot out. "Give me that. Are you so desperate for proof you resort to trickery?"

Godfrey's eyes narrowed, his thin lips wryly lifting on one side. His fist, clenched about the handle, shook a little, then, under the glare of his superior, he retreated. "Perhaps you have a bodkin?"

Mary thrust her own little sharp knife towards him. "This blade will not retract upon pressure."

Godfrey assented and took the knife. He jabbed at the mole, which obligingly bled as soon as the tip pierced the skin. "The mark bleeds. It is not that of a witch," he had to concede.

Nemis's heartbeat returned to normal as she listened for the scratch of quill to parchment. Godfrey tossed his knife into his bag, then waited, tapping his foot as the clerk finished writing the statement. After scrawling his signature, he turned to appraise Nemis and Mary. "And so it is writ. I find no devil's marks upon her at all."

"Then our account, and this examination, is settled," Lady Hanley said. She bent to retrieve Nemis's clothes, handing them to her before she crossed the room to sign the paperwork herself.

Nemis pulled on her garments in grateful silence as Godfrey and his clerk left. The gaoler took a last, lingering glance at her legs before the skirt fell, but it no longer bothered her.

"It'll not be long now, Mistress," the guard said. "Do not think this ordeal over. There are other testimonies the court will hear."

Mary's hand grazed Nemis's fingers. "'Tis over. And now, some rest and sustenance?" She glared down her nose at the portly keeper. "I believe it has been three days she has been without, so you can afford to muster up something better than the usual slop."

"There may be some bread left. I'll take her to her cell."

Although her head remained bowed, Nemis's cheeks flushed and saliva bathed her tongue, before it occurred to her how strange it was to salivate at the prospect of stale crusts. But it wasn't the thought of food which excited her, only the prospect of the torment ceasing. She had been found clean; the visions could not be induced by evil, after all.

Nemis supposed she ought to feel elated with the hurdle of the examination overcome, but instead, as she watched the men slowly pack up their papers and implements, she bit her lip from screaming for them to hurry and leave. She craved solitude and darkness. In its black embrace, she now felt empowered to examine the visions more, without fear she was succumbing to the Devil.

CHAPTER 21

SHALL WE DANCE?

Aioffe burned the porridge. Too lost in her concerns about the upcoming court session to pay proper attention, the abandoned oats stuck to the pan, filling the downstairs with black smoke. This afternoon, Nemis would face the judges. Alone. Aioffe glared at the black-flecked lump of grey as if it was entirely to blame for her bad mood, but it was the absence of any friends to support her friend's case, despite Fairfax's promises, which ached in her stomach.

Mark refused to eat the breakfast; worry for his mother cast misery across his face. Hope also turned up her nose, perhaps out of sisterly solidarity, for she was too young to fully understand the significance of the day. While Mary chided them about wasting food, Aioffe stomped about the kitchen, fretting over what to do with the morning. Already, she regretted agreeing with Nemis not to attend the hearing herself, but to stay home and mind Hope. Her tendency to announce the obvious with childish honesty could not be trusted in such a setting. Joshua and Mary were to escort Mark to the courthouse in the Castle, having cautioned him any upset would harm his mother's chances of acquittal. No-one believed McTavish's bleeding would curtail his behaviour, but both son and mother wanted to see each other, especially as it might be for the last time. The decisions about who should attend or not had not been taken lightly, and nerves made everyone snappy.

The children and Mary disappeared to up the stairs to dress. Pots and plates clanked in the washing basin as she grumbled to herself about the early hour Joshua had left for the forge, abandoning them for sake of coin. About the weather, which could have caused Fairfax's delay? About the kestrel, which surely had reached the daemon by now, but then, his kind were prone to forgetfulness. Would Fairfax giving evidence make the judges more or less inclined to believe Nemis or her accuser? And the less said about his vampire lover, the better.

She blinked back tears as she swept the floor, then glanced at the bunch of flowers on the windowsill, still blooming because of her powers. The sight did not comfort her as it should, and despite the children upstairs, solitude tightened her chest. A dark grey sky outside cast a shadow over the view from the window. What might become of their little family if Nemis swung? Her confinement gave them all reason to be here; when it ended, what then? Could she really stay here in England, build a life, all the while knowing she had abandoned her people?

A knock interrupted her thoughts. She smoothed her hair back, then opened the door. A grubby-faced lad thrust a piece of folded paper at her, then scampered off. She recognised Fairfax's handwriting.

Find us at Red Lion Inn on Merchantgate.

She pressed her hand to her stomach and sagged against the doorframe. 'Us,' the note read, and she could only hope, despite her fear, 'us' included Henry. Nemis might not be alone at the dock after all.

"Mary?" She called back into the house. "I go to find Joshua and then Fairfax. All is not lost, after all!"

Lady Hanley bustled down the stairs, face flushed with exertion. "He has come? With Fitzroy?" Mary refused to call Henry 'king' out of deference to Aioffe.

Aioffe showed her the note. "I can only presume so."

"Well, you cannot go alone," Mary said, glancing up the stairs with a frown.

"I won't be. Joshua will come with me. Can you watch the children?"

Mary hesitated. "Or we could bring them with us?"

A glance between them and a mutual shake of heads spoke the unspoken. Any meeting with Henry was likely to be difficult enough for Aioffe without the distraction of children.

Aioffe said, "Better to keep them safe here. I'll hurry back as soon as I can."

Joshua clutched Aioffe's hand as they marched away from the forge. Aioffe said nothing, although his grip pained her delicate fingers rather than filling her with the sense of support he intended to show. The greyness of the day had not lifted, nor Aioffe's mood, and rain threatened.

The river Foss babbled cheerfully beneath them on the bridge. She paused and glanced upriver. The Merchant Adventurers's wharf, close to its Guild Hall, bustled with deliveries; no sign of Fairfax's ship, the Wanderer moored nearby.

"Perhaps they came by horse," Joshua said.

"As long as he's here, and with Henry." Her wings quivered underneath her cape. In broad daylight, there was no escape. No flight to freedom. No alternative but to face him for the first time in years, since he had assumed her throne. And, for the first time as a mother, which gave her all the more to lose if this meeting didn't go well.

They crossed the river and headed towards the Red Lion in silence. The half-timbered coaching inn was quiet although midday approached. In the stables, a faint nicker of tired horses acknowledged their presence as they walked past to the front. Joshua held the door for Aioffe as they entered.

Inside, a few dock hands and cart drivers hunched over a warm repast. The innkeeper was happy to direct them upstairs to a room which he had rented to a Sir Thomas Fairfax and his companion for the week. Joshua paid him a pennie for the information but declined an offer of refreshments being brought up to the room for an extra tanner.

As they climbed the narrow stairs, Fairfax appeared at the top and greeted them. "Welcome! Henry smelled you," he said, by way of explanation. For the fae, the smell of daemon and vampire was equally unmistakable, but it was good to see his cheerful freckles again.

The quarters were at the rear of the premises, overlooking the yard. Henry stood, his back towards the door, and stared into the fireplace. A small table with a pair of chairs was positioned next to the window; upon it a pile of books and a wooden goblet. Aioffe sniffed. Blood, pie and a lingering scent of activity from the rumpled sheets on the bed.

"I appreciate how difficult this must be for you, Aioffe," Henry said as soon as the door closed. He turned, his face impassive, to face her. "And I hear congratulations are in order. A child, Illania said."

She met his gaze, wing bumps throbbing underneath her gown. Hope's face flashed into her mind, and for a moment, she wavered in her resolve to stay calm. Joshua's presence soothed her, although, he too bristled. At all costs, Henry must be kept away from their daughter. Even being in the same town was too close for comfort, but they had little no choice.

Henry's eyebrow rose. "Do you wish to dance about the subject of sovereignty, or shall we focus on the task at hand? I assure you, Naturae remains as it ever was, in good hands."

The pressure of Joshua's hand around her fingers grew, reining her in as she straightened her back. "We could dance," she said, "but it serves no purpose to deliberate who rules my realm when neither of us is there right now. But, what about Queen Illania?" Aioffe said. The ice in her voice would have frozen the river. "What has she done? Why did she go to Naturae?"

Fairfax placed a hand on her arm. "When I arrived with Spenser, she had left. It was just after Queen Mary died. We arrive straight from Elizabeth's coronation."

Aioffe's heartbeat calmed. "The less time she spends on the island, the better," she said, catching Henry's eye.

"Illania's people and Caesaria remain on Naturae," Henry added. "So the sooner we can free the witch, the sooner I can return to deal with the matter. I would not allow the fae of Naturae to come to harm."

Aioffe felt her heart rate climb again but Joshua interrupted. "Nemis's trial begins this afternoon. You have left it late to arrive and prepare."

"I am here now as I made a promise." Henry inclined his head, just enough to be polite but not so much as to indicate subservience. He stared at them both. "Which I intend to keep. Her husband acts as Regent in my absence, and is much desirous of his wife returned."

He crossed the room in long strides and picked up a slim volume from the table. "The case, I believe, will rest heavily upon whether they can prove if she has acted with maleficence as well as murder. The format of the trial, and the questions they will put to her, are likely to follow the course as set out in this... The Hammer of Witches." He proffered the book to Joshua and met his eyes. "Read it and see if you can find anything which will assist me. You know the witch best, I believe."

"Haven't you read it?" Aioffe asked. Her eyebrows crossed in consternation. Joshua's grip on her hand weakened, then dropped. She felt a strange chill where his touch had been, but put it down to nerves. "We hoped you would have a better defence than some book to rely upon."

Henry glared at her. "Of course I have, but I am open to another man's opinion. Besides, without knowing the charges, I cannot form an argument to counter. Now," he said to Joshua, "Do you understand the task?"

Joshua stiffened. "I will read it, of course. Right away." Tearing his gaze away from Henry, Joshua turned to Fairfax. "Did you bring the documents about the baptism?"

"I did." Thomas patted a satchel hanging up on the door. "Some of my finest art work."

"Then we are set," Henry said. He went over to a chest and pulled out a long black robe.

"There is one other thing," Aioffe said. The prickling sensation which warned her of danger had not abated, but she ploughed on. "Nemis continues to have visions. They weaken her."

"Spenser told me of them," Henry said. The note of seriousness in his voice made the prickles race across her body. "What is your point?"

"We're afraid they will strike her down, in front of the judges. There is a medicine which helps revive her, a tonic, but we have run out of it. The recipe is known to Maister Jeffries, but he has not been found, yet." Aioffe looked at the floor. "If she succumbs and cries out any details about what she sees, it would be considered treason."

"The prediction of monarch's deaths?" Henry's lips pursed and his eyes darkened. "I have reason to consider they might be true. While we were in London, an attempt was made on my sister, Queen Elizabeth's life. And yes, revealing the prophecy, its subject and the truth within would be problematic for Nemis, were it to be discovered."

"You're convinced then - there is a killer of queens?" Joshua said. Aioffe sensed fear cloud his aura and her fingers twitched.

"I am," Henry said. "To bear the title Queen until the matter is resolved might invite attention."

The room seemed to shrink about Aioffe; only the boned bodice of her gown prevented her crumpling. One queen dead, another narrowly escaped. Was she next?

Henry stared at Joshua intently in the silence.

As Joshua gazed back, his jaw fell slack. Still stunned at Henry's confirmation of a regicide, Aioffe's hand reached for him, but it was as if he were possessed. She could feel nothing of him. Even his familiar Lifeforce, which usually danced at her touch, lay dormant.

She jerked on her husband's arm, frowning, then she noticed the equal stillness of Henry. Why, he was suddenly acting like any other vampire. On the prowl. With a gaze so intense, was he trying to mesmerise Joshua? To what end?

As Joshua's head swivelled to look at her, a dazed expression in his eyes confirmed her suspicion. Perhaps because he had been a human once, he was susceptible?

Joshua sounded flat as he said, "We shall remain in England, where it is safe for you. The subject of Nemis's predictions will be avoided in court, if possible."

Aioffe's heart banged against her breastbone. She glared at Henry. "You are putting notions in his head!"

A slight rise to Henry's lips confirmed her suspicions.

"How dare you influence him?" She made to slap him, but Henry caught her arm easily. Their eyes met in a battle of wills.

Fairfax frowned. "Henry?"

Henry merely tilted his head to the side and looked at her. "Do you agree? Stay on these shores, or..."

Her throat ran dry. If Joshua, of all people, could fall under a vampire's influence still, then maybe any vampire could persuade him to do anything. Fae, witches and daemons were generally not susceptible to their suggestion, but Joshua... her heart clamoured in panic. Her love was a powerful fighter, strong and with magic running through his veins. Her husband alone was capable of protecting her or... overpowering her.

Before she could question what Henry was doing to Joshua, and why, Fairfax nudged him. "The time. We must go."

"Do you agree?" Henry repeated.

Aioffe shook her head. "I cannot agree to stay away from Naturae." Her chin jutted out. He hadn't finished what was no doubt a threat, and she would not give him chance to now. Thoughts of her home hovered on the edges of her fury, but Fairfax was hopping around in her peripheral vision. Nemis's life was at stake. Naturae, and Joshua's susceptibility to Henry, could wait. She swallowed. "We shall dance, but after this ordeal has passed. For now, you made a promise to free Nemis, which you must keep if you are to retain any sort of respect from me."

Her glare would have withered a weaker man, but Henry smiled enigmatically. She wanted to punch him, fly at him and tear out his eyeballs, but instead, fuming, she pulled on Joshua's hand. She pushed her love through, into him, that he might use it to resist the vampire's allure.

With a gasp, he staggered; wide eyes darted around the room as if he had just woken. She tugged on him again, dragging him to her side. As Henry and Fairfax walked casually to the door, she whispered under her breath, "Everything hath a time."

Henry glanced back briefly before Fairfax pushed him through the doorway.

Chapter 22

PROSECUTION

The manacles around Nemis's wrists and ankles clanked with every step she took. Chained to each other, she was at the head of the procession of prisoners to be arraigned that day, and determined not to stumble. "Come along," the gaoler accompanying them grumbled. "The judges won't abide delay." He jerked the lead chain, dragging them all out of the darkness of the cells and into the castle yard.

Her heart pounded. Not for the welcome sight of daylight and smell of open air, but at the crowds of onlookers gathered within the walls. They waited to see the witch, the murderers and thieves, to mock the sinners for whom justice would be dealt swift today. Shouts and jeers were ineffectively hushed by soldiers holding the spectators back. A barrage of abuse washed over Nemis as if unheard. She was the afternoon's entertainment. Head down, she focused only on placing one clog in front of the next, towards the dread the arched doorway ahead held.

They were led down a wide corridor, lined with clerks and lawyers dressed in black gowns and curled white wigs. Whispered conversation fell silent as the group shuffled along, clanking, groaning, and stinking.

The courtroom was already warmed by the bodies of speculators. The gaoler directed the prisoners past painted walls bright with biblical warnings to a narrow bench, then bade them sit. "You wait here until I bring you over to face your reckoning," he instructed with a glare. "You stay silent or I'll have to remove you from the proceedings. Throw you back into the cells with no trial, to be forgotten about. Understood?"

He pulled out the chain linking them, leaving the shackles. Only then did Nemis dare to look around.

The rectangular courtroom boasted an airy, high ceiling with exposed beams. A massive shield hung above the judges' section, ornately carved with York's emblem painted and polished. The golden lion's eyes watched her from inside the red cross on its white background. She heard rustles and scuffles of feet on the planks above their lowly station as a packed gallery settled down for the spectacle. The prisoners sat behind a tall wooden partition, which separated their bench from the main courtroom, but Nemis, being first in the line had a clear view past the judges' dais, to the small, railed dock on the other side of the chamber. A clerk's quill scratched as he scribbled at his desk. On a shelf above him, papers, ink pots, wax, a lit candle, stamps and fresh feathers.

After a nod from the gaoler, the clerk lifted his head and shouted, "Be still and quiet," at the rising volume of the spectators. He stood and strode into the centre of the room. One or two in the gallery needed a stern stare to hush them, before he announced, "In service of Her Majesty the Queen, the Honourable Justices presiding over this Assize in the county of York are Sir James Altham and Sir Edward Bromley."

Two men of similar height and middling age entered from a doorway behind the high bench. They nodded to each other and glared at the spectators, who had begun to whisper again. The first, Judge Altham, remained standing whilst Judge Bromley sat behind his desk and poured himself a cup of ale. Altham said, "The list for arraignment and trials today has been agreed with their representatives?"

The clerk passed up a sheet, names and crimes filling the docket.

Altham nodded, gave it a cursory glance, then handed it to his colleague. "Then I am bound issue a general approximation that all Justices of Peace which have taken any recognisances or examinations of the prisoners should make returns of them. All who are bound to prosecute indictments and give evidence against the said prisoners should proceed. In her Majesty's name, do we have prepared a sufficient jury of Gentlemen for the life and death rulings?"

The clerk said, "Aye, M'Lord, they await your instruction."

"Then they shall be brought forward to take their places." He gestured to a long box containing several benches and curled a finger to a soldier stood by the double doors. "Time already presses and this," he waved the list, "is an o'er full docket. Therefore, notwithstanding the absence of any witnesses, today we shall hear first the evidences against one..." He paused, eyes narrowing on the narrow script.

Nemis's stomach clenched and she held her breath. It was all she could do to keep the darkness hovering behind her eyelids from imposing itself. She stared blankly at the rounded ends of her clogs and concentrated on curling her toes inside.

But her name rolled from the Judge's lips, "Nemis Claybourne."

"As you command. Bring the prisoner to the dock," the clerk called. His head turned to the assortment of criminals sat on the bench. A wary gaze landed on her as the gaoler approached.

Nemis shuffled around the side of the jury box, head down, trying not to meet the eyes of the gentlemen who filed into their seats while she clanked across the room. Cries of "Lord save us," from the gallery, made her flinch. She pressed her lips tight, her knees like water. The chamber darkened as the gaoler pushed on her shoulders, shoving her into the dock. His keys clinked together as he locked the gate shut and, for a moment, she thought she was back in her cell underneath the tower.

The judge's voice sounded distant to her. "On what charges is Nemis Claybourne, of Hanley Hall in Beesworth, arraigned?"

She gripped the wooden railing, trying to resist the darkness creeping into the edges of her sight. A voice filled with pompousness which she recognised rang clear into the room. The Assistant Sheriff of Beesworth. The same who had dragged her from Mark and Hope.

She looked up, blinking to try and push the dimness aside. He stood, portly and officious, in front of the Judges bench and read, somewhat stumbling over his words: "If it so pleases my Lord Justices, the prisoner is accused of the following: That she feloniously had practised, used and exercised diverse and wicked and devilish acts of witchcrafts, enchantments, sorceries and charms upon one William Tunn, a blacksmith in the parish of Beesworth. And by use of said witchcraft, Nemis Claybourne did kill William Tunn."

Nemis gaped at him as he drew in a breath. The official cast his eyes around the room, confidence growing before the rapt audience. "That she did by use of incantations cause other maleficent happenings with the purpose of frightening other prisoners to do her bidding against their will." He paused, shook his head a little as if it pained him to read the next incitement. "And that she has borne children said to also do the devil's bidding."

Her palms dampened and Nemis glanced up to the gallery, scouring the faces staring back at her. She had not seen Mark in so long, had wanted him to see her moment of truth, yet at the same time, not appear diminished in his eyes. Her heartbeat quickened as she recognised, in a corner next to the door, the green woollen cap she had knitted her son. But, his head hung and he did not meet her hopeful glance. The sight of her boy so despondent made her heart ache yet filled her stomach with fire. She endured this spectacle to make him proud, so he could see her answer to the accusations like an honest woman. A mother he could be proud of.

Next to him, an arm around her boy's shoulder, stood Joshua with Lady Hanley. They locked eyes. His steady gaze reassured Nemis that as much as could be done, had been, but her legs still trembled. She felt slightly less alone, knowing he would provide for Mark, protect him, whatever the outcome. But... where was Spenser? She almost crumbled, but for Joshua nodding his support.

Judge Bromley said in a gruff tone, "Bearing children isn't a crime, unless they have been bred to be sacrificed. Do you separately accuse her of sacrifice, or the children themselves of maleficent actions?"

The Assistant Sheriff shook his head. "The children are alive and have not been questioned, your Honour. One has disappeared, a babe seen with markings of the Devil upon it, and the other, we believe, resides here in York now. We are led to believe the boy is under the care of a priest and undergoing treatment for an unnamed malady of his mind. It was decided by my seniors, after consultation with a Revered Gippes, that arresting the child could wait until he is deemed capable of answering to his crimes. There was an accusation of theft which will be brought to the Hundred courts in due course."

Altham took his seat next to Bromley. He looked across at the jury and confirmed with the clerk they had all sworn to faithfully try the defendant and give a true verdict. Satisfied, he then turned back to the Assistant Sheriff. "Do you have witnesses to attest to her crimes and the evidence you require to press these charges within this room today?"

"We do, your Honour," a slim man sat at the side stood. He approached the centre of the room. "David Newell, Prosecutor, if it pleases the court. I will be presenting witness statements and witnesses in support of the accusations herein levied." He bowed curtly to the bench and both Judges nodded their acceptance.

Nemis's head span as Newell glanced at her. Her skin crawled as his eyes met hers, then narrowed in understanding. She was to be prosecuted for being a witch, no matter what the lawful charges might state or the Treaty might dictate, for Newell stank of vampire. Nemis barely heard the judge say, "Does the accused have representation, or shall we move to the plea?"

As Altham shuffled papers in front of him during the hush which followed, Nemis shuddered. Looking to the gallery to check Joshua understood her predicament, she saw him point to the double doors. On cue, and with a bang, they flung open, startling everyone.

Henry strode into the courtroom, black gown flapping, and said, "She does. If it please your Honour, I am Henry Richmond, counsel for the defence of the accused."

Her head jerked back, as if slammed by the doors themselves. All at once, the air around her thickened. Her fingers rose to her temples as instinct drove her to resist, to hold in the wave of darkness which his arrival brought. Although Nemis had suspected the effect he would have on her, and had tried to mentally prepare herself for the sensation, the suddenness of his entrance made her reel. A peculiar mix of relief and loathing churned inside her belly. She gasped, falling back against the railing, then panted. One vampire to prosecute, another to defend her.

It was too much. She was surely doomed.

"Is the prisoner well enough of mind and body to answer for her crimes?" A distant voice said.

Her monster, the usurper who brought this effect upon her, then responded on her behalf. She forced herself to remain upright, hearing his voice muffled as if she drowned. "She is moved only by the Lord God himself, your Honour. The occasion and ordeal of this trial, the very notion of what she and her children are accused of, it is enough to affect any god-fearing person."

"And what plea do you enter for her crimes?"

Nemis screwed her eyes shut, torn between the darkness he brought and succumbing to the more familiar terrors of her mind. In her ears, the rushing of her blood swelled in volume, so she could hardly hear his response.

"Not guilty to all counts, your Honour," Henry replied for her.

A touch to her fingertips, gripped on the railing, jolted her back into the present. "Look at me," Henry ordered quietly. "For I am here at your loved one's behest. And I will not fail you."

His words reached her. Beguiling. Seductive when all she wanted was to flee. The pressure of his cool stroke soothed her savage breaths. Oh God, he was powerful. Even more so than she expected. More than she had foreseen. Did he know? Most vampires couldn't touch a witch, let alone try and mesmerise them. Innately, she resisted his allure, but her stomach clenched at the thought that others might not be so capable.

Henry was her only hope, Aioffe had said. Motherless Mark, her heart said. She could not leave him thus.

Nemis opened her eyes.

CHAPTER 23

PERSECUTION

Henry stood next to Nemis at the dock as both judges peered over their glasses and frowned at her. He noticed Newell, for the prosecution, was the only other vampire in the room, and smiled. The witch, of course, a daemon or two he smelled in the gallery, but at least the jury was entirely human. Perhaps this would be easier than he had anticipated.

Judge Altham stroked his slim beard and asked her, "Do you agree to this plea, Mistress Claybourne?"

She swallowed, then her head rose. "I do. Not guilty."

Henry felt a curious flush of pride in his charge. Perhaps if she showed some backbone, he would prevail. He squared his shoulders and set his jaw. "May we proceed, your Honours?"

Bromley and Altham glanced at each other, then nodded to the prosecutor. "Let it be known," Altham stated in a loud voice to the court, as Newell gathered his papers, "that the confession of a witch doth supersede any evidence which may be represented. Has she made such a confession?"

Newell grunted, "No."

This seemed to bewilder the Judges. "A shame. We might have saved ourselves some time. I presume she has been examined properly?"

"Aye, your Honour."

"Do you have the statement by the Examiner?" Bromley asked.

The prosecutor handed a sheet of paper up to the judges. "The findings of Master Godfrey, an expert in such matters," Newell replied, his lips tight as he glowered. "Such that it is. He is available to bear witness if necessary."

Altham read it silently then passed it to Bromley.

"Are we sure the correct procedure was followed, such as may offer the accused the chance to confess and repent?" Bromley asked while his eyes scanned the document.

Henry interjected, "Your Honours, by correct procedure, would you be so kind as to clarify for the court whose guidance or which rule of law you intend to follow in forming your judgement upon the matter? Since we have a new monarch, I thought it best to check if there has been any change? I have been out of the country, you see."

Bromley took another swig of his ale. "Her Majesty, upon her ascension, has not yet had cause to change the law regarding such cases. We therefore are still minded to rely upon the discovery and treatment as set out by the theologians in Malleus Mallificarum. The Hammer of Witches, the guide is also titled." He glared at Henry, daring him to object.

Henry glanced up to the gallery and met Joshua's gaze. "Excellent," he said.

And indeed it was, for Henry had read the book from cover to cover on the journey up from London, and found many things in it of use in Nemis's defence. His instruction to Joshua may yield something further, but until they heard the detail of what Nemis was accused of, he could not know.

Bromley flattened the statement before him, then mumbled, "Master Godfrey's statement reads, We in humble abeyance to your Lordships have this day, in the presence of Gaoler Marcus Bennet of York Castle, Lady Mary Hanley of Hanley Hall, Beesworth, and myself, Master Godfrey, examiner of the county of York, performed a diligent search and inspection upon the accused. On the body of Mistress Nemis Claybourne, we find nothing unnatural, neither in their secrets or any other parts of her body, nor anything like a teat or mark. Not any sign that any such thing hath ever been."

Henry breathed a sigh of relief. He glanced at Nemis's shaved head, bowed and still, and wondered what other horrors she had endured to be granted an unequivocal statement of her cleanliness.

Bromley harrumphed, then said, "This all appears to be in order. Master Godfrey, known well to us, has certified with witnesses the accused is clean of any devil's marks. Therein, no need for us to question him in person. Since the witch has refused to confess," he waved the prosecutor forward, "you may present any other such evidence as you have, that we may then determine whether there be any truth to the accusations."

Mr Newell crossed back to his desk and picked up a sheaf of paperwork. "To the matter of the death of William Tunn, I have here a sworn testament by his widow, Margaret Tunn." He surveyed the room, his gaze landing on a haggard-looking woman with wisps of mousy brown and grey hair straggling out from her headscarf, sat in the audience. "Please, approach the bench, Mistress, and I shall read your statement for the benefit of all gathered herein."

As Margaret Tunn walked to the front, she glared at Nemis. Her hands shook as she crossed herself, then kissed a rosary.

Henry smelled the fear wafting from her, and concluded the ostentation, not to mention the crowds in the room and seriousness of the occasion might give the widow some reason to be nervous about speaking of witchcraft and her husband's death so publicly.

From the corner of his eye, he caught Nemis wilting down on the stool. The gyves which shackled her wrists clanks together as her hands trembled. He sensed no guilt or malice, nor did her crumpled comportment suggest regret. Only weariness. Perhaps she was innocent of wrongdoing.

In truth, he cared not; only that the proceedings moved along at a pace which meant he could return to Naturae as quickly as possible. His gaze roamed over the witness again, judging how best he could manipulate the situation to bring this to a swift conclusion. Mistress Tunn had been convinced enough of Nemis's murderous intent she had sworn to it under oath, but she refused to meet his eye.

Mr Newell waited until Mistress Tunn had found her position to the right of the judges' bench before he read in a solemn voice:

"I, Margaret Tunn, being of sound mind and body, do make this statement of fact that Mistress Nemis Claybourne did, by use of witchcraft, take the life of William Tunn, an honourable member of the Guild of Yorkshire Blacksmiths, in Beesworth.

On the Sunday before Midsummer in the year of our Lord 1554, my husband said he felt most stricken during the evening Mass held at St Mary's Church of Beesworth. He told me then, he was unable to walk and could not receive the holy sacrament. As we walked home, a great black dog crossed our path. It went into Market Street and shortly afterwards, Mark Claybourne, Mistress Claybourne's son, ran back past us. Therein, I saw the Devil's magic transform the dog into the boy."

The crowds in the gallery gasped; people turned to each other and muttered. The judges glared at them until silence fell again and Newell could continue.

"Shortly thereafter, when we had returned to our house, William was taken with shaking and fitting, and with great pain to his stomach. I sent my eldest child to fetch Father Thomas, as I was afeared he be possessed with a spirit most evil. Foul, gibberish language did pour from his mouth and he sayeth wickedness hath entered."

Henry noticed, while the testimonial was being recited, the widow clutched her rosary to her chest and shook her head. There was something more to this tale, he ascertained.

Newell's voice turned accusatory. "Whilst I was at my labours tending him, my child returned with Mistress Claybourne instead. Mistress Claybourne is known in these parts to invoke the spirits to aid her with the cause of midwifery which she, being also a cunning woman, is said to be proficient at. Mistress Claybourne had not been at the Mass earlier and wore no hat or mantle upon her. She brought with her an ointment which, she said, would ease my master's great pain. I confess, I, being with no other master to advise me otherwise, paid her for the ointment and ministrations, and did allow her to strip my husband of his shirt. I was not in the room at the time to hear what incantations she uttered over him, for she bade me fetch warm water. When I returned, I saw she had rubbed this ointment upon my husband, and five days after, my husband and master died. When I next saw her, it was Midsummer's Eve, and she did not deny his death."

Henry ducked his head to hide his smile. If this was the extent of the evidence which they could produce, he was confident he would have no need of persuasion to win.

The clerk took the paper from the prosecutor and placed it on his own desk. Newell turned to Mistress Tunn. "Do you have anything else which, subsequent to making this statement, you now wish to detail to the court?"

She shook her head, fingers pulling the rosary through her hands.

Newell plucked another paper from his sheaf of papers, then turned to Henry absently. "I presume all is in order with the statement and I can move on?"

"I would ask some detail of Mistress Tunn, if it pleases the court?"

Bromley glowered. "If you must."

Henry approached Mistress Tunn and smiled convivially. "Did you happen to keep any remains of the ointment which Mistress Claybourne applied?"

Mistress Tunn glanced at Newell. "I did."

"Do you have it here that we might examine it?"

She nodded and withdrew a small bottle from a pocket in the folds of her skirt.

"If it please the court," Henry asked the judges, "I would like an expert to ascertain the contents of this tincture, to understand if indeed there is any poison within."

Altham gave a curt nod. "I'll allow it."

Henry turned again to Mistress Tunn. "You said Mistress Claybourne recited incantations over your husband while you were fetching hot water."

"Aye."

"And how far away would you have been then?"

Margaret shifted her weight around then shrugged. "We do not have a large house, maybe a few yards. But I was near the fireplace to heat the water, so it was a bit noisy."

"But you would have heard what was happening in the bedroom, could you not?"

"I suppose so."

"And your child - did they hear anything?"

She shook her head. "I sent them back out to fetch Father Thomas."

"So it was just you, your husband, and Mistress Claybourne in the house."

"Yes."

Henry tapped his fingers to his lips then said, "The incantations, can you repeat them for the court?"

She pouted. "As I said, I was out of the room when she applied it, so I cannot say for certain what she said."

"So, you cannot swear to the fact that she incanted or invoked anything at all, especially not the Devil."

"I suppose not, but I hear she usually did with her treatments. That's what other folk have told me."

Henry tapped his lips. "Hearsay isn't the same as actually hearing it yourself." He glanced at the Judges, who glowered back at him. "Tell me, did your husband make Confession before he died? With the priest you called to your home."

She stared at the floor, fingers slipping the rosary beads through her hands.

"Mistress Tunn? Tis but a simple question, which might indicate whether your husband was indeed possessed by evil spirits, so I must press you for an answer."

"He did not."

"Did he attend confession usually?"

Her lips pressed together.

"Mistress?"

"He was of the new faith, sir. He did not believe in confession."

Henry noticed her hands clutched the rosary even tighter. "Or taking the sacrament, I presume. And this was a matter of some disagreement between you?"

"Aye."

"So, he didn't confess, not because he was possessed, but because he didn't share your faith?"

"Aye. He were a good man." She began to sob. "But all sinners must repent."

Henry leaned closer to her. "I have no doubt. So, was there any disagreement between you prior to him falling ill at church?"

"He refused to take the sacrament. I asked him and begged him, every Sunday, but he would not."

"And for how long had he believed differently to you?"

She muttered, "Several decades."

"A matter which caused some disturbance between you? Arguments and the like?"

"Aye. We argued." She glanced at her hands. "I only wanted what was best for him."

"And for how long had he suffered these pains to his stomach?"

"A few years, perhaps."

"Had Mistress Claybourne offered treatment or even encountered your husband before this night?"

She grimaced. "No, but I knew of her from others whom she'd assisted in Beesworth."

"And Mistress Claybourne, how long had you known her by this point?"

"Some months. She'd just appeared in the town, staying at Hanley House." Mistress Tunn glanced at Henry. Her eyes hardened with the understanding of where his questions led.

"If he had ailed for many years before she arrived, then this malady was not something Mistress Claybourne could have instigated. They did not know one another, or indeed, your family for very long. Could you think of any reason why Mistress Claybourne would wish ill to your husband, then? Some slight perhaps? Or, are we really to believe that a simple salve applied to a long-suffering man, who she didn't know well, was really to blame for his passing?"

When she said nothing, his eyebrow rose and he looked at Altham saying, "Your Honours, your time is precious. Perhaps this case should never have come to your courtroom, for it seems there is little by way of evidence here?"

The judge stared impassively back, his lips tight.

"She's a witch," Mistress Tunn blurted.

"Unfortunately, that is irrelevant," Henry said, his head whipped back to her. "Being a witch is not against the law. The question is whether she did cause any harm by the practise of witchcraft, and so far, you have attested to her provision of an ointment as proof of this accusation. She had no prior connection with your husband. No reason to wish him ill.

No charms or incantations were said. Could you be mistaken, I wonder, as to the cause of his death?"

"But the dog? Her son?" She wailed, casting tear-filled eyes around the chamber. "Her babe, who is marked by the Devil."

"Did you actually see the dog change into a boy? In the darkness after leaving evening Mass."

"Well, no." She pursed her lips. "But it was only moments. The dog went into the street and then he emerged."

"No-one else witnessed this occurrence?"

"Not that I saw, sir, no."

"Or the accused applying the medicine and calling forth the Devil?"

"No."

"What about your husband's death? Did anyone else witness his passing?"

Mistress Tunn's head sank as she shook it.

"Let the record show there were no witnesses to any of these occurrences save the accuser herself. In order to condemn a witch for maleficent actions, the Hammer of Witches states very clearly there must be two witnesses."

Henry glanced at Newell, who paled and pushed his bottom jaw out.

Striding across the open space towards his desk, Henry said, "So, to clarify for the record, it was night, and Mistress Tunn was struggling home with an ailing husband with whom she had recently argued on matters of faith. I put it to you, Mistress Tunn, that it is co-incidence you saw a dog, then a boy."

Henry opened his satchel and fished out some papers. Holding them up, he said, "These records attest to the fact that the children in question have been accepted into the loving arms of Christ by baptism. All sin cast out from them. Besides, they were not present at the passing of Master Tunn. You were."

His eyes narrowed on Margaret. "A wife at odds with her husband for many a year. What it must be for any God-fearing woman to see her husband struggle so, without the comfort of confession. A man so sickened and still scolded by his wife, he would try any salve to ease his pain. No-one else to see the suffering. And no-one else to witness his easement. To blame is easy when one grieves."

Mistress Tunn let out a sob. Her eyes darted around the room in search of support. Henry wasn't about to give it to her. "I put it to the court," he said, his voice dangerous and low, "that perhaps, it was Mistress Tunn herself who murdered her husband."

Chapter 24

TEARING THE DOXY DOWN

A ripple of whispers spread through the gallery after Henry's accusation. Joshua could not help his small smile and he squeezed Mark's hand. By proposing an alternative killer, the well learned vampire had cast doubt upon the most serious of the charges against Nemis. He looked down at the pages of the Hammer of Witches book, his fingers tracing the words. If he could only find the right ones to refute the second charge, Henry might get the case dismissed in entirety.

The Judges banged their gavels and called for order. Mark shuffled in his seat next to him, white-faced and clutching his favourite rock, while onlookers shushed each other. Mr Newell blustered about Mistress Tunn, then retreated to his desk, red-faced with fury.

Bromley snapped, "We are not here to try the witnesses, only the accused. I will have silence in my court."

Altham said, "Move on and present the evidence you have in support of the other allegations, Mister Newell."

"I... I will perhaps return to this... woman," Newell stammered. "But, here, my witness will detail Claybourne's various incantations, causing of celestial occurrences and testify they frightened many a prisoner."

Bromley nodded his head and said, "Many?"

"Many," the prosecutor replied, gathering himself. "And other happenings which did occur thereafter as a result of her incantations and the like." He dragged out another sheaf of paper. "In addition to the testimony from the gaoler here, I have a statement from one Sarah Fell, also of Beesworth, who did travel from there to here in York with the accused and personally suffered as a result of her bewitchment."

"Is that witness present today?" Altham asked. He frowned. "The name seems familiar to me."

"She is not, your Honour," Newell said stiffly.

"If I may ask," Henry interrupted. "Is this witness a felon or an official?"

Newell muttered, "She was in the same transport... yes, as a prisoner."

"Oh yes," Altham said. "We tried her already, didn't we?" He glanced at Bromley for confirmation. "Persistent drunkenness and theft. A doxy wench to boot." The curls of his wig shook as he burst into laughter. "Mr Newell, this statement had better contain something of worthy substance, for I do believe your witness was sentenced to a week in the stocks, if my memory serves."

Newell's fingers curled, almost crumpling the papers in his hand. "She attests that the accused did mutter incantations while in Beesworth gaol, your Honour, and that thereafter there were lights in the sky which," Newell glanced over his glasses and looked around the room for support, "we may all recall. Many calamities, including the death of our beloved late Queen Mary and the sweating sickness which swept the land, have happened as a result of the witch's enchantment."

Altham peered at the prosecutor. "Are you suggesting the witch hath caused the death of the late Queen Mary? Set a plague upon the land?"

Newell looked grave. "I have the testimony of not one, but two witnesses that unholy incantations were said. And we all know what happened afterwards."

As soon as the hint of treason was mentioned, whispers started in the gallery. While the judges called for order, Henry's brow furrowed. He knew there was no way in which she could have been involved in the attempt on Elizabeth's life, being imprisoned in York at the time. To claim Nemis caused the death of Queen Mary and plague was so tenuous, the lawyer hadn't even included it in the list of charges, but the judges could, if they were so inclined, add to them if more information came to light.

He ground his teeth together. The suggestion of treason had to be swiftly quashed, in case it triggered Nemis into a fit and everyone would witness her prediction. As for what she might have made the prisoners do with her 'incantations' was yet to be determined. The charge of using witchcraft to make prisoners do her bidding and causing other calamities seemed, from the tone Newell struck, to be wrapped up with the celestial lights of years ago. Henry remembered the panic in Naturae, and Fairfax's unease, and then he understood the vampire's strategy. It was intentional, casting such aspersions, to make a witch more significant and scary than in reality she was.

But, the coincidence of the prophetic lights could be explained, dismissed even with the help of the Hammer of Witches. As for making people do her bidding, even a true witch could no more make people do what they wanted than stars could. Their potions and concoctions were temporarily suggestive at best, and the effects wore off. Only vampires could influence behaviour to any lasting degree with mesmerisation.

He smiled wryly then said, "If it pleases the court, could we check on the availability of the Sarah Fell?"

"Very well," Altham ordered. "Find the doxy and bring her here." The flustered clerk scurried out and proceedings paused.

Henry glanced at Nemis, who seemed frozen on the stool. She had not moved for the entire time Mistress Tunn had given her evidence, nor reacted when Henry had cast aspersions. Lifting her shaven head, Nemis stared not at him, but up to the gallery. Tension lined her pale skin and eyes darted along the crowd as if seeking someone up there.

"Perhaps we could hear from the gaoler," Mr Newell said, interrupting Henry's thought process. "I have the Assistant Sheriff's statement here."

"Proceed," Bromley said.

As the official moved to stand at the front of the court, the clerk of the court rushed back in and whispered something to the Judges. Altham then announced, "As I suspected, the next witness is serving her punishment, but she will be released, temporarily, to appear before us."

"Your Honour," Henry strode forward. "Are we seriously to entertain the word of a convicted felon as reliable and reputable?"

"We must be thorough, Mr Richmond," Bromley snapped. "The seriousness of the allegations warrants it. This is not a manor court dealing with petty theft or non-payment of dues. This is a murder trial. Indeed, it could not be more serious, especially if this witch is responsible for causing the death of the late Queen." He shook his head. "If we cannot satisfy ourselves of her innocence, I would consider adding in the charge of treason, for which I'd be inclined to refer the case higher, to the Star Chamber. The highest in the land."

Henry gaped. The often arbitrary court, judged by members of the Privy Council, could impose whatever punishment it deemed suitable, without recourse or appeal. The mere mention of treason or regicide would almost certainly result in Nemis's death. Given who he was, or rather, who he had been, there was nothing he could do to affect the outcome.

"Then, I welcome the opportunity to bring forward my case in Mistress Claybourne's defence, and prove her innocence," Henry responded.

Newell began to read the statement. "I, Alfred Cooper, Assistant to the Sheriff of Beesworth, testify that Nemis Claybourne was held at the prison in said town from Midsummer's night, June 1554, until her transfer to York Castle, in early May 1556. I was also responsible for Mistress Claybourne's arrest and witnessed the disturbance she caused with her babe, marked by the Devil to the face, and her son, being possessed by the Devil."

The crowds in the gallery started whispering, so both judges rapped their gavels and called for silence.

Newell continued. "While detained in Beesworth Gaol, the witch was much afflicted by her circumstance, caterwauling all hours. Many times, she plied her cunning knowledge to other prisoners. During the transfer, I escorted the covered cart containing Mistress Claybourne and Mistress Fell through day and night. Mistress Claybourne was much agitated during the journey. Then, as we were hastening to our destination, a fearful wind arose. The sky did grow bright with lights, even though night had fallen. I heard her muttering incantations, which did frighten and influence the other prisoner, Sarah Fell, into lewdness and lascivious behaviour when I stopped for respite. Upon our arrival at York, I opened up the cart to find Mistress Claybourne shaking and possessed of a malodorous stench. This is my sworn statement: Mistress Claybourne did affect the stars to aid in her devilish cause, and did incite the Sarah Fell into lewd behaviour."

Henry clenched his teeth together and glared at the fat man at the front. With flushed cheeks and almost purple lips, not to mention the smell of wine on his breath, the Assistant Sheriff had no doubt dosed himself well with liquid courage before his appearance. "I have a few questions, your Honour."

Bromley sighed. "I expected you would."

Henry chewed on his lip for a moment. To query the circumstances of Nemis's arrest served little purpose other than to bring back into question her children. One glance at her stony-faced child above, so fond of Fairfax and so unreliable, reminded him of the impracticality of putting young daemon on the stand.

"Mr Cooper, would you please elaborate how you know Mistress Clay-bourne had influenced Mistress Fell into the lewd behaviour you observed. Please describe, if you will and in Christian terms, precisely what happened. What was said and so-forth."

After smacking his lips together, the official puffed his chest out. "I was up at the front, so all the noise she made , what she said, was all behind me in the cart. There were only the two women in there. We stopped. Mistress Fell was climbing out of the cart when she said, very clearly, 'She made me do it' before she... offered herself to me. The innkeeper heard it too."

Newell slapped his hand on the desk. "'She. Made. Me. Do. It.' What could be clearer?" He looked to the jury for support and found several nodding heads.

Henry pursed his lips as he appraised Cooper. No wedding band. No doubt a drunkard. "And, did you take up Mistress Fell's offer? You may speak freely, as she has already been proven a doxy by these same judges."

Mr Cooper's eyes widened. "I knew immediately this was the Devil's work, sir." He turned his head towards the jury. "For is it not always the case when an unmarried woman offers her favours? Rolled up her skirts and spread herself, she did. A doxy at least would wait until we were private before showing herself." He rolled his shoulders back.

"You have not answered the question, sir. Did you act upon Mistress Fell's offer?"

The official thought, his jaw masticating as if he chewed on a thorny twig. He glanced at the Bible on the Judge's desk then admitted, "I fell victim to her wiles, yes. Perchance, being in the witches' proximity made me weak. Perhaps t'was the Devil at work. Tempting me, you see?" He shrugged. "I'm a god-fearing man, not a learned one, so I could not say for sure."

The judge's nods indicated their acceptance. A man could not be held responsible for being tempted by a woman, which irked Henry.

"And these incantations, can you detail those for the court?"

Mr Cooper shook his head. "I cannot. With the wind, and them being inside the cart, you see. The specific words I could not make out."

"Then," Henry said, "how can you swear they were incantations?"

"What else would the wails and moans be?" Cooper's chest swelled fit to burst through his jacket. "Upon my word, I have never heard the like of her noise. No-one could be near the shrieks she made. They sent a chill through me, I say. An unnatural chill."

"A chill which was nothing to do with the wind, apparently. So, you heard no specific entreaties? No mention of the Devil or his minions? No crying out to the heavens, to make them light up?"

The official shuffled about. "Well, not specifically, no. But she did make an ungodly racket, and there was the smell."

"From the covered cart? Unopened and unclean after several days of travel. Carrying prisoners who had been living in your gaol for months, doubtless without any facilities to wash."

Cooper's eyes shifted from side to side.

Henry pressed his point. "I suggest, so stinking is it inside the cart, that when you do open the door, the stench of your lack of care would have billowed out. And you maintain, during this horrific, foul-smelling journey, Nemis Claybourne not only influenced a known whore to offer herself to you, but she moved the stars in the heavens as well." He glanced at the jury, incredulity flaring his eyes.

The Assistant Sheriff said nothing, only looked at the prosecutor for support.

Newell's lips tightened, then he said, "Is there a question, Council, or are you merely making statements to infer my witness was negligent in his care? Perhaps you would like to accuse him of murder as well?"

Henry smiled. "Well, as our learned theologians made clear in Malleus Maleficarum, 'every alteration that takes place in a human body, for example, a state of health or of sickness, can be brought down to a question of natural causes, as Aristotle has shown in his seventh book of Physics.'

And," Henry paused his quotation to glare at Newell. "'The greatest of these is the influence of the stars. But the devils cannot influence the movement of the stars.'"

He faced the judges. "I'm certain your Honours agree with the esteemed authors, priests themselves, when they attest, 'This alone only God can do.' If we are to believe the testimony of Mr Cooper, here, then we must turn our backs on the accepted wisdom of Aristotle, the Pope and countless others who confirm that a witch, as an agent of the Devil, cannot influence the stars."

He drew in a breath, fully aware he had the attention of the entire court and he could not fail now. "Your Honours, and the learned gentlemen of the jury, this clearly identifies, nay separates, the difference between all these causes, circumstances, and happenings, and the allegations made here about Mistress Claybourne. Even if she were in collusion with the Devil - which she is not, and no witness thus far has been able to confirm they heard any such entreaties - she could not have affected the stars' movement. Which, in turn, means she cannot be held responsible for what happened afterwards."

Judge Altham's eyes shone, but Bromley gazed down at his cup then, with deliberation, took a sip.

"Mr Richmond." Bromley's stern expression dismissed any notion Henry would be so easily victorious. In a powerful voice, he said, "In my court, it is not entirely unusual for the defence to assassinate good characters. This is the second time which you have achieved this feat, and yet, I find little to commend your behaviour and obvious relish in doing so. The prosecution's witnesses may lack moral judgment, but you, sir, have not yet convinced me their statements are without merit." His hand swept down to the dock. "Your own witnesses must be beyond reproach, and the accused must explain herself, or she will hang."

Henry swallowed as his mind ran through the options. He was confident he could rubbish the testimony of Sarah Fell easily, yet overall, this wouldn't be enough if Bromley was minded to find Nemis guilty regardless. If he interpreted Bromley's order correctly, to win, he needed a character witness of impeccable standing. Unquestionable morality. An expert in explaining away the behaviours of someone as pitiful as Nemis.

Who did he have? He dismissed the idea of Lady Hanley immediately, a disgraced fae spy he barely knew. Her standing in the human world may be good by virtue of her title, but, being female, she was inferior as a character witness. He considered Fairfax. A daemon who unwittingly caused chaos wherever he went, yet could play the part of Sir Thomas Fairfax and lie convincingly, if he were so minded to. Too unreliable. And Aioffe and Joshua were no use, as persons of unknown standing in York.

Or, should he move straight to putting Nemis herself up to be questioned? Could she bear it, plagued as she was by visions which they dared not detail? Or would the threat of the Star Chamber would indeed be made real and his name included on the records which might end up in the hands of the Privy Council?

The situation was, he admitted to himself, as dire as it could get. He needed a miracle.

CHAPTER 25

MEDICINE OR MEDIATE?

As luck would have it, someone of impeccable standing knocked on the door of the house on Blossom Street. "Good day," the tall, bald monk on the doorstep called. "Lady Hanley?" He rapped again.

Aioffe bade Hope to stay in the bedroom and dashed down to answer. Her face flushed with relief and she grinned. "Maister Jeffries! At last," she opened the door wider. Although Joshua had mixed feelings about the former monk, having been used by him to transport illicit copies of Bible translations, both Mary and Nemis thought highly of him. Aioffe hardly knew him, but given the situation, any assistance was welcome.

"Thank you for coming to Mary's call, she isn't in at the moment. We met, on Naturae, some years ago. You came with Fairfax."

"And Henry Fitzroy, for my sins." He dipped his head. "Your Highness. I can only apologise for the delay to my arrival, it was… unavoidable. Then, I thought it better to come in person rather than simply send a recipe for Nemis's medication."

"Where have you come from?" She stepped back to allow him entry. The scent of herbs and magic trailed in his wake as he swept into the kitchen.

"It does not matter as I'm here now. How is Nemis?"

Joshua had warned her Jeffries could be infuriatingly enigmatic. "She's already in court. Henry Fitzroy is representing her." She shook her head. "I'm not sure which affects her the most - prospect of the noose, or facing his darkness." She shrugged. "Either way, she was frightened her visions would overcome her, and in public."

"Then I am where I am supposed to be." He lifted a grey eyebrow. "I also took the liberty of preparing the tonic in advance." He rummaged inside a travelling bag and pulled out a little bottle. "The only pertinent question is how we get it into her."

Aioffe pressed her lips together. "We'll have to go to the court. Lady Hanley, Mark and Joshua are there also, watching. Perhaps her case hasn't been called up yet and I can persuade someone to pass the tonic to Nemis, somehow."

"I'm sure I could find my way to the Castle, but persuasion of strangers isn't my strong suit," Jeffries said. His eye flicked to the stairs. "And you have duties here, it would seem."

Aioffe wheeled about. Her daughter was perched in the middle of the staircase. "Hope! I told you to stay upstairs!"

"I wanted to see who it was, Mama." Hope bumped on her bottom down the remaining steps. "This is the man who makes Nemis's medicine?"

"Yes." Jeffries waggled the bottle. "And an old friend of her family."

"He's a witch too," Hope stated, then stared at him with a frown on her face. "But you smell of death. Who died?"

Aioffe noticed her wing bumps flutter, causing the heavy linen of her smock to billow behind her shoulders, and a shiver of unease crept into her tone. "Who died, Maister?"

"You need have no fear, little one," Jeffries said, smiling at Hope. "While I am a healer, not everything can be cured." His eyes flicked to meet Aioffe's, hooded and dark with secrets. "Perhaps we ought to go to the court, and I can tell you all of my travels when Nemis has been freed?"

"Put your cape on, Hope," Aioffe said, understanding that what he might impart was not suitable for children's ears. "We must make haste."

It irked Henry that Sarah Fell held up under the barrage of his questions far better than he expected. She had recounted her experiences of Nemis's peculiar behaviour both in prison and during the cart ride to York with surprising clarity. The jury in particular was repulsed by her graphic description of the fits and seemed to believe the doxy's claims of being spell-struck, so he stopped short of prompting for specifics she may have heard in Nemis's screams, lest any detail about Queen Mary's death spill from garrulous lips. Adding treason to the charge list was still a possibility. Henry was left with little choice for his next attack to the prosecution's case.

Having dismissed her with a tense, "Thank you, that is all the questions I have for you," he restrained himself to a withering glance at her low-cut top. As she sauntered out, he caught her mimicking his words, playing to the crowd above.

He turned to the bench. "Your Honours, I move the testimony of a woman of such low moral standing cannot be taken into account." He gestured at the shreds of cabbage leaf which still remained in her hair as she spun back to glare at him. "Why, this whore would say anything in return for a respite from the stocks, or even a mug of ale and coin. To such a person, it means nothing to swear upon the Bible that her word is fact, for she clearly has no respect for the sanctity of the word of the Lord."

Neither did he any more, but that was irrelevant. These humans still held dear their faith. This was their weakness, and he would exploit it.

Newell sighed in frustration. "Just because Mistress Fell has not attended Church in a while does not mean she lies. She did not deny the behaviour for which she was found guilty of this morning. Your Honours, and the gentlemen of the jury here, can judge for yourselves if she speaks the truth when questioned. We had all seen, and cannot deny, the fear which struck her, nor dispute her testimony that she was caused to lewd behaviour by the command of the witch. There is no suggestion anyone has paid her to make this statement. She has done so voluntarily so the court might know of the foul and unnatural behaviour of the accused. She is the second witness which the counsel pointed out was needed to convict." He shot Henry a smug look. "Her testimony and statement I submit to the court as sworn truth, and with it, conclude my presentation of the facts."

Bromley nodded, "Agreed. The testimony stays on record." He addressed Henry. "As I do not see any witnesses ready to leap to the accused's defence, do you wish her to stand before us and try and explain her actions?"

Henry sensed Nemis would not deny her behaviour, but could she prove no harm had been caused by her actions? Looking at her, shaking on the stool, he doubted she would be able to withstand the pointed questions Newell would doubtless pose. She appeared to be in another world entirely. He gritted his teeth and dithered; had he poked enough holes in the prosecution's case to refute the claims of murder? His gaze slid over the jury, assessing the mixture of expressions. Not yet, he surmised. Then he looked at the judges, considering if now might be the time to try his skills on Bromley, but the judge was distracted shuffling papers.

A loud cough came from the balcony. Henry glanced up. Perhaps Joshua had found a loophole.

Next to a spluttering Joshua, a tall, bald man stood in monk's robes, gazing steadily at Nemis. A healer whose face Henry knew quite well, having eased his death before being made vampire two decades earlier. They'd crossed paths several times since then, as Maister Jeffries moved in high social circles with many influential contacts. A worthy witness perhaps?

In his hands, Jeffries held a small bottle. Maybe it was the restorative medicine? Would it give her the strength to stand up to Newell though?

"Your Honours, if it pleases the court, I would like to ask for a small break to the proceedings."

"On what grounds?" Altham's eyebrow rose. "I would remind you, we have many other cases to hear this afternoon."

"On the grounds that the accused should be offered a final chance to confess her sins, before she answers to her alleged crimes." He gestured towards the balcony. "I see there is a holy man, and an expert physic known to me, now present in the gallery. Having heard the accusations levied against her, Mistress Claybourne might wish to change her plea. This would, as you suggested earlier, bring the proceedings to a swift conclusion, would it not?"

Henry met Bromley's eyes and felt the frisson of energy pass between them. With a subtle push, Henry's will took hold.

The Judge's mouth twitched as he glanced up. "If a priest is willing to hear the witch's confession, I'll allow it."

The monk bowed his head in acquiescence, then turned and made his way from the gallery.

"Is there a private room?" Henry asked Bromley, staring into his eyes once again. "There may be more she wishes to confess in order to unburden her soul."

Bromley gestured to a door behind the bench where the other prisoners sat. "The clerk of the court has a small office. Be quick though," he said, breaking eye contact.

"Bless you for your consideration, your Honours. I am Maister Jeffries," the monk said in deep tones as he glided through the chamber towards the bench. "I presume there is paper and quill therein?"

"The witness was not listed before and therefore should not be approved," Newell interrupted. He met Altham's eyes and repeated, "He should have been presented beforehand."

"This is highly irregular," Altham said, siding with Newell. "And I will not stand for it in my court."

Henry's heart sank. While he had been wrestling with the quandary about whether to put the witch on the stand then mesmerising Bromley, Newell had exerted his influence over the one judge who appeared more sympathetic to Nemis.

Altham continued, "Mistress Claybourne has been afforded many an opportunity before today to confess. We have other cases to hear. The accused shall take the stand," he ruled. "Now."

CHAPTER 26

THE STAND

The note of finality in Judge Altham's voice broke through Nemis's reverie. She itched her forearm, eyes darting wildly about the courtroom. Henry, so recently the cause of the ache within her, looked at her with what seemed like compassion. Her gaze shifted, and her heartbeat steadied.

Jeffries, pillar-like in the gallery, stared aghast at Altham. "Your Honours," he protested in a deep voice which rang with authority. "The opportunity and sanctity of the confession should always be preserved."

"Is it not so writ in the Hammer of Witches?" Henry added, glaring at Bromley.

"She can always confess," the judge said, looking down at his papers. "When found guilty, there will still be time before she hangs. Proceed if you have anything further, Richmond."

Jeffries put his hands on the Judge's desk. "I will stand for the accused. Testify to her character. I have known Nemis Claybourne for many decades." He pointed his finger at her as his voice grew louder. "First, as a healer within the sacred walls of Tynemouth Priory. She is..."

The gavel banged down. Both Nemis and Jeffries started.

"Enough!" Bromley shouted. "This witness is not on the list. His testimony cannot be entered."

"But your Honours...." Henry's entreaty was to no avail. The gavel banged again.

"Is the jury ready to rule?" Bromley growled.

"I'll testify," Nemis whispered. Henry's head whipped around. She had not spoken loud enough for the court to hear, but his acute hearing caught her words. "I shall speak for myself."

"That is not wise," he said, as he looked into her eyes.

The darkness she found in his gaze beckoned, and for a moment offered comfort. But it was not to be trusted. Not entirely. She glanced around the courtroom. Her skin felt cold, as if she had been trapped in the chilly outside when all she wanted to do was enter the sanctuary inside. What was the worst which could happen now? The blackened edges of her dread crept together, threatening to pull her back into the vision. Into the night. All she could make out as she turned her head was the pale, accusing stare of the lion on the shield above the judges' bench.

Mark's face - white save the dark hollows of his eyes - swam before her. He was on the inside, looking out at her. Seeing her for who she was. Estranged, but he needed her. Her heart thumped. It should not be this way. She was his mother and should be with him. The crimes she was accused of would forever taint his life, and she could not accept that. He had to know of her innocence, even if the noose was almost a certainty. There would be no other opportunity to tell him, and she would not, could not, allow this chance to pass.

Yet, the yellow of the painted lion shimmered, golden, warm and comforting. She stared at it, imagining instead the sunlight which brightened each day. How Mark loved to walk in the sunbeams, catch them as they danced through gaps in the leaves. Like a lioness, she had to have the courage to tear down her accusers, defend herself and her family. This was how all mothers protected their young in the face of adversity in nature. Nothing else mattered but her singular desire to protect what was dearest.

She stood. In a quiet but controlled voice, she said, "My name is Nemis Claybourne, and I am a witch." She paused, and the clerk shushed the crowd.

"Here is my testimony, and I pray God one and all hear it well. I have recited many incantations, but with the voice of the Lord God by my side. Not the Devil. I have seen many stars, but only wondered at their movement. Many pains have I eased through my medicines and prayers, but, I stand before you innocent of all the crimes I am accused of."

The courtroom fell silent as she straightened her back. Her eyes narrowed on Margaret Tunn, sat on the front row, threading her rosary through her fingers. Nemis then turned to face the jury. "Innocent of murder, but guilty of easing the suffering of a man afflicted by canker who only wished to ease peacefully into heaven. To think that I, grown from child to adult in the sanctity of religious houses, would defy the natural order for when a person is taken into the Lord's arms is false. It is true, I am a cunning woman, dedicating my skills as a healer to the preservation of life. A midwife, birthing many a babe, each as precious as mine own. I have also held many a hand of those who pass from this life into the next, so they might know they are not alone. Prayed with them. Mourned with their loved ones and eased their suffering where I can. This is all I did for poor Master Tunn. Ease the pain so that he could pass in the company of his family without distressing them."

She drew in a deep breath before continuing. "There was no black dog, only a boy, then a dog. I do not know, but I have never seen magic which can transform a person into a creature. Just like there are no devils marks upon me, because the Devil cannot scar those who truly believe in the divine light of the Lord's forgiveness as I do. These are claimed fancies of a troubled, grieving mind, and no more. I am sorry for the loss of a husband, a father, and a kind soul, but I had no part in his death. That was the Lord's doing in calling him to heaven before his family wished for."

She saw her words held the attention of the jury and pressed on. "And of the incantations you heard reported, I am innocent. Guilty only of pained prayers to the Good Lord."

When she glanced at Henry, she noticed his mouth had dropped sightly open and he examined her with eyes which held respect within.

Tilting her head in contrition, she cast her gaze along the line of gentlemen, for somehow she knew it was they who needed the most persuasion. Her fate lay in their hands, not the judges. She had to appeal to them as honourable folk, with the words of a woman and mother. The warmth and courage of the lion filled her being. Her vision cleared.

"How many of you fine gentlemen have watched the passing of a loved one and wished for an end to their suffering? A parent, perhaps, or a sickly child. Who amongst you has heard a woman's cries of labour and not hoped for a successful outcome? Does not every cry make you more fearful? For fear when you are already frightened only heightens."

She noticed a few of them shift uncomfortably in their seats.

"And, when you are in those moments, pushed to the edge with desperation for some respite from the agony of waiting, watching, and hoping, who amongst you has not muttered a prayer? For that is all an incantation is. A prayer to a higher being, in hope the Lord listens. In your prayers, you paint a picture of what might be. What you wish would happen. How you wish you could feel. But, emotions borne of pain, I feel more deeply than most because I am a witch. A mother. A healer. And so, I offer my healing to ease the suffering, that is all."

She spread her fingers, lifting her arms slightly as if offering them that same plea for hope.

Her eyes rose to meet Mark's, then Joshua's on the balcony. Next to them stood Aioffe with Hope in her arms. In the moment, her love for her family infused her, driving away the remnants of her vision from the fringes of her sight.

"I am a godly woman and I stand proudly before you and in the light of the Lord, without the shadow of sin to cast darkness over my conscience." She turned to Jeffries and said, "I have no need to confess, for I have done nothing wrong in our Lords eyes or the law."

She fell silent and looked at the floor like a penitent.

The courtroom was hushed for a moment. Then, Newell stepped forwards and cleared his throat. "Mistress Claybourne, you stand accused of using witchcraft to murder William Tunn. What was in the ointment you used to poison him with?"

She lifted her head. "That was no poison, sir. It was a simple ointment to relax the muscles he had held tense. The canker within his belly had swelled so much, nothing I could have done would ease it or change the time of his passing."

Jeffries snapped, "As a Maister and physic of wide repute, I can, if the court so pleases, confirm the contents of the ointment if you have it?"

Henry produced the small bottle. "Mistress Tunn did indeed bring it with her. This is my independent expert." He glared at Altham. "The use of which was earlier approved by this court."

Altham stroked his beard and nodded imperceptibly. Bromley frowned.

"Having served at the pleasure of their Majesties Henry VIII and Edward VII, and most recently consulted with the late Queen, I am certain you will not find many physics of better repute," Jeffries said. He pulled out the stopper and sniffed. "Rosemary, sage, leaf of mint, and, I think, a touch of chamomile. A most common remedy to be applied to a midriff which is swollen due to unbalanced humours. Nothing in here which is in any way poisonous."

He tipped the bottle to his lips and drank. "See? I do not fall to my death, nor will I."

Newell harrumphed and turned back to Nemis. "And what incantations did you say in the presence of William Tunn?"

"I only offered a prayer for his soul, sir."

Newell's eyes narrowed. "No incitements, or offering to exchange his soul in return for favour from the Devil?"

She shook her head. "Never."

"And yet, both the gaoler here, a fine man and an official sworn to uphold the law of the land, and Mistress Fell, have testified that they saw you in unholy communion with the Devil. Making a racket with your charms and incantations. What say you to these charges, witch? Do you dare to refute a man's word?"

Nemis looked along the jury's faces. At their beards and jackets, their trousers and bald spots. Realisation dawned upon her. As a woman, she would always be subjugated so a man could feel more powerful. Always inferior, for that was what men were taught. She'd seen it many times before: men gaping at the mysterious nature of women, granted the power to birth life itself, who then proclaimed their own prowess at the result. Healers who by the power of touch and concoction of potions could restore health.

And, as a witch, she was even lower in the 'natural order' of humanity.

But ultimately, as she looked around the courtroom filled with males, her persecution came down to mens' inescapably low opinion of her gender. She wasn't on trial for being a witch, although the accusations implied it so. A man had died, and herself been blamed, because of grief said it had to be someone's fault. The charges embellished because of a deep-rooted fear of her ability to change the state of a person. Heal or harm - as a healer she could do both.

She saw then the battle ahead was not one which a courtroom would change, but one all women would fight for in the years to come. Nemis looked at her fingers, interlaced with each other and realised, her only hope was to show she knew her place.

"I do refute it, but not because it is a man's word. If I appear peculiar to you, or to those who have accused me, it is not because I am a witch, but a woman. Weak, and subject to all the foibles and delinquencies of my gender."

She gazed into the eyes of the judges and jury, certain she was correct calling them out for persecuting womankind. Although it shamed her to do so, therein lay the only way she saw to escape the noose. She smiled, deliberately at the older gentlemen who wore rings and looked well-treated, as she sensed she might gather more sympathy from them with her explanation.

"Gentlefolk, especially those among you who are married, you may know this. There are times when a woman in her middling years undergoes a transformation, from being able to bear children, to her later, quieter time of life. For some, this is a trial, others less so. A woman's mood can flip from rage to tears. In my case, I am also troubled with flushes and irrationality. With faints and pains."

There, she thought, let them be uneasy with the mysteries of womanhood. She dared not glance up to see the flush to men's faces as she sighed deeply, conscious her cheeks reddened. "I am not myself in those moments. I know they will pass but, being held in captivity, these untimely concerns which should remain within the privacy of a home, I have endured in public. In a prison, with unkindness and illness all around. As I said, I feel too deep the emotions, too much the pain of the change, and it overwhelms me. I shall never again bring forth life from my womb, and I grieve for that loss. The shame in my condition stems from those less as kindly disposed as your good selves, and from misunderstanding."

An uncomfortable silence fell over the courtroom.

She felt a touch to her shoulder and knew Jeffries leant his tacit support. "Oh dear lady," he said, in gruff tones. "How you have suffered. The late Queen Mary also endured such maladies. I'm sure there is not any here who would judge you simply for your femininity."

"There is no crime in being a female, or a witch," Henry stated. "Your Honours, Mistress Claybourne cannot be prosecuted for the misfortune of feminine troubles in her advancing years."

Then Nemis looked at the judges, her eyes brimming with tears. This variation of the truth, skirting around the details of what was happening to her, pained, but it was her last thread of hope. "I ask the court's forgiveness in bringing into my testimony the unforgiving and shameful nature of my position, but there is naught I can do to prevent it."

And there wasn't, she realised. All her life she had tried to resist the visions, shied away from them, even when they offered comfort. No escape could be found. Why had she resisted them for so long? Only now, when her very life was on the line, did she understand the gift she had clearly for what it was. With the support of her friends and family, she understood then her abilities were to be used to protect them. Save them and other perhaps, through foreknowledge. It was the only way to face the terror: she had to use them rather than resist their dark call.

With this acceptance, her skin stopped itching. The greyed edges to her eyesight remained, like the whisper of smoke which could be drawn in as a veil by her bidding. She stuck her head up high, stared calmly ahead and awaited the verdict. It mattered less to her now which way the jury judged her. She had already won the battle and could do no more.

CHAPTER 27

VERDICT

"Do you have anything further to bring before the court?" Altham asked Henry. On the other side of the courtroom, Newell grunted with dissatisfaction.

Henry swallowed. Nemis had surpassed his expectations, turning the courtroom on its head by playing on their discomfort about the unfathomable nature of women. Studying their sombre faces, she had been successful in eliciting sympathy from the jury. It was a strategy he hadn't even considered, nor, as a man, would he have used. He wondered: was it enough to free her? He was no lawyer, and had never claimed to be. Henry had, though, done his best to bring into question the accusers, point out the inconsistencies in their testimony and discredit the foolishness of them.

"Your Honours, Mistress Claybourne has sufficiently answered to the accusations. The witnesses - so called - have not, as I have demonstrated, given sufficient evidence to convict her unequivocally of murder, the most serious of the charges levied against her today, having failed to show intent or indeed, means. Nor can it be proven, beyond any reasonable doubt, she used incantations to cause maleficence, since no-one of any repute heard what she did cry out. I cannot speak to her feminine suffering, only that as men, we should be sympathetic to such matters. To be a witch is not a crime. She has committed no crime, nor have Nemis Claybourne's actions been proved beyond doubt to be maleficent. The defence is content to leave the decision of her fate to the esteemed gentlemen before me in the hope that they perform their duty well…"

He stared, wide-eyed, along the row of men. "And with the mercy which all good Christian men should show."

Bromley glanced at Newell, who shook his head, then he growled, "The Jury may discuss their verdict."

Henry gave a slight bow to the bench then, as the jury began whispering amongst themselves, he turned to see Newell scowling at him.

"This isn't the last of it," he sneered under his breath. "And you are out of your depth, casting a desperate line when I have a net. The blemish of witchcraft will not spread through England whilst I still live and breathe. I will find another to make an example of if this one escapes the noose." He tapped the side of his nose. "I can smell a fake, Richmond, even if they," he flicked his fingers to the jury box, and said in a low voice, "are too human to notice your influence. Clumsy. Risky. This is my world and if I see you in it again, there will be consequences at the highest level."

"Your persecution jeopardises the Treaty," Henry hissed.

"I act within all laws, whatever the ruling." Superiority and disparagement rolled from the prosecutor as he turned to his desk and began shuffling his papers together.

Henry's fingers curled into a fist, his ire barely contained. This vampire was a simple lawyer; he was a king. His tone was intolerable. Why he…

Jeffries touched his arm. "Do not rise for the bait. This pond is not yours."

"What do you mean?" Henry saw red but Jeffries squeezed his fingertips around his limb, then replied in a hushed but forceful tone, "This is a mere battle when the war is to come."

Henry exhaled, his glance falling on Nemis, who had taken her seat on the stool while the jury passed bits of paper between themselves. She looked calm. Dignified. He forced his fist to unfurl; the monk was right. Violence would accomplish nothing here but draw attention to himself and away from her moving testimony. He had a kingdom to return to, a kingdom far away from these petty matters. The persecution of witches was of no concern to him.

"You will need to decide upon which side you fight," the monk continued, then sighed. "Divided loyalties are the hallmark of those who rule." His brown eyes wrinkled as he smiled. "But perhaps you already know this?"

"You speak in riddles again, old man. I should have you..."

"Has the jury reached a verdict yet?" Bromley boomed, interrupting Henry's threat.

The clerk scuttled over to the jury stand and conferred with an elderly bearded man at the end. He nodded to the judges and returned bearing a box filled with scraps of paper. Altham and Bromley sorted through the notes in silence, all eyes upon them except for Nemis, who stared at the gallery. Her lips moved soundlessly, and Henry wondered if it was in prayer or a spell. Her heart clamoured fast, so loud to him it was like a pulse in his ears.

"On the matter of the wilful murder of William Tunn by the practice of witchcraft," Altham said, then cleared his throat, "the jury finds Nemis Claybourne..." He glanced sideways at Bromley and his eyebrow rose.

Henry couldn't determine whether his query expressed relief or loathing.

"Not guilty."

Henry caught his breath while Bromley's brows drew together in consternation. Nemis's eyes shone with tears.

"On the charge of use of incantation to cause other maleficent happenings with the purpose of frightening other prisoners to do her bidding against their will, the jury finds her also, not guilty."

Immediately, a noisy disruption broke out in the gallery. Newell pinched the bridge of his nose and squeezed his eyes closed.

Henry looked up. A scuffle broke out and benches tipped over, thudding to the floorboards. Mark was being restrained by Joshua, his arms wheeling wildly as if he were reaching out for his mother. On the other side of the observation area, several people howled their frustration and fear. Cries of 'burn the witch,' rang through the room. Others were crossing themselves, shaking their heads and muttering to each other. He allowed himself a small smile. It was the sort of scene Fairfax would have relished.

"Now this matter has been concluded," Jeffries said, appearing once again by his side. "There is another I would bring to your attention. A most suspicious pair of deaths, which you, along with the fae, ought to be aware of."

As they left the courtroom, Henry pressed Jeffries. "My sister, does she...? Is she...?"

The Maister shook his head. "She is in the rudest of health, as far as I know."

Henry demanded more information, but Jeffries refused to elaborate further until he could speak plainly. The monk then followed Henry and Fairfax in silence back to their accommodation, his head down as if he were reflecting upon the gravest of matters. A happy, reunited family dawdled behind them, having been invited by Thomas to join them for a celebratory meal. Lady Hanley had excused herself on the grounds that she had to settle the accounts with the clerk for the prison fees.

After crossing the bridge, Fairfax bounded ahead to organise a feast for them all, and source some fresh blood. His lover's joy at seeing Nemis set free and reunited with her son grated, and he couldn't quite place why he did not share everyone's relief. Henry reminded himself he had held his end of the bargain with Spenser, yet his failure to hold Newell to account for his disparaging remarks lingered like a cloud. Perhaps it was pent up frustration, not knowing what was happening on Naturae, which tightened his chest. And Fairfax had already refused to set sail on today's evening tide.

Aioffe's silent presence a few steps behind him was equally a pressure and, he determined, just as uncomfortable for her as it was to him. They had yet to dance, although the night was still young. He glanced back at Aioffe, watching her carefully tread over the cobbles, and sensed from her tense shoulders and averted head, she was as reluctant as he to skip around the subject of who held the right to rule Naturae. There was also the small matter of a murderer to consider. Were these deaths Jeffries mentioned connected? Whether she was frightened of being next to fall to the killer's hand though, he could not ascertain. She had said little this morning for him to judge, even when he confirmed their theory, and Nemis's predictions, had merit.

Holding Aioffe's hand, a small girl skipped alongside, her face marred by a blood-red blotch in the shape of a butterfly wing across her cheek. Unfortunate for the child. He presumed this was the baby - now grown - which Illania had referred to, and wondered if she had wings. Like all fae in human garb, hiding wing bumps was made easier by the use of blousy undershirts and capes. With white blonde hair and the simpering smile of the young, she met his eyes as they passed underneath the arched stable yard entrance. Henry almost jolted to a stop, for the vivid greenness of her gaze seemed familiar. It was almost like looking into the gaze of someone he knew very well. As familiar and dear to him as.... As Fairfax.

He frowned and resolutely directed his eyes to the inn doorway. His mind raced. How was that even possible? Had Thomas betrayed him? The similarity in the cast of its eyes was uncanny. His throat constricted and he glanced at Joshua. Did he know? Were they both cuckolds? He determined to question him, under his influence, at the earliest opportunity.

Yet, with the same breath, he yearned for nothing else but to toss his belongings into the Wanderer and set sail immediately. He had been away for too long. Caesaria and his own potential nuptials to secure his kingdom awaited. And an answer to Thomas's proposal had also been promised. Their relationship might be illegal in England, but on Naturae, they could be free to love one another and build a life together. Henry sighed, frustrated with himself for his inability to decide between them both.

The group corralled in the back room of the bar, where Fairfax had persuaded the innkeeper to put out a spread for those who ate food. It wasn't quite the banquet which Henry was accustomed to, but he smelled a welcome jug of fresh blood at the head of the table. He strode over, ignoring Thomas's attempts to slap him on the back with congratulations, and poured himself a large cup. He downed the blood and turned to Jeffries.

"Maister, waste no more time and tell us what you know."

The monk pulled out a stool and said, "The matter is not for the moment." He inclined his head to the children. "Let us celebrate the freedoms we have and be grateful for those we love." He poured himself a goblet of wine and lifted it. "To Nemis Claybourne. May all witches be so fortunate as she in escaping the noose and flame."

Gathered around the table, everyone's cups rose in a toast. Henry poured himself another drink, the scent of blood filling the air as he avoided looking at Thomas's wounded expression.

CHAPTER 28

THE SECOND CROWN

Much later, with full bellies, the children nodded off in comfortable laps. Polite conversation about the weather and anything and everything but trials, prison and future plans tailed off. Jeffries bade Henry join the group of fae and Thomas by the fireside. Henry, broody in solitary contemplation, deigned to stand by the mantelpiece, rather than pull up a chair.

"The news I have to share with you all," Jeffries began in his deep, rumbling voice, "is not the news I would want to bring to such a happy occasion. It concerns deaths."

Nemis paled. "Of Queens?"

Jeffries' grey gaze turned to her and he frowned. "Not quite. But I fear there is more to these deaths than will be made note of in official documentation. In many ways, the victims are nobody of significance."

"Then why tell us of them, if they are nobodies," Henry said. "People die all the time."

"Because their passing has the potential to shift the balance between our kinds." Jeffries' long fingers rose and he began to check them as he spoke. "One, although unremarkable in themselves, what follows next might be of consequence to you, in particular, Fitzroy." He glared at Henry, then continued.

"Two, should the manner of their passing become common knowledge to the vampire council, it would fall under the banner of interference with humankind." He shook his head. "And thirdly, whilst I have no particular love for the ruling authority, upholding the Sation Wars Treaty has kept the peace between our kinds for over a millennium. Any risk to this stability should be known by the leaders of all creatures."

He looked at Fairfax, Aioffe and Nemis in turn. "While you may not be elected officials or wield much influence with your peers, within this room, all four unnatural beings are represented. I bring this information with you in the hope that you act upon it."

"Who has died?" Aioffe asked in a quiet voice.

"Firstly, Amy Robsart, wife of Robert Dudley," Jeffries' glance slid back to Henry. "Earl of Leicester and favourite suitor of your half sister."

"Elizabeth knows she cannot marry for love," Henry snapped. "The Privy Council would not allow it."

"She is wilful enough to do as she pleases. Having been at her court, she is undoubtedly in love with Dudley." Jeffries shrugged. "It is unfortunate the main obstacle preventing her from acting upon her desires has 'fallen down the stairs.' To her death."

Aioffe gasped. "Do you think Dudley's wife was pushed?" Her heart pounded, while her head screamed, 'not a queen, not a queen.'

"I have been unable to find out the exact circumstances of her death, other than all the servants appear to have been given the day off while Mrs Dudley remained at home in Cumnor Place in Berkshire. Apparently alone. However, the convenience of her demise strikes me as problematic. Our Queen walks a fine line between the faiths as it is without the shadow of her suitor's wife to muddy the politics." Jeffries' arched his eyebrow, wrinkling his forehead. "The second death I know more about, having been there, and may yet tip the balance of power between nations and creatures."

He drew in a deep breath. "I have just come from the deathbed of Mary De Guise. She had recently been made a vampire, but it was to no avail in the end." In the stunned silence which followed, he shrugged. "I know not who decided to extend her lifespan, nor who abruptly ended it."

"De Guise, the regent of Scotland?" Joshua said. His shoulders dropped, and he cast a sorrowful glance at Nemis and Aioffe.

"Her death will mean the return of another queen to Shetland's shores," Henry's voice deepened, sounding more dangerous. "Why would someone make her a vampire only to kill her? Her daughter, Mary, will want answers when she claims her birthright."

Jeffries said, "I suspect so. She has no reason to stay in France now her husband, King Francis, has died. My suspicion is the Church turned De Guise so she would be stronger in resisting the change of religion which Moray was gathering support for, finally. Someone else didn't want the resistance. Mary Queen of Scots remains human as far as I know. For now."

"And, if she finds out her mother succumbed and agreed to be made vampire, or that she was murdered, Mary would have little reason in either case not to push forward the Catholic cause in a country so recently committed to the Protestant cause," Joshua said as consternation spread across his features.

Jeffries nodded. "Her half brother remains committed to change, but unrest has plagued Scotland these last few years despite his influence with the ruling clans. Mary's likely return will prompt renewed sympathies to the Catholic cause, yes."

He glanced at Henry. "And Elizabeth will feel the threat of Mary's claim to England's throne anew if she is closer. It may prompt her to react rashly."

Henry tapped his finger on the mantelpiece, interrupting the reflective, silent shock which fell. Aioffe's fists balled in her lap; the machinations of human politics was something she had long ago learned to avoid. But Jeffries was right. These deaths had wider implications for creaturekind.

"Neither of them bore the weight of the crown, though," Nemis said, reaching for Aioffe's support with her hand. "Perhaps this is nothing to do with the prophecy."

Jeffries' eyebrow rose. "A prophecy? One of yours?"

While Nemis closed her eyes, Aioffe explained, "Nemis has had visions plaguing her since the celestial lights in 1555. They are hazy, but, we believe, England's late Queen Mary was a victim, as the circumstances, as were reported, match what Nemis saw."

"And I prevented another murder," Henry said. "An attempt to poison my sister at her coronation." His fingers curled together with a snap, as if he struggled to control his anger. "Elizabeth has been warned to be wary."

Joshua's head hung and he studied the rushes on the floor intently. Aioffe wondered if it was because of his lingering catholic faith, or if there was something else he knew.

"I did not see anyone falling down stairs," Nemis said, opening her eyes and looking around. Relief eased the tiredness lines from her brow. "Nor are these queens."

"A Regent is a queen, of sorts," Joshua asked, his voice tense. "How did Mary de Guise die?"

"Horribly." The lump in Jeffries' neck bobbed up and down. "I fear she was poisoned. I suspect by daemon blood." He looked at Fairfax, who had been uncharacteristically quiet this whole time. "Not sold any recently, have you?"

Thomas shook his head. "Ever since Henry accidentally had some of Mark's, I've not been bled."

Aioffe glanced at Nemis's lap, where Mark slumbered peacefully.

Henry shuddered and reminded them, "A newly made vampire might not know any better, such is the thirst for blood."

He recalled the pain of ingesting just a drop of Mark's blood by accident upon arrival to Naturae, and the effects were both violent and terrifying. His life was saved by Jeffries' intervention and magical healing. Often used to cure humans of various ailments, there was something within daemon blood which was addictive to fae, and deadly for vampires.

Jeffries said, "I smelled its difference when I was called into her chamber to see if I could heal her, and shown the bottle she drank from. But I was too late to do anything. She was in the throes of the toxin by then."

He did not look especially sorry about this, but they all knew Jeffries was a monk who wore the black habit when it suited him, rather than out of any allegiance to Catholicism.

Nemis said in a voice which shook, "I smelled a stench with one death, in my visions, and the haze cloaking the Queen was red. Details return easier to me, now I am less frightened. Was there a window in the shape of a cross?"

Jeffries nodded. "Through which the light had a red hue. From the stained glass, I thought. At the time."

Nemis paled. "Then de Guise was one of the deaths I saw. I felt."

Joshua crossed the floor to Nemis. Taking her hands in his, he searched her face. "Are any other details returning to you?"

"Some. I come back to choking in red water," she said, then frowned. "I'm sure the first is a drowning, but there is great pain there as well."

"Anything else?" He asked.

"Then there's the one who was bloated, writhing on a bed where the incense made the cloud. After that, the one with a flagon and echoes of music, although... it's been some time since I saw it, and I can hardly recollect it."

"They could be Mary and the attempt on Elizabeth," Henry said.

"If Elizabeth didn't die, perhaps that's why it's fading?" Jeffries approached her as well. "What's the next?"

Nemis swallowed. "In a room with a red, glowing cross, the stench is terrible and the cries penetrate the air. It's like being blinded by noise. I cannot even hear what they say, for the voices are overwhelming."

Jeffries nodded. "The atmosphere in de Guise's room was thick with wails from her maidens as well as her screams. No-one could have mistaken the agony she endured."

"Daemon blood is excruciating," Henry confirmed. He glanced at Fairfax. "No offence."

"None taken," Thomas replied, then smiled at Henry. "We are what we are."

Henry's face remained like granite.

"What about the next vision?" Jeffries inquired.

Nemis glanced sideways at Aioffe. "All I saw was a blade of some kind. Slashing down. Stabbing, perhaps?"

"Any others?" Jeffries prompted.

Nemis stiffened.

"Tell us what you know, please, dear friend. Anything could help."

"The last is the worst." Her lips tightened into a line. She was so thin, when she shuddered, her whole being seemed to vibrate. "The silence. The sheer absence of anything except... the sensation of being dragged. Pulled almost, from the inside out."

In Nemis's lap, the hand not held by Joshua twitched. Aioffe stared at it, noticing her friend's fingers strain then curl. Involuntarily, her own began to do the same, and she suspected then the manner of the last death.

Only a fae pulled Lifeforce deliberately.

And as far as she knew, only one fae alive killed like that.

Aioffe's heart pounded. She shot a desperate look at Joshua, whose stricken face matched her own. All she could think of was Spenser, who had suffered the pulling hands of Illania until close to death. How on earth could the fae queen be involved in all of this? It wasn't possible. Henry said she and Caesaria had been on Naturae when Mary of England died. Or was there another, Princess Tamara, perhaps who could drag Lifeforce from a person? Yet, until a fae queen died, her offspring were not supposed to come into their powers. She thought she was the exception, and her powers had certainly increased upon her mother's death. Besides, the spies would surely have told them if Tamara had entered the realm.

"This is wasting time," Henry spat. "Thomas, we sail at dawn."

"For Naturae?" Fairfax replied. "Where she is. Caesaria." He gulped and looked anxiously at Aioffe.

Henry's head swivelled, following the entry of a young serving girl to their room. "Where my future wife is." Then he took in the gaping faces seated about the fireplace and glowered. His gaze stopped on Nemis. "I shall then release Ambassador Spenser back to you."

"I haven't had a chance to thank you," Nemis said. "For what you did for me."

Henry gave a curt nod. "As long as your husband has kept up his end of the bargain, there is no need." His eyes flicked to Aioffe. "But if he hasn't…"

Aioffe clamped her lips together and fumed through her nose. "There is much to discuss," she began. "Queen Illania, where is she? And about…"

"I don't know!" Henry exploded, then wheeled on his heel towards the door. "And I can't do anything if I'm stuck here!"

"You can't just leave," Joshua cried, and she remembered the peculiar sway he had over her husband. She stayed him with her hand, hardly able to breathe as she considered the implications of Illania, Caesaria, and Henry. In Naturae. In cahoots?

"Watch me," Henry said, advancing across the room with an angry, human speed.

Aioffe knew he could have darted out but a serving girl had had entered to clear the table and would notice. "What about our dance?" She called in a deliberate, deceptively gay voice. "You promised."

Henry flicked a low finger at Thomas as if pushing him away. "Trust is everything if you are to be partners." He paused and turned back to Aioffe. "Besides, leading a dance, at such a dangerous time to be a queen, would be very unwise."

"Very true," said the monk.

Nemis hung her head and muttered, "He's right, Aioffe. Until we find out the culprit, to resume your.... position... would place you directly in danger."

She noticed Joshua's lips tighten but relaxed as soon as Henry shut the door behind himself. He had left before she could caution him about the European Queen!

Aioffe heaved a breath in and out and tried to regain control of her emotions and fears. She glanced at Hope, still asleep on her lap. What of her responsibility to keep her safe? "Then what do we do? What next?"

Fairfax shook his head and looked around ruefully. "Well, don't look at me for answers!"

"Actually," Jeffries said, "perhaps we should. Where in London would you go for..." he glanced at the serving girl's back as she made her way out of the room with the platters. "Poison?"

Thomas shrugged. "Any old apothecary, I suppose. Why?"

Jeffries shook his head. "Too obvious. If Elizabeth had died, the first people they would question are apothecaries. I meant, a man such as yourself, who operates in the shade, who might want to keep your deeds a secret. Where would you go?"

Nemis's head rose. "He wouldn't. He'd get the ingredients from lots of places and then find someone else to bind them together." She glanced at Jeffries. "Someone like us."

"Yes, you're probably right, my dear. But, I doubt your usual cunning woman or even an infirmarian like I used to be, could be so precise in the art of poisoning. Such an important target, and on such an occasion, you would need to be sure it had the desired effect." The Maister sniffed.

"There would have been many at the coronation who would have wished for the poison to work. And not many who could have sniffed out the problem before it was drunk. It is fortuitous Henry adores his sister." He stared at Thomas. "More detail about what happened would help us get to the bottom of it."

Fairfax sighed noisily. "I'd better go and see if he's calmed down." He rolled his eyes. "And I thought I was the queen of all drama." Flinging his hands in the air theatrically, he minced out. "I'll write..." he tossed over his shoulder as he closed the door.

Jeffries muttered, "That daemon has been spending far too much time in the playhouses. I shall return to Scotland, to speak with Knox, vile man. Poor face of the faith that he is. He despises female rulers. Maybe he will know more of who was behind De Guise's turning, and it is entirely possible he knows more about her death. He maybe even played a part in it," he growled. "There is likely much change upon the horizon north of here; I will keep you informed of anything I discover."

He rummaged in his bag and drew out the vial of Nemis's medicine and passed it to her. "Keep this safe. As you know, in the wrong hands, it can kill."

Joshua stroked his chin, his brows drawn together. "Makes me think. How would the poisoner get into both Mary de Guise's rooms or Elizabeth's coronation in the first place?"

"John Knox would not be allowed close to Elizabeth. That much I do know," Jeffries noted. "She apparently read his First Blast of the Trumpet Against The Monstrous Regiment of Women, then threw it on the flames. Her sister Mary was of the same mind. But would he go to such lengths as to order a death, I wonder?"

Aioffe recalled Lady Hanley reading the booklet and doing just the same with the text. "These are the sort of questions we should be asking ourselves," Aioffe said. "Any queen is a target for the likes of him." She clutched Hope in her arms. She did not notice Joshua's jaw tightening.

Nemis said, "Not only do we have to find who is responsible for the deaths we know about, we must prevent the others which may not yet have happened."

Joshua dropped his hand on Aioffe's shoulder. "Then we start by going to London and investigating."

Aioffe frowned as he stood and picked up his cape. Hope stirred in her arms.

Joshua said, "I can't just sit around here, mulling what might be or might happen. We should see what we can find out about the Queens we are fairly certain fell afoul – or were meant to – of the killer. Mary and Elizabeth. Once we understand more about their deaths, maybe we can get ahead of the next by catching the murderer. Only with detail can we stop them from striking again."

She understood his reasoning and felt reassurance replace her fear. Her beloved always had a plan, and any plan was better than this sensation of helplessness. "Perhaps I can persuade someone who was there at the coronation, or a friend to Queen Mary, to talk to me. We'd have more anonymity in a big city as well." Much as though she disliked it, for this task, staying hidden was imperative.

Nemis shook her head. "I cannot go with you, even if I could fly. Mark needs me and hates cities. I want to put York behind us. There's no reason to stay. We should return to Hanley House with Mary, if she'll have us. I want to be there for when Spenser returns."

"I can't see any reason why she wouldn't allow it," Joshua said. "And Mary can reach out through the spy network for any other information about his release."

"Also," Nemis said, with a determined expression on her face, "I must face my accusers, now I'm proved innocent." She reached over and touched Aioffe's fingers. "Please understand, I would come if I could."

"No, no, of course you should stay with your family," Aioffe urged. She glanced at Hope and her eyebrows drew together. "I worry for her in a city. She's getting older now, and a struggle to keep safe. Keep people from staring at her."

Nemis offered, "Then she should stay with us. We will watch her in Beesworth until you return. They know her face there. She won't be such an oddity, not now."

"It would be safer," Joshua said to Aioffe, but her heart wrenched at the prospect.

"I just hate to be parted from her," she said, gazing at him. "Together, we can face anything."

"We will be a family again soon enough," he replied. He bent and stroked Hope's cheek. "Wake up, little one. We need to get you to your bed."

"Home," Hope whispered, opening her green eyes to meet his. "Are we going home, Papa?"

Aioffe blinked and looked at Joshua. "Soon, my sweet. When it's safe."

He sighed, similarly avoiding answering the question of which home.

CHAPTER 29

COST OF A UNION

Naturae

"I hear your halfling sister claimed her throne," Illania called across the waves, then tittered. "Quite the occasion, very satisfying."

Henry looked around, barely pausing rowing the oars. She waved a chubby hand, glittering with gems. Caesaria stood on the jetty, dressed in green like a stick insect, next to her chariot. His heart sank as he glanced to the mist. The Wanderer and Fairfax were thankfully nowhere in sight, as he had disembarked in silence before the ship entered. He stared into the grey wall, jaws clenched as he rowed until he felt the bump of the prow hit the posts. His mind whirled. Satisfying? Halfling?

He reached over the bench and grabbed the coiled rope, then tossed it onto the jetty. Thane, with a face like thunder, threaded it through a ring. "My liege, it is good to see you home once more."

"Is it?" Henry muttered. He clambered out and left the advisor to beckon over a worker for his bags. After rolling his shoulders back, he nodded to Spenser, who lurked on the beachhead with other Council members.

His regent visibly sagged with relief as Henry strode towards Illania and Caesaria. "I'll thank you not to insult my sister. Halfling or not, Elizabeth is the rightful Queen of England and deserving of her crown. It shall not be taken from her while I still live until the day she naturally dies."

Illania looked taken aback. "How is it an insult if it is the truth?"

Why was she even here? He glared at Caesaria. "How many fae have pupaeted in my absence?"

Her thin lips twisted into a sneer. "I told you, such powers cannot be bestowed unless I am made queen."

"And I told you, without proof you can perform the role, then you will not share my crown."

"Come now, children," Illania tittered. "There is no need to argue. Caesaria, Henry has barely set his feet back on Naturae and you greet him thus?"

"I greet him as I would any other vampire, mother."

"A good wife would tend to his needs first, my dear. Perhaps if you acted like one, this whole courtship can progress." She curled a finger in the air behind her. "A vampire after a long voyage always needs sustenance."

Henry thought about the awkwardness between himself and Fairfax, the affection he hadn't been able to show after an argument about Hope's parentage. Even though he had been persuaded of Thomas's innocence, he still couldn't give his love the commitment he sought. Then, arriving at the mist, the strangeness of their parting hadn't healed the still-open wound. He did not know he would again see his love. No sustenance could salve heartache.

A European handmaiden flew forwards, bearing a jug he did not recognise. Another followed with a tray of fancy goblets. Until they stopped in front of him, Henry hadn't realised just how hungry he was. The smell of fresh blood brought moisture to his lips and he stared at the offering, eyes widening with anticipation and desire.

Thane placed his hand on Henry's arm. "My liege, we've kept a deer safe and aside for your return. It wanders on the south side of the island." His expression asked him to choose.

Easy choice.

"I can take care of my own needs," Henry snapped at Illania. "Mollycoddle someone else." He strode straight past the tub, to pallid-faced Spenser. "She is freed, and we shall talk before you leave," he snapped, then darted into the woodland.

As Henry sank his fangs into the deer's neck, drinking deeply, a flush of gratitude accompanied the warmth of the blood. The hunt, then the chase, had been brief, but satisfying. His fae, at least, knew how to welcome him home.

He drained the deer dry, then left the carcass to rot into the ground. Feeling more himself, and fortified for the confrontation which lay ahead, he sat alone for a moment. No other animal made a noise, only the faintest rustle of the vegetation in the breeze. Despite watching and listening, he heard no rapid heartbeats, smelled nothing but the flowers, and it pained him.

In his absence, the land had been stripped bare of sustenance, just as his advisers had feared. He gazed between the tree trunks. Straight and tall, like the bars of a cage, he wished, just for a minute, to be able to fly straight up to escape.

The entire voyage here, he had been consumed with his own indecision. Unfortunately, like his situation in the woods, he could see no easy way free. Although his morality would happily allow him to continue his relationship with Fairfax and be married to a fae to provide for his realm, doing both would satisfy no-one. If he chose Caesaria, Thomas would never return, for he had made clear his feelings on fidelity right at the start of their relationship. But Caesaria, foul creature though she was, could provide the future fae Naturae needed. Could perhaps create the heir his people wanted. An heir as Aioffe already had.

Henry shook his head, auburn hair falling over his forehead. Bind himself to Caesaria, and her dreadful mother, forever; that was the cost of a union, and a high one. Forever was too long a time to deny his truest nature as a lover. From what he had observed of Joshua and Aioffe, he suspected fidelity was valued by the fae. There simply was no way he could be both lover to Thomas, and husband in every sense of the word to Caesaria, simultaneously.

The only solution he could see wasn't really a solution, but his only advantage, and Fairfax's disadvantage. He had to play for time, which he had more of than mortals. And he had to get Illania and her people off of his realm before they destroyed what was left of it.

The Council were waiting for him in the near-empty High Hall upon his return. As was Caesaria. As he strode through the chamber, his fists balled. She sat in his chair, presiding at the head of the oval table. He stepped up to the dais. "Get out of my seat."

Caesaria turned to him, the model of serenity. "My liege, we were not expecting you to join us so soon."

"Why? Do you presume to know my mind? My movements? My needs? For your mother presumes these things when she knows nothing about me." His gaze flicked the grey, gaunt faces around the table as Spenser stood.

"Princess," he said, with a slight bow to Caesaria. "I will escort you to your chambers whilst the King is briefed." He shot Henry a glance. "My liege, perhaps I could seek an audience with you in your chambers when you have concluded?"

Henry pulled out his chair with a jerk, unseating Caesaria. She recovered quickly by taking to the air. Swirling around, above the table, one side of her mouth tilted up in a haughty half-smile. "I'm sure we will have ample opportunity to discuss our future plans," she said, looking down at him. "This quaint way of ruling has delayed the arrangements for our nuptials, so I have much to do."

Henry rose to his tiptoes, ready to pounce up at her, but she twirled up then darted out of the hall. As soon as she had gone, he sat down and pursed his lips. Some of the Elders hung their heads. Thane shifted in his seat, and Henry could see him struggling to find a suitable opening sentence, so he did it for him.

"They've depleted us." Henry spread his hands wide across the table. "And for that, I can only apologise for my extended absence." He looked at the Captain. "How do our forces stand?"

"Hungry," the whiskered fae replied. "But ready. We have plenty of fish still, but nothing upon our lands." He glanced at Thane. "It has not been easy, my liege, for Naturae to support so many people."

Henry nodded curtly. "And the pupae?" He addressed Thane.

"No new ones, and those which were hanging are still stunted from lack of blessing."

As Henry expected. He breathed out through his nostrils in a long whoosh. "Where is Issam?"

"Occupied," Thane said, as he met Henry's eyes. "As the spies reported in, they were promptly commandeered by Caesaria. She… pressed them for information. Too hard."

Henry glowered. "And?"

"Issam is caring for them. Elsewhere."

"Where?"

"He would not say, my liege. For their safety, he said."

"So how have you kept abreast of developments in the wider realm?"

"We have not," the Captain said. His fingers curled into a fist on the table top. "With respect, my liege, we have barely been able to stay alive ourselves, let alone wonder at what is happening beyond these shores."

Henry's eyebrow rose. "How so? You have fish, resources… I left Spenser in charge. What has happened?"

Thane answered. "The Ambassador was weak when he arrived, my liege, and weakened further as he tried to get Caesaria to work with us in the management of the realm." He shrugged. "No matter what he said or did, she made her own decisions and has her own priorities. Her people are different. Aggressive. Itinerant. Self serving. They refused to stay within the island's boundaries, so our soldiers were constantly occupied with escorting them to the other islands to feed once our supplies dried up."

The Scottish Elder spoke up. "They have no care, no concern about being seen. Our trading relationships are ruined. Caesaria allowed her fae to simply take what they want. No matter what the Ambassador said or did, she expects everyone to serve her, and her alone. And her appetite is…. voracious."

Just as he'd anticipated, Henry fumed silently. He did not blame Thane or the Elder for ranting, only felt the weight of the responsibility fall onto his shoulders. He had hoped Spenser would have been more effective, but he saw now how much of an awkward position he had left the Ambassador in. No matter, he thought. This was what ruling was all about. Taking difficult decisions. "When did Illania return?"

And why had she stayed?

"Not long before you, sire," the Captain answered. "And it is clear from whom Caesaria learned her ways."

"I want them gone," Henry growled. "Now we just have to figure out how without causing a war between tribes."

The Captain glowered at him. "But we need a Queen to recover our populus! Sire, we must search for Aioffe."

Henry thumped his fist on the table. "I forbid it." He looked down and adjusted his tone. He needed them on his side and saw no other way than to admit the truth. "I met with Aioffe while I was in England."

The Council all gasped, then clamoured over each other, "Where?"

"She lives! Blessings upon us!"

"Is she well?"

"Why has she not returned?"

Henry stood, slapping the table to bring them to order. He swallowed and took his time. "I saw Aioffe, and she is well. As is Joshua. But...." He glanced around, then said with as much sincerity as he could manage, "She and her husband will not be returning to Naturae."

"She cannot abandon us. Her duty is to us!" Thane sounded more perplexed than hurt.

"She has other duties now. To her family. And... for her own safety."

Heads shook, and Henry knew he needed to confide in them to rebuild the trust they had in him. "I ask for your silence - say nothing to anyone else about what I tell you for it will cause unrest among the populous." He leaned forward and dropped his volume. "There is a murderer at work. Specifically, someone killing queens. My half sister Mary was the first. I averted an attempt on Queen Elizabeth, and I am told the Queen Regent of Scotland, Mary de Guise, could also have been a victim. It is possible, predicted even, more queens will die."

Thane asked, "How do you know this? Aren't they all humans?"

Henry spoke quickly. "The witch, Nemis, saw the deaths we know of in a vision. Details which we have since found out to be true, such as Mary de Guise. She was made vampire shortly before she was poisoned." Henry's eyes darkened as he stood unmoving. "There are other deaths in Nemis's vision which have yet to occur. If Aioffe returns as a queen, then she too would be at risk."

The Captain pushed his chair back. "We would keep Queen Aioffe safe." He clenched his fist. "No-one would harm her here."

"She has made her choice," Henry replied. "Now, especially, she does not wish to be your queen. I ask you to respect that, for her sake. Is it not better to know she is alive and well, than dead because of her title? Would you have her risk her life by returning?" He shook his head. "No, I cannot ask it of her, and if you cared at all for her, you would not, too. It is a death sentence to be a queen at the moment. Naturae is fortunate to have a king," he reminded them.

"So, where does that leave us?" Thane asked. "Naturae needs a Queen."

"But no-one wants the one on offer," the Scottish Elder whispered. "Caesaria. We are doomed."

"Not doomed," Henry said. He smirked, "Although naming her Queen would also put her at risk, I suppose." Which wasn't an entirely unattractive option, now he thought about it. Perhaps knowing the risk would bring her in line?

In the meantime, he stuck to his plan. "But I ask for your tolerance while we explore other options. If there is one fae tribe, there will be others, surely? Does anyone know where?"

The Council members glanced at each other, blank expressions on their faces.

"The spy network might know," Thane offered.

The Captain studied Henry from underneath his bushy eyebrows. "Or the Vampire Council?"

"A good thought," Henry said. "I shall write to them and enquire." He smiled, recognising the familiar control and decisiveness return to himself. "For now, focus your energies on what Naturae needs to recover and we will discuss your plans tomorrow."

CHAPTER 30

BEAR BAITING

London

Within two weeks of their arrival in London, Aioffe and Joshua realised their investigation would take far longer than planned. After ingratiating themselves with locals in the Clink district of the city – notorious for the light-fingered thieves operating in the shadows of the nearby prison - they compiled a lengthy list of people to speak to.

"It's hopeless," Aioffe said to her husband, in the solitude of the tiny room they rented. "And I miss our Hope."

"I, too," Joshua said as his fingers rubbed the back of her neck, "but it isn't hopeless. We still have some leads left." He glanced down at the sheet where they had carefully written down names to find, based on rumour and what little information they had gleaned from gossip in the local inns. Three-quarters had a line through, having been located, persuaded to talk, and found wanting of anything useful. His nose caught the smell of the blood as it drifted through their open window. It reminded him of not only the nature of the entertainment they planned to go to that evening, but also of their need for sustenance. "We should change into looser clothes.

After we have been to the bear baiting, maybe we should head out of the city, to the woods and hunt."

"Tomorrow, I want to return to the seamstress we visited today, on Lombard Street," Aioffe said. "I know it took ages to walk there, but I'm certain I can find out more about her client, the wife of William Cecil, with a light touch. Where we might find her, intercept her, and casually ask about her daily business."

"I think we need to move to the other side of the Thames, for it takes us too long to traipse from one end of London to the other. Perhaps find somewhere in Smyths Field, or the Strand, where her husband resides, or even around St Paul's would be better. We should live where the wealth is, not the paupers, even though we cannot afford it for long."

She nodded. "Aye, makes sense."

Joshua's hands moved up to her hair and he began pulling out the pins which fastened her headdress on. "If we can only find out who served Mary upon her deathbed, then check their names against a list of who attended the coronation, we might have a chance."

"That's precisely the sort of information someone like Mistress Cecil, who has served both Queen Mary and Queen Elizabeth, might know. If we can't lay our hands on a complete list, then it's a question of working our way through these names until we do." Aioffe turned to Joshua, taking her hood from his fingers and laying it on the bed beside her.

He cupped her face in his hands and stared across her skin. "You look pale, my love. Paler than usual. What worries you?"

She sighed. "It's just so noisy here. So dirty. So many people."

"Perhaps we should find a playhouse instead of the baiting? Fairfax always said they were a feast for all senses. Maybe there's enough Lifeforce there for you to replenish?"

"These last few weeks, with the trial, then flying here, getting settled, have worn on me, I admit." Aioffe reached behind and tugged on the laces of her bodice. He gathered her into his chest, reached his arms around and peered over her shoulder as she relaxed into him. "I think I'm homesick," she said, as his nimble fingers untied the knot. "I never thought I'd say that about Naturae."

He laughed softly. "It was always me who wanted to stay in one place and settle." He pulled back from her and she sighed as the restrictive corset released. "I miss it too."

She drew in a deep breath, then exhaled before smiling. "Funny, I don't miss ruling, but I miss the people. The freedom."

"Naturae's not entirely lost to us."

"I just don't know what's the best thing to do for Hope."

"Doesn't every parent worry for their children?"

She stood. "I suppose they do. I sense she has great powers, which will only manifest as she grows. She should have a happy childhood before she chooses what she wants to do." After a shake of her head, Aioffe then glanced through the window. "At least she can fly, although, I wouldn't be happy if she decided to stretch her wings and hunt on her own. Oh! What if she gets lost? Or flies off to find us?"

"She won't, don't fret. If there's one thing we've taught her, it's caution, especially among humans. Spenser will fly with her as often as she wants to go out, and he's well versed in keeping his true nature hidden around humans." Joshua trailed his fingertips down her back, along the ridges of her covered wings. "Our job as parents is to keep her safe until she discovers how to use her skills to survive in the world around her." He grimaced. "Sounds like just the sort of statement a human couple might make. Remember William Tunn's aspirations for his boy?" His fingers tightened unintentionally on her skin. "But keeping them all safe was always their priority. All parents just want what's best for their child. I imagine my family would have said something similar to me, if only I could remember them."

She whirled around, and he thought he saw what looked like guilt flash across her face. Reaching for him, she buried her head in his shoulder.

"Now, don't you worry about her," he said, stroking her hair. "Hope's perfectly fine with Mary and Nemis. I'm sure Spenser is there right now, to accompany her if she wants to fly. She knows not to go off wandering on her own."

Aioffe mumbled something into his chest, then shook her head furiously. He pulled her back and stared deep into her bright blue eyes. "She's fine! We'd have heard if there was a problem."

But Aioffe looked away. She stripped with efficiency, freeing her wings. Busied herself re-dressing in a lighter skirt, looser bodice and flinging her cape over her shoulders.

Joshua hastily made similar preparations, glancing all the while at his wife. Her movements were economical, even though they were not late for the start of the show. He reached out to her with his mind, hoping to sense what lay behind her sudden and overwhelming emotion since she would not voice it, but there was only a void, as if she closed a door.

Perhaps she just needed to eat, he decided, as he retreated. Focus, he told himself. Put the conversation aside until there was less of a time pressure.

Joshua held Aioffe's hand as they entered the wooden stalls of the nearby Southwark bear and cock baiting arena and climbed the creaking steps to the gallery. Two pennies each bought them bench seats in the gods; those who wanted to be splattered with blood could pay less to stand on the edge of the action. Below, in the centre of the sandy pit, a blood-stained post with a ring on the top stood like a lonely sentry in a desert.

The stalls filled with Londoners from all walks of life jostling together, chattering, jeering, and chanting in anticipation of the entertainment ahead. The air was ripe with the scent of dogs and hops as the ale slopped from flagon to cup. Coins dropped into sweaty palms as bets were placed. Rumour had it, the Queen often visited the arena, and had ordered the construction of two new, dedicated rings close by, such was her enamour with the sport. Since Joshua had earlier ascertained the court was in residence at the nearby Palace of Whitehall, just across the river, they were determined to attend as many of the nightly games as possible. Aioffe reasoned Elizabeth would seek her entertainment with her closest friends, and access to them would be easier in a crowd.

Aioffe's face was nonetheless wary as they listened to the gossip around them, hoping to hear familiar names being discussed, but all she caught was the bear's names - Blind Robin, Mad Besse, Harry Hunks and Sackerson. The various beast's virtues were debated with respect bordering on reverence, whereas the numerous dogs who would attack them seemed unworthy of mention. Her fingers twitched, aching to pull from the crowd's anticipation.

With no preamble or announcement, a huge, shaggy-haired bear was led into the ring by his bearward. The beast lifted his scarred nose, pink-rimmed eyes wildly darting about as he sniffed. With a spear shaft, the bearward whacked the bear's rear and it stopped ambling across the sand.

The bear grunted, in seeming resignation to the change in its location from cage to pit.

The crowd roared, and, as if in acknowledgement, the beast's paw rose. While the keeper affixed the chain to the post, the bear stood on its hind legs and began to postulate, playing to its audience with a series of grotesque thrusts and grunts. At the laughs and claps or acknowledgement, it shook its great head and growled into the air. After a final jerk to the leash to test its security, the bearward clapped his hands, the noise of which was entirely drowned out by cheers. He cast a sorrowful glance at the bear, then hastened back through the hatch from which they had emerged.

The bear sensed his solitude and stopped his performance. A hush fell over the crowd, listening for the sound of the barks. From underneath Aioffe and Joshua's vantage point, enormous mastiffs and bulldogs dragged their masters into the ring. Panting, growling, dripping with saliva; on four paws, the largest of the dogs stood hip height to a man. They formed a circle around the edges of the arena, prompting a flurry of bets within the masses.

The bear dropped to all fours and wheeled around, his lips wobbled as he snarled.

"He's blind!" Aioffe exclaimed, just before the dogs began to bark. The beasts strained at their rope leashes, rearing up on hind legs with snapping jaws. She covered her ears against the cacophony of noise which erupted.

Joshua's heart began to thump in his chest as the rumble of their deep barks spread their excitement.

A keeper released his hound. Gazelle-like, the beast sprang towards the bear, launching itself towards the bear's neck. Jaws open, paws stretched, it landed on the bear's back.

The bear lurched back onto its hind legs, standing and tipping the dog straight off onto its rump. As the mastiff wriggled its back to twist to its feet, another dog pounded forward. Just as it leapt, the bear swiped it, mid-air, away with its paws. The crowd oooh'd as the second dog hit the sand with a spray and a whimper. But the first had re-grouped and sunk its fangs into the bear's leg.

"Oh no!" Aioffe said. She stood and gripped Joshua's arm. "This is barbaric!"

"It's not over yet," he said in a tense voice.

More dogs were released, swarming towards the bear.

"I can see the bear's Lifeforce, and its confusion." Aioffe sounded distressed. "I can't watch." She looked away, gazing instead at the rapt faces in the crowd. She scanned the audience, studying their attire, for it would indicate their status better than any gossip could. "Have you seen anyone important yet?"

Joshua couldn't tear his eyes from the pit, his belly tight and a grimace on his face. It was one thing to kill animals for food, quite another to take pleasure in a spectacle of such brutality. Aioffe always calmed their catch, so it felt no pain, but this was all about how much pain the bear could stand. In his head, he knew the entertainment relied upon the bear staying alive, but neither of them wanted to witness any prolonged suffering.

Agitation soured her expression. "This is their new church," she said. Her lips curled in disgust as she appraised the chanting audience. "Their passion for this sport could sate me, but the cost of it..."

She froze. "Oh..." then her head snapped to the bear. Not taking her eyes off the pit, she pushed past him and down the stalls.

Joshua noticed her wing bumps vibrating beneath her clothes and he tried to follow. His way was blocked by a man's arm, pumping the air with excitement as the bear roared angrily. "Aioffe," he shouted, but his call was drowned out by the crowd cheering and she'd disappeared from sight. His chest tightened, suddenly fearful for her. He shoved the man aside and clattered down the gallery stairs.

Aioffe had frozen midway down, staring across the ring. Joshua grabbed her arm, "I thought I lost you!" But, his voice tailed off as their physical contact allowed him to share what she saw. The bear was surrounded by hounds, snapping, tugging on its fur. Around the beast's body, a purple haze of pain caused by its wounds.

She flinched as it yowled, pinned down, at the end of its tether. The bear's head wrenched around as if trying to see where the next attack would come from, but it was hopeless. Its long brown fur heaved with the mass of twenty or more dogs, all trying to grab a nip. Ripped skin flapped as it writhed, exposing more parts for the frenzied hounds to snap their jaws into.

Joshua staggered back, dropping Aioffe's hand, but still watching as the keepers closed in. They poked the dogs with spears to prise them off, but as soon as one was hauled away, another hound took its place or pounced upon the weaker dog. The frenzy was a seething mess of fur and claw, jaw and spike. Yips, cheers and clamour fuelled the chaos in the pit.

The irony-tang of spilt blood assaulted his nose. Snarls and shrieks pounded in his ears. His stomach clenched, feet shuffling apart as he automatically balanced himself. Braced for the onslaught.

The individuals in the surrounding crowd faded away, and he stood alone. Black air thickened with the stench of gunpowder and peppered with flickering torches in the distance. Battle cries. Screams. The thunk of blade against poleaxe shaft.

He was under attack! Soldiers, hundreds of them, were swarming towards his position. He reached over his shoulder, seeking an arrow, a bow, which should be behind him. But his fingers felt nothing but empty space. His hand dropped to where a sword should be by his side. Nothing.

Yet he knew, with absolute certainty, the blood and cries were from his comrades. His fellow soldiers. Falling. Dying. He had to save them from the slaughter! Had to protect...

"Joshua!"

Aioffe's voice. It sounded far away, like she was on the other side of something. Somewhere. Was she trapped? She sounded muffled, yet he knew in his soul it was his wife calling. He had to get to her!

"Joshua!"

Who was she calling for? He felt her tug on his arm. He frowned, his hands balled into a fist. Why wasn't she calling his name? Tarl. He was Tarl.

"What's wrong?"

She sounded closer now. Her breath a welcome warmth on his cold cheek. Her fingers curled over his fist. Was she safe? He turned his head, looking down to where she ought to be. By his side, not over there, on the battlefield.

Through the darkness, she stared up at him. The vivid blue of her gaze washed away the memory. His throat felt dry, and he blinked.

"Where are you?" She asked.

"I don't know," he answered. What an odd question, but pertinent. He looked down at himself, then around. Where was he? His body felt displaced, his clothes just wrong. With sweaty palms, he patted himself down. "I could have sworn I brought a sword."

Joshua met her eyes, his mouth gaping as he reached for more words to express his confusion. He started, there was something on his back! He recoiled, stumbling on the floor as he tried to look over his shoulder to see what it might be.

"Shh," she whispered. "They're yours... You're with me. Just look at me until you know it."

He gaped, but, as his eyes traced the familiar outline of her jaw, her heart-shaped face, the noise of the crowd returned.

Her fingers crept down his arm, interlacing into his. "I felt you go," she said, then rolled her lips together. "I think I know where you went."

Joshua shook his head. He wasn't altogether sure, but he trusted Aioffe. Always.

"We should leave now." She tugged on his hand.

When he resisted, she turned back to face him.

"I don't understand," he said. "What's happening?"

She swallowed and glanced at the bear. "I think it maybe something in your human past re-entered the present." Her eyes shifted to stare beyond him. "But here is not the place." Dragging him down the next set of stairs, she said, "We will find another way to find those we seek. This is too provocative."

Outside, the crowd thinned. They walked swiftly through the streets, without talking. He clutched her hand, his insides still quivering with upset. Despite their physical connection, he sensed her blocking his mental enquiries. The determined set of her chin told him she would not relent, or speak, until she was ready.

Miles later, they reached the sanctuary of woodland. Pushing their way through the undergrowth, they came to a clearing and he pulled her to a stop. "Here," he said. "Please, tell me now."

Her face was drawn as she glanced at the sky. "Up there." She began to loosen her garments to free her wings.

He stared at the black night above, twinkling with stars and sighed. Her wings unfurled, capturing his gaze in a shimmering with a rainbow of colours, shining under the moonlight. As always, when their eyes met, she took his breath away. But, as she launched herself into the air, and hovered wearing only a shift and a smile, all he saw was an angel. His stomach clenched, for she was so pure, innocent, and he so unworthy of her. What kind of a man was he?

His hands clenched on his lapel. A deceiver. He thought of the note which he had kept hidden from her in York. Of his own culpability. 'The devil is an angel fallen,' ran through his mind.

The burden of keeping the threat to Aioffe a secret sank heavy into his gut. "You fly," he said. "I'll hunt for us instead."

Her gentle smile faltered. "Are you sure?"

He nodded. "I think better with a full belly. Go! Be free, my love."

She stared at him, eyes silently urging him to follow her. But he couldn't. What would happen if his wings failed? If he fell from the sky, who would care for Hope? He averted his eyes, then turned and gazed into the woods.

Without saying anything more, she shot up and within moments, disappeared from his sight.

Joshua sighed, then looked around. Hunting. This much he could do, and perhaps it would help to ease his conscience to provide for his wife, while he still could. She may no longer be queen, but he would never stop worrying. Never stop trying to protect her.

CHAPTER 31

THREAT OR PROMISE?

Only when Henry called, "Ambassador," did Spenser look up from pacing outside the royal quarters. The fae's wings dropped as he crossed his arms and looked down the hallway with a pensive expression.

"You are free to leave Naturae whenever you like," Henry said, unlocking his chamber door. "As I am returned, and your wife freed, it only remains for us to decide upon your future role."

Spenser followed him in. "Precisely what I came to discuss. Hurry, for Queen Illania merely awaits fresh bearers to bring her also to your door."

"Hmm," Henry said. "Rather presumptuous."

After a quick glance down the corridor to ensure they were not observed, Henry closed the door. He turned to the Ambassador. "I gather it has not been easy to balance the needs of your princess with the business of Naturae." He did not blame him, not now he understood the extent of the burden he had left Spenser with.

"My wife, sir. Tell me of my wife."

"She, your son, and her fae friends are all safe and well."

"Her visions?"

"A reality. De Guise was the third. Nemis has seen others. More queens dying."

Spenser sighed. "Naturae has been kept blind by Caesaria."

"Controlling knowledge," Henry nodded. "A typical strategy for ruling." And one he himself frequently used.

"The spies were in a terrible state after she intercepted them." Spenser's hands shook. "She has not the powers of her mother, of a queen. Yet. So her methods of extracting information are violent and archaic. It took quite an effort to get them away from the island."

A rap on his door prevented Henry from demanding he elaborate. "It is critical we ensure the spy network is operational again. I must be kept informed." He shot Spenser a warning glance. "If you know where they went, tell them I'm back on the throne and their service is required."

Spenser nodded as the door swung open.

"Her Highness, the great Queen Illania," announced the mottled green winged fae with the squeaky voice. Henry noticed his ornamental robes had been smartened and repaired, no doubt by Naturae's skilled workers. He scuttled out.

Henry and Spenser bowed as Illania's tub entered. Once the bearers gently landed on the floor, she dismissed them with a flick of her wrist.

"My favourite gentlemen," she cried as soon as they had left. Henry caught a glimpse of her guards stationed outside before it closed.

"Your Highness," Spenser said, his face pinched as he straightened. By this side, his hands shook a little. "Since King Henry has returned, I ask your leave to visit my family."

Illania's eyebrow arched. "I shall consider it. But first, Henry, there are arrangements to be made. Formalities."

"I will not wed your daughter," Henry said stiffly. "Not yet."

"Why wait? Your realm needs populating." She sniffed.

"Well, there are no new fae to welcome because Caesaria hasn't performed. In the meantime, your people have raped Naturae of all resource!" Half true at least.

"Then expand your realm! There is no shortage of land. Take Scotland as your own."

His jaw tightened.

She held a hand in front of her face and pretended to examine her nails. "The Vampire Council would have no complaint if expansion was by one of their own, would they?"

She glanced at him and blinked. In that instant, he realised their plan had always been to force him into such a position. Henry darted next to the tub. He glowered down at her, considering how quickly his hands could wrap around her throat. How long it might take for an immortal to wilt.

Illania stared up at him with surprise. "Isn't that what you've always wanted? To rule over the humans? You've not exactly abided by the Treaty thus far."

She cackled as he gritted his teeth. Spenser coughed.

Henry forced his arms to stay by his side. Her insults had to mean nothing. He pivoted instead. "Your daughter has hardly covered herself in glory in my absence."

Her eyes narrowed. "Your absence meant a lack of discipline. Once you get to know her, I'm certain you will find her more pliable."

As malleable as a rod of iron perhaps, Henry thought, but he grabbed the half offer. "Then perhaps we should spend more time together now I am returned, before we commit to an eternity in each other's company?"

Illania pouted. Her fingers pinched and played with the frills on her skirt. "Or maybe," she paused, then pointedly stared at him. "You harbour some hope another fae princess, or queen, will appear?" Her eyebrow arched. "Or reappear?"

Henry gaped. Had she a spy in the Council, he wondered?

"But," she shook her head almost playfully. The curls around her cherubic face bounced. "If Aioffe were to return, she is already wed. Your presence here - superfluous." She wriggled her fingers in the air, as if wafting away a non-existent fly.

Henry's eyes narrowed as he said coldly, "Aioffe will not return."

"Can you be sure?" Illania's lips pressed together briefly, then she clapped her hands. Her bearers hurried into the room.

Henry met Spenser's eyes as the tub retreated, then he frowned. He darted to the door and locked it. "Warn Aioffe," he said in a low voice, quiet enough that no-one else would hear. "Tell her, the music plays off-key. It is not yet time to dance."

The Ambassador looked perplexed. "Is that a threat, or a promise?"

Henry shrugged. "Neither. Both. But," he sighed, "if I keep Illania and Caesaria here, somehow, then, if another queen dies, we know it isn't their doing." His fingers tightened on the doorknob, as if the cold metal of the handle would warm the chill from his heart. Let it not be Elizabeth, let it not be Lizzie...

CHAPTER 32

THE DANGERS OF RESEARCH

4th June, 1561 London

Aioffe stared at the list in her day book. Courtiers' names crossed through, a few more added at the bottom of the page. She closed it and glanced at Joshua, resting on the bed. Most nights lately, he slipped into nightmares, rank with sweat and crying out his pain. Respite was impossible for them both until, in these early hours, his mind and body quietened. The dawn light bathed his pale face, reminding her of a marble statue laid straight and still. In the deep, meditative state of the fae, akin to a human's sleep, his exhausted stillness reminded her of watching over him while he transformed. The noise, closeness and stench of London couldn't have been further from the dank hut in deepest France over a century ago.

And yet, she still had not told him much of his life before. She dared not. To voice how she had soothed away the memory of his battlefield trauma made it seem as if she shrouded the truth from him. To have not mentioned it for so many years now looked as if she deliberately deceived him. The fact was, his rebirth to fae had unwittingly obscured all recollection of his human life, although he had since wrestled with his faith as if it were so embedded within him, it was innate.

She had only ever intended to ease his trauma, but perhaps time as it slipped by, frayed the veil she'd woven? Through the ragged holes, his past experiences were seeping through. Aioffe had a suspicion the bear baiting ring heralded those memories returning, which was why she had tried - unsuccessfully - to remind him of what it was to be fae. To fly and be free. To hunt and be sated. On her lap, Aioffe's fingers twitched, as if in response to her guilt. Perhaps it also had something to do with the glimpse she thought she had, of Father McTavish, seated across the ring. It unnerved her to see a familiar face so far from York.

Since that night, Joshua had not pushed her for answers, or a clarification of her blurted excuse for his funny turn. In truth, she knew little about his history or family to impart. Even if she did tell him what he was, what happened when they met, and their harrowing journey, had enough time passed? Could time and love truly heal the wounded mind?

With a sigh, she stood and crossed to the window. No good could come of worrying about the past, could it? She considered how she had intended to help Tarl in his pain, and how fine the line was between kill and cure. A little like Nemis's medicine - which would kill a human but cure a witch of the after-effects of a vision. She frowned. Medicine, or poison. Both were as intimate a way of killing, and could only have been applied by someone close to the monarchs. Someone they trusted to be with them during their vulnerable moments.

She glanced once again at her journal and tapped her lip. In her heart, she was losing faith in Joshua's logical theory that the deaths, or almost deaths, stemmed from a religious cause. Elizabeth was a Protestant, while the Marys were staunchly Catholic. As the weeks stretched into months, they had crossed out most of the names on their list because, after questioning them, not one person had been present at Queen Mary's court, Elizabeth's coronation, and Mary de Guise's castle in Scotland.

At least, not one person still alive.

Seized with an idea, she strapped on her dagger and tied her purse to her belt. She scribbled a note to Joshua saying where she was heading on a torn-out page, then pocketed her journal. With a last glance at her husband, she crept from their room and into the rising heat of the day.

Holding her nose as she stepped carefully down the narrow Pissing Alley, Aioffe emerged from Paternoster Row into Paul's Cross Churchyard. Ahead, St Paul's Cathedral stood surrounded by gardens and market stalls. Long viewed as a symbol of the reigning religious climate, for five hundred years, the building had withstood riots and demolition at a pace unheard of in the quiet countryside Aioffe and Joshua usually hid in. At its centre, the tallest spire in England cast a long, lazy shadow over the graveyard.

As she crossed the cobbles, she suddenly felt uneasy. She glanced behind, but saw nothing except the booksellers readying their wares. Snatches of conversation drifted across the open space; French, Dutch and German mingled with the newer English press, who hawked wares made by the recently formed Royal Company of Stationers. Having been granted the lease on the Charnel House and chapel during King Edward's reign, booksellers flourished. Here, the tradition of selling books, plays and pamphlets, which offered insights on everything from battles to topical ballads, embedded itself as the paper heart of London.

An advocate of learning, Aioffe loved perusing the stalls, although experience taught the fae to avoid voicing an opinion on such human preoccupations. For between tuppence and sixpence, the price of a pound of beef or a visit to the theatre, anyone could read a folio of discourse about almost anything. If you couldn't read, then someone could regale you with its contents in one of the many inns nearby, or you could listen to the fervent debates in the churchyard. It was thus no surprise or coincidence that, despite changes of monarch, St Paul's remained at the heart of religious controversy.

As her eyes darted around, not watching where she trod, her shoes toe caught on a cobble and she stumbled. Her arms flailed, but, as she recovered, Aioffe flushed as several book-sellers stared at her. Noticed again.

She jutted her chin forward. A woman walking with such a determined gait, despite her fashionable middling class of dress, could be considered an anomaly for the time of day, but confidence was a mantle she had grown comfortable feigning since becoming a queen. Her fingers clutched her purse strings as she straightened her headpiece and continued.

To one side of the gardens, a row of long, several stories high buildings butted close to the entrance to the cathedral. Therein, she had heard, Cardinal Pole and Queen Mary's favourite, Bishop Bonner of London, presided over trials of heresy, hanging and burning hundreds of Protestants. To soften the acrimony, Elizabeth had banned use of the words heretic and papist, but if records of their deaths were to be kept anywhere, Aioffe considered it would be here.

Her pace quickened as she passed the huge carved doors to the cathedral. This early, with the June humidity already rising, the newsmongers, the Paul's Walkers, had yet to congregate inside, to share the latest gossip in the cathedral's nave. She hoped to be about her business before it grew too busy with Londoners seeking a cool respite beneath its lofty arches.

It took only a touch and a gentle smile at the old priest who guarded the records office for him to forget someone, especially a woman, was being permitted entry. Finding the right record took longer. Lost in the scrolls and ledgers, her fingertips blackened from tracing the Latin script, she hardly noticed the growing humidity until a thunderclap echoed through the stacks. The windowless room offered no breeze and it was impossible to tell, other than by the rumble of thunder, what nature of storm was brewing.

She looked up, suddenly aware of the presence of another in proximity. A low pant, which for some reason sent a tremor down her spine. Leaving the ledger she had been reading - a list of people present at the condemnation of heretics from a court session in 1557 - she pushed back the chair and stood. The urge to flee battled with her sense of propriety; causing a scene would impact her ability to continue her studies.

Her lips pinched together, head down, as she walked as fast as she could down the stacks. The candle by the doorway had been snuffed out, leaving only a tendril of smoke wafting in the breeze between door and frame. Her heart pounded, fingers reaching for the knob. Just as her fingertips closed around it, she heard a shuffle of footsteps behind her.

She wheeled about, but a covering rammed over her head before she could see more than a glimpse of jet black. Aioffe screeched, her hands grabbing at the fabric.

Then bony fingers gripped her neck, squeezing the air from her throat. She kicked out, gratified to hear a small "oof" as her foot made contact with flesh. Momentarily, the pressure lessened. Her fists rained down on the assailant.

Unseen, a blow thwacked her head. Darkness painfully swallowed her.

Loose fibres caught in her throat as she heaved a juddering breath in. Aioffe coughed, then tried to bring her hands to her face, but discovered they were bound. With her fingertips, she rubbed together the cloth and realised she had been wrapped in her own cloak! She blinked, attempting to take stock of her surroundings, but her sight was obscured by the rough fabric which scratched her cheeks. Worse, a tightness about her jaw told her she had also been gagged. All she could make out with her night vision was shadows, tones of grey and black. The darkness was only lighter in a small line, a crack, towards her feet.

She forced herself to still and listened. Wherever she was lay mostly silent, save a shuffling, slapping sound somewhere above her. She jumped as thunder rumbled. The deep, ominous noise sent her heart clamouring in her chest, yet the notes of its music sounded deadened, as if the earth itself had absorbed the noise.

Aioffe wriggled her legs - bound as well. Her toes curled, oddly liberated although still stockinged, and she wondered why someone would have removed her shoes? She shunted her feet around to gauge the extent of the space. The top of her head was chilly; her toes could touch something solid and cold when pointed.

Stone walls enclosed her entirely. A sarcophagus.

Thunder clapped again, closer this time.

Panicked, she reached out with her mind for Joshua. No words formed in her thought, just the distress of captivity which she knew he would understand. To be trapped in the dark, bound and immobile, was the worst of punishments. Worse, a lingering stench of decay which seeped in through a crack in the lid told her where she was.

She sighed as she felt his reassuring touch - a flood of warmth and longing. Her mind formed one word to Joshua, "Crypt."

CHAPTER 33

LIGHTNING STRIKES

At Aioffe's mental touch, Joshua's head reeled. How could she be trapped? He'd read the note upon waking and was already pacing through alleyways towards the cathedral to join her. He was close, but not close enough. Poking through the grey sky, he saw St Paul's spire. Joshua ran through the streets, forgetting about the gathering clouds as his mind kept the tenuous link to Aioffe. With every step, he tried to reassure her of his proximity, his drive to reach her, but he felt her panic nonetheless. His hose stuck to his thighs, undershirt drenched with the closeness and the air was hard to draw in. The rumble of thunder sounded terribly near.

As he pelted down Bower Rowe towards St Paul's courtyard, the sky flashed. From the dense grey which cast the city into gloom, blue-white lightning forked down! He skidded to a halt in horror. He spun around to see where it landed. The Church of St. Martins on Ludgate, which he had just run past, was struck!

Scores of people froze where they stood as falling rubble pounded to the ground.

His mouth hung slack, the metallic taste of the storm acrid on his tongue. Already, flames licked the singed roof timbers, but he could not stay to help. Not yet - Aioffe was still trapped close by. He turned towards Lollards Tower, and set off.

Another jagged fork seared down. If he hadn't been gazing straight ahead, he might have missed the sight. Tentacles of energy splayed, landing on the lead gulleys, high on the cathedral spire.

The lightning jumped from gutter to gully, crackling as it sought a route to earth. A clap of thunder sounded as the searing fork hit the ground, a terrifying, deafening sound.

Yet still, the destruction of St Martin's caught more attention from the Londoners on the streets.

Joshua glanced up, his gaze tracing the lightning path back up the building. As if slashed by God's wrath, a jagged black wound scorched the spire. On the edges of the slash, flames curled around the wooden slates. Around the courtyard, the close air suddenly chilled. The dry tinder caught, and with a whoosh, the fire gathered pace, spreading around the spire. His skin prickled.

Aioffe!

As his long legs raced across the cobbles toward the door, people streamed into the cathedral! Even if rain followed the humid storm, it would not be enough to douse the flames on either church. He pushed his way through them, shouting, "Fire! Fire on the spire!"

Little scared townsfolk more than fire. Everyone knew its danger. Whole cities could be wiped out in a matter of hours, yet often, only rudimentary preparations were kept to hand. The size and significance of the cathedral may provide false hope a disaster could be averted. Few believed such a sacred place could ever be struck down with the wrath of God. But, having worked with fire all his life as a blacksmith, he knew no amount of prayer would save the spire, or, perhaps the entire building!

"Get out!" He cared not that everyone was staring at him as he raced up the nave. "Get out of here!"

Some ignored his cry, despite him repeating it, and continued to loiter and chatter as if nothing was wrong. He shook his head and darted past the dazed expression on other's faces. The smoke would soon enough confirm his warning, and maybe then they would decide the storm was safer than the mighty pillars of their sanctuary.

The last time he had been in here, a freshly restored rood screen had separated the altar from the aisle, but now he saw the barrier had once again been removed. His eyes sought the figure of Christ, which still loomed above the altar suspended by thin ropes. Joshua's heart thumped as he stopped at the aisle's apex, underneath the spire. Unconsciously, he crossed himself.

A scent he recognised wafted down - melting lead. Above, as the spire burned fierce, its bells and the roof flashing were melting!

He reached out with his mind again, searching for some sense of direction from Aioffe... where in all that was holy *was* she?

His prayer must have been answered as letters spelling out "Crypt," formed in his mind. A sweat broke to his palms. Where was it? He turned this way and that, looking for an entrance, but all he saw was a freshly painted sign hung above a stone archway on the right of the choir stalls, saying 'St. Faith's Church.' A church within a cathedral? It struck him as odd, but then he remembered where he was. Where better to hold a forbidden mass than directly beneath the obvious?

He wrenched open the door and almost tumbled down the stone stairs. At the bottom, he emerged into a wide, low antechamber, in complete darkness. Several arches led into further chambers, each mouth looked more ominous than the next. Where was she? For some reason, he felt the metallic sourness in his mouth again, but this time, it reminded him of blood. He blinked, and wondered why he could not see clearly, as a fae should.

A sense of dread, as if he had been here before, churned in his belly. A chilling fear, verging on panic, swept through his body…. was it his or Aioffe's? The mental connection between them rippled; he wasn't sure where he began and she ended. Heart thumping, he paused, listening hard. He frowned, all ambient noise which he might have used to orientate himself with sounded muffled, as if the pounding of his own blood drowned it out.

A scratch, and he whirled around. A rat scuttled past, its long tail flicking his ankle.

Joshua crept towards where, from his impression before he fell down the stairs, he thought the largest arch was. With each footstep, he told himself he was drawing closer to his love, guided by her, but in truth, the darkness blinded his usual night-sight. His hands stretched out, face scrunched listening for any noise which might give away her location.

Another pace. And another.

Then, the smell of smouldering wood drifted towards him. It must be coming down the stairwell from the cathedral above! His fingers stretched, and with blind faith he reached for the wall, a column, a casket. Anything solid, so he could shuffle closer to her. The further in he went, the more he realised he was as blind and deaf as a human once more.

A thud!

He felt along the edge of whatever he was touching, heart thumping. A muffled voice! Urgency overcame his caution. With haste, he ran his hands over whatever was in front of him until he could identify the shape of a casket. "Aioffe!" He cried as he found a small crack in the stone.

He plunged his fingers through the narrow gap, scratching them until he could get a purchase on the stone crevice, then he pushed. The granite would not yield. He gritted his teeth, confused as to where his usual strength had gone, and shoved again.

She called to him once more, her voice muffled, laced with panic. The sound echoed around the chamber, and for a moment he wasn't sure he was even at the right sarcophagus! He dragged his hands out to push afresh on the slab. His biceps screamed in red hot pain and tears sprang to his eyes. He had to be able to move this! Or, was he wasting time on someone else's resting place? His mind whirled with confusion. Could he trust his own senses?

Since the crack wouldn't widen, he rammed his fingers in as far as he could, hoping for confirmation it was truly she. Something warm brushed against his fingertip, almost immediately retracting. He registered it was cloth. A stocking, perhaps?

He felt skin brush his fingertips. This time, she kept the connection. He closed his eyes with relief. He felt her tug, and all at once, his body flooded with her warmth. She was not taking, but giving!

Her Lifeforce invigorated him in a heartbeat. His skin tingled and her strength surged through him. He heaved the stone, now as light as paper and pushed the lid entirely from the casket. It clanked to the floor and shattered; the noise to him so loud the echo clattered around the chamber like thunder. He opened his eyes.

Aioffe lay trussed up in her cloak, like a joint of meat, in the stone box. Only her feet were exposed, stockings torn as if she had been dragged. Her head, he saw now, was covered in a black sack. Holding it in place was a stole, the scarf-like vestment worn by the ordained, gagging her. She wriggled as he loosened the gag and pulled off the hood.

"I knew you'd come!" Her skin seemed to sparkle, brightening the darkness and her eyes were aglow. "Hurry! The storm!"

"The spire is alight," he replied, grinning with relief, even as he imparted the bad news. "We may have to find another way out."

She sat up, her hair dishevelled and wild about her face. He bent into the casket and untied her hands. Once freed, she flung her arms around his neck and he lifted her out. Relief surged through him, but he resisted his desire to clasp her to him forever. He settled for breathing in her unique smell, and his heartbeat calmed.

"Who did this to you?" He asked, feeling about her waist through the folds of her cloak for the knife she always wore behind her on a belt. His hand came up empty. She frowned. It was missing.

"It happened too fast." She shook her head.

He whipped out his own blade and the rope which was wrapped around her legs quickly fell free. "Who did this?"

"I didn't see. A vampire, I think? Where is my knife?" She peered into the casket, pulling away from him, then plucked out the priest's stole which had secured the bag over her head.

Without warning, his blood rushed, pulsing in his ears and he staggered. His head span as he reached for contact with her again.

Her fingertips gripped his arm. "I think I have to tell you," she whispered.

"What do you mean?" He'd felt something like this in the bear pit, but the terror which gripped him now was different. He hadn't wanted to pressure her into telling him then, for his own secret and fear for her pressed upon him as well, and he had to protect her. "Tell me what this is now, for I cannot take much more! I... I'm as weak as a human!"

"Our past, your past... I think it's trying to break through to the present again."

Her hand grabbed his, and she yanked him with her as she took off across the crypt. Her touch alone jolted him back into their current quandary. They pelted up the staircase, then pulled open the door.

An old priest stood, a look of surprise on his face, in the doorway, as if he had been about to enter. He looked faintly familiar, but Joshua in his panic, couldn't place him. Behind, smoke billowed, peppered by red-hot embers falling to the flagstones. Joshua noticed in his hand the priest held a small bottle, filled with a dark liquid. He thought he caught the distinctive whiff of vampire, but with all the smoke and fumes, it was hard to be sure.

"You!" Aioffe exclaimed. She squeezed Joshua's hand tighter.

The priest's eyes narrowed as they darted between them both. When they alighted on the stole, still dangling from Aioffe's fingers, he froze. "You…"

Before he could finish his sentence, the vampire pirouetted, then rushed away, quickly enveloped by the billowing clouds.

Above, the spire's timbers groaned and cracked. Shrieks of "Save us!" and wails echoed through the nave. Their corporeal forms were mere shadows in the haze.

Joshua's breathing grew ragged as he inhaled the hot grey confusion. He clutched his wife's arm. Only Aioffe's touch kept his mind in the cathedral. He knew, were they to separate, he would be dragged into the hell of his nightmares.

Before he could ask for a moment to gather his wits, Aioffe pushed him out of the doorway, straight into the smoke!

CHAPTER 34

MEMORY

Joshua's fragile state of mind concerned Aioffe the most. Not her capture, not McTavish. Not the fires, nor even the storm which prompted the crowds to gather inside the cathedral. Certainly not the murderer. Above all else, she could not fail her love now when he needed her the most. Clutching his hand, she ploughed through the throng of people towards the exit. She could not tell him what she knew here, not when everything he saw could trigger his descent into a kind of madness again.

As they approached the great double doors, it seemed half the city gathered inside. "It's those lights in the sky," a sodden, red-faced lady proclaimed. "I said they'd bring trouble. I'd rather face the Lord's wrath indoors and know I'm safe under His roof."

"Foolish woman," the man beside her growled, catching sight of the grey plumes of smoke which filled the ceiling and billowed into the nave. "No safer inside. Do you not see?" He pointed to the blackened timbers. Aioffe dragged Joshua past them into the torrential rain outside, just as the fellow remarked, "John Knox was right. 'Tis the blight of having a Queen."

Their lamentation reminded her of her mother's terrible prediction. Her mother Lana had died thinking she had brought a blight to Naturae, but that Aioffe was the light who could scour their realm clean. Some light she was, Aioffe thought as she squinted through the torrential rain. The storm had darkened midday London so completely, the daytime was like midnight, bringing with it all the filth which had accumulated over the hot summer. She should have illuminated Joshua's past so he could face the present before it got to this stage. It was her fault he suffered so, and her guilt had weighed heavy on her heart for too long.

Joshua slipped on the wet steps, jolting her back to their present predicament. His hand gripped hers, as she once clasped his for balance when she was unused to walking. "I wish we could fly," she muttered as he held his leg up and rubbed it. The pain on his face suggested he was still more human than fae. She stuffed the priest's stole into her pocket. She wasn't sure why she still kept the horrible, tatty reminder of her abduction, but better to have a hand free in case they stumbled again. "Lean on me." She tugged him along.

His skin was ashen as he winced stepping on the foot which had twisted. "As usual, wife, your answer to everything is to flee from the problem," he snapped. As he pulled her to a halt, she saw the conflict in his face. He wanted to run as well, so why was he resisting her?

"No more," he said. "Talk to me before I lose my mind again."

The rain streamed down their faces as they gazed into each other's eyes. His words cut, but she could not deny the truth in them. "Before I made you fae, you were human."

"This much I know." He stared at her, hard. "Why do I keep feeling like I am one again? A troubled, fearful, weak one."

"You were a warrior, and still are." Her voice was deadened by rain pounding the cobbled square. "When you awoke, after being cocooned, you had no memory of your life before. I thought I was doing you a favour - sparing you."

"Sparing me from what? What could possibly have been so terrible I needed to forget it?"

She swallowed and glanced up at the spire, which blazed through the darkness like a beacon. "War."

Memories ran flicked through her mind as images - of being trapped in Harfleur under siege, of his immobilising fear, and of the men who fell. As her recollection of the attack flooded back, it infused her voice with sorrow. "The brutality of it. The friends you couldn't save. The blood spilt in the name of King Henry V." Her eyes rose to meet his. "Human war's destruction. Every night, from the day you rescued me after the siege at Harfleur, you were plagued by recollections of what you saw. You could get no rest, as a human."

She looked down at their sodden clothes, remembering the heavy downpour the night before Agincourt's battle. "My love, here, now, you get no rest either. I think the bloodshed we saw then haunts the present."

His head hung as the anger left him. "But I am no human now, I don't even feel like a man." He looked at her with pained eyes. "I've struggled ever since we went to the bear pit."

"Maybe the gory sight, perhaps the noise there, triggered the problem. And just now, even though there was no violence, only fires and chaos like war, your... weakening happened again."

Although guilt dragged on her heart, she had to get him away from the fire so his fae-ness could return. She glanced down Bower Rowe to see a crowd of people half heartedly throwing buckets of rainwater on the flames which consumed St Martin's church. There was no way out in that direction. They splashed towards the records offices instead, to loop around the cathedral and then their lodgings. From the corner of her eye, she caught a sight of a still flaming wooden roof tile falling from near the tip of the spire. Tossed in the driving wind, she watched as it drifted over to the houses and rooms opposite. "Oh no! The records!"

"What of them?"

"I was searching for someone who might have been there at all the queens deaths. I thought, perhaps we were looking for a Catholic, when really we should have been looking for a heretic, in the eyes of Mary at least. So, before I was captured, I was going through the notes about the Protestants she tried, in case one of them went missing from the death notices. We couldn't find anyone else who linked both Queen Mary I and Mary de Guise and would have reason to want them dead. And the attempt on Elizabeth was when she tried to bring something of the Catholic Mass into her coronation."

"Which could mean they are Protestant. I see your logic. But," he shook his head, "it doesn't explain how that person could be present at the deaths?"

"I know," she said. "The manner of killing is so intimate, and we have eliminated all the close friends and courtiers. Who else would be there at someone's deathbed?"

"Well, Jeffries was."

"As a high level priest, even though he hasn't been one in years."

They gaped at each other.

"A priest!"

"You don't think it could be Maister Jeffries, do you?" Joshua said, his eyes narrowing.

"No!" she gasped. "Why would he tell us about Mary de Guise and Lady Dudley if he had killed them? And, he has nothing but respect for Elizabeth."

"Hmm."

"Funny, how someone is innately trusted just by what they wear, though," she said, as they reached the churchyard with St Paul's Cross in the middle. They paused as the rain pelted down and the flames on the spire shot up.

A group of clergymen were having a heated debate about the spreading disaster. All around, people were valiantly tossing leather buckets of sodden river sand and water at the thatched roofs of the houses, in no way getting close to quelling the fire. The entire area was in chaos: booksellers hurriedly trying to pack away their flammable, ever wettening wares with faces tight with hopelessness; onlookers with uncertain expressions deliberating over whether to escape the rain inside the stone, sacred building, or go home and leave the mess for someone else to sort out.

They skirted the edges of the churchyard, both eyeing the clergy with suspicion now. One of the priests was arguing for blowing up the surrounding buildings to create a fire break, while another had fallen to his knees in prayer. She couldn't spot McTavish among them, but perhaps that meant he was still inside? She let out a small sigh of relief as they moved past the curates virtually unnoticed, but checked over her shoulder as they walked, worried he had followed them out.

"There's nothing we can do here," he said.

She knew he was right, yet still, she lingered. Her natural inclination was to help, but, amazingly at the moment, no-one seemed in need of healing assistance or calming ability.

They both turned towards the cathedral, just as a loud creak came from above.

"Run!" Joshua said as one of the long, flaming rafters tilted, then tipped. Like a giant, glowing spear shaft, an entire side of the spire fell - its fiery tip aimed straight at them!

CHAPTER 35

ESCAPE

Missing them by only a few feet, the rafter crashed across the church-yard. Sparks shot into the air as the blackened timber broke across gravestones. Screams of terror echoed around as Joshua limped and Aioffe pelted towards the bell tower on the far side. In the crush, he gripped her hand as they pushed and shoved their way through the low gate and onto Paternoster Rowe.

As fast as was feasible, given the weather and hordes of people dithering on the street watching the fires, they dashed to their lodgings. Joshua felt himself grow stronger and sturdier with every footstep away from the chaos behind them. They hastened up to their room on the top floor at the back. Only then, in their temporary sanctuary, could he pull her into his arms and whisper, "I nearly lost you."

"Luckily, I'm fairly hard to kill," Aioffe mumbled into his shoulder. She pulled away. "I knew you would come for me though, in the crypt. You saved me before me in such a place. A church in Harfleur. I fought a vampire, who had taken a child I was fond of. We were fond of." She swallowed back a sob at her own recollection, which she had learned to live with, but was new to him. "I had to draw from your strength then, as a human, but your Lifeforce gave me power when I was weakened. After what happened in Europe with Illania, I now know there's always a cost when Lifeforce is taken not given."

His eyebrows drew together. "And what became of the child?"

She smiled. "Happily, he survived. You saved us both when I drew from your Lifeforce, as I gave you mine just now. Benediet, the boy we saved, was taken in by a couple on the campaign with us, who couldn't have children. They were returning home after Harfleur surrendered. Instead of having to live as an orphan, alone and scratching around for food in the devastated ruins of his home, he went to Wales with them, and I presume, lived a long and happy life. We both missed him greatly."

He was silent for a moment, then took a pace across the room to stare out of their tiny window. "I don't remember it, or him, at all, but now you tell me, it seems familiar somehow." He turned to her, brows drawn together in consternation. "Why didn't we take him? We could have been a family."

"You and I then were too young, too troubled and too different. Your indenture to King Henry V had still to be fulfilled. It was too dangerous to bring a child with us as Henry pressed on with his campaign. We did what was best for him."

He sighed and his shoulders sagged. "We're getting nowhere and our family needs us. We should leave London."

"Agreed. Now." She pulled off her sopping and heavy wool cape and started to undress.

He went to the chest and pulled out their travel bags. "What else haven't you told me about?"

She paused mid lace pull and thought. "The priest we saw in St Pauls?"

Joshua frowned. "You know him. I saw it. Do I?"

"He was there when we first met." She snorted. "Father McTavish. Without his interference, we would probably have gone our separate ways. I was the oddity. A winged girl who knew nothing, and revolting to you."

"But you said we met in my village... You had hurt yourself and I took care of you. We fell in love."

"I said that because it seemed easier than explaining that he was the one who suggested you take me to the authorities at he Church. Then, a century later, I met him again, in York. He was there in the church when Reverend Gippes told us of Mary's death. He was the one who bled Mark. I think he's a reformed character now. Something, or someone, gave him back his sight."

"Why didn't you tell me about him before?"

Her mouth dried. After over a century together, telling him might separate them again. "To protect you. From yourself. From suffering the pain of your past." She brought his hand to her lips and kissed his knuckles in the hope her touch might calm his rising ire. "Please understand, I never meant to cause you harm, even when we knew the truth of one another. Tarl Smythson, as you were known as then, was in trouble. Wanted. You were a thief, even though I think you only stole the Church's silver to pay for your mother's burial."

He stiffened.

"The priest, Father McTavish, caught you red-handed in the church you were robbing. Caught me too, for I was injured and seeking shelter. To atone for your sin, he told you to take me to the authorities. Our world, the very notion of vampires and fae, was entirely hidden from you before. You struggled to understand that everything you thought you knew was not what it seemed. I don't think you fully understood McTavish meant the vampire authorities, and that I would almost certainly have been used as a pawn by them. You didn't know who I was or how valuable a hostage I was. I didn't tell you, or anyone, because both our lives would have been in even more danger. By the time I realised what you were instructed to do and who you intended to hand me over to, I had fallen in love with you. Even when you loved me back, you were still fearful of what I was, and then, when I tried to heal you, you turned into a fae. All I wanted was to take away the fear from your life."

"Sometimes I wish it were still hidden to me now," Joshua said, somewhat ruefully. "Life was probably a lot simpler as a human. A home, a family, a profession."

"We have that now. Or we could have."

He sighed and reached over to help her finish pulling the stiff laces from her corset. "What do you know of my family?"

After laying the wet garment on the bed, she dropped her skirt to the floor then pulled off her damp undershirt. She sighed as her wings stretched out. "You loved them very much. I think your father was a blacksmith, and died when you were younger, but he taught you how to smith. Your mother had died recently as well. You told me, you stole to pay for a Mass to be said for her soul. To help guide her to heaven, even though she was accused of being a witch, and had committed suicide."

"*Was* she a witch?"

She bundled up her skirt and packed it at the bottom of her bag. "I don't know. But, there is something magical in your blood, in your Lifeforce, I'm starting to think. When you were mortally wounded at Agincourt, I only thought to save your life. Save our love, not make you into something else. I always thought it was my love and belief in you which made you the way you are, but perhaps your magic is the reason why you turned into a fae."

He pulled his jacket and shirt off to free his own wings. "Instead of getting well, I grew these."

She nodded. "And you have other powers too, ones which I don't have. How when you touch me when I'm Blessing, you can see what I see. And, the bow and arrow which you can pull forth in battle?"

He nodded. "And the armour." He glanced down at his bare chest and almost smiled. "Maybe I am a warrior after all."

"The ability to manifest didn't come from my line or Lifeforce, so what else but witch magic?"

He frowned, unconvinced. "I thought that was something to do with your magic, from when you made me."

They both reached into the chest to find dry clothes. Wearing the clean linen shirt with the specially widened neckline at the back to allow for his wings, Joshua shook out his old black jerkin with similar adaptation at the shoulders. The letter he had carried with him from York dropped out of the small pocket.

Trying to be tidy, Aioffe bent and picked it up.

He froze. "Don't."

"What is it?"

"A letter. A threat intended, I think, for you." His breath juddered and he wrapped his fingers tightly over hers. "In York."

"You knew I was a target?"

He caught his lip between his teeth. "I didn't want to worry you, or Hope, or anyone. I thought I could protect you."

She pulled away and unfolded the note. "'*One queen downed by unclean hand, but whych queen is next. The devil is an angel fallen, so sayeth a learned text.*'"

He hung his head. "I don't know of anyone else but a fae who could be compared to an angel. Or another queen."

"Except Illania."

His shoulders bunched. "And a learned text could be either the Malleus Mallificarum Henry gave me, because of the 'witch,' or the Bible. Either was what made me think a Catholic was behind the killings."

"You kept this from me?" She waved the paper. "Even though I'm not a queen any longer, all this time, you didn't think to warn me?"

"I tried to protect you. To keep you from worrying needlessly."

She stomped her foot. "We are husband and wife. There should be no secrets."

"Except when it suits you to keep my past from me?"

Her mouth clamped shut and they glared at each other for a moment. "Who sent it?"

"I don't know. It's not a hand I recognise."

She whirled away and started to ram the belongings into the bag. "We should go to York then and find out. Clearly, someone there knew who I was and where we lived."

"Perhaps we already know that," he said quietly, taking the note from her hand and putting it back in his pocket. "Didn't you just say Father McTavish was there?"

Aioffe turned on her heel and stared at him. Her face paled, then she upended the travel bag onto the bed. Her hands worked furiously through the thick fabric to find the secret pocket where she had stashed the stretch of material.

As she pulled it out, Joshua frowned. He caught the end of it and ran the thin stretch of fabric through his hands. She had thought it black, but realised the darkness came from the material being wet, and it was actually a dark green.

Her eyes widened as he wound the stole around his hands to display the end. "I've seen this before. I saw it in York!" She pointed to the embroidered motif on the tips. "It's McTavish's. It was in his workshop when I took Mark there to be bled."

"And yet this is the same item which I untied from you in the crypt." He growled, "Where is he?"

She raced to the window as if she could see as far as St Paul's Cathedral from miles away. Her wings flapped but he grabbed her arm. "Wait!"

"We have to know!"

"Know what?"

She exploded on him as if he were to blame. "Where McTavish is!"

"He threatened you, then attacked you, nearly killed you, and you want to dive straight back into his clutches?" Joshua yelled back.

She pulled her arm away. "This is our only chance to catch him!"

"Whether he stayed in the Cathedral or not, it doesn't matter now we know it is him. We have to get you to safety."

Everything in him wanted to flee with her, but, he was filled with fear that his weakness would prevent him from protecting her.

She made to climb out of the window again. He grasped her waist. "No!" They stumbled together, away from the opening. "It is too dangerous. Please," he gazed down into her wide eyes, "do not pursue this. There must be another way."

"He's got to be stopped! Maybe he's responsible for the other deaths!"

"I do not care about the others, only you." He forced himself to calm, in the hope that logic would overrule her impetuosity. "We cannot just fly back across London in broad daylight, half dressed, to hunt a vampire without any weapons and," he drew in a breath, "in the middle of a catastrophic fire. Besides, he took one look at us coming out of the crypt and disappeared. He could be halfway out of London by now."

"He could still be there. I didn't see him outside the Cathedral."

He softened his voice. "That is precisely the point. He knows what he did and he escaped. We are ill-prepared for a chase. We have nothing to capture him with. And, he can run anywhere faster than we can."

"He doesn't know we know what he's done."

"All we know right now is that he attacked you. That's enough for me to want him dead, but, we have no proof he was involved in anything else."

Her eyes narrowed. "But we have the proof he captured me, and..." Her eyes shifted from side to side as she organised her thoughts. "He was newly arrived in York when we met there first so he could have been anywhere before then. His workshop at the leper hospital had lots of equipment and potions. He could have brewed poison there easily, and he had Mark's blood."

Joshua's fingers tightened on her arm. "Poison for Elizabeth and Mary, and Jeffries said Mary de Guise was killed by daemon blood."

"So he could have supplied it, or used it."

"It's feasible, yes. Normal poison wouldn't work on Mary de Guise if she was a vampire. But how could he even get close to them?"

"We thought earlier that a priest might be welcomed at a deathbed. Especially a Catholic one. Queen Mary probably surrounded herself with them, and Mary de Guise."

"And Elizabeth?"

"The coronation was a mixture of both religions, as we have discovered in our research here."

Joshua thought for a moment. "I can't see the connection between them all yet. Or why he didn't strike at you earlier, if he intended to kill a queen."

Her lips pursed. "Does the why matter, when we know who? He'll escape. He could leave London and we'll never get another chance." Her eyes blazed with defiance.

Joshua bit his lip as he studied his wife's face. He couldn't help but feel a flush of pride in her resilience. "All I want is to keep you and Hope safe. Please, let's just get out of here now." He slid his fingers down her arm and gently pressed her hand. "He could trace us to here, and, unprepared, I'm in no fit state for a confrontation."

She sagged against the wall, defeated. "I robbed you of your strength when we need it the most."

He buttoned up his jerkin, then slung his bag over his chest. "Although I have no doubt about your formidable fighting skills, for once, your usual instinct to run is right." He picked up her clothes and started to help her into them.

She huffed, but her fingers began to tighten her clothing around her. "Being safe is knowing the man who attacked me has been stopped. He must be caught, before he attacks me or someone else again, or we'll always be looking over our shoulder."

He stuffed all her remaining clothing back into her travel bag and handed it to her. With a reassuring grin on his face, he said, "We will. We have to out think him to capture him."

"Out think him?"

A smile played on Joshua's lips. "We have some advantages."

She frowned.

"Nemis's visions? And a spy network. If we can work out who is next, perhaps we can get ahead of him."

"And set a trap?"

"Exactly."

"And in the meantime, we prepare. Nemis said the next death was by a slashing blade, and your knife was taken by him. We can only assume that's what he meant to do to you."

She shivered. "My grandmother was stabbed. Not even that killed her though - her betrayers had to cut off her head to finish the job."

He pulled her closer and fixed her cape around her shoulders. "That's not going to happen, not while I'm around. I'll sheath you in the finest silver-steel under-armour. Now we know you are a target, you'll not be alone. Not ever again, until he is caught. Wherever we go, I will be with you."

"We need to speak to Nemis, and we must warn Hope. If I die, then she will become queen."

He swallowed and said with conviction which he did not truly feel, "You won't die. You cannot."

She stepped back to the window and stuck her chin up. "To Hanley House, then?"

He nodded. "We dart straight up, through the storm and fly above it."

CHAPTER 36

VINEXPLICITY

Naturae

"Double our guards outside Illania and Caesaria's chambers through day and night, reporting to me every four hours," Henry ordered the Captain in the lowest of voices, as soon as the council session came to a close. He hoped the bustle of parchment and scraping of chairs would obscure his whisper from reaching where Caesaria sat.

"My liege," the old fae said. He bowed as his wary eyes flicked to their unwelcome guest before he bustled away.

Henry straightened his shoulders and approached his intended. His purpose was clear - remind her of her obligations under the guise of spending time getting to know each other. "I thought perhaps we might visit the Pupaetory together?"

Caesaria's black glare met his. "If we must."

Henry offered his arm in the traditional courtly gesture, expecting her to take it, but she took to the air and flew off ahead of him. He glowered at the snub, then wandered through the High Hall, noticing how his fae shrank from her and now, by extension, him. For all that he tried to soften the impact of the European presence, there was an 'Us and Them' culture settling in which he could not see how to bridge. Nor was he certain he wanted to. Even if he married Caesaria, he certainly didn't want Naturae to become another tribe's permanent home after all.

Worse, with so many wild fae about, it was too dangerous to invite Fairfax for a reconciliatory visit, and he could not leave Naturae's shores. His strategy of playing for time began to look more and more like indecision instead, and that invited rebellion.

Earlier in the day, during a private meeting with Thane, ostensibly to discuss renewed trading arrangements, the unofficial leader of the workers had been blunt in his appraisal. "They fear her wrath," he had said. "Her treatment of the spies didn't help. We all heard their screams. It's rumoured her mother is worse though." His face tightened. "We lived under a tyrants' rule for centuries, and there is little desire to repeat the experience. We have learned. Our only strength is in our number and claim on this land, and patience runs thin."

Henry had tried to brush Thane's warning off with reassurances that no such torture or lack of being heard would happen while he was here. Keeping an eye on their leaders suited his purposes, but he could see as the weeks went by with both fae tribes co-habiting on one small island, it could not last for long. A sense he was missing something - a reasonable way forward where he could both keep an eye on Illania and Caesaria, solve his people's problems and feed them all - festered. His mind circled around the question of why the Europeans were here, in his realm at all, without finding an answer.

Queen Illania, since his return, had been the model of consideration and co-operation. She ordered her workers to assist with the rebuilding work, which had started again. More and more of the conical treetop homes were erected - although there were still questions about who would live in them when no new pupae grew, and the Europeans made no move to leave. Henry was keen to demonstrate his command could lead to greater prosperity, so he made sure to express his royal gratitude for their labours in frequent visits. The foreigners' camp on the far side of the island was reportedly kept tidier. He also ordered all workers and solder fae follow a diet of fish alone, implementing and enforcing a system of everyone fishing for themselves in the hope of curtailing trips to the mainland. On the face of it, Illania concurred with his orders, echoing his desire for her people to blend into the Naturae environment, as he presumed they would anywhere else on the continent, even though it looked and sounded to him like they were settling.

Once the Princess had left the hall, Henry darted down the stairs, across the clearing and up to the Pupaetory landing platform. He arrived just as Caesaria swooped down. Sleeking his hair down, he grinned to himself just a little. It was good occasionally to remind everyone he was a vampire. She smoothed her floaty dark green gown as she ambled over the planks towards him. Her pale skin shone, moon-like, amidst her long black hair. Henry had to admit, the effect of her arrival in the treetops was dramatic and beautiful. The smile he welcomed her with grew more genuine as she held out her slim hand for a kissed greeting.

He obliged, but, any thought she might be softening vanished with her snide tone. "It's entirely too primitive, dangerous even, to house all the vines in one building."

"Why's that?"

His enquiry met with disdainful scorn.

"If one vine suffers a blight, it will spread."

He bit his tongue, reminding himself he could not be expected to know everything. Perhaps she didn't know much about vampires either. "Oh? And what would you propose?"

She sniffed. "Our vines are given individual containers. Then, they can be located to sunnier climes or kept separated should one vine become afflicted."

That explained the barrels with tall yet bushy growths he'd noticed being shuffled around the island by her workers. The Naturae guards had discretely followed Queen Illania to various locations in the forest but been banished from observing what she did there by her own soldiers. Where the young fae, the pupae, were kept was a mystery to him, as he hadn't spotted any among the hoard, as if the entire tribe grew straight from vine to adulthood.

A glisten of gold approaching caught his eye. Caesaria turned to Henry with a peculiar glint in her eye. "Mother is, of course, the expert."

Henry considered bowing as the tub landed on the platform, but Caesaria stiffened by his side. He decided against obsequiousness; he was the king, and it was high time they were reminded of his status.

Illania rolled out of the chariot with more gracefulness than he expected someone of her stature could, then drifted towards them. "What a delightful day to tour your vines, Henry."

She attempted to walk in front of the procession, but Henry strode ahead. "Indeed, and how kind of you to join us," he said, as the guards held open the doors. The Pupaetory opened out into a wide atrium, several stories high with a glass ceiling. Plinths of varying heights, green with scented creepers, ran along the hall, reminding him of Roman temples and abandoned monasteries. Sounds of laughter echoed through from the rooms on the balconies lining the sides, but there was no-one learning how to fly today. The current pupae had all but grown, and would soon join their vine siblings as productive worker fae.

The schooling and residential area of the Pupaetory were not of concern, although the absence of activity pressed the issue upon him.

At the far end, a small doorway with the key still in the lock seemed innocuous, but within, there ought to be the beating heart of the next generation.

He gritted his teeth and unlocked the door.

Inside, the summer sun dappled the leafy stalks and the air was humid. Heady scents mingled in Henry's nose, almost overpowering. The vines grew tall, thick with leaves and with fat stems. The ground had been well composted, the windows clean so the sunlight could stream through. Although he had not been in many greenhouses, the lush growth here surely was a good sign of vitality. Given the right kind of royal 'blessings', the vines would soon be laden with pupae. What these actually looked like, he didn't know, but surely, they would grow safe and strong here?

As pride surged through him, he spun on his heels, arms outstretched as if he were bestowing the greatest gift. "Come in, come in." But Illania and Caesaria paused just inside the doorway, staring at him. Horror stretched across their faces.

"What's wrong?"

"Your vines!" Illania squeaked. "What a disaster!"

Henry glanced around. The plants soared into the roof, palm-like leaves reaching for the sunlight.

"Oh my, this will never do," Illania tutted.

"An abomination," Caesaria concurred. As she reached out her arm as if to touch a leaf, her mother slapped it away.

"What's wrong with my vines?" Henry charged over to them.

Illania's chubby paw wafted towards them. "Can't you see?"

Henry frowned.

"These are not at all healthy," Caesaria said. "While you were away, I was concerned about as much. Perhaps if I had felt more like a Queen... Still..." She shook her head. "I'm not to blame, of course."

His eyes narrowed, wondering what game they were playing. "Specifically, what is the problem?"

Illania bent towards him. "You should have done something, a gesture at least, to make my daughter feel at home here."

"My vines?"

"Oh, apart from the absence of any cocoons? Of pupae? Your vines are suffering, dear boy. It's a wonder any of them have survived."

"They look perfectly fine to me," Henry retorted. "And the lack of pupae is exactly what you are here to remedy."

"Only a true Queen can impart the necessary Blessings," Caesaria said. She peered down her nose. "And you have thus far failed to make me one."

"I think I've made myself perfectly clear," Henry said, drawing himself tall. How many times did he need to repeat his order? "Until there are new fae growing, I will not marry you."

Illania sighed. "Nothing will grow on these vines." Her shoulders rose a fraction. "They are too far ill. Left unattended for too long, I worried this might happen."

"Vinexplicitity," Caesaria said, knowingly. "Mother, I thought you would concur with my assessment."

Nodding her head vigorously, Illania said, "Quite, quite." She slapped her hands together as if dismissing the entire grove.

"How do you know?" He asked.

"The leaves, dear boy. See how they stretch to the sun?" Illania shook her head. "Too many of them, and look at their colour. Green!"

"Plants are supposed to be green!"

Caesaria tittered. "Not all over. These are fae vines!"

"Did you think them grapes, or ivy perhaps?" Illania joined her daughter, laughing as the pair shook with mirth.

Henry clenched his jaw and glared at the floor. How could he have been so stupid? Of course plants which grew people should look different. Quite how, he couldn't imagine, but it was clear he had done something very, very wrong. "What do we do about it? How do you make them... better?"

Illania abruptly stopped laughing. "Well, I suppose....."

"Mother..." Caesaria's hand flew out to stay Illania, but retracted it as quickly after a glare.

"I suppose I could assist."

Henry's heart sank into his stomach. There would doubtless be a price. "What would you do?" Illania's smile narrowed as it spread into her cheeks. "What only a queen can." She wriggled her finger at the nearest stalk and her face screwed up in concentration.

As he watched, the vine seemed to straighten. The leaves at the base rippled with yellow, briefly, then wilted. Illania drew in a deep breath of air, clenched her fingers into a fist then tried again.

The yellow within the leaf spread, bleeding straight through the edges! Then, it shrivelled, turning brown, drying into a husk before his eyes.

"You've killed it!" Henry said through gritted teeth.

Illania turned her face up to his, innocence beaming through her bright blue eyes. "It is too far gone, dear boy. There's nothing for it. I did not kill the vine. Vinexplicitity has already blighted the entire orchard. The grapes would be soured, so to speak."

Caesaria's face whitened. "Oh, Mother.... What shall we do? Even if I were queen and could bless, these vines are useless. They could never bear a cocoon." She took a step towards the door, then turned back. "Unless..."

Illania let out a long sigh. "It's the only chance they have." She nodded to Henry. "They shall have to be removed, quickly." Her gaze wandered around the chamber. "It's altogether too light in here for them to ever recover." She splayed her hands. "And of course, once restored, each vine will need to be kept isolated, in case the blight spreads."

She beckoned Caesaria closer. "My dear, this is a perfect opportunity for you as well. Henry needs to know how to support a queen in her role, and - Naturae can see the pair of you working together as one. Should solve the disharmony I keep hearing about. Now, let's see if my workers have some spare barrels..." She stepped daintily towards the door.

Henry fumed through his nostrils. The building looked like it had stood here for eons, and Aioffe had obviously managed to make it work for her. Did she really think him so foolish? "You will not dig up my entire Pupaetory. Prove to me this works on half of them."

Spreading the risk was prudent. Kingly. Responsible. Barrels were portable; it was bad enough he was stuck with a supposedly sickly orchard - if he let Illania take them all, Naturae could be left with nothing. His trust in the Europeans reached a new low, but what choice did he have?

Illania twirled back to him and extended her hand. The smile on her face wasn't reassuring yet she said, "Deal. I make no promises, but, for the sake of our newly formed family alliance, I will try to restore them, so Caesaria may arise to fulfil her destiny. As your queen."

Henry shook her hot hand but could not meet her eyes.

"Oh, and there's one more ingredient we'll need. A curative. A fertiliser, if you will."

"Which is?"

Caesaria said solemnly, "Royal blood. A sacrifice must be made."

And there it was, Henry thought. How they meant to bleed him dry. "Mine, I presume?"

Illania snorted back a laugh. Caesaria failed to restrain hers as she emitted a loud Ha!

"Oh no, that would be a catastrophe! Vampire blood for a fae vine, can you imagine? He'll suggest a so-called saint next!"

The scorn in her voice quelled his fear for only a moment. "Then whose?"

The queen shared a conspiratorial glance with Caesaria.

Let it not be a daemon's, Henry thought. A chill tightened his heart. Fairfax. Lizzie...

"Don't worry," Illania said in a diplomatic tone. "Since there's no living alternative, it'll need royalty. It only needs to be a minor. Should be a simple enough matter. There's plenty close by in Scotland. One royal, to save an entire garden."

Henry blinked. Who did she want to sacrifice?

"How very efficient, mother." Illania patted her daughter's hand as she led them out.

And then Henry thought he knew. With a last glance at the jungle, then the wilted vine, he waited until they left before locking the door behind him and pocketing the key. His jaw ached from biting his tongue.

He strode from the Pupaetory, already mentally composing his note. Aioffe and Joshua had to be warned.

Or... he paused at the threshold of his chamber. Was it simply 'efficient'?

CHAPTER 37

THE PLAN

Beesworth

Returning to Hanley House was a homecoming of sorts. Joshua and Aioffe arrived just as the sun streaked across the sky, where they found Nemis and Hope preparing oats for the break of fast in the kitchen. Their daughter had grown an inch since they'd been in London, but was still small enough to fling herself into her parents' arms as soon as they stepped through the door.

"I hardly recognise you," Aioffe said in a choked voice. She trailed her fingers down her daughter's face wistfully. Hope's birthmark seemed to throb and flush with her touch. "You're getting so big now!" She swept a curl behind her ear and hugged her again as if she never wanted to let her go.

"She's been learning all her letters," Nemis said proudly, turning away from the porridge pot. "And has developed green fingers too! Not quite like her mother, but the garden blooms nonetheless."

"And how does Mark fare?" Joshua asked. The boy was nowhere to be seen.

Nemis scratched her short hair. "He's distant with me." Her shoulders rose then dropped. "But at least he has Spenser and Mary, and Hope, of course."

"And you, dear friend, how does Beesworth treat you?" Aioffe released Hope to embrace her friend. Joshua sat and lifted Hope onto his lap.

Nemis took a moment to respond. "I'm getting there," she choked out. She burrowed her head into Aioffe's shoulder. "No, I'm not. I'm glad you're back." She pulled away, her eyes brimmed with tears. "It's.... difficult. Being in Beesworth. They stare at me. At us. The unhinged, the odd, and the unwanted." Her shoulders heaved and she didn't meet Aioffe's eye. "And, despite the medicine, I still have the visions. I thought they might stop when I was free'd, but..."

Aioffe stroked her shoulder. "What can we do to help?"

Nemis pressed her lips together, then smudged her tears away with her free hand. She seemed unable to voice anything else for fear she would unravel. After a few seconds, she nodded almost to herself. She gave a gentle squeeze before releasing Aioffe's fingers, then stepped across to the cupboard.

"I don't think there's anything to be done," Nemis said, all business, with her back to her friends. She pulled out platters and started laying the table. "We are safe here, at least. Mark is as settled as I think he gets. Lady Hanley is..." Her eyebrow rose as she looked at Joshua.

"Mary," he finished off with a wry smile.

"How about the predictions?" Aioffe asked. "Have you remembered any more details?"

"Not really."

Aioffe's lips pressed together then she said, "We have news..." She glanced at Joshua, who shook his head over Hope's.

Nemis ignored his unspoken suggestion to wait. "What do you know?"

Before Aioffe could detail their discovery, Joshua interrupted. "Why don't we get everyone fed and we can talk?" He eased his daughter up from his knees, but she clung to his chest.

"Papa, don't go again!"

Heartbreak flashed across Aioffe's face, hardening the resolve in her voice. "We are here now, sweetheart."

As if she sensed they would leave again soon, Hope launched herself from Joshua into her mother's embrace. Joshua's lips tightened. Much as though they had both desperately missed their daughter, no-where was really safe until they could catch McTavish.

A kestrel rapped on the window, just as Lady Hanley bustled in from the hall. "Good morning," she said, as if she expected to find Joshua and Aioffe in her kitchen. "Well, let it in then," she snapped at Nemis.

While Nemis opened the back door, Mary turned to her guests. "About time you returned. I've a barn full of broken spies. A household filled with creatures, in a town which crawls with hostility toward us." She threw her hands in the air and stomped over to the pot. The smell of burnt porridge wafted through the kitchen as she stirred. "I cannot live with this kind of disruption. It's intolerable."

"We interrupted the cooking. I'm so sorry," Aioffe said to Mary. "We should have let you know we were coming, but we didn't have time."

Mark appeared in the doorway. After a surly grunt of a greeting to Aioffe and Joshua, he sniffed and rolled his eyes. "Not again, Ma."

Mary sniffed. "You'll eat what's put in front of you and mind your manners, young man." She slopped a ladle-full onto a plate and shoved it across the table. Mark crossed his arms and glared around the room.

His black mood soured the air until Spenser emerged through the back door, clutching the hind legs of a brace of live rabbits. With ruddy cheeks and a bounce in his step, their friend appeared restored to his usual robust health. His skin still glowed from the hunt as he put an arm around his wife and pecked her on the cheek. Nemis melted against him as she stroked the kestrel's wings. He beamed at Joshua and Aioffe, exclaiming, "Good morrow, one and all! What an unexpected delight we are all together once again."

Aioffe and Joshua's faces lit up with matching grins as his presence warmed the frosty atmosphere.

He passed a brace to Lady Hanley and ruffled Hope's hair as he made his way around the table. "Have you all fed? I can always find a couple more if you are tired." His dancing brown eyes assessed Aioffe. "Long flight? You look pale." He frowned. "Where's your knife?"

Aioffe's arm fell to where it usually hung and her face drooped.

"We're fine," Joshua replied, shaking his hand. "And we have much to report." His gaze darted to the youngsters so Spenser would understand why they did not elaborate.

Aioffe slid Hope from her lap and bade her eat, then approached Nemis to retrieve the bird. While she unwound the note from its leg, Spenser fished out his purse and counted out some coins. "Children, would you be so kind as to fetch some beeswax candles from town for us? There should be enough there for a mutton pie each as well." He winked at Mark, who perked up and began to gobble his porridge.

Aioffe scanned the message and gasped. Hope's fingers reached up and touched the back of the note. "Henry Fitzroy," she said in a disappointed tone, although she could not see the writing inside. Her eyes widened at Aioffe. "Mama? Promise you'll be home when I return from town?"

Aioffe glanced at Joshua. "How did you know who it was from?"

Hope shrugged. "I touch, and I know where something comes from, and whose it is."

Aioffe rolled up the scrap of paper and passed it to her daughter. "What else does it tell you?"

Her daughter rubbed the tiny roll of parchment between her fingertips. "The ink is fae, but the paper, that's from somewhere in Scotland. It's not old, perhaps a few years or so. And only Henry's fingers have touched it.

I can tell from the smell." She wrinkled her nose as if the odour pervaded the entire room. "He's a vampire and they smell fusty, even if they aren't old." She held the little note towards the fireplace.

Joshua plucked the message before she could drop it in the flames. His expression contorted from shining pride in his daughter's strange new ability to bewilderment as he read the message for himself. He glanced at Lady Hanley. "How many guests are in the barn? And how capable are they of being put back to work?"

"Enough and, for their true queen, I think they ought be well motivated to try."

Aioffe said, "I shall go and see them right now." She bent to kiss Hope on the top of her head. "We shall fly together later, little one. Hurry back from Beesworth."

They gathered around the kitchen table as soon as the children left. "We know who the killer is," Aioffe said.

"He attacked Aioffe, and we think intended to kill her." Joshua added. "He got away from us, though."

"Who?" Spenser looked murderous.

"Father McTavish," Aioffe said, glancing at Mary. "The same priest I took Mark to be bled by in York. He had the means - he's clearly a healer of some kind - but until he attacked me, we didn't connect him to the killings. Then we realised a priest could have poisoned the Queens without being noticed."

They explained how they had come to this conclusion after all the dead ends they chased, then the circumstances of their escape and McTavish's disappearance.

"What we cannot work out is, knowing the who, the why. What does McTavish stand to gain by killing queens?" Aioffe turned to Lady Hanley. "I've asked the spies to disperse across the land, to find out what they can about McTavish and his whereabouts. If he realises I've left London, it would be easy for McTavish to trace our family to this house. All he has to do is return to York to discover our association with Nemis, and that Beesworth is where Lady Hanley usually lives, and therefore we might reside. I can show my face in the town easily enough."

Joshua said, "We thought to set a trap. It's the only way to capture a vampire."

"With you as bait?" Spenser said. "Announce yourself as being here so he comes, with the children here as well?" He flopped back in his chair. "You forget you are still wanted for murder yourselves."

Aioffe and Joshua shared a look of concern. Their friend had orchestrated a show of confidence, dressing and acting as the gallant, energetic Ambassador he once was to conceal his worry over his family. He had also pointed out the several flaws in their idea.

Joshua pulled out the kestrel's note. "That was originally our plan, although it meant sending the children somewhere else for safety."

Aioffe sighed. "It seemed reasonable a few hours ago, but the closer we drew, the more unfeasible we realised it was. Proclaiming who I am and where I am also breaks the Treaty. We realised then, we should remain hidden. We came to seek your advice, however temporary our staying may be." She glanced at the glum faces around the table. "We still need to trap him, but where?"

Joshua cleared his voice. "This may influence our decision." He unrolled the parchment, frowned then read. "Henry says, in his usual unhelpful and enigmatic way: *Scotland. Royal blood needed to cure vin...vin...*" He stumbled over the word then enunciated, "*vinexplicitity*." His eyebrow rose as he met Aioffe's eyes.

"I have no idea what vinexplicitity is," she said, frowning. "Could he mean a royal in Scotland is needed for something?"

Spenser frowned and blinked. "Vinexplicitity? Can that be right?"

"Oh! Mary Queen of Scots?" Mary jumped in. "One of the spies told us she has returned to reclaim her throne. The Catholics are cock-a-hoop and think she should replace Queen Elizabeth in England, of course, but I don't see that will pass. Still, she resists the reforms her bastard half brother, the Earl of Moray, imposed, and it's rumoured she herself keeps to the old ways. That old goat Knox would have her stabbed for failing to convert."

Nemis paled. "Knives. The next one is knives."

Lady Hanley drew herself up and snapped, "I only meant stabbed as a figure of speech."

"To stab is an intimate manner of killing," Spenser mused. "One would have to be very close to the intended victim. I cannot imagine Knox would be allowed anywhere close to her court, but a priest..."

Joshua said, "Careful, let's not run away with ourselves. You have assumed royal blood means a queen, which it doesn't necessarily have to be. Countless people claim royal lineage. There is nothing to suggest the queen killer, McTavish, is linked to what Henry says. Rather, the note implies the opposite. I'm sure Henry would have mentioned if he thought it was related, given he knows the threat of murder."

Aioffe wet her lips as she thought. "Then why is Henry telling us this? He didn't even write who the message was for on the note - the kestrel could have found any one of us."

She looked around the table at their bemused faces. After a moment, Spenser offered, "Issam's told me before, Henry distrusts the kestrel system, so perhaps that's why he's oblique. Also, before I left, Henry told me to find you, Aioffe, and say the music plays off-key. I'm assuming it means more to you than it does to me."

"It is certain that he does not want to relinquish Naturae back to me," Aioffe replied. "But I cannot return to dance about my throne with Henry now. And before I was attacked, I would have agreed it was wisest not to be queen, but now I'm clearly a target anyway, for McTavish at least." She tightened her lips. "How are matters on Naturae?"

"Henry still plans to marry Caesaria, but only if she can show she can Bless the vines, which she still hadn't done, at least, not while I was there," Spenser said. His sombre tone did nothing to ease their fears. "He walks a delicate line with Illania and her people as guests. He intended to keep Illania and Caesaria there so he could be sure they weren't responsible for killing his half sister if - when - another queen falls." Spenser stared around the table. "If McTavish is the one killing queens, there's no reason for Illania to be watched by Henry, is there?"

"I'm not sure we should even tell him; he wasn't concerned before unless it's to do with his sister," Joshua said. "And he should still be afeared of them both and want them gone from Naturae." He sighed.

Spenser said, "You are under no obligation to tell him anything." He turned to Nemis. "I know you are affected by the visions and from what you have described, and what's happened so far, I can't help but think the queen's deaths somehow feel personal. You have to be close to poison, or stab. Not with you, Aioffe, but to play the long game with Queen Mary and Mary De Guise? A vampire has time on their side, unlike mortals. Perhaps McTavish attacked you for another reason?"

Aioffe tapped her finger to her chin but said nothing.

"I did wrong him," Joshua elaborated. "McTavish is the same priest who was there when we met. When I was a human, in Wrye, over a century ago."

Huffing, Aioffe retorted, "He ordered you to take me to the Church authorities, then tried to feed upon you before he attacked me again. You left him tied up, not staked, as was my suggestion at the time. Regardless, it still doesn't explain why he didn't try to kill me in York, nor why he killed Queen Mary, or de Guise? I could understand why he'd want revenge for what we did - even though he feigned to ask forgiveness - but what could those other queens have done to him?"

He shook his head. "My past is still strange to me, obscured by cobwebs."

Spenser started. "Wrye, did you say?" His eyebrows drew together. "Illania was encouraging Henry to expand his lands into Scotland itself. I thought nothing of it, a throwaway comment she made, but now I wonder." He rubbed his temples. "The other Orkney islands were rich with magic at one time. Hmm, and now, vinexplicitity..."

"The why of history may be connected to the why of the killings, and vampires can have long memories," Nemis said.

Aioffe snorted. "Funny, McTavish alluded to as much when we met in York. I should have staked him right there."

"It wasn't your fault," Joshua said broodily. "How could you have known what the future would bring because of the past?" His bitter tone hinted at the disaccord between them.

Nemis reached over to touch both Aioffe and Joshua's hands. "If I have learned anything from my foresight, it's that destiny can be re-written. Together."

"Is there a tonic you can make Joshua to clarify his memories?" Aioffe asked, then said carefully, "He hasn't been himself while in London."

"That's Maister Jeffries' area of expertise," Lady Hanley said.

Joshua grumbled, "But Lord knows where he is now."

"I will send a kestrel to find him," Mary responded primly. She glanced to the window, where the sun blazed high in the sky. "The children return soon, and we still do not know what our next steps should be."

Joshua turned to his wife. "We wanted to set a trap for McTavish, but I think it not safe to delay here, my love. There are too many innocents..."

"Nowhere is safe," she responded, shaking her head. "But you are right, we cannot endanger anyone else." She glanced at Mary. "Too many people dear to us who cannot fly up and away from danger on the ground."

Mary concurred. "It is best you all relocate somewhere else. I have enough to contend with. Go, and know I will keep the spy network operational here with Uffer. We shall communicate by kestrel and coded faelore messages only." She stood. "And it is better you decide where to spring your trap without anyone else's knowledge. That way, if McTavish does arrive, no-one here will be able to advise him of your whereabouts."

Aioffe grasped her hand as she swept past. "Mary, you are wise and the truest of subjects. Your support shall not be in vain."

Her lips pinched together. "My Queen, I only ask that when you are restored to your rightful throne, a home be made for me once again in Naturae. Until then, I will perform my duty for my people, and stay here." She glared at Joshua. "I presume you'll need more money?"

Without waiting for an answer, she left the kitchen.

Joshua met Aioffe's eyes. "What if Mary is right, and Henry is directing us to Mary Queen of Scots?"

Her eyebrow rose. "Go to Scotland then? To find answers."

"And protect a queen," he replied. "And perhaps there we will lay our trap."

She stretched across the table and took his hand. "Together."

Nemis said quietly, "Spenser, we ought to go as well. We have tried to rebuild our lives in Beesworth, but none of us can say we are happy. Or safe. More queens will fall, I'm certain of it. Until McTavish is stopped, I have to live with this constant fear. I would rather feel like I'm doing something, anything, than simply biding my time suffering their deaths over and over."

Her husband was silent for a moment, then said, "Edinburgh is a fine city." His gaze met Nemis's. "Many witches live there. Perhaps other se'ers can be found, who could help us. Help you." Spenser's hands curled into fists to hide their shake. "And being closer to Naturae would be wise. I cannot say what my other Mistress has planned."

"Like birds, we shall return north then," Aioffe said with a slight tremor in her voice. "To trap a killer."

CHAPTER 38

CASTLE

Naturae, 1564

"It'll be magnificent," Henry said to Thane as the Advisor approached. His fingers trailed along the smooth stone wall, as tall as he was.

Thane nodded. Somewhat stiffly, he said. "When it is finished, my Liege."

Henry's lips tensed. It had taken months to persuade the Council of wisdom in building this castle, followed by time-consuming negotiations with villages all up the coast of Scotland. Henry had run himself ragged, organising the trades and persuading humans to part with their supplies. To get the materials necessary to create his design onto the hidden island, and equip the fortification with the most modern of weapons was no less of a logistical feat. The workers had re-trained in stonework rather than carpentry, and the soldiers trained even harder. Naturae was a hive of craft, alive with the ringing of hammers and what Henry thought was happy chatter.

True, they were behind on his schedule, but that could hardly be helped when over half the workforce had disappeared one night a month ago. Illania and the majority of her people vanished without warning, taking their barrels, and leaving behind those transplanted vines which originated in Naturae. Caesaria and a few guards had remained, claiming her mother had left to find the cure for vinexplicitity and citing fears of the disease spreading as the reason why they took their barrels with them. "Mother and our people will return, in due time. But of course, I stayed, for I do not run from a challenge," she had simpered when Henry confronted her about her mother's abrupt departure. "Besides, why would I leave now, when you build me a castle to celebrate our forthcoming union. It will be ready soon, won't it?"

Illania had yet to reappear on Naturae's shores with the promised sacrifice, and he couldn't quite work out if that was a blessing or not.

Thane said, "I regret to inform you, the last of the worker emissaries you appointed who were sent out to search for other fae tribes have returned."

"And?"

"They have not managed to locate any other fae, after years of hunting."

Henry's lips pursed and he breathed out slowly. "So, no other available Princesses, no Queens who might support us and, no bridges built."

"I did warn you my Liege, ordinary worker fae are not cut out for such long distances. We have to stop so often to rest. The spies or the Ambassadors are who we should have used. Alas..."

"They are lost to us as well." Henry turned to his advisor. "What else? Speak plain, for we are not in company."

Shrugging, Thane paced forward and then spoke carefully. "While you managed to convince the Council this construction would bring us together... Unite us and defend us, was the phrase you used, I still don't see it as enough progress. It's not a solution to all our problems." He gestured across the cleared landscape, to a cluster of vine barrels under the shade of the treeline.

He drew in a breath and said, "Yet none of you can offer me any alternatives, not even when I have asked." He sighed. "Thane, I promised, when I started my reign, that I would do everything in my power to protect my people. Building this castle is more than a statement or gesture to appease Caesaria. More than just a defensive building. The creation of it and its purpose protects our future."

It made Naturae his domain, like his forefathers had stamped themselves on their lands.

Thane's hands closed into a fist. "And if making Caesaria feel like a Queen doesn't work, what then?"

Henry bristled. "I will not marry her, bed her or place a crown on her head until her mother or she solves the vinexplicitity issue. I'm increasingly convinced they did something to the vines themselves, but on the Council's advice, I cannot banish them entirely from our shores in case it triggers a war. Unfortunately, these Europeans are both problem and solution, so I am left with no alternative: I must give it a chance to play out." He seethed inside as he glanced at Thane, noticing his agitated wings. He could not afford to have the leader of the workers use his influence to stir up trouble.

"Besides," he leaned in confidentially, "admit it. Although we need Caesaria, she has not endeared herself to our people, has she?" A marriage made too hastily might upset the reverence with which his people viewed him. Henry was determined not to make the same mistake his father had by marrying the unpopular Anne Boleyn. Still, he lacked options at this point.

"She is cruel, and will not learn our ways, that is true." Thane looked sideways at Henry. "We all understand your dilemma."

They rounded the corner and headed towards the already built gatehouse. Thane paused and said in a quiet voice, "I had wondered whether there was some truth to the rumour our beloved Pupaetory was somehow the source of the malaise." He shook his head. "After pupaeting fae for centuries, I could not see what had changed. I confess, there was a time I thought it was because of you - because you cannot Bless or because you are a vampire. If it were only the lack of Blessings, Queen Illania could have solved the issue and at least proved the vines were capable still of bearing pupae. We could have waited."

With a grimace, Henry said, "The problem with the plants is not me, how can it be? Anyway, she demonstrated how she imparted Blessings to me, before the vine wilted before my eyes." He clenched his jaw. "Ours is now a battle of wills - the Europeans must fix the problem they caused."

"While Naturae suffers."

Henry's head swivelled to glare at Thane. "You are hardly suffering. Naturae has never been so prosperous. Besides, time is different for those of us who live long lives. A few years is nothing to wait. You lasted centuries with a defunct Queen before Aioffe came back. The issue will be solved. Illania has promised a cure, and we must be patient." He turned back to admire his magnificent tower. Strong, decisive leadership was always admirable, Henry reminded himself, and what could be a better demonstration of his authority than a castle? "And in the meantime, we build."

He ignored Thane's glower.

"Yes, my Liege."

CHAPTER 39

DISGUISE

Four years had passed since Aioffe and Joshua left London, and although they were still viewed by many as peculiar - 'not Scottish' - their family established themselves into Edinburgh with modest success. They remained vigilant to the threat of discovery and the killer every day, but a life had to be made while they kept watch. Aioffe influenced herself into ideal work as a seamstress to Queen Mary of Scotland, and got Joshua a job as a blacksmith at the Castle. Hope grew and grew, taking an interest in learning healing from Nemis, who plied her services to humans as a cunning woman and midwife. The witch's cures were held in high regard and, due to almost continuous debilitating visions, she worked all hours when she was well. Mark was taken on as an apprentice and seemed the most settled he had ever been, surrounded by his family.

Spenser, although relishing the stability of family life in the capital, recovered sufficiently to resume some of his Ambassadorial duties and darted around the realm re-building his connections with human society. He occasionally flew over to Naturae, stayed as briefly as was polite, then hurried home with tight lips. As yet, he had brought back nothing of

McTavish's whereabouts or news from Naturae, other than Henry was building himself a castle. Aioffe didn't want to know - surviving in human society, supporting a family and looking for ways to capture a murderer before he could strike again took up all her energies. The time slipped by, marked only by the rituals of church and state, which their lives revolved around on a daily basis.

Everyone's nerves were especially on edge today. After bidding farewell to Hope and Nemis, Aioffe and Joshua left their top floor lodgings as sunrise broke over Edinburgh. Together, they wound their way down the fourteen staircases, across the tiny, stinking courtyard and left the tenement.

The narrow wynd towards the High Street was thick with sludge, baked onto the earth and already filled with a noisy hustle of people. City living did not suit the fae, but limited housing options meant little choice. Everyone wanted to stay within the defensive walls, and those who did not were viewed with suspicion. Life was only bearable at night, when they could emerge from their windows and fly to the hills.

Aioffe gazed down Canongate towards Holyroodhouse Palace. The dawn light bathed the dormant volcano, known as Arthur's Seat, an inviting dusky orange, but to her, the colour signalled a warning. The elegant windows of the palace, still being renovated, were dark and shuttered. She sighed, brow furrowed with reluctance to attend her duties.

Joshua noticed her hesitation. "It's just a day. A wedding day, but still a day." He brushed his lips across her cheek. "And Queen Mary will host dancing and revelatory afterwards. Spenser has charmed himself an invitation to the festivities, so you will not be alone. We must remain vigilant, but it might not happen after all."

"I know," she replied. "Years of waiting, and still no sign of McTavish. Do you think we got it wrong?"

He shook his head, then rubbed the back of his neck. "Everything we know about his methods would suggest he'll choose a moment such as this, inherently dramatic and loaded with significance. He did with Elizabeth's coronation, and Mary de Guise's rebirth as a vampire. When there's potential to slip her poison with so many people around, I don't see how he can resist."

Aioffe sighed. "To serve and protect a Queen then I go, bearing nothing but my wits and wood." She touched his arm. "Take care yourself, at the Castle."

"It's heaving with Earls, Lords and clan leaders, and all their men at the moment," Joshua said, as he glanced up the royal mile, towards the grey towers overlooking Edinburgh. As if it had grown from the craggy cliffs the castle perched upon, the mighty fortress watched over the city.

This short walk was the only time she was away from his side and not safely in a heavily guarded palace. He'd prefer it if she simply stayed at home, safe, but that idea had been quashed as soon as they arrived. "If I can find a reason to join you at the Palace, I will. A cast shoe, or to accompany the guards in case of my being needed to fix something else. I'll try, but if you see anything, or anyone suspicious, just reach out." He lowered his head to touch her forehead. "I'm but a heartbeat away, my love. Forewarned is forearmed." He swallowed the lump in his throat. "We have a plan; we just have to have the patience to stick to it."

His reassurance did little to quell their nerves. He patted his jacket pocket. "And we are as protected as we can be. Godspeed and good luck today."

In her pocket, Aioffe's fingers curled around the stake she always now carried with her. Underneath her corset, stitched with steel and silver plates, her heartbeat steadied. While at work as a seamstress in the palace, she did not eat nor take refreshment, focusing only on providing the finest stitching and the most diligent watch over Scotland's young monarch as was feasible. Queen Mary of Scotland had no idea an insignificant servant to her colourful court, another queen watched over her, convinced that either one of them was McTavish's next target.

After bidding Joshua a final goodbye, Aioffe hurried towards the Palace, gnawing on her bottom lip. If McTavish was going to strike another female ruler, he would do so when it would cause the most amount of chaos. They had to assume it was Mary, and trust Henry would be able to guard or at least warn his sister, Elizabeth, in England somehow. Given the political situation in Scotland, not to mention the religious unrest caused by a catholic queen in a new, Calvinistic, Kirk, parallels with Queen Mary of England and her subsequent death could not fail to be drawn.

But would McTavish take his time as he had before, she wondered? Or would he make it a quick kill with knives, as Nemis had foreseen?

She rounded the Kirk of Holyrood Abbey, quiet since it would not be used today, and across the quadrangle towards the north-west tower. Inside, she found her employer, Servais de Condé, or Condez as the French master of the wardrobe was known, as he fussed with the decorations to the extra seating set out in the queen's chamber.

"This velvet will need stitching to stay," he exclaimed, as he tugged on the crammosy velvet covering a pair of old stools. He threw his hands up in exasperation as the slippery fabric rumpled as soon as he sat down, then stuck to his breeches as he stood. Tutting to himself, he then caught sight of Aioffe. "You! Fit this correctly, or she'll have us thrown out."

Aioffe bobbed a curtsey. "Of course, sir." As he wandered off, she heard him mutter the biblical quote he so often resorted to in times of tension. "With man, this is impossible, but with God all things are possible."

A brief smile touched her lips; his words were particularly pertinent today, for it was a day when faiths of all expression would be sorely tested. Mary was marrying another Catholic, without dispensation from the Pope to wed Darnley, her first cousin. Neither was she waiting for permission from Queen Elizabeth. The nuptials were due to take place also without the support of many of her protestant-leaning Privy Council. Mary would need her God on side, Aioffe thought, as she scuttled away to find a matching red thread from the wardrobe storeroom.

As she passed whispering servants, the hushed murmurs of unwelcome news followed her down the long corridor. "They say, last night at Mercat Cross, she proclaimed he would be named and styled King!"

Her heart sank; Aioffe found Mary's intended, Lord Darnley, Henry Stuart, arrogant and oafish. A poor King he would make. Despite the fact that he bore more than a passing resemblance to Spenser, he had none of her friend's wisdom or wit. At barely twenty years old, long-legged Darnley carried himself with an unerring projection of entitlement, which grated upon most of the nobles at court. He was frequently inebriated, and several servants, both male and female, had been subjected to his sometimes violent advances. She wondered how many of Mary's loyal subjects would support this English born and educated 'King' Henry, when his father had been exiled for treason until very recently and his mother was still held in the Tower of London by order of the Privy Council of England. But, Mary was besotted with the blond boy, who was one of the few people taller than her six foot of height, and as striking and opinionated.

The dawn brightened quickly into a sunny morning, filled with trifling jobs like the sewing of ruffs and taking up hems. She was sent from bedchamber to state room, her eyes watchful and her senses tingled with the constant stream of people arriving to watch the wedding or pay their respects. The first time Aioffe had to pause was when the staff were ordered to a halt around six o'clock in the morning, that they might kneel as Mary descended from her chambers to enter the palace chapel.

Dressed in black mourning clothes, for her late husband the French Dauphin Francis, the Queen was escorted by Darnley's father, the Earl of Lennox and the Earl of Atholl. After she had swept past trailing incense and perfume, Aioffe crept around to the lesser used North Door and snuck inside the vestry, while the congregation awaited the groom's arrival. From there, a crack in the door was just large enough for her to see the proceedings.

Mary stood before the altar, a dark stately pillar of black with a wide mourning hood amongst the red and white of the décor Condez had chosen for the occasion. Regally she waited, head bowed and with the seated crowd silent, while Darnley was fetched by the pair of Earls. Aioffe's eyes narrowed as she examined each of the clergy in turn, just in case McTavish lurked in disguise. With the assortment of pomades, incense and creatures in attendance, it was hard for her to sniff out any lingering scent of a poison. Could it be in the chalice, as Queen Elizabeth's had been at her coronation? Or, was McTavish in wait, ready to stab her as she walked out? Aioffe began assessing the guests, pew by pew. The chapel was not large, perhaps a few hundred people had been squeezed in, and appraising them from behind was not ideal but she dared not move. Only wait, until they turned for Darnley's entrance.

Her breath drew in sharply when one of the hatted heads swivelled in her direction, as if it knew it watched. Henry Fitzroy's dark eyes met hers and her heart began to pound. She broke the contact and screwed her eyelids closed, pushing 'Fitzroy is here' to Joshua.

CHAPTER 40

A WEDDING

Henry Fitzroy felt Aioffe's gaze as a touch of the familiar. Caesaria's continued presence on Naturae had honed his ability to differentiate the scent and tingle of being watched by fae, vampire or daemon. He swallowed, glad in one sense Aioffe survived, but now he set eyes on her too-white face again, frustration and resentment flushed through his veins. He blinked and she melted into the dark room, leaving him to simmer and stare at a closed door.

Spenser, ignorant of Queen Illania's location and on one of his infrequent 'duty-led' trips to Naturae's shores, had informed Henry about this wedding. He had not mentioned Aioffe would also be here. Backed into a corner by the Council pressing for a solution, and without Fairfax to relieve his tension, Henry decided here, a royal victim would surely be amongst the numbers who would be in attendance. Perhaps it was the illusion of having a choice - any choice - which spurred him into action; perhaps it was desperation.

In his lap, Henry's hand balled until his fingernails dug into his palm. Illania had failed to provide royal blood for his vines. It had been a year since the Europeans vanished. Not even a recent exchange of letters with the Vampire Council could tell him where she'd had gone.

Worse, thanks to Caesaria's over-violent tactics, the absence of reports from the spy network about Illania's movements or anything else going on in the wider realm, Henry and his Council were left isolated.

Although the castle neared completion, Naturae's options for future generations withered month on month, until now, the brown stalks in both the barrels and the Pupaetory were bare. Desperate and frustrated with his refusal to commit to her fully, his bride-to-be killed the aging Captain in a fit of rage. Henry had taken extreme measures in response and locked her away in the newly constructed dungeon. This gave them all a measure of security so he could voyage here and solve the vinexplicity problem himself.

All he needed was someone vaguely related to human royalty who he could mesmerise and entice back to Naturae. He could not waste this time. He must not, for too much depended upon it.

Relaxing his fingers, he faced the altar once more. Too long staring behind him might give away Aioffe's secret vantage point. He wished her no ill, but he had a mission of his own as no-one else was going to solve Naturae's problem for him. Pride prevented him from asking her for help with his vines. Above all else, he would demonstrate how perfectly capable of ruling over fae he was.

Still, he could not prevent a frown from darkening his brow as he stared diligently forward at the veil covering Mary. Clearly, he realised now, he'd underestimated Aioffe's obsession with finding the killer of queens, for why else would she be here at Holyroodhouse? In truth, Henry had been happy in his ignorance of their hunt, having enough to deal with on Naturae. Any queens who died were not his concern, except Lizzie. As long as his sister was safe - that was all that mattered. He trusted her guards, and trusted her to be wise to the presence of unfamiliar creatures. It was also for her benefit he attended today, so he might write an account of the proceedings. This marriage strengthened Mary and Darnley's claim to Elizabeth's throne, after all, a fact both Queens and cousins would be acutely aware of.

Subtly, Henry scanned the crowd, searching for Ambassador Spenser. When Henry had sent his message to Aioffe, warning out of the kindness of his heart, that Scotland might provide the royal sacrifice for his vines, he'd been deliberately cryptic - such was his mistrust of the kestrel system. Henry thought the fae would have understood he meant for them to avoid the danger, and been sensible enough to stay south. Apparently, his warning had been ignored, for where Aioffe was, the rest of her rag-tag family were also sure to be around. Perhaps he'd been too cryptic, and they had come to Scotland believing he offered them a clue? The more he considered it, the more he realised his simple note could have been misinterpreted.

With clenched teeth, Henry attempted to concentrate instead on the ceremony before him. The Latin liturgy of the Catholic service was a stark contrast to the brief and heartfelt promises his father had made to Anne Boleyn all those years ago. Theirs was the last wedding he had attended, and his own ought to be next.

The bride stood, and Henry almost gasped. Mary was tall - taller still with the towering mourning hood she wore, and matching her lanky husband in height. Bright red hair, a shade darker than Elizabeth's, curled artfully to frame a pretty face. At twenty-three, she appeared an age more mature than her nineteen-year-old spouse. Henry noticed, disconcertingly, that Darnley, in profile, looked distinctly like a younger Ambassador Spenser! Then, as he turned his head towards the crowd with a cocky expression upon his face, the resemblance was gone.

As three rings were placed on Mary's finger, the middle one a glittering diamond, he glanced down at his own hands. No band signalling a bond with Caesaria yet, nor a sparkling bauble to remind him of a promise to his beloved Fairfax. His heart ached with loneliness, for he had not seen

Thomas in many a year, and would not until he could promise himself to him in good faith and a safe home. And he could not do that until his own advisers were appeased and his realm returned to prosperity.

He breathed out through his nostrils as the audience politely clapped, signalling the end of the formalities.

Having never met Mary, and secure in his disguise as an Earl from the Highlands paying his due respects, Henry had no qualms about meeting the monarch's happy gaze. She paid him no heed, which both offended and mollified him, for Henry disliked wearing disguises of any sort. What a shame he could not present himself as of equal status, a King in his own right, but, she smelled entirely human. Ignorant of creaturekind no doubt, and he would not risk exposure and thus break the Treaty.

Arm in arm with her new husband, Mary left the chapel, and Henry's mission to mingle could begin in just a few short hours when the celebrations really began. While they soaked in the adulation of the crowds of well-wishers outside, he filed out with the rest of the congregation, without even glancing at the vestry again.

While Henry was engrossed in stalking a deer for himself in the nearby estates later in the morning, he unexpectedly glimpsed Darnley once more. The newlywed, adorned in brightly coloured and regal attire, had forgone the nuptial Mass his wife planned, and instead, embarked on a hunting expedition with his entourage. Their hullabaloo was enough to frighten off any prey from the vicinity, which told Henry all he needed to know about Darnley's prowess. He sized him up from afar, wondering how much of a problem it would be if the young king, along with all his royal human blood, were to disappear before the marriage could be consummated.

With only a few lords accompanying the king, surrounded by open landscape far from civilisation, the happenstance was almost too good to be true. By necessity, his friends would have to die lest they tell the tale of Darnley's disappearance. To act upon his impulse was therefore not as simple as it first appeared, and he was not certain of success felling mounted knights, even with his extraordinary speed. If he had his throwing knives on him, perhaps they could be toppled from their horses a little easier, but Fairfax still had them.

He watched the king swig frequently from a hip flask, his voice growing loud and wild with liquor. His obscene gestures and overtures ceased to be so amusing to his fellows the more he drank. Henry felt a sliver of sympathy for Queen Mary, for he recognised the unsubtle flattery and body language. Darnley was too interested in men to make his promises of fidelity worth anything. Uncomfortably, Henry pushed to the back of his mind the parallel, given his own situation with Caesaria and Fairfax. If he could only get close enough, the removal of this upstart might bring his sister some peace as well.

His chance to attack disappeared, for while Henry contemplated the angles of his approach, a page galloped up and informed the King of the need to return. With a whoop and a whack of his whip, the king took off on his massive bay without having shot a single arrow.

Henry gave up on the idea of hunting and ambled back into Edinburgh. Plenty of others who could claim royal lineage would gather at the palace to feast. He'd find one there. The streets were still busy, an air of celebration toppling up the tankards as quickly as the alehouses could pour them. From the corner of his eye, he spotted Joshua's tall blond head. The fae walked down High Street on the opposite side to Henry with a glower on his face and purpose to his step. As Henry paused, wondering if he should make himself known, the gunners fired a salute from the castle. The simultaneous booms echoed across the town.

Joshua flinched, then cowered against a nearby building. He braced himself with hands over his ears, knees quivering until long after the noise faded. Something was clearly very wrong, Henry realised as he darted over. Joshua's face drained to a ghostly white and his lips moved, whispering to himself. A prayer, which seemed to provide as little comfort as Henry's hand as it fell on Joshua's shoulder. "Save us, Lord, for only in thine arms will we find true salvation."

Over and over, Joshua whispered his plea, as if he was entirely unaware of his surroundings, lost to the street around him. Lost in another time, perhaps, Henry thought, as he pieced together how long Aioffe and Joshua had lived. How many battles they might have witnessed. Decades ago, he had heard tales of soldiers suffering similarly - having survived battle, they relived it in their dreams and sometimes their waking hours.

"Joshua!" Henry said, shaking the fae's shoulder. "It's just a salute. Every state occasion is marked thus."

His fingers tightened their grip, putting pressure on a sensitive part of the muscle until it would cause physical pain. Finally, Joshua's face, pale and tremulous, turned to him. His eyes were clouded, unfocused.

"Look at me, Joshua." Henry's gaze bored into him, exerting his will to obey only his command. "Tell me where you are?"

"H-Harfleur," Joshua stumbled out.

Henry frowned.

"Edinburgh man. You are in Edinburgh."

The fae stared at him and the hazy fog in his pupils dissipated as Henry forced awareness in. Strange, Joshua didn't appear alarmed by Henry's presence; he was that far inside his own torture. Or perhaps Aioffe had somehow told him. Henry said, "I warned you. Why are you in Edinburgh?"

Joshua's head dropped, breaking the gaze. "Aioffe. McTavish." Then his head shot back up again. "We have to trap Father McTavish!"

"Who is this man? Why do you want to capture him?"

Joshua looked stricken. "Aioffe, I must get to Aioffe!"

Henry's fingers gripped Joshua's shoulder hard again. "Why?"

"She needs me. I can feel her panic. He could be here, killing again."

Henry straightened in the blink of an eye. The fae was clearly shaken and in no state to tackle anyone, let alone someone intent upon killing. "Then we go together."

Joshua allowed Henry to pull him away from the building and down the street. His voice sounded less strangled as he added, "Spenser should be there by now."

Henry set a brisk pace which would not seem out of place to humans. "Damned right he should be."

CHAPTER 41

SPENSER

Henry strode past the gatehouse guard, glaring at him. "This man and I will be permitted entry," he said and carried on. The soldier's jaw gunned for a moment as he stood aside. Although he could hardly see through the haze of pain which had grown during their rush to Holyroodhouse Palace, Joshua understood then how Henry's vampire persuasiveness surpassed Aioffe's for speed and efficiency.

His gratitude was short-lived. Passing the four-storey tower with its conical roofs, built by Mary's father, James V, and where she had her apartments, Joshua and Henry entered the palace. Once inside the courtier-filled hallway, Aioffe's presence in his head intensified. The scent of her filled his nostrils, as if she were close. He reached to comfort her, not realising one of his hands had instinctively stretched behind his shoulder, seeking the bow which should be there. He had to protect her!

Henry's fingers gripped his elbow, yanking it down. "Have a care!"

Joshua caught Henry's darting eyes, widening as the silvery bow appeared slung over his shoulder.

"What the..." Henry hissed. "Get rid of it!"

Joshua's breath exploded out of him in a short, hard pant. "I cannot!"

Henry dragged him into a doorway. "Get a grip," he said, staring deep into Joshua's soul. "You cannot walk around a banquet armed for battle." The vampire moved in front of him, shielding him from prying eyes.

Joshua glanced down, horror sweeping across his face as he saw his own panic had brought forth the shining suit of magical armour and glowing bow. The last time this peculiar power had surfaced, Aioffe and Joshua had been battling their way out of a dangerous encounter with Illania and her daughters. As soon as they had escaped, with Spenser and Hope, the armour had faded back inside him. He had never quite figured out how to bring it forth again.

Now was not the most appropriate time for its re-emergence, Joshua realised. The palace was swarming with nobility, dressed in their finest in expectation of a lavish matrimonial banquet. Many of the men wore ceremonial swords - an accessory his outfit lacked - and no-one brought a bow and arrow to a feast.

"If you cannot make this," Henry's hand swept down Joshua's body, "disappear, we'll have to find a room to take it off in. A knight in fine shining armour is an invitation to dual for the Queen's hand, and we have better things to do with our time here."

Aioffe's panic inside his mind waned as Joshua held the vampire's steady gaze. "It doesn't come off, only... in."

"Breathe," Henry ordered.

He panted and focused only on the dark eyes boring into him until the pain subsided to a dull ache. When his breaths came easier, he patted his chest with trembling fingers. The armour had gone, replaced by the dark leather tunic he had dressed in this morning.

Henry smiled, wolfish as he showed a hint of fang. "For a moment there, I thought I was going to have to strip you." His head swivelled to see up the corridor. Hats and decorations blocked their view. "Without wishing to cause your.... over-protectiveness to emerge again, do you have any idea where your wife might be now?" He turned back to Joshua. "Because I last saw her in the chapel."

Joshua's fists clenched. "She is only a seamstress. She should be where Mary is. Why would she be there?"

"I can only presume she was there to keep watch on who attended the ceremony, hidden in the vestry," Henry replied. "Do you think she saw someone? This Father McTavish?"

"We had a plan, to capture or kill him," Joshua admitted, then shook his head. "All I could sense was her panic. McTavish is a vampire." He thought it prudent not to mention the stakes they carried at all times - the only sure way to be rid of such a creature - lest Henry took offence.

"Then we try the vestry first."

They sidled back into the crowded hallway, then entered a lobby where refreshments were being served. High windows opened onto the inner courtyard, the fountain at its centre drawing as much admiration as the circulated wine. Hastily, they pushed their way through the revellers, down corridors until they reached the chapel.

Inside, it was dim and quiet. Joshua scanned the aisle, his senses on alert. Then, he heard the muffled sob. He wheeled around on his heel, eyes darting behind and landing on a small door.

Henry's hand stayed him. A finger rose to his mouth and with his gaze, he gestured to the altar.

A priest emerged from a doorway at the rear of the couch. His head bowed and he shuffled down the aisle as if in a daze, a cloth dangling from his fingers. Before Joshua could move, Henry had bolted towards the priest and wrapped his hands around the man's neck.

"Is this he?" Henry growled.

Joshua's eyes narrowed. The priest's legs kicked out as Henry pulled him higher, up onto his chest. With a young, pale face and a full head of gingery hair, Joshua knew it could not be their target. "No."

Released with a huff of impatience, the priest dropped to the floor and scrambled behind the altar, whimpering.

Joshua strode towards the closed vestry door and put his ear to it.

"My love?" Aioffe croaked.

He tried the handle. Locked. He turned to find Henry already by his side. "Stand back." He heard a shuffle, as if something was being dragged.

One well-placed kick and the lock was punched through the timber frame. He hustled inside to find his wife, on the floor, staring up at him.

Cradled in her arms was Spenser's body.

Tears streamed down her face. "I can't save him," she wept.

"What happened?" Joshua knelt, one hand grasping hers, the other tracing his fingers down his friend's face. The grey skin had been pulled taught as if his insides had been drained. Clothes hung on a skeletal frame. Joshua's heart pounded against his chest as he glanced over her. "Are you...?"

She nodded. "I'm fine. I tried to give him some Lifeforce back, but... I think he's too far gone." Her shoulders shook as she pressed her fingertips into his neck and screwed her eyes shut. Her eyebrows gathered and she bit her lip as if straining. Then her hand drooped and she wailed, "And I don't know what else to do now."

"Is he...?" Henry asked.

"He's not dead," Joshua said, studying Spenser's immobile face and seeing the faintest of movement underneath his skin. He heard an occasional faint heartbeat and sighed with no small amount of relief. Spenser did look far worse than he had when they had rescued him from Bavaria, but at least his body was still, sort of, intact. "If whomever did this meant to kill, he'd be dust. My love, tell us what you do know."

Aioffe drew in a heaving breath. "I waited until everyone had left the chapel. There were a few stragglers, just twittering amongst themselves, so I closed the door and hid behind the cassocks in case someone would use the room to change in. I stayed until everything fell quiet. I didn't want to be caught when I slipped out. Then, just as I went to leave, Spenser was shoved in through the door! Someone locked it and," she gestured around, "there's no other way out."

The room, which was more of a closet, had only the smallest of windows, neither of which anyone could have squeezed through, and both of which were internal.

"This is either the work of a very skilled vampire, which would be peculiar without a fight," Henry surmised. "A case of mistaken identity, perhaps, or something else entirely. Who or what could shrivel him so?"

"Another fae," Aioffe replied. "Illania."

She sounded so sure, but Joshua could not see the logic in it. "Perhaps it was poison? But, any fae can do this. Remember what was left of Alice after Lyrus attacked her?"

"She was a human child," Aioffe said. "Spenser is fae, and knows better than to drink anything he does not know the providence of. He would have fought an attacker, but there's nothing to suggest he did. His clothes are not torn, his hair barely ruffled and his wings are intact. This was done by someone he knew, I'm certain of it."

"But why suppose it was Illania, then? He was her Ambassador, and she seemed so attached to him," Henry asked in clipped, guarded tones.

Aioffe shrugged. "She toyed with him before, for his loyalty to me."

"Maybe it was a lesson?" Joshua said. "Or a warning." He glared at Henry. "You should have told us if Illania was here."

"I did not know myself," Henry retorted. "She left Naturae a while ago. No-one knows I'm even here, except Spenser could have guessed, so it's not a warning for me. Besides, there's too many people around here and no hiding Illania and hundreds of her fae."

Aioffe glowered her acceptance of his point while Joshua gathered Spenser in his arms, as he had all those years before. He weighed even less now. "What can be done for him?"

"What do we tell Nemis?" Aioffe asked.

Henry stood. "There are too many people to simply walk out of here with him looking like this. We can't even pretend he's had too much to drink. Stay here." He strode out of the door and reappeared a minute later. "Aside from the main entrance, there's a side door which leads to the Queen's chambers."

Aioffe shook her head. "I'm known there, and Mary will be changing for the feast, if she's not already consummating her marriage." She shuddered. "Darnley - I cannot look at him without seeing Spenser in his prime, but he is as human as they come."

"The priest also told me there is a vault, at the back of the chapel, where the altar goods are kept. Spenser should be safe in there until this spectacle is over."

"We still don't know about McTavish," Joshua said as they followed Henry into the chapel.

"Indeed," Henry replied. "It seems prudent for Aioffe to stay with Spenser."

Aioffe agreed. "Lock me in, please."

Joshua's heart wrenched as he carefully laid Spenser down on the tiles. "We will search for McTavish, and Illania, or any other fae," he promised his wife. "And come back for you under cover of darkness."

As he stood, she clasped his hand. "We must get word to Nemis."

"To say what, though?"

"To prepare."

"How can one prepare to be a widow?" Henry said.

Aioffe cried, "Stop talking as if he's dead. He's not."

"He might as well be." Henry stretched tall, seemingly filling the low chamber with his presence. His eyes glittered jet black. "We need answers first."

"Vengeance even," Joshua said, his jaw set. He felt the weight of his armour reappear, but, when he glanced at his arm, he saw its faint shimmer underneath his tunic. With clear eyes, he turned to Aioffe as he stood in the doorway. "This ends tonight."

CHAPTER 42

TREACHERY

9th March 1566, Holyroodhouse Palace, Edinburgh

A hell-like existence followed for the household, except Henry Fitzroy, who disappeared like a snake slithers into the bushes as soon as Nemis laid eyes upon her skeletal husband. For nine months, each night when Aioffe returned home, the sight of her dear friend Spenser lying on the bed, silent and shadowed, was a constant reminder of the price he had paid for their failure to find answers. Life was hard for them all, Aioffe told herself, but at least she could choose to leave. Spenser's was a different sort of purgatory: unresponsive to Aioffe's blessings or Nemis's ministrations, with no prospect of recovery without a miracle or a higher form of magic than any of them possessed. No-one could fathom why he had been attacked, although Aioffe was convinced Illania was behind it.

No sign of McTavish, Illania, or any other fae, had been found that fateful wedding night, although Joshua and Henry searched the palace until their soles bled from running. After the royal couple had been sent to their matrimonial bed, they fetched blankets from the palace stores and bundled Spenser up. Their escape from the vault could not warm the chill of fear which had shrouded them all.

Still in service to Queen Mary, Aioffe and Joshua maintained their vigilance, watching over her for as many hours in the day as it was possible. Ever alert to visitors to the palace, or wherever she went on her many progresses and battles. It was a task made harder by shifting politics at court and their lowly status as servants. But guilt and fear kept them focused. If it hadn't been for Spenser's attack, they might have concluded they had picked the wrong queen to protect, but the daily reminder of his silence kept their resolve from weakening. McTavish had been patient before, so they must be now, Joshua often said.

Much had changed in Scotland since the wedding. Mary's husband was deeply unpopular with her people, and with the court, most especially with the commander of her army, Lord Bothwell. He was a powerful witch, according to Nemis, and his lands on the border ensured Scotland was safe from invasion by the English. Darnley was so frequently away hunting with his falcons, the Queen made a stamp of his signature so that she could continue to pass legislation. An Italian musician turned Queen's personal secretary called Rizzio kept it in his desk.

The King's boyish charm had quickly waned with the Queen, as his violent and boorish tendencies became evident to all. Hardly anyone afforded him the respect he felt due as king; he was called simply Lord Darnley, or the Queen's husband. His sway was thus limited over court matters; something Aioffe had overheard him complaining about to Mary frequently and bitterly.

But Aioffe and Joshua knew he was not the greatest threat to her crown. Each day, Aioffe watched over the now pregnant Queen as diligently as was feasible, expectant of another encounter. As a woman, a servant, Aioffe was not party to much except court gossip, and certainly not anything political.

Nemis, in her new capacity as one of the Queen's midwives, had more intimate access, but it was not seemly for her to be present all the time either. As the royal pregnancy progressed, Aioffe's concern for Mary's vulnerability grew, along with her perhaps irrational certainty that Mc-

Tavish would strike when the Queen was weakest - as he had with Mary of England. Birth was a dangerous enough time for any human, and this queen was driven more by emotion than logic. Her favourites, those she would allow near her, depended entirely upon whim and fancy. Rumours already abounded that the father of her child was, in fact, Rizzio, who she dined with most evenings. Some said the love triangle between the Queen, her husband and their lover, was at breaking point.

"This ends tonight," the King, Lord Darnley, shouted, weaving as he staggered up the privy stairs. Aioffe kept her head low, hoping he would pass without noticing her. His hands were known to roam freely over the servants. When drunk, he became the devil incarnate. Aioffe pressed into a cold stone wall, Mary's torn nightgown in hand and her head down.

"Tonight for vengeance!" He rambled on, his words echoing up the narrow stairwell which linked the Kings and Queen's apartments in the tower.

His assertion reminded her of Joshua's bold claim in the chapel; a claim which had not come true. How she wished the terror had ended that wedding night, Aioffe thought ruefully.

Above her, Darnley's drunken vitriol echoed down the privy staircase into his presence chamber. Her fingers tightened on the silky night shift and she hoped there wouldn't be another fight, but it seemed likely. She rushed down the main spiral stairs in the turret and pushed open the forestair yett, in front of the drawbridge between tower and palace.

Aioffe started; several of the Confederate Lords, passionate protestants who she knew to be at odds with Mary's position on religion, advanced across the bridge. Including the Earl of Morton and Lord Lindsay, she guessed almost eighteen courtiers strode the planks with purpose. Noticing the grim looks upon their faces, Aioffe's heart sank as low as her customary curtsey. The Queen's cosy supper with Secretary Rizzio, her half-brother Lord Stewart, the Countess of Argyll, her half-sister, and a few others, looked like it was about to be further interrupted.

"Go!" The Earl of Morton shouted at her. "Get out of here, by orders of the King!" His hand curled around the pommel of his sheathed whinyard, as if he were about to draw it on her!

Soldiers, some she did not recognise, marched behind them onto the drawbridge. They brandished their swords at her, and she caught the whiff of vampire among their number.

The narrow bridge crowded with people, pushing and shoving to get to the tower door. "What's happening?" She cried, determined to stand up to them, even though their numbers would overwhelm her if she tried much.

"Begone, wench!" Lord Ruthven said, shoving her down onto the bridge as he pushed past her. She sprawled on the slippery boards, mentally sending her alarm to Joshua. Glancing back through the boots, she glimpsed the Lords striding up the stairs. Then, the soldiers formed a line, guarding the entrance to the tower and thus the Queen's chambers. The only one way up or down was now blocked, for those on foot.

Her heart thumped. Shifty glances between the soldiers suggested this was a greater threat than a palace intruder or some upsetting administrative business. Something in their stance told her the guards were not here to protect the Queen's life or spare the bickering couple's blushes.

Aioffe scrambled to her feet, darted down the bridge and into the palace. She reached the stock cupboard at the far end, seeking to shed her clothes and liberate her wings, when shouts erupted from the tower. She wavered, fingers clutching the door frame, as the horrible thought occurred to her: every man entering the turret had been armed with a blade. Had McTavish been one of those in the crowd of courtiers? She'd been pushed down by Ruthven, and unable to study each man's face. Had she smelled vampire? She wasn't certain; being outside in the wind at the time of the encounter, it was certainly possible, and suddenly seemed likely.

Ought she to go back to the drawbridge and fly up to the windows to see what was going on, or, wait and see who left? The tower slits had red painted bars on, so she would only be able to observe, not enter.

Her hand fell to her pocket; the stake tip jabbed her thigh.

Wait and watch, she decided, feeling the reassuring touch of Joshua close by. She could not be everywhere, so best to observe from below and spring him as he exited. McTavish, if he had slipped past her unnoticed within the crowd of people traipsing into the apartments, needed to be stopped, for surely there was no preventing someone's death now. Was there?

CHAPTER 43

DOUBLE-EDGED DAGGER

Joshua flung himself from the horse as soon as it had clattered into the stable yard. As he ran around the small moat at the foot of the tower, seeking a way into the palace, he glanced up. His keen eyes focused on the drawbridge between the Queen's apartments and main building. Flaming torches lined the gangway, illuminating the shine of armoured guards. Why would there be soldiers, he wondered? Through the bars on the tower windows, angry accusations drifted out on the breeze.

Aioffe's alarm touched his mind, his fist clenched in response. He screwed his eyes closed, seeking her whereabouts within the walls of the palace, then flew open as he realised she was tucked behind the door, at the other end of the drawbridge! Her confusion about whether McTavish was close perplexed him, but, he could hear Darnley's vitriol pouring from above.

Tonight, something unusual was happening.

Reassured Aioffe was safe and keeping watch over the forestair, he returned to the stables to remove his jerkin and free his wings. As it was his habit to wear black, his spring into the night sky went unnoticed. He flew high, then darted down to hover a distance from the second-floor window.

The bedchamber was shuttered from inside, so he shifted along the wall and peered into the chamber the Queen used as a dining room. Chairs knocked to their sides, plates of half-eaten food upended on the floor, and Mary, pinned against the crimson and green wall hangings by her husband. Her hands circled her belly, fat with child, as she wrestled against his clasp on her shoulders. They argued, her pleading with him, but to no avail. Then, his head whipped around, and for a moment, Joshua thought he had been spotted.

Darnley's gaze landed on the closet door, and he paled.

Joshua dipped then rose again close to the next, smaller window, around the corner of the tower. A single candle provided scant light to the privy closet. Inside, a crowd of men huddled together in the near darkness, their backs to him. Far too many bodies crammed into such a small chamber, he thought, for anything good to be happening, and in the Queen's dressing and toilette room! He could not make out their faces as they jostled with elbows jabbing, grunting with effort.

The stench of fresh blood wafted through the grill.

He gasped, unable to see who the victim was. The Queen, he knew with some relief, was still in the adjacent chamber. Was she to be next?

The huddle broke up, then the men piled out of the door, back into Mary's chambers. Joshua flew closer to the window and peered through the bars.

David Rizzio lay on the floor. Inert. Blood pooled through his fine clothes, soaking the rush matting. Daggers and short swords had been left, stuck proud in his lacerated body.

Joshua felt his armour and bow appear. The hunt was on, although there appeared to have been multiple killers.

Why Rizzio? What about the Queen!

And where was McTavish?

He was about to dart back to the bedchamber window, when Mary rushed into the privy room. Her hands flew to her mouth. Joshua's heartbeat thudded in his ears, his fingers reaching behind his shoulders for the bow and arrow. He was ready for McTavish to jump out and stab her too. Hovering outside, his eyes narrowed as he drew his weapon.

Mary let out a whimper, then fell to her knees. She cradled Rizzio's head in her lap, wailing. Joshua wanted to shout a warning through the bars, but he bit his lip and steadied his bow instead. Surely now...

Any moment...

He glanced again at the body. So many stab wounds - his chest was entirely black-red with blood. His eyes widened; the hilt of one of the daggers strangely familiar.... What was it?

Cloudiness crept over his vision and he faltered, mid air. He gazed down at a man. A distance away, Joshua yearned to help but was too far away. Blood, oozing out of a body, brutally attacked with no provocation. The wind whipped his hair in the darkness, and he was too distant to stop the next attacker.... His wings froze, head spinning. He couldn't help, couldn't stop what was about to happen. He'd been here before...

Joshua began to plummet.

A scent, a familiar fir and witch hazel, comforted him. A touch. Her touch. Fingers gripped his biceps. Warmed the chill in his heart, and his limbs burned. Her heat sliced the blanket of memory blinding him.

His wife jerked on his arm again, pulling him higher in the air. The clouds of his vision parted. He saw her straining, carrying the weight of him. Immediately, his wings pulsed, then beat again. The relief on Aioffe's face was instant. He reached for her, drawing her body close as they soared up.

"The Queen," Aioffe gasped. "I couldn't see McTavish." She glanced down; the palace beneath them was aglow with torches moving through the grounds.

"Neither could I," Joshua said. He shook his head. "There were too many of them. If he was one, there were others killing as well."

"The Queen is dead?"

"Not as far as I know." He peered down, but she pulled him back up.

"Then whose blood did I smell?"

"David Rizzio. The knives, they left their knives in him."

Aioffe's eyebrows crossed in consternation. "Why would they leave evidence of their deed?"

He shrugged then met her gaze. "One of the hilts, the shape of it, seemed familiar."

"Do you think it was my dagger? The one McTavish took?"

"No. But I felt like I knew it."

She sighed. "Maybe McTavish wasn't involved, and this was just a human plot. Still, we must see if the Queen lives."

He swallowed and it was painful. He looked into her eyes and knew he had to admit the truth. "Aioffe, I... I don't think I can protect you. Every time..."

"Every time there's violence, you lose yourself." She nodded. "I don't know why."

"I'm broken." The lump in his throat wouldn't go away.

"You aren't broken." She traced the outline of his jaw then rested her hand there.

Her tenderness touched him more than he could express. All he could do was pull his love into his arms. "With you, I'm not alone." He felt the warmth of her sigh into his chest. "Without you, I am frightened."

"Together, we will end this and be free again," she said. "Perhaps not today though." She pulled away, tugging on his hand to swoop down to the tower once more. Peering through the windows, they saw Mary being helped to her feet by the Countess. Darnley stood, overlooking the body, his jaw gaping.

"The dagger," the King said in a shaking voice. His finger pointed at a knife with a hole at the end of the handle, left protruding from Rizzio's waist. "They meant to implicit me, not place me on the throne."

Aioffe glanced at Joshua, who whispered, "He wasn't even in the room, I saw. Or at least, I think I saw."

"Well didn't you mean for this to happen?" Mary rounded on her husband. "Or was it me you planned to finish off?"

Darnley shook his head. "I never…"

"You fool," Mary cried. "Incompetent wantwit." Her shoulders rolled back. "Of course they implicated you - just as you intended to stab me in the back. You failed." She glared at Darnley, who fell to his knees.

"Forgive me," he said.

Mary strode out to her bedchamber, cradling her belly.

"I want that knife," Joshua called as he flew up, over the conical roof turret. He glanced down, the barred windows impossible to slip through. Frustrated, he returned to find Aioffe hovering outside the dining closet's window. "The guards are still blocking the drawbridge. No-one is allowed entry."

She stared inside at Mary pacing, wringing her hands together. Aioffe whispered, "The Queen and her babe will need checking, after such a traumatic event. They cannot refuse a midwife, surely?"

"Let's go and find Nemis."

"Perhaps she can recover the blade?"

Joshua suppressed his shudder. "It had a curved edge and handle, like a drawn out 'S' - I'm sure I've seen something like it before."

Below, the echoing sound of church bells rang out in a tocsin to rally the watch.

She said, "Make haste, before they remove the body."

CHAPTER 44

A TOUCH OF HOPE

Joshua and Aioffe sat, owl-like perched on stools, clutching each other's hands as they faced the window. Their wings simultaneously rose at the sight of Nemis traipsing along the street below. They remained thus until she entered the room, red-cheeked from climbing the endless stairs. "Did you see the Queen?" Aioffe asked. "Is she…?"

Nemis dropped her equipment sack on the floor and hung up her cloak as she laboured for breath. "The unborn babe and Queen are well, surprisingly so after what they have endured." She glanced over to the pallet bed where Hope's wide eyes watched her parent's every move. Even though it was the early hours of the morning, no-one slept except Mark, curled up in a corner snoring softly. Spenser remained still and silent on the far side of their cramped quarters.

"I'm glad," Aioffe said, rising and relaxing her wings. "Who else was there? Did she ask for a priest?"

McTavish could still do it, she thought for the hundredth time. Strike Mary down at a point of great weakness.

"She's alone, save her husband and handmaiden," Nemis replied. "I had to argue my way inside. Apparently, Lord Bothwell tried to enter the Tower, but was repulsed. He's disappeared. However persuasive McTavish might be, he cannot affect all the guards. There are no exceptions. No-one gets in, especially not a catholic priest when 'tis likely some of the Lords of Congregation were behind the attack."

Aioffe's shoulders sagged. "Small relief, and at least she still lives. Between the watch still circling the tower with their spears, and those guarding the entry, half of Edinburgh wants to know what's going on."

"Do you have it?" Joshua asked, his voice loaded with tension. "The knife I described?"

Nemis nodded, picked up her bag, then tutted to herself as she emptied its contents onto the table. "I gave the Queen something to help her sleep, although how she's supposed to rest when the dead body of her friend still lies on the other side of the apartment is beyond me. It's morbid. Unhealthy." She pulled out an object, wrapped in the linens she used to wipe down her patients. "I think this is the one."

As she made to pass it to Joshua, she hesitated. "Hope should perhaps touch it, though, before you."

Aioffe gestured to her daughter. "That's an excellent idea."

Hope crossed the floor, staring at the bundle curiously. "Open it," she suggested to Nemis. Her fingers reached for the blade, but Aioffe's hand flew out to stop her.

"I've seen this weapon before!"

Blade and handle flowed together in an elongated curved 'S'. At the end of the grip, a steel circle the size of a thumb. The knife edge was smooth and a dusky red blotch marred the top of the wrapping.

Joshua frowned. "Where?"

"Fairfax! When he found us in York, he was supposed to bring a letter, but it, and a blade, were missing from his roll of throwing knives."

"I remember now! This matches the rest of the set." Joshua said. His eyebrow rose, then he shook his head. "Except that makes no sense."

"I didn't smell Fairfax among the crowd," Aioffe confirmed. "Only humans and maybe vampires."

"Then how did this get here?" He asked. "And why not use it on the Queen?"

Hope's hand curled around the knife and she plucked it from the wrappings. Turning it this way and that, so the low moonlight caught the bloodstains, her eyes widened.

Aioffe asked, "Daughter? What do you see?"

Hope's lips moved together soundlessly for a moment, her gaze absorbed in the glinting steel. "This knife has killed magic," she whispered. "Do you see? The stain of it remains in the metal."

They all peered closer, unable to see what she described.

"Many, many years ago, it's barely there, but I'm certain." Hope continued as her hand began to shake. Her fingers clenched the handle tighter. "Father! I sense something else. It's as if you are marked on it. Your Lifeforce, but not the same.... And Henry Fitzroy!" Her eyes flared and met Aioffe's. "His mark is upon it too!"

Joshua's jaw clenched and he snorted. "How can he be involved? How can I be?"

Nemis said quietly, "The knife does look quite old."

Aioffe replied, "Henry is too young a vampire. Unlike McTavish."

Hope dropped the knife. It embedded itself upright in the floorboards and they all stared at it as if it were alive. Hope recoiled, leaning into Aioffe. Her wings quivered against her skirts and she buried her head into Aioffe's chest. "It's ancient."

"So is he," Aioffe said. "At least as old as your father is, if not older. And from Wrye." She glanced at Joshua, but he remained focused on the knife. There were too many links to the island for it not to be important, she realised. Joshua's family had lived there, his mother was buried there, and they had met in the small church McTavish was connected to.

Joshua said, "Do you recall Fairfax saying he thought he was being watched?"

Aioffe's head tilted, a thoughtful look crossed her face. "Yes. And Naturae, where Fairfax sailed from, is close to Wrye. Perhaps he made a stop there."

Joshua said, "If this is the knife missing from his set, which we can assume came from Henry, as it was supposed to contain a letter from him to Spenser, maybe McTavish stowed away on Fairfax's ship then stole it?"

She bent and picked up the knife. "I think you should hold this. See if anything comes to you." He leaned over and touched the knife's edge. His fingers jerked back as if it burned, then he reached for it again. He took it from her then balanced it on his palm. "I... I thought something might happen if I touched it," he shook his head. "But nothing." He frowned, curled his fingers around the handle, and closed his eyes.

"Don't you feel anything?" Hope asked after a moment.

His eyes screwed tighter. "I don't know." Then he huffed and looked at Aioffe. "It does seem familiar, somehow, but, now it's not sticking from a corpse, my only kinship with it is how well the blade fits my hand." He examined it closer. "Fine workmanship, though. A blacksmith or weapon master could be proud of creating such a set."

Aioffe couldn't help but feel relieved he hadn't disappeared into some kind of enchantment or panic again. Perhaps the knife in itself wasn't the cause? Aioffe swallowed, more sure than ever his past was the key to his cure, if only he could remember it.

He looked at Hope. "Are you sure you felt something of me?"

She nodded solemnly. "I don't want to touch it again." She scurried back to the pallet bed. The wood creaked as she sat, cupping her chin in her hands and looking mournful. "I don't like the taste of it. Of death. Vampires. And magic."

Nemis crossed to sit with Hope. "Magic shouldn't be scary. Remember, you are born of a witch."

As Hope grinned at her birth mother, Aioffe looked sideways at Joshua. He spun the knife around by the circle at the end of the handle, concentration crinkling his features.

A notion lingered, a memory of his creation. Of how unique he was. How no-one else had ever become fae, and no-one else could magic up a bow and arrow. His reaction to the knife, which Hope said had killed magic before, only added to her unvoiced and unproven theory that Joshua was part witch.

"We need to know more about the knife's history," she said. "But, we can't forget, McTavish is still out there. A Queen will die."

Joshua stopped spinning the blade, catching it neatly in his palm, edge down. "I don't suppose, if we keep the knife, he'll stop."

"If he means to kill, this knife, or my dagger, any blade, would do. Or we could be entirely wrong," Aioffe replied.

Nemis stood. "I've searched and searched my visions. I cannot tell which knife, which queen, will be next." She laid her hand over Joshua's. "But I can say it will happen. The watery death I see first... but perhaps that's already happened, as it always comes to me at the start. Mary of England we know about, Mary de Guise as well." Her voice caught. "Surely another Mary will follow." She turned back to look at Aioffe. "We have to protect her."

"And we will," Joshua vowed.

Aioffe pressed her lips together, then asked Hope, "Could you get a sense of who the knife had killed before Rizzio?"

The blotch of red on Hope's cheek seemed to darken as she flushed. "If I could, I would have said." She knotted her fingers together, her head dipped as she stared at the floor. "Mother, I'm frightened. The magic I saw was powerful. Ancient. It seemed to flow around the blade. I... I almost don't want to know."

"It sounds a little like how I see Lifeforce," Aioffe said. "Ripples of light, like ribbons." She beamed at her daughter, delighted at last they had a power in common.

Hope's eyes shone. "Sort of. Does that make it fae magic?"

"I don't know, but I think we need to find out." She turned to Joshua. "I think I have to return."

"To the palace?" Nemis asked.

"To Naturae," Joshua said, his face tight. "We should go quickly."

Aioffe touched his arm. "I should go. Alone."

Enough dallying around. This part of their quest had to be hers.

Hope and Nemis cried out, "No!"

"I must," she said. "Joshua and Nemis, you have to stay and protect Queen Mary. Find out what happened, why she wasn't killed when they had the chance." She crossed her arms. "We still don't know why the queens are being murdered. Just because McTavish didn't kill her this time, doesn't mean he won't. It could be this latest incident was a warning, like the letter, Joshua. To show us how close he can get to me, or to the Queen. Toy with us, like pawns."

She shook her head and glanced at Nemis and Joshua. "That's the best reasoning for what happened I can come up with, so you both need to discover what you can. It's not enough for us to spy and wait any longer. Meanwhile, I have to find the answers we need about this knife's origins and Henry's involvement. I'll be quick, I promise. A kestrel and message won't be enough though - I want to look into his eyes. Also, there are records I can scour in the Scriptaerie. Perhaps there will also be something there to help Spenser."

She didn't need to remind them she was the only one who could find her way around Naturae's vast library, a catalogue of fae history, written in faelore and dating back thousands of years. Nor did she want to subject Joshua to any more of Henry's disturbing ability to influence her husband than necessary.

Surly of face, he acquiesced. "Perhaps you will also be better protected on Naturae. Better than I can protect you here, clearly."

"I know you try, my love, but time isn't healing your wounds. It was my actions which caused the unbalance to your mind. You are fae, and feeling human weakens you when we need you at your strongest. It is not your fault, though. I blame myself, yet we cannot fix any of this without knowing more. If we are to stop your past from haunting you, we have to know what it is."

"I should go. Maybe being there will help unlock what I knew?"

"I understand, but what if it doesn't? And, in both of us being absent, McTavish is free to strike again?" She caressed the worry lines on his forehead and said, "We have to play to our strengths to defeat this demon, and time is no longer on our side. You can get as much from the town gossips as I, and Nemis will no doubt be needed more at the palace to watch for any unusual activity there. I'll be there and back as fast as I can."

She fluttered across the room as her daughter let out a forlorn wail. "Hope, we need you to be strong and care for Spenser and Mark, while we are out. I'll be home before you know it, all the quicker knowing you and our family are safe here. You are our guardian angel now. Please, can you do this for us, my brave child?"

Hope lifted a tear-streaked face to her, but her eyes were clear and resolute. "I can mother."

Joshua gazed out of the window. "Mary's still not safe, even with all the guards." He turned back to the room. "I don't trust anyone now, not after this. Darnley's head is too easily turned, and her half brother, Moray, spins the political web too well."

"Make a plan then, my loves," Aioffe urged. "For you may be all that stands in the way of murder."

CHAPTER 45

GRAVEYARD

Within an hour, Aioffe had packed her bag and flown through the window. Joshua and Hope watched her ascend, then she pirouetted, waving goodbye. Her heart almost broke at her last sight of them, daughter nestled into her father's shoulder, as they half-heartedly waved back.

She darted high into the orange sky, above the clouds, tears streamed down her cheeks, but she stared straight due north. How quickly the situation had changed, with no warning, and how fortunate she had a long flight to digest it and prepare for what lay ahead.

Aioffe allowed herself a small diversion in the Highlands, replenishing her energy, before she crossed the sea to the Orkney Islands. The sun had begun its descent into the horizon when she recognised the familiar, craggy coastline of Wrye. Here, she hoped to begin her investigation. She swooped lower, searching for the landmarks she hoped were still there.

The church, where she had first met Joshua a century and a half ago, had fallen into disrepair. Its low slate roof crumbled within the stone walls, leaving only a greening whitewashed carcass. She smiled as she landed on the same cove their small fishing boat had beached upon, remembering how strange it had been to be in the company of a human for the first time. How revolted Joshua - Tarl - had been by her nakedness. Her wings. Her oddness. Who would have thought they would have had such adventures together since? They'd barely survived their first voyage without killing each other!

She walked across the flat landscape, pulling her cloak over her wings and head, not so much against the chill of the evening, for it was comparatively balmy, but having learned the lesson. Hiding and disguise were second nature and more necessary than ever.

The graveyard she sought was overgrown with dandelions, long flowering forget-me-nots, and creeping tendrils of ground ivy and gorse. Aioffe stood near the porch, which somehow seemed smaller, yet she had not grown taller. Her gaze swept around the assortment of gravestones, seeking the one she knew marked Tarl Smythson's mother.

It was still there, askew and shaded by a pine sapling which had taken root. She ran her fingers over the stone, peeling off the moss which covered the inscription.

'Mary Smythson' it read. 'D. 1513.'

Simple, but not terribly informative. How old was she? What was she? Other gravestones announced more detail – beloved wife, father, husband - forever etching that the person whose bones lay beneath had been cherished by someone.

Poor Tarl. Perhaps he couldn't pay for the extra carving? But then, he hadn't been able to afford the grave at all, she recalled.

But a Mary, that was of interest.

She scratched off the rest of the moss, out of respect, exposing the cross within a circle she remembered noticing when she first visited. Before she even knew what a gravestone was, and before she could read the human's language. She glanced to the church roof, checking the same shaped cross was still there as well. It was - weather-beaten but still proudly jutting up from the apex, proclaiming Christian dominion over what had been

Viking lands. She frowned as her fingertips traced the engraving on Mary Smythson's slate again. They weren't the same shape, really. She hadn't realised it before, but the horizontal bar on the gravestone's cross was lower than usual, as if it were upside down.

Aioffe sat back on her haunches, mentally reviewing all the symbols she had seen in all the religious sites over the years. An inverted cross was used to crucify the apostle Peter, supposedly at his request, but it meant something entirely different to the vampires within the Catholic church. It marked Mary as different, associated with them.

Her skin prickled. How did this tie McTavish, a vampire they had met here, to Tarl's mother, possibly a witch? She thought back to their exchange but could recall nothing of significance, other than the sneering tone McTavish used, saying he 'knew of her' when he accused Tarl of thieving to pay his debt for the burial. Since it had been her first encounter with humans, and she barely spoke their language, had she missed something?

She shook her head to herself. Returning had brought few answers and more questions. Her skin crawled as her fingertips stroked the grassy knoll. She gently pushed her fingers into the dry earth, as she had before, to push the forget me nots up, in remembrance of Tarl's mother. This time, however, as she drew forth the tiny seedlings, she felt a wisp of something else enter. Remnants of a Lifeforce so familiar to her now it eased her disturbed mind. Delving deeper, Aioffe examined the strands, closing her eyes and focussing on the sensation as they entered her.

Strange, it wasn't just one Lifeforce she caught the hint of, but several. In a peculiar way, the mixture of essences brought Hope to mind. Joshua definitely, the sense of his Lifeforce was strong. Stranger yet, was a sense of the darkness Aioffe associated with Lana, her mother. Although she couldn't pinpoint what it was, there remained in the earth both magic and blood, as if it had seeped out over time as poor Mary Smythson decayed. She understood then how Hope had seen her father in the magic from the knife, for the Lifeforce strands were related; they tingled and fizzed in the same way.

She couldn't understand why she felt a sense of her own mother, though? And the magic, dynamic even after a century or more, reminded her of Nemis's frenetic energy when she was having visions.

As she retracted her fingers and wiped the dust on her skirt, there was little doubt in Aioffe's mind that Mary Smythson had been a powerful witch, and that Joshua was also touched by magic.

CHAPTER 46

MOONLIT FLIT

Edinburgh

Hardly a day had passed since David Rizzio had been murdered, and rumour was rife that the conspirators planned to seize the throne. The complication was Mary still refused to grant Darnley the 'Crown Matrimonial' which would ensure he could rule in the event of her death. According to the Watch commander, this fact alone was all that kept the Queen safe from her vicious husband and his co-conspirators. For now.

"Queen Mary must be taken to safety. Away from Edinburgh, today," Nemis said, sitting bolt upright on the bed, roused by Joshua shutting the door behind him. Spenser, beside her, did not move, and Hope and Mark were both out at the market. "I've seen the knives still slashing."

"It sounds like your visions about the queens are becoming clearer," Joshua said. "And you haven't needed your medicine this time." He cast his eyes over her, noticing her usual ruddy cheeks and controlled hands, then smiled.

"I looked for it specifically," she said proudly. "I thought, given the near miss in that Mary lives despite the attack, my vision might have faded, like when Elizabeth was saved, but it's still strong."

"I'm pleased, sort of, but it doesn't help unless you can tell us when or why. The watch hasn't dispersed, and people still want sight of their Queen. With the crowd that holds vigil for her, getting her out unseen could be a problem."

"I must go." She scuttled around the room, gathering her belongings. "I'll make the case for escape directly to her, and tell her our plan. At the very least, some fresh air would help her and the child." She turned to Joshua. "Have you made the arrangements?"

He nodded. "The kestrel has returned, message delivered."

"Then Queen Mary just has to agree," Nemis said. "And heaven help us if she doesn't see the wisdom."

"We'll be there at midnight," Joshua replied.

Joshua pulled the cloak lower over his forehead and leaned against the wall to shelter from prying eyes. Much depended on disguise, and the darkness. Canongate cemetery, close to the Abbey walls was deserted and quiet, with barely the hoot of an owl to break the peace. His horse's bit jingled, the animal suddenly skittish in the eerie silence. Joshua stroked its nose and murmured endearments to calm it.

John Stewart of Traquair, the Captain of Mary's personal guard, stood stiffly by his mount. "Erskine, are you certain this is what the Queen wants?"

Joshua replied in an imitation of Erskine's voice, "Aye. Just watch, she'll be oot." He pointed to the low door in the distance. Erskine himself slept soundly in his bed, thanks to Nemis's sleeping draught, and Traquair wouldn't have been here at all were it not for him interrupting Joshua saddling and loading the horses an hour earlier and insisting he accompany him when he recognised Mary's luggage.

They waited, stroking their mount's noses to settle them. With the moon high in the sky, the clear night was near perfect for the plan, but Joshua's heart thumped regardless. This was a brazen move, endangering them all. A niggling voice, a sense perhaps, cautioned him about being watched, yet he couldn't see nor smell anyone else in the graveyard who ought not be there.

Finally, the wine cellar door creaked ajar. Four figures stealthily crept across the cemetery, arms wide for balance over the uneven earth. Joshua huffed, his plan shaken by the addition of two extra people.

One of the figures stumbled on her skirts, knees falling onto the freshly dug grave just yards from where Joshua stood. He dropped the reins and darted over to help, but Mary had already recovered. She brushed the dirt from her dark red gown in disgust. Keeping his head bowed as he offered her his hand, she asked, "Is it his grave?"

"Aye, m'Lady," Joshua growled. "Master Rizzio rests in peace now."

She did not acknowledge him at all, merely glared at Darnley.

Ruefully, her husband commented, "In him I have lost a good and faithful servant, the like of whom I shall never find again."

Joshua snorted as Darnley continued to plead with his wife. "I have been miserably cheated."

"Hush your mouth," Mary snapped. "That you should feign remorse now and put us even more at risk."

Joshua had bigger problems. Anticipating only Mary and perhaps her gentlewoman, Margaret Carwood, to escape, the arrival of Darnley and the page meant he hadn't enough horses. Doubling up was required; Erskine's was the largest horse, and she was a tall and pregnant woman. He put his boot in the stirrup and swung his leg over before reaching down to Mary. "Ride behind me, my Lady," Joshua suggested. "Let my body be your armour."

Mary settled herself in the saddle, wedging her swollen stomach against his wings. If she noticed anything peculiar, well, that couldn't be helped, Joshua told himself. He was just grateful the Queen was a fine horsewoman and could not, because of the belly bulge, wrap her arms around his torso for grip.

Nothing about this night was ordinary.

Darnley shook with fear, but he mounted the horse intended for Mary; his page, Standen rode pillion behind. Traquair helped Mistress Carwood up, and then they were away.

They trotted through the near silent streets of Edinburgh, following the route Joshua had already ascertained would avoid the night watchmen. After leaving the city, he urged his horse into a canter and hoped Mary would be able to hang on.

Several miles passed without incident, and he began to breathe a little easier. He was so focused on keeping their mount smoothly weaving around the potholes in the road to Seton, the appearance of horsemen blocking the way ahead surprised him. He pulled back on the reins, and behind, the others clattered to a stop as well.

Darnley panted, "Come on!"

Joshua felt Mary tense as they peered into the darkness. Moonlight streamed over the shadowy figures, and he smiled.

"Come on! By God's blood, they will murder both you and me," Darnley said, unable to see what Joshua could. His arm stretched towards Mary.

Joshua's head whipped around, just in time to catch Darnley spurring his mount on with buffoon-like kicks. As he passed, the King swiped his lash on Joshua's horse - viciously and so close to Mary's belly the tip almost grazed it!

"Have a care!" Joshua snarled, reining in the rearing mare.

Mary clutched her babe and pleaded, "Do not harm the child!"

"In God's name, come on!" Darnley cried, urging his mount ahead. "If this one dies, we can have more."

A look of loathing crossed Mary's face. "Push on, and take care of your own self. As usual."

Darnley's lip curled, and with every deliberation, his heels dug into his horse's flank.

But his way forward was barred by pistols and swords.

"My Queen," the leader of the men called as he trotted closer. He lifted a broad-rimmed hat to reveal his face. "We are here to escort you to safety," Lord Bothwell said.

He nodded curtly to Joshua; no need to elaborate on how they knew to meet on this particular road, for the kestrel system was strictly between creaturekind. Bothwell travelled with ten armed guards, so Joshua hoped to pass his charge into safe enough hands.

Keeping his own head low, he muttered to Mary, "I leave you here, my lady, and pray I deliver you 'tae welcome hands."

Her fingers gripped his arm as she leaned forward and swung her leg over the hind. "With the Lord Commander of my forces, I am always welcome." She slid from the horse and strode towards the witch. "Dunbar by breakfast, I presume?" She beamed, radiant in her relief. "I'm in the mood for eggs."

CHAPTER 47

FIRST STEPS OF A DANCE

Naturae

The mist surrounding Naturae embraced Aioffe like a long-lost friend. Her wings quivered as she lingered within, fingers caressing the sparkling droplets, cleansing her of apprehension.

Home. Aioffe had no doubt the mist's message was to remind her of her place and duty to this land.

But anxiety returned as she fluttered towards the shoreline. The trees loomed dark and ominous in the night sky, quiet save the faintest rustle of leaves. Even the waves clawing the pebbled beach were silent of the gentle rattle familiar to her.

She flew over the treetops, deeper into the heart of her homeland. A chill crept up her arms as she tried to reassure herself Henry was taking good care of her people. Certainly the building works had progressed, for new houses perched in the treetops, and the ground beneath flushed with spring colour. Her heart leapt into her mouth when she saw the outline of a massive grey structure, spiking high into the sky like a spire. This must be

Henry's castle. She looped around its five sides, topped with crenellations with turrets to each corner. Shining mini cannons poked out of window slits on the top floor, some six stories up. Rising from the centre, a cone with yet more cannons, with strange wide mouths. At the base of the walls, rising as high as the trees and embedded between the stones, pointed stakes like thorns spoke of the defence it was meant to provide against vampires.

It was quite the ugliest building Aioffe thought she had ever seen. Entirely utilitarian, Henry had created a stronghold with little light and style. Oppressive silence suggested it was unoccupied, so why build it at all, she wondered? Guilt swept through her - would the fae have needed such a defence if she were still Queen?

Desperate to get away from its foreboding presence she soared over the treetops towards the older buildings. Her heart broke a little more with every beat of her wings until she reached the two ancient ash and elm trees. They, at least, flourished with new leaves, and their greenery broken up by colourful message ribbons still dangling. Aioffe considered dipping to read them, to gage a sense of her fae's fears and hopes, but, the continued quietness perturbed, urging her to the citadel. Where were the gentle voices, singing the pupae to sleep in the Pupaetory, or the happy chatter of youngsters? Where the low chuckles of gathered workers, sharing the news of the day at it's close?

And where were the sentries? She had returned unnoticed, unannounced. Not that she wanted fanfare, but anyone could invade and no alarm had been raised.

She alighted on the palace landing balcony and strode through the atrium. At the tree trunk which marked the junction between the High Hall and various corridors which led to the other chambers, her fists balled. "Henry!" She called. Her voice echoed down the passages, unanswered.

She glanced to her right. The carved double doors to the High Hall were closed, a heavy chain wrapped around the handle. She pressed her ear to the wood, her heartbeat escalating as she felt the warmth exuding from within. Muffled sounds of snoring! Many snores, deep and light.

Aioffe let out the breath she had subconsciously held in. But why were they locked inside? She jolted about as cool fingers curled around her arm.

"Aioffe," Henry said, with barely veiled fury. "Why are you here?"

"Why are my fae locked in the High Hall?"

"My fae. For safety and rest," he said. "I provide their protection during the dark hours."

In the darkness, his eyes gleamed like limpid cesspits as they roamed over her, but she detected relief in his tone. Who had he been expecting, if not her?

Her stomach clenched. "Who do they need protecting from? And why aren't they safe in the monstrosity you built?"

To disguise the tremor in her voice, Aioffe's hand wandered up to adjust a missing crown.

Henry was silent for a moment, then he pulled on her arm. "This way. The fae save their energy and recuperate peacefully, in familiarity." He stepped towards the atrium. "It was Thane's idea."

When she resisted his tug, his dark gaze stared into her. "I do not think you need fear, Aioffe, for what lies in the shadows you and I together are strong enough to bear." His head bowed. "Strength was never the problem for you, but you would be safer off the island nonetheless." A smile hinted, a flash of his white fangs.

But, she misunderstood his threat.

"Before you are sniffed out, by my intended Queen," he said. His teeth disappeared behind unsmiling lips.

"Where is she?"

Henry's head jerked towards the castle. "Locked away. Do you really wish to see her?"

Aioffe shook her head. If Caesaria was anything like her mother, intervention or discussion was useless. She recalled also the madness which had overtaken Caesaria in Bavaria when even familial bonds had been tested in the Princess's quest for power. Hollowly, and not entirely wanting to hear the answer, she asked, "What has she done?"

Henry sighed, his gaze still low. "The better question would be, what have I not done, for them?" His shoulders sagged and Aioffe sensed his sorrow. "And the answer would be, not enough. I find myself torn. My sworn duty is to keep them, my fae, safe, from her, although she, being a queen, is the answer to what ails them as a race." He shrugged and met her eyes.

Aioffe realised Henry, peculiar proud creature that he was, wrestled with the truth they both knew. But it had to come from him, and as she stared at him, eventually, it did:

"I thought you might be...." He shook his head. "Never mind. The truth of it is, I am wrong. No matter what I do, I am simply the wrong king."

His admittance softened her stance, for to admit this spoke of new humility. She gripped his elbow, silently urging him to continue.

"I tried to capture Darnley, to sacrifice royal blood onto the vines because Illania didn't bring me one like she said she would. Then, Spenser was attacked, and, like you, I thought perhaps she had done it. I believed she would then return to Naturae and cure the vines with whomever she had captured, for why else would she be there? I hurried home, but Illania wasn't here."

His lips pressed together and he searched her face. After a moment, he said ruefully. "I was convinced Caesaria, a fae queen under my control, could make up for what I lacked as a King. I have made too many assumptions about what people would do, and all the while, Naturae has suffered. The weight of this crown is... heavy."

Aioffe's mind harked back to that first belief ceremony she had held on Naturae. In her desperation to prove she was a worthy Queen herself, it had taken her husband to remind the fae of the importance of belief, and self belief. Only then had the hearts and minds of the Naturae fae willingly released their Lifeforce for her to gather. It was a stark contrast to the taking method employed by Illania when she had need of Lifeforce, and Caesaria had doubtless learned from her that it was easier to take than to ask.

"She could, in theory," Aioffe said. "But a Queen is only supposed to come into her full powers when she ascends to the throne. But she has to be a true Queen, in body, mind, heart and soul. I'm not convinced that simply wearing a crown would be enough."

Henry snorted, "And Caesaria, like me, has no soul. I'm evermore sure of it the longer she stays."

"Perhaps she once did…"

Aioffe could not help but feel ashamed she had left. That she had put the needs of herself and her family before the needs of her people. Although she had oft thought of those who remained on Naturae, she hadn't acted. She hadn't the courage, she supposed, to face their questions, to bear their adoration, and to reclaim the burden of ruling. Henry had borne that for her, and she had been happy to let him.

As if he could read her reluctance to admit her own truth, he said, "There is little point in pretending. We should have danced years ago, you and I. Perhaps then this would not be so… awkward."

She whispered, "Except I did not wish to. When I returned to England, a new mother to Hope, you were already here. Their accepted king, I was told. I have a family now to consider, and I do not want my perceived destiny to be laid upon such young shoulders as Hope's. She should know freedom, and have the choice I was never afforded. Time passes differently for immortals, and I never thought my absence would be permanent… I just…"

His eyebrows knitted together. "Could not bring yourself to face the problem, eh? We dance different steps then, for I can. Yet, for all that I have done, I cannot give Caesaria what she desires when my heart belongs to another."

Aioffe's lips pressed together as she ruminated.

A screech echoed through the atrium and down the corridor, interrupting her thoughts. He glanced in the direction then sighed. "She's securely locked away, but hungry. Always hungry."

"Then I have little time to waste. Please, let me go now."

"Dawn will come soon enough," he said, leading her to the Atrium. "The workers will hunt the seas to provide for her and you cannot be here."

Aioffe bit her tongue. The memory of being forced to eat cold, dead fish in the Beneath during her own captivity surged into her mouth, sickly and sour. Did Caesaria deserve such a fate? Probably. Henry wouldn't have kept his intended wife locked up if he trusted her to hunt for herself, if she even could. Aioffe could not recall ever having seen another Queen - her mother, Illania or the Princesses - source their own food.

Outside on the balcony, Henry turned to her. "If the fae see you, then you can never leave them again. They would not allow it, and chaos would again ensue." His eyes narrowed on her. "I will not give up this throne, this responsibility, so easily, and they deserve better than a half-hearted attempt at ruling. I am one and they are many. If they decided to revolt against me... there will be chaos once more."

Henry was right, and Aioffe flushed with shame. In her hasty decision to return, for her own purposes, she hadn't even considered the impact on her people. On Henry's otherwise stable rule. Although, Naturae in reality wasn't quite how she had envisaged his custodianship to be. Shaking her head, she acknowledged their tenuous accord. "I am not ready to return as Queen. Not today, perhaps not ever. A queen killer is still at large, and my daughter still needs a mother."

"Then we must be allies after all," he said. "You ought to protect her. In your daughter, there is at least an heir, should the worst happen to me or to you."

That he considered Hope his heir was encouraging. "What do you propose?"

He tapped his finger on his neat short beard. "You could leave now, and the status quo continues."

Aioffe snorted. "That solves neither of our problems."

"Or, you stay, cure the vines of their blight, the vinexplicity, and.... we find a way to co-rule." His forced tone implied this was a last, desperate resort. She wasn't entirely sure she believed him.

"I don't know anything about vinexplicitity, what it even is, or how to cure it. And, if I returned as Queen, Henry, you would be left King in name only. Like Lord Darnley. Is that what you really want?"

Returning permanently certainly wasn't what she wanted, not to mention Joshua and Hope might have something to say about it.

"Then why have you come back?" He snapped.

"I need answers."

"To what?"

She touched his hand, for there was no cause for animosity. "In the Scriptaerie, I think there might be records which could help clear something up, and I want to know how your mark could have been left on a knife used to kill an Italian courtier in Scotland."

His face turned surly and he pulled his hand away. "I haven't done anything. Clearly. I have not left these shores for months."

"I know," she said. "We are fairly certain McTavish is the killer, but we have yet to find him. I return now because a knife which has both magic and your mark on it was at the scene of a murder, possibly also an attempted murder of Mary, Queen of Scotland."

"Attempted? You missed him again?"

She ignored the slight. "It was used to kill someone close to Mary Queen of Scots, but there were many people there. She survived, but imagine our surprise to see a blade Joshua and I recognised as Thomas's."

He leaned on the balcony railing and gazed out across the clearing. Aioffe reached into her bag and withdrew the knife. "We saw he was missing one when he visited."

"I gave him this set." Henry took the weapon and twirled it around. "A gift. A reminder of happier times."

"Where did you get them from?" Aioffe asked, keeping her eyes on the spinning blade and attempting to sound casual.

Henry's lips tightened as he slapped the grip firmly into his palm, blade tip down as if he meant to stab with it. "I traded for them."

"Traded what?"

"Healing." He shrugged. "Some human girl on Rousay had burned herself. My blood eased the pain and prevented scarring her. The family offered grateful recompense."

"Were they blacksmiths?"

He nodded. "Forge fires need charcoal, but she'd put green wood on whilst left minding it on her own. The sparks spat out and caught on her dress. I heard her screams while I was there, hunting. The knife set was a family heirloom, they said. I didn't really want to take it, but they insisted. Fairfax and I used to practise throwing them together."

Aioffe's heart raced. Perhaps Joshua still had family on Wrye!

"Does that answer your question?" Henry said.

She almost leaned across and squeezed his hand, but his growl warned her as much as the blade he still held. "More than you know."

"Then," he gestured to the brightening sky, jabbing at it as if he were about to launch the knife twirling into the horizon. "We need to decide what next. I must unlock the High Hall doors soon. Daytime is quite normal, I assure you. Caesaria is most active at night, and most lazy during the day."

Filled with hope, Aioffe flicked the edges of her cloak back to free her wings and backed away. "May I return tomorrow, when it's safe?"

"If you must."

Her wings began to beat slowly. "I need to visit the Scriptaerie. I can be quiet and hidden there while I research."

"Let me know if you find anything about vinexplicity," he growled.

She nodded. "Perhaps then we could discuss... a choice of music? I don't think we could ever be dance partners, but maybe I can help somehow."

Abruptly, Henry stuck the dagger through a loop on his belt, and turned away. The bob of his Adam's apple betrayed his relief as much as his fingers curling around the knife handle as if drawing reassurance from its presence. The sentiment she could feel sympathetic towards, for the burden of ruling alone was great.

"Then I shall trust you to return, and grant you permission to search for what you seek as long as you remain hidden. I shall see you anon," he said. "Godspeed."

CHAPTER 48

TRUST THE WITCH

Edinburgh

Nemis knew she was writhing - her belly was on fire, and she had spewed hot blood in an attempt to rid herself of the pain. Her eyes burned like a drill boring into her mind, but she could not feel her hands to scratch them.

But in the dark, she wrestled with the vision. A part of her tried to separate herself from the living death which trapped her. Identify something, anything which she could cling onto and remember as a clue this time. She told herself to succumb, to be willing to exist in the moment. If she could only experience it truly, while being more conscious about what was happening to 'her' then perhaps... But the agony was too great.

Just as she felt the vision slipping away, sliding into the shadows, another presence appeared close to her. She started, sensing magic, but not her own. Her retreat had already commenced, the experience of dying as this queen was nearly passed. Within a heartbeat, Nemis separated into her own entity once again. From a distance, she lingered, watching the shadow arch over the body, vigorously rubbing at the limbs which were so recently her own. The figure's movements as it circled, massaging and kneading, seemed familiar, but she could not place it. The presence was not tall, but slim and dressed in a long, dark shift. Dangling strips hung like a shroud, wafting in the air as it moved around, but its face remained elusive.

Then, it reached into a pocket and withdrew a vial.

Nemis scrabbled mentally to cling onto the sight, but a warmth she recognised as her own medicine dripped through her veins. "No!" she screamed. "Wait..."

Before she jolted back into reality, she noticed the body on the bed relaxed. Crownless, her face turned to the shadowy form. Queen Mary reached out to touch it! "Better," she whispered before her hand fell to a flat stomach.

Nemis's fingers curled in a death grip so tight her fingernails drew blood from her palms. Hope and Joshua watched, feeling helpless. For safety, Joshua had gathered Spenser in his arms, clutching his friend close as if that would in some way shield him from the horrors his wife endured. Sometimes, Nemis thrashed around or flung out a limb in the throes of her pain, and hurt her beloved. His body was cold, inert, but still with a slow heartbeat.

As the fit passed, Nemis's body relaxed. Hope leaned over the bed and dripped a few drops more of Jeffries' elixir between her lips.

"A bad one," Hope said, glancing at Joshua with dark eyes. The birth-mark darkening the side of her face paled, for none of them had rested much these last weeks. "She suffered this time."

Joshua nodded. "I thought she had more control over them, but..."

Nemis stirred, slurring, "A witch."

"Still with us," Joshua reassured her. Not for the first time, he wished he could say she was 'fine' or 'well.'

"Trust the witch," Nemis muttered. "We have to trust the witch."

Joshua's blood ran cold. "What do you mean?"

As he placed Spenser back down on the blankets, Nemis said, "I saw a witch there. A new vision - definitely Mary - and she is saved!"

"Another attempt?" Joshua asked. "When? Do you know anything else?"

Nemis straightened her cap, which had fallen askew while she had been fitting. "Only that it's definitely our Queen Mary, and extremely painful." She looked up at Joshua, eyes wide in alarm. "Poison! Tis the only explanation."

He frowned. "Not a stabbing, then?"

Nemis swung her legs over the side of the bed. "I still see that one, but this is different. One I've not seen before." She swayed as she bore down on weakened legs. "I must go to her. The babe..."

Hope darted over to help her stand straight. "You're recovering so much faster," she said, rubbing Nemis's arms with affection. "I remember when it took you days to revive. I shall walk with you though, just in case."

Nemis gazed at Hope's red wings. "In the vision, I wondered for a moment if the shadow was you, but now I see the goodness shines too bright in you for it ever to be cast in shadow." She staggered over to her bags. "The birth of a prince draws near; I must protect her."

Hope threw her cape over her shoulders, enveloping her appendages, then opened the door for Nemis. "Pray for a safe delivery," she said, looking at her father.

"I pray for us all," Joshua replied, his face grim. "And I will prowl through the night until I find that priest, have no fear."

Chapter 49

KIDNAP

Naturae Henry gripped the bannister as he awaited Aioffe on the landing balcony, watching for her huge wings to appear through the cloudy night. For weeks, every night without fail, Aioffe appeared and closeted herself away in the Scriptaerie scouring scrolls and deeds, then disappeared each dawn. He still had no idea what she searched for; she refused to elaborate.

Tonight, he asserted to himself, he would not draw comfort from her company and gentle platitudes to soothe away the day's frustrations, but voice them. Demand answers. Then, demand her sacrifice. He would no longer consider alternative Queens, or how to hunt down a human royal. It had to be Aioffe's blood, he'd decided. Born of Naturae, no-one else could provide for it as well as she. She had a duty to care for the fae as much as he did. Yet, when in her presence, he could never seem to find the words to ask her. Although they hardly spoke, except to exchange pleasantries as friends might, their nightly routine consoled him; she made no demands upon him, just accepted him for who he was. He could not mesmerise her into doing the deed.

As he stared into the night sky for her, Henry's conflict crystallised around a sour fact: her silent companionship was welcome. He'd grown more at ease with her presence on his island, and nearly forgotten his plan. He snorted, thinking how ridiculous he had become, anticipating her arrival as one might a lover returning from a day's work. Yearning for the calmness which arises from familiarity.

But it couldn't continue. After a confrontation with both the Council and Thane earlier, along with their continued lamentations about their former queen, keeping her visits a secret weighed on his mind. Worse, the Elders had begun to notice his rule was more relaxed of late, and that would not do. They might take liberties with his authority. Given his tenuous grip on power, which Aioffe's mere presence every night reminded him of, he could not tolerate this impasse any longer.

She touched down on the balcony, nodded to him, then walked by his side into the palace. Howls echoed along the far hallway as Caesaria vented her rage and hunger, but they ignored it. At the Scriptaerie doorway, he bowed curtly.

"All fae safely resting, as usual?"

He nodded, his jaw too clenched to speak. How weak he was now, how indecisive her friendship had made him. He hesitated, in her presence torn once more.

To fill the silence, she asked after the fawn she had brought from the mainland only the day before.

"Well settled into the herd," he replied, stiffly. "And Thane has agreed new training grounds. We prosper, except for the one thing which would bring us all hope in the Pupaetory."

"When I have found what I seek, we shall dance." Her standard reply.

Enough. As she made to enter the Scriptaerie, he caught her arm. "When?"

Her blue eyes flared at him. "I told you. When this other matter is resolved. I cannot perform the role of a Queen until I know my family is safe. That I am safe."

His eyes narrowed as they scanned her guarded face. "Tell me what you know of the wider realm."

She had the audacity to pout a little, until he shook her.

"I have heard from Joshua by kestrel," she admitted. "He reports your sister is grievously sick."

He blinked. So the spy network was still active. A part of him felt relieved. "Is it poison?"

"According to the spies, it is a serious illness, but not sinister. Nemis hasn't seen her die, in her visions."

"What else?"

"Queen Mary of Scotland has born a son, and is now away on a Progress."

"And the so-called killer?"

Her fists clenched. "McTavish remains uncaptured." She glared at him. "Even Naturae is not safe. He could sail in, unnoticed as the shores are unguarded, if he knew I was here." She shook her head. "The only way my family becomes secure and Elizabeth and Mary are saved, is to solve this riddle for once and for all. Perhaps discover why he threatens female rulers, and put an end to his schemes."

She glanced away and he knew there was more to her search than that. Why did she have to be so obtuse about what she sought to know? He shook his head. Naturae was not safe for her, much as though it pained him to be the reason for it, but he had little choice. So why couldn't he just demand her sacrifice and be done with it all? His fingers tightened on her arm. "I thank you for the update, but you leave me no option."

Her eyes flicked to his grip, then met his. A ball of fury resolved as his stomach tightened. He shoved her into the Scriptaerie. "You'll stay in here until you find what you are looking for then. Safe for now."

She gasped, but he slammed the door, locked her in and withdrew the key.

Muffled bangs on the wood suggested perhaps he had gone too far, but, he reasoned, she needed to learn his patience had dried. That made three prisoners, and he had never considered himself a gaoler before. Yes, he too was trapped on this blasted island. Trapped spinning a never ending web of secrets, lies and plots of his own. His fingers tightened around the key. Why hadn't he kept his resolve? These fae had weakened him. Aioffe's indecisiveness must be contagious. His hand wandered up to his crown, which felt tighter around his head than ever before. Fuming at himself, he stomped away from her cries. She ought to be grateful it wasn't the dungeon.

CHAPTER 50

SMOKE

O   Joshua hurried across the wide stable yard at Jedburgh Castle carrying a warm poultice in a bowl. The Queen's mount, a grey gelding named Jock, whinney'd a welcome from the stalls. "I know it still hurts, boy," he murmured as he applied the thick paste to swollen front fetlocks. Under contract to the Crown as a farrier on Mary's Progress, between Nemis and himself they had thus far managed to keep a protective eye over her and tend to the health of hundreds of horses.

Until the events of the last few days, at least. The entire Progress ground to a halt while Queen Mary lay abed.

As he wrapped fresh bandages over the herby poultice, Nemis poked her head over the stall. With a face pale from exhaustion, she leaned on the stall and said, "Thought I might find you here. Despite the fever, she's asking after her horse."

"Jock's not the only one suffering, but he's recovering," Joshua said. Rough terrain, ridden over at speed, meant many of the mounts used needed a good rest, but Jock had sustained an injury and could not be mounted for many a day. "How fares his mistress?"

"Not in a state to be worrying about her horse, that's for sure. After yesterday... I cannot help but wonder if we missed something." Nemis's lips pressed together and she shook her head. "I'm concerned it could be poison."

He huffed through his nostrils. "I couldn't be there all the time, and I did not see anything suspicious, aside from the Queen tumbling into a bog, that is. The entire episode was more comical than dangerous."

"Well, it's not normal to vomit blood so much, near sixty times in one day," Nemis said. "The emesis seems to have stopped now, but her fever comes and goes, as does her mind. Sometimes she complains she cannot see." Her hands wrung together. "I keep asking myself if it's all connected. Tell me again what you saw. Perhaps we missed something. Someone."

He stroked Jock's mane and thought. A few days ago, word reached the Queen that her friend and ally Lord Bothwell, Commander of her army and defender of the Borderlands, had been attacked by thieves and malefactors. Initially, his death was reported, but clarification arrived hours later that his wounds were severe yet he still clung to life. He was not expected to live long. Mary hadn't hesitated and the next morning she set out for Hermitage Castle. Everyone knew if Bothwell died without an adequate plan for a transition of his powers, the English might invade the troublesome Borders, even though Joshua didn't think Elizabeth would order such an act from her own sickbed.

Although he had not officially been one of the small party accompanying the Queen on the sixty mile round trip, Joshua had watched over Mary's journey from above. The route was treacherous and robberies commonplace.

"They left before dawn, as you know, and the ride there was arduous but uneventful. I couldn't enter the castle, for it was surrounded by Bothwell's men. I couldn't even land close. She visited for about two hours; just her, the Earl of Moray and a few other Lords. Then, on the journey back, Jock stumbled. She fell into the mud, and Moray and her maid took her to a farmhouse to clean up. It was a diversion no-one could have foreseen."

He bent and re-tied the bandage ends on Jock's legs, then stood. Nemis's downcast expression bothered him. "I'm sorry, but I don't see how she could have been poisoned. The message that Bothwell lived came late in the evening, and Mary left by dawn the next day. It was a last moment change of plan. I saw everyone she interacted with the entire journey, and the farmers were just as shocked to find a bedraggled Mary on their doorstep as you would expect."

"Perhaps not in the farmhouse then, but what about inside the castle? Couldn't you have searched there beforehand? Checked it was safe?"

He knew she was tired from nursing the queen - who was prone to taking to her bed for days at a time on occasion - but the accusatory tone of her voice irked him. "I cannot account for what happened in there. Bothwell, we have trusted before, and he is no particular friend to the Catholics as far as I'm aware. And, with the change of plans so swift, how could McTavish have got wind of them, then journeyed before she did? Vampires may be fast, but still..."

"Unless he was at Hermitage Castle beforehand." She shrugged and stepped back from the stall. "Some say this is Darnley's doing - his mere presence and demands for conjugal rights a week ago has soured her humours. What the Queen suffers from is beyond my healing abilities to cure. Her malady is similar to what I saw in my visions, only, I know I am the only witch in the room, and I can do naught to help her."

"We must find out if this is an attack, then," Joshua said gloomily. "Let's rule in or out one cause of the sickness before we worry about the other. Darnley left before she fell ill, so if it was that poxed pillock to blame, then McTavish or someone got to him. Or, it's all in her head. Maybe seeing the witch so wounded upset her? I'll go to Bothwell myself, before it's too late, and see what I can find out."

"Be quick," Nemis said. "Before the king finds out his wife ails and decides to press his advantage. With the Prince barely two months old, and not yet baptised, I'll warrant Darnley will think he has the power."

"Stay by her bedside." Joshua gave Jock a pat goodbye. "But, send a kestrel to Aioffe updating her. Perhaps it will prompt a reply."

"We've had no word from her lately?"

"Not for days."

And that, he realised, was at the heart of his unease.

Hermitage Castle's unnatural squareness made it seem alien, and thus even more isolated, plonked in the rolling Middle Marches. With a river running to one side, the oppressive building was built on a site long rumoured to have been occupied by witches. As he flew down, through the low clouds, and neared the H-shaped fortress, Joshua glanced into the high, narrow windows at the top of the towers, hinting at deep impregnable walls. Near darkness inside betrayed little about its occupant's state; was he too late?

Outside, the sides of the mound above the moat swarmed with even more guards than he'd noticed a few days before, and in the fields around, armies camped out, performing drills, cooking or maintaining their kit. Bothwell must still live then, if more men had rallied to their Lord after his attack. If he had died since Mary's visit, they wouldn't be as relaxed; orders would have been given to actively defend the castle.

Swooping up through the cloud, he could not shake a sense of entering forbidden territory, perhaps like anyone passing through the mists of Naturae, he supposed. The notion comforted him, for surely a vampire would think twice about trespassing on lands sacred to witches?

He landed some miles away in a copse, stripped to his bare chest, then re-dressed with his wings underneath his shirt once more. After retrieving his forged papers from his satchel, he walked down a track towards the vast rectangular gatehouse. Flashing them before a soldier, he announced he had an urgent message from the Queen, and where might he find Lord Bothwell?

"Abed," the guard said with a jerk of his head. "Yer can wait with the others. He'll shout down when he wants an audience. Or a wench."

Bothwell must not be as close to death as was reported then, if his voice could be heard through these thick walls. Joshua entered a dank corridor and emerging into an equally dark chamber in the heart of the castle. A small fire glowed at either end of the high ceiling'd windowless room. Archers blocked what little light there was from the slits between the stones, perched on narrow boards above. No wonder Mary hadn't wished to stay long, he thought. A more inhospitable accommodation for a Lord he hadn't often seen.

A few messenger boys lounged in front of the fires on musty rush matting; his arrival prompted only a glance before they resumed their conversation. "They say t'was his own escaped prisoners wot did 'fer his Lordship,' one of them remarked. "That, an' the Elliotts." He shivered. "And now the Armstrong and Johnstones are out, it'll be another clan war before you know it."

"I heard they're still roaming," the other lad said, fiddling with his leather scroll case. "I've nothing to thieve, so perhaps they'll ignore me when I go back. Think there's any chance of some grub?"

Their ruminations were interrupted by a bellow for wine, echoing down unseen stairs from the corner of the room. The eerie effect made the jumpy boys shake, and Joshua smile. A serving girl appeared from behind one of the moth-eaten wall hangings, scuttled across the hall with a jug, and disappeared into a dark hollow.

A few moments later, another shout for messages prompted them all to follow in the wake of the servant, who nearly collided with them in her haste to dart back down the stairs. The smell of decay and herbs lingered in the stairwell. Joshua let the boys go into the tower chamber first, for theirs was a simpler delivery task.

When they left, Joshua knocked on the door and waited. Receiving no reply, he knocked again. "Enter," a weak voice said, then coughed.

Inside, the air was thick with incense and burnt plant. Lord Bothwell, normally a rugged-looking stocky man in his thirties, was hunched over a desk like a man twice his age. The surface was littered with vials, pastes, and dried herbs. Shaking fingers wafted the fumes of something burning in a pewter bowl towards his face.

"Close the door," he ordered, then broke into a fit of coughing again. His forehead and chest were swaddled in bandages, but even in the low candlelight, Joshua could see dark purple and red bruises mottling his entire body. On his thigh and left hand, large gashes had been stitched together, then left exposed to the air to heal.

Bothwell bent over the bowl for another inhalation, then leaned back. He held a finger up then let out his breath. His face unclenched and serenity smoothed his swarthy features. The witch glanced at Joshua with dark eyes, added a pinch of something from a bottle to the dish, before dousing the concoction with wine.

Thick smoke filled the room, clouding the smug smile which spread over Bothwell's cheeks. The pungent odour of the mysterious substance hung, overwhelming the previously stale scent of illness. With each hazy breath Joshua took, a tickling sensation scratched in his throat, making him retch. His eyes darted around seeking fresh air, but the dark chamber was windowless.

"Speak," the witch commanded. "The vapour will do you no harm."

"My Lord Bothwell," he began, before having to clear his throat.

"But you are no Erskine today, I see." Bothwell shuffled in his chair, then puffed out a plume of smoke. He turned to Joshua, eyes bright and focused, and with movements which seemed less pained than they ought to be given the extent of his injuries. He had a small moustache, untidy and in need of a trim, and dark cropped hair which curled appealingly at the nape. "Who are you really, fae?"

"Joshua Meadows." Good god, what was in that smoke? He coughed, unable to prevent his wings rustling beneath his shirt.

"Was it your bastards who attacked me?"

Joshua started. "I heard it was your own prisoners?"

Bothwell shook his head. "They'd already escaped during my absence from this castle. There's no reason to ambush me when they were returning to their clans regardless of my movements. There were a few men on the ground to keep mine occupied, but I was the main target - to kill."

"Why would you even think the fae would attack?" Joshua's stomach clenched as his fuzzy mind flashed to Aioffe, to Henry and Naturae.

"Because it takes wings to strike from above." Bothwell peeled back the bandage on his forehead. "Although I barely saw it, this was sliced by someone upside down, and so fast with silver and green, I thought at first I was dreaming."

The skin had knitted together well, but the shape of the wound curved, as if someone had intended to scalp the man.

Bothwell re-arranged the wrap with steady fingers. "If I had not dodged and cast a protective spell, I would not live before you now. Fortunately, flesh wounds are easy for me to heal."

Joshua's fists curled as he shook his head to clear the haze. "I know nothing of this, or why any fae might attack you."

Bothwell scowled. "Do you call me a liar?"

"Not at all. I cannot explain it."

Bothwell rubbed his ribs while Joshua coughed. The magical truth-drawing vapours seemed to swirl around them. They stared at each other with unveiled and mutual distrust.

But, 'trust the witch,' Nemis had said. Under this witch's dark, probing gaze, hitherto unspoken secrets spilled from his lips without his inherent discretion. "You should know, there's a killer of queens. Hunting, haunting this realm. He's already killed Mary of England and Mary de Guise. He's almost certainly behind the earlier attempt on Queen Mary when Rizzio died."

Bothwell's face darkened. "Really?"

"My wife and my friend - Queen Mary's midwife - and I have been guarding her. And now, we think she has been poisoned. She lies very poorly, near death, at Jedburgh."

"Yet I have just this moment received letters from the Queen. They seemed perfectly lucid, and in her hand." He glared at Joshua, flicking his fingers towards the papers resting on the bedspread.

"Since she wrote those, a violent malady has overtaken her. She cannot move, and consciousness comes and goes. My friend Nemis, who is also a witch and a healer, can do no more for her. And, before you say it, as I know he is not well liked by many, we can't see how Darnley can be involved. He has not visited for weeks."

Bothwell's teeth clamped together as he searched Joshua's face, seemingly assessing whether to believe him.

He had to give more to bring this man to their side. Joshua remembered his mission. "There's a priest, a Father McTavish, who we suspect is behind it. Have you seen a vampire lately?" Even saying it sounded ridiculous to Joshua, but the effect of the magical smoke prevented the subtlety he usually preferred, and with Mary so close to her death, every minute counted.

"No vampire would dare enter this territory." Bothwell harrumphed, then coughed. "But then, I never thought fae would dare to either. I was not very lucid when Mary came, I admit. To be honest, anyone could have come and gone and I would not have noticed. As far as I was aware, nothing happened of note here while she and I spoke."

"The Queen fell off her horse and into a bog on the journey home. That's the only other unusual thing to occur before she became ill. That, and your untimely attack."

"I must go to her." Uncoiling from his chair, Bothwell staggered to the chest at the end of his bed. Flinging it open, he rummaged through his clothes. "When... do you know when she ingested the poison?"

"Around the time she visited here, we think. She has been sick ever since."

"Then we do not have long." As he pulled a shirt over his head with a fluidity incompatible with his wounds, "If my lack of awareness allowed an interloper, a vampire at that, to strike... No! She shall not die. Not under my watch," Bothwell growled. He flopped on the bed and began to push his boots on. "I have also just had word the Prince is taken ill as well. She must know this threat and fight on to bear another heir."

Bothwell entered Jedburgh castle on a horse litter in the dead of night. Saving his strength, he said, but Joshua could smell the stench of his potions wafting on the breeze as he circled above. Once Bothwell was assisted into the small castle by his men, Joshua plummeted down to land behind the stable yard. After he had re-arranged his attire and checked on Jock, he went in search of Nemis.

In the kitchen, a surly baker pounded the day's dough. Joshua enquired - as was expected of all servants - after the Queen's health. The baker said he knew not, only that Lord Bothwell attended the Queen, alone. He grumbled about impropriety, for the queen had only a local clergyman to watch over her while the maids rested. While Joshua wondered where Nemis had disappeared to, the baker crossed himself. "T'will be a long last confession," he moaned, shaking his head. "She's in no state to resist him."

Bothwell or McTavish? Stricken with a sudden fear, Joshua muttered, "God bless the Queen," and dashed out.

Taking the tower stairs to the top floor where Mary's rooms were, he withdrew his dagger and burst in without knocking. The witch knelt by Mary's bedside; his head whipped around to see who entered. Their eyes met and Bothwell's startled look dissolved.

Joshua snapped, "Where's the priest?"

"There was no priest here when I arrived." Bothwell wiped Mary's brow with brisk, economical swipes and continued, "But find your witch friend, and send her up. I have need of some medicine which I will instruct her on how to blend."

Still ill at ease, Joshua glanced around, poked in the cupboards and down the hall. No sign of McTavish. He breathed a little easier while Bothwell vigorously rubbed Mary's arm. The sheets were splattered with bloody effluence, and the chamber stank. As stiff as a board, the Queen lay straight and still, eyes open, staring up at the canopy and apparently ignorant of their presence in the chamber. Bothwell stood, bent over her pale face and whispered something low over her lips.

Joshua froze, memories of Jeffries saving lives by the power of his breath alone swam before his eyes. The mental pictures made him feel uncomfortable, as if he missed something, but what?

The door creaked; Joshua wheeled around, dagger in hand.

Fingers clenched the frame as a spotty, tonsured head edged through the opening. "Begone!" Bothwell shouted. "There is no need for a witness, no impropriety occurs here."

Joshua crossed the room in a few long strides, flinging open the door to reveal the startled monk. Not McTavish. He slid his knife hand behind his back. "You heard what his Lordship said. Go!"

The monk dithered for a moment, sizing up the two strange men in the Queen's bedroom.

Bothwell growled, "Do I need to repeat myself?"

The monk fled.

As Bothwell turned his attention back to Mary, he snarled, "Meddling fools. Do not allow anyone else to enter. The poison's progress will not make for pleasant viewing."

"Are we too late? Can you save her?"

Bothwell glanced at him, crafty with dangerous, dark eyes. "It is well you brought me here in time." He continued his ministrations, pounding his fingers up and down Mary's limp arm. "Hurry! Find your witch and, in my name, fetch guards to the door."

CHAPTER 51

PLOT UNCOVERED

A few days later, the Queen's health improved. After catching her breath on the bed once again, she beckoned for Nemis and Lady Margaret to help her stand. Groaning with every step, her cheeks flushed with the exertion as she staggered across the bedchamber to the stool by the dressing table. Although still weak, Mary had determined to receive her brother, the Earl of Moray, and select members of the Privy Council sitting upright and in the main hall of Jedburgh Castle.

As Nemis brushed out Mary's long red hair, she whimpered as strands caught in the comb.

"Gentle!" Lady Margaret reprimanded.

Nemis apologised. "You are still not well, my Lady."

"She's well enough to show her face in public," Bothwell growled from a chair next to the dressing table. His wounds had almost healed, leaving only a rakish scar across his forehead. "This way, the narrative is controlled and secession guaranteed." He stood and glared scornfully at Nemis, as if to remind her of his political prowess and her low birth.

Lady Margaret tutted underneath her breath. No other servants had been allowed into the chamber since Bothwell's arrival but now he insisted the lady in waiting assist with dressing the Queen so that gossip could be laid to rest.

"Dear James," Mary whispered in a hoarse voice, reaching a pale hand over Bothwell's fist. "After all you have done, the Privy must see I am alive. My son also lives, and all shall be well. That is what matters."

No-one was convinced; both witches knew threats to her rule would continue as long as McTavish and his poisons were still at large, and rumours about the King continued. Lady Margaret, oblivious as she supervised the placement of Mary's headdress, muttered, "All that matters. The Prince."

All those present were all anxious the meeting should go well, yet not tire the Queen so much all their labours would be undone. It was no small comfort Mary hadn't vomited blood or fainted in days now, and was able to eat morsels of food. Better yet, the Queen's mood had improved immeasurably since word arrived the baby Prince James had survived a normal childhood malady, and would be able to be baptised as planned in a few weeks' time.

A rap on the door was answered by Bothwell.

Joshua stood there, smartly presented in a borrowed pages' uniform. "Is her Majesty ready?"

Lady Margaret nodded, then Bothwell addressed Mary. "I will gather the Privy Council whilst Master Meadows escorts you down. Do not leave his side. You do not know him well, but I vouch he is here to ensure no harm comes to you in my absence." Bothwell flashed Joshua a warning glare which spoke of his new obsession over the Queen's safety, then disappeared into the hallway.

Joshua bowed before the Queen. As he stood, he noticed the room seemed brighter, no doubt from the removal of Bothwell's oppressive presence. A talented and powerful witch, who had doubtless been responsible for bringing Mary back from the brink of death over the last few weeks, no-one could accuse him of a comforting, warm manner. Rather, Nemis grumbled after he had described her sleeping draught as 'no more potent than warmed milk', he was as cold, calculating and as dark as his magic.

Mary clung to Joshua's arm as they descended the steep steps of the tower. Nemis followed, then waited for him as he led her into the temporary Presence Chamber. Once seated at the head of an empty long table, the Queen said, "I shall not drink here, fear not." Reassured, and further comforted by two guards at either entrance, Joshua joined Nemis in the hallway again.

"This level of watching over her cannot continue," he whispered. "For sure, when we return to Edinburgh, someone will question who I am and why she has need of a farrier to accompany her everywhere."

"Better you than Bothwell the bulldog," Nemis replied. "And let's hope we go home soon." She glanced down the corridor, checking it was empty. "Lady Margaret told me the King was turned away the other day!"

Joshua nodded. "Darnley was here, but for only a few hours. Bothwell and Moray refused to let him see her."

"Probably wise. She remains convinced he plots against her and was the cause of her sickness. This meeting is to sign the papers putting her crown into the Prince's hands if she dies."

He sighed, weariness and homesick catching up with him in the brief moment of relative quiet and friendly comfort. "I doubt paperwork will stop McTavish from trying again."

Without warming, Nemis inhaled sharply. "Oh!" She staggered against the wall hangings.

Joshua grabbed her waist. "Another vision?"

Her eyes rolled back and her body sagged. Of course, the first chance they were alone and not in Mary's presence, Nemis's tight grip on her visions would relax. He should have foreseen this possibility, after so long holding them at bay! Worse, this area of castle was not designed for privacy; there were no handy side chambers to haul his fitting friend into!

He glanced around, spotting Lord Bothwell appear at the end of the corridor. Behind him, a score of men clutching papers. Without looking guilty of some wrong-doing, the best Joshua could do was put his arm around a wilting Nemis and prop her upright as if she were merely drunk or sleepy. The procession of Lords approached, chattering amongst themselves. Perhaps they wouldn't notice?

He hung his head, jostling her body a little so her head also flopped forward as if bowed. In moments, he knew she would begin to convulse.

He grit his teeth as long robes swooshed past his lowered eyeline, into the hall. When they had all passed, he looked up.

Bothwell had stopped at the chamber's doorway, staring at them both. His eyes narrowed on Nemis, then he pulled the doors closed behind the Privy Council members. "What is wrong with her?"

"A vision, I think."

Bothwell pinched the bridge of his nose and huffed. "Why didn't she tell me about them before?"

"How else do you think we knew about what was to come?" Joshua's patience ran dry. "Can you help me get her somewhere safe? I have a treatment she uses."

Striding towards them, Bothwell frowned. "Does she have them often? Worsening?"

"Frequently enough to be debilitating, but she hasn't had any since the Progress started. I hoped it was because we were here preventing the murders, but...."

Bothwell grabbed her head and yanked it back. He breathed over her lips, a dark wisp flowed over her face. Then, just as fast, he inhaled the wisp. Consternation uglied his eyes. He leaned over Nemis again...

"Stop it!" Joshua cried, pulling her tighter.

"You must concede," Bothwell murmured into her ear. "Give in to the sight to control them."

To Joshua's surprise, Nemis's body tensed. She blinked; her eyes cloudy, swirling with darkness. She shifted in his arm and he felt her bear her own weight. Then gazed around lucidly, although the whites of her eyes were now entirely black.

"Paper... plots...." Her voice sounded steady, measured. Then she ducked into a crouch so quickly Joshua nearly lost hold of her. Her hands flew up to cup her ears.

"An explosion! A fire." She paused, turning her head in another direction as she stood again. "There's Aioffe's knife! Sticking in a back. I'd know it anywhere."

She frowned, head turning left to right, searching. "But... I don't see her?" She gasped. "Too late..."

"Too late for who? Aioffe or Mary?" Joshua said. He gripped her shoulders. Usually by this point in a vision, Nemis's body would begin jerking and writhing as she experienced the pain of the murder. He had to know who was dying!

Nemis mouthed soundlessly, and Joshua began to panic. Her face contorted, and he knew the death sequences she saw were starting to play. Sucking her into their dark web, she could be lost inside them for hours! He had to get them both out of the Palace before anyone saw or heard her screams. Candles in their sconces flickered, and shadows seemed to creep along the walls. Towards him.

"Touch her skin," Bothwell said.

Did he say it? Or were his words a voice in his mind?

It was an order, spoken so softly as to imply a suggestion yet, when Joshua met Bothwell's eyes, his face had a curious cast. Joshua suspected the witch knew something, or had done something which could not be explained. The hairs on his neck rose.

"Touch her now!"

Joshua's heart clamoured, thudding like a hammer inside his chest. Bothwell's lips had definitely moved... this was real, not his own trauma resurfacing. He blinked, and the claustrophobic sensation receded.

But, to interrupt Nemis in the thick of a vision sometimes caused her to lash out. She became a danger to herself and anyone around her.

"You are clearly dear to her, fae. Connected somehow. I have opened her mind, now you must touch her to complete the circle!"

Calling him fae, when he had lived so long among humans, jerked Joshua fully back to the present. Despite the dangerous edge to Bothwell's tone, Joshua hooked his fingertips over hers. Her skin, which was usually clammy when she had a fit, warm and soft to his caress. The tingle of their connection reminded that through touch, he could conduit, sometimes share Aioffe's powers. How this ability could be connected to Nemis was beyond him, but they had shared so much, this intimacy would be forgiven.

She lifted her hand and gazed at his fingers interlaced with her own. "Joshua! She's the bait!"

Her eyelids dropped, her body sagging against his. He withdrew his hand and stroked her hair. "Hush, dear friend. All is well," he crooned, all the while worrying who was the bait? His heart ached - Aioffe had not touched him in so long; was she safe, wherever she was?

Nemis stirred in his arms, as Bothwell tugged on his own short tuft of beard. "There is a plot to rid us all of a pest," he said, then pulled them both away from the wall. "But it is not what, or whom, you think."

Nemis fixed Bothwell with a stare. "It is not Mary who dies next," she mused. "But she is the bait for your plan." She beamed and turned to Joshua. "And she must be the bait for ours as well!"

"A plan for capture hidden in a plot to kill?" Joshua said. "Sounds like something only Fairfax could dream up." He grinned, amazed at the clarity in her recollection. "I tire of being on the back foot. Perhaps it is time to honey a trap."

But Bothwell stepped aside. Keeping his gaze on Joshua, as if he expected him to pounce and cry traitor, he began to walk backwards down the corridor, towards the Hall. "Mary cannot know when, or where. She would never approve."

"There is still a danger," Joshua said, understanding then the witch played a larger, longer and more political game. "I have sworn to protect the Queen until the killer has been caught."

Bothwell nodded, the model of calm efficiency again. "I will send word of when and where." He spun on his boot and marched through the doors.

CHAPTER 52

DANCING

Naturae

The key scraped in the Scriptaerie door then it swung open. "How much longer?" Henry growled at Aioffe as he entered and proffered a cup of deer's blood, still warm.

She took it graciously. When the gaoler offers you food, only a fool would refuse it. She'd learned that much over the years. At least it wasn't cold, dead fish. "As long as it takes."

Henry closed the door then drooped against the door-frame. There was something almost sad in his expression and his aura a moody grey fuzz. She hesitated, then reached out.

"Another turbulent Council session?" She asked, because he had been the one to break their silent stand off.

His hooded eyes slid over her face and he wet his lips. "You could change everything, you know."

"It's not that I don't want to." Really, she was tired of being cooped up in the Scriptaerie. "But for me to do what you want and bless the vines, I need my energies restoring with a Blessing Ceremony. And that would mean letting everyone know I was here."

He stared at her. "There's no other way? I can set you free long enough to hunt? Won't that do?"

Still, there was something he was not telling her. Conflict flashed across his features, twisting them.

"I know a hunt revives your vampiric energies, and yes, I can survive on blood alone, but," she sighed then said, "Imagine: you have to fill a unique bottle with invisible elixir, before you can pour out fae magic. Just as you need to capture a deer, or a person, before you can feed. For a queen, it's not just to quench a thirst, it's what I need to do every time I have to bestow my energy, or Bless. It's exhausting." She didn't mention how depleted she currently felt. She had not given Blessings in so long, or drawn Lifeforce from another, but, to show any weakness was not wise when she was this close to the edge of sanity.

Henry said, "Then how does Illania keep her vines growing? She doesn't do ceremonies."

A shiver of fear chilled her arms. "She does, only not like mine."

He huffed, then looked at her through half lowered eyelids. "Caesaria says it can be done with a few fae."

"That's because her mother drags the Lifeforce out of her fae without them having any choice in the matter! I've seen it. I know. You know. Any fae can drain a human or an animal, and some can take Lifeforce as sustenance from other fae. You saw what happened to Spenser and the Captain, with your own eyes. When the Lifeforce is mostly, but not all, drained from a fae, only a husk survives. Illania can take it either as a trickle or pull it like a flood, and control whether the 'donor' lives or dies as a result."

It wasn't because Aioffe couldn't drain Lifeforce like that. She just wouldn't. She preferred the sweeter taste of freely given strands of Lifeforce which drifted out of a person without them knowing it. Another thing Henry didn't need to know, especially if he was consulting Caesaria. And she still hadn't found a cure for Spenser's condition.

Henry's hand clenched around the doorframe. "A few sacrifices could be made, in the name of the greater good."

The note of desperation in his voice irked her. Were things really that bad here? "And who would you designate to be the victims?" As he looked at the floor, she continued ranting. "Alice the housemaid, or perhaps Pauleus the gamekeeper? How about the Council, being as they seem to trouble you so much." She shook her head. "I can't believe you would even ask this of me. Of the Naturae fae. Every life is precious. Especially when you don't even know if the vines even can recover."

Because he hadn't even let her see them, she too had no idea how far the rot had penetrated.

She turned away from his scowl and stomped into the centre of the Scriptaerie. After draining the cup, she leaned on the table.

"This situation is impossible, Henry. It cannot go on. Either you believe me, or you believe Illania." She back to look at him. "Illania hasn't returned with the sacrifice she promised as a cure, has she?"

Henry gasped. "Not quite..." He jerked his head aside and stared into the distance as if he were pondering a choice.

She thought she knew what bothered him. "And you will never be able to give your heart to Caesaria and make her your true queen. It's just not who you are or who you love."

His lips tightened and she noticed his clenched fists, but continued regardless. "The sooner you accept these facts, the sooner Naturae can move forwards. It took a rebellion for me to learn how to capture Lifeforce and transform it into Blessings. I'd never done it until I was made Queen. I'm sorry, I know no other way than mine. You have to find another solution for yourself."

"I tried. Then, I thought I had one," he said, then flashed dark, sorrowful eyes at her. Before she could ask what he meant, he darted out. The door clicked as he locked her in.

She sighed and tried to calm herself by examining the table top. As she stared at the swirls of the ancient wood, she began to think more rationally. It was all well and good to spell it out to Henry so there could be no misunderstanding, but knowing a problem didn't solve it. How long was it going to take to find the answers she needed?

She had other people depending on her, a family of her own. Just as important. She swallowed the lump in her throat. Being here, away from them, ached. Did her beloved even know where she was? Every night, some hours after Henry brought her evening sustenance she allowed herself a break in scouring the records. She thought of Joshua, and reached for his loving reassurance. The hope of their minds meeting was the only thing which gave her the strength to carry on searching.

Tonight, maybe tonight, would be different. The right scroll would answer her call, and she could send Joshua a mental picture of their reunion. An image of joy at finding the solution. She blinked away the tears of loneliness and wondered why she had become so combative with Henry. It had not been wise, she decided, to spell out the truth to him thus. He'd been angered, and anger clouded judgement. The only thing he could do to change the situation was to set her free, but that didn't solve her problem, or Joshua's problem, either.

Just keep searching, she told herself. That was the plan. The stakes were too high to not complete her task, and being a captive hadn't changed anything, only given her more time to study.

She was just about to take flight to the highest shelves in the cavernous trunk library, when the lock clicked again. Aioffe whirled around, surprise flushing her face. Henry stood in the doorway, his eyes so dark they were black holes in his pale, pinched face. He reached behind and dragged a large bundle in.

"Perhaps he will change your mind."

"Who?"

The sack wriggled. "Is it really her?" Thane's deep voice rumbled. "Our true queen?"

She darted over, fingers untying the rope which secured the opening as fast as she could.

"I apologise for the deception, Thane," Henry said, as Thane's hand burst out of the sack. "It was necessary. If Aioffe does not comply, then the fewer people who know where she is, the better."

Thane dragged the covering off. "My Queen!"

She stood back, grinning so broadly at the sight of her friend her cheeks hurt. "It is good to see you." He looked older, greying, and his musculature seemed smaller as if he wasted away. But, as his twinkling eyes met hers, she knew him no less diminished in wisdom and presence for all the weight he had lost. He reached for her hands, his smile matching her own, then dropped to his knee and bowed his head.

She rubbed his fingers in hers. Both fell silent in their reunion. In his aura, she saw green strands of relief replace the jagged orange of confusion.

Aioffe knew then - she could resist no longer. She was needed here, but there had to be a way she could serve without permanently returning. After a moment, she turned to Henry. "What would you tell them? I cannot return to rule."

He shrugged. "It is time for you and I to dance. There can be no more delay. If anyone can help find a solution, it is Master Thane."

The leader in question exhaled loudly. "Your people will be pleased to see you as I am." He glanced at Henry and Aioffe. "They will be as conflicted as I, though. Nobody wishes to see their Queen unhappy, it serves no fae." He stood from his kneel. "Why are you here at all?" His eyes flicked to Henry. "And why didn't you tell us she was on Naturae?"

"Henry allowed me to search the records here," Aioffe said, wafting her fingers towards the stacks of scrolls. She met Henry's glare and decided it served no purpose to mention her recent captivity. "And it seemed better to keep my presence on the island unknown. I am a target, you see."

Thane nodded. "My Liege told us."

"My being here endangers you all. So, it was better I stayed hidden from everyone while I searched the records."

Her old friend's eyebrow arched.

She continued, "For something which might explain how my mother was involved with a witch. She died over a century ago. And what her death has to do with vampires."

Her fingers traced the whorls on the tabletop as she avoided Henry's gaze. "It's all connected, somehow, to a killer." She met Thane's eyes. "A vampire has murdered queens across the realm. Their deaths, and others to come, were foretold by Nemis, but we don't understand why. And, until the killer is caught, I'm not safe."

"You are safe here!" Thane said. "We can protect you."

She might as well give him the complete picture. "No queen is. I cannot be a queen. Too many lives depend on it. Ambassador Spenser was attacked and lies close to death. Father McTavish, the killer, is clever, a master poisoner. We're trying to find him, to capture him and put an end to it. Joshua, my daughter and Nemis... I fear they are all in danger if we cannot stop him."

She noticed Henry grimacing but carried on. "I'm less concerned about my life. Others, my family, are relying on whatever I can find out. Especially Joshua."

"What's wrong with him?" Thane asked. "Why isn't he here searching as well?"

She swallowed. "When I made Joshua fae, I inadvertently took his memories as well, but their absence is destroying him. When I am threatened, he becomes as weak as a human. I think he needs to be reminded of his past, to know about his mother, a witch, for him to heal. She died on Wrye, not long before I met Joshua."

She chewed on her lower lip as Thane studied her intently. He crossed to the table and pulled out a chair and sat, processing what she said. "But you haven't found anything in the histories here to help?"

Aioffe pressed her lips together briefly, then admitted, "No. There's nothing written down anywhere about that period."

Tapping his finger to his chin, Thane asked, "So the death of his mother was around the same time as your disappearance? Prompting the Great Hunt. I never asked, why did you go?"

Her eyebrows drew closer as she recalled why she left. "We'd argued, again. My mother and I. Our only interactions were arguments back then. She threatened to send me away, to Illania's court, except she was torn. Illania had demanded a piece of the Naturae realm in return for my upkeep. And, my mother didn't trust me to be good and stay with her. Didn't trust anyone."

She sighed. "Then, while we were fighting, a report came in which upset her even more. Something about a crown being lost," Aioffe's hands flew to her head, "but she burned the note before I could see it! Refused to tell me anything else except to accuse me of ignorance."

Thane said, "Is that why you left Naturae? The arguments?"

"I thought, if I could just see some of the realm, I'd understand why she wanted to keep hold of it so much. Political matters, other creatures, didn't seem important, but I should have realised... In truth, I didn't want any part of it. The destiny everyone expected me to have - I was never asked if I wanted it."

"That explains it. You wouldn't know, because you weren't here. Neither was I really, I was too young and just a worker fae. Your mother was too distressed to keep up with records then, and no fae would have written anything down about that time, for we were not allowed to learn faelore." He gave her a gentle smile, seeing her downcast face. "Not until you came into power."

Henry butted in. "Then where could one find out about what happened? The humans would hardly have kept such records, and the vampires would never let a fae read theirs."

Thane shrugged and said, "You would have to ask someone who was around then. I was too young and never left the island." His head bowed. "The Captain is gone, though. The Elders would only know about their territories, and there is no-one representing the other Orkney Islands anymore."

"Spenser would know, perhaps," she said mournfully. "But he's..."

"Unavailable," Henry finished.

All that time wasted. Fruitlessly searching for an answer to saving Spenser's life as well as Joshua's past. She should have thought... Spenser might have known all along what had happened. Something about his situation, his attack, niggled in the back of her mind.

"And Issam and Uffer are... no longer around."

"Uffer!" She cried, then wheeled around to face Henry. "You have to let me go!"

Thane frowned. "Let you go? Uffer lives?"

Henry glowered. "Not until this is resolved."

"I'll come back, I promise!" She must get to Uffer, in Beesworth. Her wings rose. "Let me out, Henry."

"It's not that simple. We had a deal. We are to dance. You have to help." He looked down his nose at her. "Your people need your help, and I'd prefer it to happen willingly."

She inhaled deeply, held in her breath, then exhaled slowly as Thane joined Henry's side.

"Please," Thane said, begging her with his eyes. "You cannot leave us like this." He looked at Henry. "Even though you ambushed me, it was worth the discomfort. I will not betray the trust you have shown me. Letting me see the secret which has been eating at you these past few weeks." He smiled. "You are not as unreadable as you like to think, my liege."

Henry dropped his gaze.

Thane looked uncomfortable. He hesitated a moment, then said, "Henry... you have done well by us, and you are a just and fair ruler. In many ways, you have delivered on your promises to us. But it isn't enough. Your protection, your castle, and the progress we have made to keep the realm stable, despite all these things, we find ourselves again living in fear."

Without acknowledging Henry's glower, Thane's eyes turned to bore into Aioffe. The chastisement she expected would cut, but she stared straight back at him.

He took her hand and said, "My Queen... Aioffe. We cannot exist like this much longer. Under your mother's rule, we feared and we revolted. Chaos ensued. Then, you returned to give us hope again. Do not withhold it now, or history will repeat itself. We will find a way for you and my liege to work together if you cannot, or will not, sit on the throne again. We must."

Aioffe's eyes darted between the pair of them, pleased in a way that they stood united. Once she had thought Thane her ally, save for a moment when he hadn't believed in her. The consternation on his face showed the lengths he would still go to as an advocate of the worker fae. She had to get him to believe in her once more. "I will return as soon as I have spoken to Uffer. I know where he is. A day or two, that's all I am asking for. I can then send word of what I learn to Joshua by kestrel before I return and decide how we go forward." Her heart ached for putting her people through the delay, but she had to be sure her family were safe. They had no soldiers or castles, and they were the ones risking their lives to stop a murderer.

Thane appeared to be considering her suggestion, but Henry's scowl deepened until he looked more like a gargoyle than a person.

Another solution dawned. "While I am gone, I will see if I can replenish myself on human Lifeforce, enough to try to impart some Blessings. It won't be enough, and it's not fae in origin, but at least it's something.

That way, we might know if the vines are sickly, and Illania is right about vinexplicitity, or if they can be saved by simpler Blessings."

Henry's jaw unclenched and he gave a curt nod. "If you do not come back, as promised, then I will hunt you down myself. The fae can fly me across the water, and I can run the length and breadth of the country."

He was a fool if he thought she couldn't disappear, untraceable, if she wanted to, but she nodded. "I understand. May I go now?"

"If it will prompt a swift return, then yes." He stood by the door and gestured with his hand for her to exit first. Thane smiled, and it all seemed as amicable as it could be, for a prelude.

Aioffe tried to walk as sedately as she could along the hallway, but containing her enthusiasm to leave was harder than she imagined. Her feet seemed to dance along and before she knew it, they were through the Atrium and heading for the double doors to the landing platform.

Behind her, Henry said to Thane, "Once she has left, unlock the doors, rejoin the others and say nothing about what has happened." He passed him a large black key.

"I will," Thane replied, as he darted ahead of Aioffe to open the atrium door. "Hurry back," he said to her with a grin.

As he pushed the handle, a hum reached her ears. Aioffe stopped short, but Thane had already opened the door.

On the landing platform, a golden tub sat, gleaming in the moonlight.

"Leaving so soon?" Illania cackled. "I don't think so."

Aioffe looked up. The air was filled with soldiers, like a mottled silvery web of blades and wings. A thousand spears pointed at the doorway.

At her.

Chapter 53

THE WITCH'S WARNING

Sunday, 9th February 1567, Edinburgh

Few people knew where the cunning woman Nemis and her peculiar family lived, and none would dare to visit. They had carefully put around the rumour that a leper sought treatment from her, which was enough to deter most folk from approaching and keep their home a sanctuary. A knock at the door was therefore unexpected. In the middle of giving Spenser a bed wash, Nemis hastily flung the blanket over him. With Joshua and Mark out working, Hope answered the call.

"How dare you?" she cried, when Bothwell strode inside without introduction. He wasn't even the slightest bit out of breath despite the climb.

Nemis exclaimed, "My Lord!" Then frowned. "Why are you here?"

He glowered, flashing dark eyes around the room, skirting over Spenser's body on the bed. As they appraised Hope's face, the tension lines softened. "What a shame such beauty is so marred." He pulled his cape around himself as if it would protect him from their poverty.

Hope hung her head, hands wringing her threadbare skirts. Nemis's jaw clenched as she picked up the wash bowl and stood.

Bothwell's gaze returned to Spenser's obscured form. "What's wrong with him?"

Nemis looked back, and adjusted the blanket so it covered the edge of his wing which, in her haste, she hadn't managed to obscure. "He was attacked. Drained of Lifeforce."

Bothwell sniffed. "What have you tried?"

"The usual tonics and remedies I know of," she said, shaking her head. "It was a fae, but not even the magic of another fae can help restore him to us."

Bothwell leaned over and flipped the cover from Spenser's face. In the evening light, the shadows in his gaunt cheeks made his grey skin appear darker. The witch leaned over and sniffed again, deeper. He exhaled and a wisp of black smoke left his lips. "An infusion of freshly drawn vampire blood might work." He turned his head to address Nemis. "Cut him deep over the heart to pour it in. Directly in, and do not use leeches afterwards."

"I will try," she said. Her heart clamoured at the possibility of her husband returning to them. Years had passed already with no change, but a fae could live trapped forever in the in-between, Aioffe had warned. Her brother Lyrus had suffered the same fate, starving and injured, until he was rescued from where he was buried. Nemis was ready to attempt anything to save Spenser.

Hope said, "What did you come for?"

Bothwell straightened, staring straight at her as if he had forgotten she was in the room. "Tonight, it happens. As promised, I am here to warn you the trap will be sprung." He stood and walked the few short paces to the doorway and Hope.

Nemis saw her shiver as she shrank into the wall. "Where?"

"I have let it be known about court - Mary will be at Kirk o'Fields tonight, where she will pay a last visit to her husband before he is due to move back into the palace, in the relatively unguarded Old Provost's Lodgings. Within certain circles... blood-thirsty ones... the opportunity this provides for access to the Queen is rare and to be taken advantage of. Although I do not know the man you seek, perchance he will take the bait. As I intend to as well." He grinned, but somehow it looked sinister as his dark eyes flashed towards Hope. As they grazed over her slim body, her wings and then back to her flushed face, he said, "You would be wise to stay indoors, pretty one, and forget you ever saw me."

Nemis frowned. "We're ready."

Bothwell replied, "See that you are. Scotland will awaken with a bang to the dawn of a new age. The age of the witch." He sneered. "And fae-kind will not be welcome."

Before Nemis could ask anything else, Bothwell strode out. As his boots clattered down the stairs, Hope slammed the door shut.

"I don't like that man," she said. "He's creepy."

"He is very powerful," Nemis replied, frowning. "But how did he know where we live?" She retrieved her cape from the hook on the wall, then glanced back at Hope and Spenser. "I don't like it. I don't like it at all." As she tied the frayed ribbon, her face paled. "Hope, I think you should leave."

"I don't want to."

"You must. There's something... a wider plot perhaps, which I cannot fathom." The predatory way Bothwell had looked at Hope perturbed her. Nemis went to her husband and tenderly stroked his hair. "For all the hope he has given with a possible cure, I cannot help but worry for you all."

"Why would he harm us?" Hope's voice wavered. "He just offered help."

"Joshua told me it was fae who attacked Lord Bothwell before. He has every reason to despise them. I think he means to drive them - you - all out. He is not known for his tolerance." She squeezed Spenser's cold hand. "If it ends tonight, and we can capture the man we seek, then we should all leave. But you should go now, and not get caught up in whatever plot is to come. Mark can borrow a cart so Spenser can be laid down and hidden. Go to Beesworth, where Mary and Uffer will protect you."

"Have you seen something?" Hope's eyes narrowed accusingly.

Nemis shook her head. "This is purely a mother's instinct. A witch's. I must find Joshua and warn him. Quickly, fetch Mark and be on your way. We'll catch you up on the road, don't worry."

"At least wait with Spenser until we return," Hope pleaded.

"I'll pack while you're gone. Hurry!"

CHAPTER 54

THE TRAP

A murder of crows shot past Joshua and alighted half a mile away, on the Old Provost's Lodging's ridge line, cawing and clucking as they settled on their perch to overnight. He paid them no heed, flying above the track leading from Holyroodhouse Palace to Kirk o'Fields. His day had been spent lurking in the palace grounds, while Mary attended the wedding of two of her favourite servants. Blessed with extraordinary hearing, he overheard one of her handmaidens, one of the four Lady Mary's, say the Queen would spend the night with the King at the Lodgings. Now dressed in warm, dark clothes for camouflage during the clear, frosty night ahead, he watched for Mary's exit like an eagle in the sky. Slung, dangling, across his chest was an ordinary-looking satchel which he always had to hand, containing a selection of tools for day work and a variety of other items in readiness for his night job.

Around nine o'clock when the bells at Kirk o'Fields peeled, he caught sight of the Queen's distinctive red hair, glinting with jewels as she walked the path from the palace. Bothwell, ever-present these days, ambled by her side. She had changed into an elaborate dress more appropriate for an evening's entertainment - the masque'd ball due to begin later, he supposed. The party of courtiers accompanying them were in good spirits; even the witch seemed light of step as the group wound their way along the quiet track to the King's temporary abode.

Mary visited several times a week, but not usually so late at night. Darnley had been ordered to stay put in the undisputed 'cleanest of air in the city' until he recovered from his great pox. To live with her at Holyroodhouse risked passing the painful disease onto Mary, or worse, Prince James. Herbal baths and mercury treatments were rumoured to be working well, and Darnley was apparently pressing to return to her side, and bed.

The Lodgings were unguarded at this time of night, so Joshua waited until the party was admitted before alighting next to a warm chimney breast. If the witch was close, there was less risk to Mary; Bothwell had proved he would lay down his life to protect her. Joshua decided to rest and check his 'Trap Kit' as he called it, just in case.

With slow movements, he shuffled against the bricks and brought his satchel into his lap. He reached inside, touching the items Nemis and he had gathered in readiness. A bottle of holy water to subdue or scald - a shot in the dark really, as they had no idea if it would actually work on such an old vampire. A long silver rope. And of course, a stake. End of game for a vampire.

He rummaged for his main weapon for capture: a net, reminiscent of a large gladiator's rete. Joshua had fashioned the silver and steel mesh over many nights, and practised with it each dawn when he hunted, until he was confident he could use it correctly. Every pennie they had was spent purchasing the raw material. It was weighted at the edges and so fine it folded like silky nightshirt. The weapon could be tossed over a vampire from above or used to wrap him, should he need subduing.

His fingers stroked the soft metal as he stared up at the moon and thought about Aioffe. Was she still wearing the steel panels and silver undershirt they had made? He tired of waiting, following the Queen around in a near constant state of readiness. What if they were wrong about McTavish? About his next target? Was Aioffe in his sights instead?

He reached with his mind, feeling for the reassurance of her mental touch. Although they were hundreds of miles apart, he sensed something different tonight. She was there, yet, unresponsive. Pre-occupied perhaps?

They had not spoken in weeks, not in person, nor by message. Yet, he knew through this nightly touch, she was alive and well, and, he suspected on Naturae. The very instant he could not connect to her thus, he would drop everything in Edinburgh and fly straight there. But the biggest threat to her was McTavish, and he had to capture him before they could be reunited. His eyes snapped open as he heard the door latch.

Mary laughed somewhere beneath him.

"Our last night of freedom," he heard her whisper. "Let's put the newly-weds to bed, then retire ourselves."

Joshua peered over the roof tiles, and met Bothwell's dark eyes looking back up at him. "Indeed," the witch said to Mary, a wry smile spreading over his face as he glanced back to her. "But, after you have put in your surprise appearance at the ball, we should discuss next steps. Stay close and you will be safe."

"Whatever do you mean, James?" Mary scoffed in a low voice. "The King is insistent. He moves back to my side tomorrow, although... he was strangely not upset that I didn't stay with him tonight as planned." She sighed, doe eyes fluttering at him. "How clever you are to give us one more night together."

"Then tonight everything changes," Bothwell said. His eyes flicked up to Joshua again then behind, to the other Lords staggering out of the Lodgings, then back up to Joshua. He grabbed Mary's hand. "To the music..."

They dashed ahead of the group, giggling like a pair of children playing hide and seek, leaving the others to scramble behind them. Joshua leaned back into the chimney, legs braced to spring up into the air as soon as the coast was clear.

As their laughter faded into the distance, his fingers curled, suddenly realising then what Bothwell had done. Everyone expected Mary to stay with Darnley, in the unguarded Lodge. Yet, at the last minute, Bothwell had spirited her away... without any forewarning.

Joshua wondered whether this was an ingenious, or if Bothwell intended, from his eye signals, for him to follow Mary? Was the trap supposed to be tonight? He grimaced. Regardless, he was ready, if a little disappointed Bothwell had not tipped him off. Worse, if the witch's plot was intended to coincide with their plan to catch McTavish, then the double-crossing witch had removed the bait!

He muttered a curse under his breath, and decided he would stay close to the Kirk. So far, McTavish had used poison and there was little to suggest he would change methods. 'Trust the witch,' Nemis had said, and so far, Bothwell hadn't let them down - except for his failure to warn Joshua about taking Mary away from the designated location. That was surely what those significant glances had been about, he told himself. Even if Nemis's vision was correct about the next death being a stabbing, and McTavish somehow ambushed on Mary's way home, then Bothwell would intervene, glued to her side and under the covers of her bed as he was. Joshua had his own task and a tingling in his fingers told him this was the opportunity they had been waiting for.

He checked the group of courtiers had disappeared around the bend in the path, withdrew the silver net from the satchel, then took to the air. His heart raced but the clear, crisp night could not be more perfect for a hunt. Hopefully tonight, their nightmare would end. All he had to do now was keep focused and watch...

An hour later, Joshua considered that perhaps the better place to observe the grounds for a while was perch among the crows on the roof. His fingers were cold from holding the net, and his wings tired as the temperature fell. He was about to swoop down for a rest, when the kitchen door creaked. He frowned; no-one had approached the quadrangle of buildings adjacent to the church and everyone, including most of the servants, had already left the house.

A dark head peered around, followed by the broad shoulders of Darnley's valet, Nelson.

He giggled then dashed out to the south garden. Joshua froze. His heart sank when a few minutes later when Darnley appeared in the doorway. He breathed the night air and cleared his throat. After re-tying his deep red robe, he ambled across the square towards an outbuilding, breathing heavily. "Where are you?" Darnley called in a low voice.

Joshua glanced over the garden. Nelson lounged against a tree trunk. "Our usual spot," the valet whispered loudly. Darnley grinned and changed course. He paused, leaning against the timber corner of the barn and jiggling inside his robe as he stared toward the garden. A determined expression spread over his face.

Just then, Nemis rounded the outbuilding! Before Joshua could ask himself what in heaven's name was she doing here, she ran smack into the king! Darnley wheeled away from the wall and lashed out. The blow he landed sent them both staggering apart. With a cry, Nemis fell onto the mud.

Joshua gasped and quickly stood. He was about to leap down, when he caught a glimpse of something shifting on the other side of the Lodging. His head whipped around, hand clenched on the net. A trick of the light, or someone else? He craned his neck, still the edge of the roof blocked his view. Joshua leaned further, his black wings invisible as they rose, balancing him in readiness.

He stared hard on the one side of the Lodging. The crows suddenly took off, screeching a warning. In the blur of their wings, Joshua was torn – investigate what was happening at the front, or tend to Nemis and Darnley and reveal himself at the back?

"Get away!" Darnley shouted, his words slurred. "Begone with ye. Spying for my wife, are you?"

Joshua looked down just in time to see Darnley weaving over Nemis, labouring for breath as his fist unclenched. She lay curled into a ball, hands to her face, whimpering. He flapped his wings, shot up, banking on Darnley looking down at his prey, then landed behind the outbuilding.

He heard a slap of flesh then she squealed. Tucking the net into his satchel and his wings under his cape, Joshua ran the length of the barn. Reaching the corner, he whispered, "Goody Nemis! I told you, the King has no need of healing now." He spoke loud enough for the pair to have heard, but hopefully not so loud it would alert anyone else to his presence. Nelson was too far away and out of sight in the orchard.

As he turned the corner, he saw Nemis glower at Darnley as she scrabbled away from him in the mud.

Joshua ignored the King and went directly to help her up. "I'm so sorry, your Highness," he said. "She meant no harm. Her concern is only for your health before your return to the Queen..."

Nemis picked up on his cues. She rubbed her cheek. "I see now he's recovered, Master Meadows. Sir," she addressed Darnley, "Your Highness... I beg forgiveness for my intrusion."

Joshua gripped her arm. "I'll see her home," he said, genuflecting towards Darnley as he pulled Nemis backwards.

The King's head tilted back as he drew himself up to his full height, still weaving slightly. "See that you do." He gave them one last, haughty glare down his nose and swaggered towards the garden.

Joshua's eyes followed him until he was far enough away not to hear, before he looked at Nemis again.

"It's tonight, she said quietly.

Joshua reached for the satchel. "I was ready. I am ready. But Bothwell has removed our bait under cover of the darkness."

"He came into our home with the message earlier. But I knew you'd already be watching over her." She touched his hand. "Bothwell surprised us. Frightened us."

"Did he hurt you?"

When she shook her head, Joshua frowned. "Did he see…?"

She nodded. "But he also suggested a cure for Spenser, once he'd breathed him like Jeffries does. One we haven't thought of."

"What?" Joshua growled.

"An infusion of fresh vampire blood."

He swallowed, lips pressed together. The memory of Bothwell's strange scented potions soured in the back of his throat, yet he could not deny he was a healer as good as Maister Jeffries, if not better.

She continued, "So you can't kill McTavish when he arrives."

"I make no guarantees," he said. "It'll be hard enough to catch him, let alone restrain myself for what he has done."

"You must." She released her grip. "Hope, Mark and Spenser are already on their way to Beesworth."

Joshua glanced about the empty yard. "A sensible plan." Together they walked back around the barn, towards the streets.

"We can catch up with them when we have McTavish. Mark has a wagon."

He shook his head. "You cannot let them make such a journey alone. They need you."

"The children are together, and Mark is a man," she said, gently.

Of age officially and outwardly he may be fully grown, but, Mark couldn't change who he was inside. A fighter, he definitely wasn't. Hope regularly beat him at archery and sword play, but she was young and pretty, and no matter how well disguised, often attracted unwanted attention.

"He's still unpredictable and it is a dangerous road for anyone." He reached into his satchel and pulled out the net. Weighing it in his hands, he looked at her through lowered eyelids. "Nemis, you should be with them. Please. It's not safe for you here either." He glanced back in the direction of the orchard. His sensitive hearing picked up intensifying groans of pleasure. "Once the King has finished…"

Her fingers touched her raw cheekbone. The King's rings had left a small cut below her eye. "I know." Her eyes met his. "Will you be safe on your own?"

He nodded. "Go, catch them up."

She turned to leave, but then, a cry rent the air. Joshua jumped up, wings beating to propel him into the sky then he swooped towards the orchard. Another screech, from between the trees!

He saw a hooded figure tussled with the King. A flash of steel glinted in the moonlight. Darnley screamed again. His valet looked on, frozen, naked from the waist down.

Joshua whirled the net, spinning it around his head just as he'd practised. He launched the shimmering web at the hooded figure just as the knife rose again for another slash.

As the silver wrapped about the torso, a shrill, unnatural cry pierced the night. The corner of the net thwacked bare skin on McTavish's face. Only his raised arm remained uncovered.

A second later, before the net could slide off, Joshua catapulted onto McTavish's back. His knees drove into the vampire's torso, punching him down on the frosty grass and, in doing so, shoving Darnley away. He reeled, clutching his chest, both hands around the hilt of a dagger.

Untrapped by the silver net, the vampire's arm twisted on the grass, trying to lever himself up. Keeping his gaze on the loose arm, Joshua's fingers found eye sockets through the metal. "Yield!" Joshua shouted. He pressed, hoping the pain would halt further resistance.

The vampire was strong, jerking his body as he tried to roll the unwelcome passenger off. Joshua's wings beat, pinning him in place. His knees slid to either side of McTavish's chest, gripping and squeezing as he bore down.

He felt ribs crack, such was the force of his assault, but Aioffe had warned him a vampire's bones could be almost entirely broken and they would not die. Once placed again in correct alignment, a vampire could heal astonishingly fast.

"Do you think if you kill me, this is over?" McTavish rasped. "It won't stop..."

Why wouldn't it? "It stops you!" Joshua jabbed deeper into the vampire's eye sockets, fingers tightening around the skull and bore down again.

McTavish shrieked again, the sound dying in his throat as Joshua's wings thrashed. More ribs broke, a hip, and still the vampire wriggled. Being unable to draw breath had no effect, even though Joshua knew his weight combined with the drive of his wings would flatten most people.

"Aioffe... is next. And her heir..."

At the mention of her name, Joshua's wings dropped. His arms ached with the effort of holding the vampire down. He glanced at McTavish's covered face; through the thin web, he saw McTavish sneer. Fury boiled in his blood. How dare he threaten his wife? Murder innocents?

Joshua considered adjusting his hands so they could wring the scrawny neck, perhaps break a few bones there as well, before his strength left him. The vampire's next buck nearly unseated him. He panicked - although he hadn't been submerged by his memories, already he felt himself weakened, as if his fae essence drained by the conflict alone.

It was no use. He'd have to stake him. Another vampire would have to cure Spenser - this one was too dangerous to leave alive.

He moved his left hand so his palm pressed McTavish's chin and, with his right, reached for the satchel. Keeping his eyes on that ever-wandering arm, he fumbled inside...

"No!" Nemis shouted, as she thumped a log onto McTavish's forehead.

Instantly, all the fight left the vampire.

Joshua hung his head, heart thudding in his chest. What had McTavish meant - Aioffe was next? It won't stop? He shuddered, unable to process the threat. He panted, overwhelmed by gratitude for Nemis's action, and that, in the one moment he needed all his strength, he hadn't entirely let himself and his family down.

Nemis muttered a curse under her breath - they had more immediate concerns.

Joshua asked "D... Darnley?"

She darted over to the King's body and cursed again. "He's gone." They glanced around the silent orchard. The valet Nelson, as if released from a spell, tottered towards the Lodging, and away.

"Got to catch..."

Just then, an enormous explosion boomed. His wings jarred as the expulsion of air rolled across the garden. The force of it sent Nemis sprawling to the grass. Shards of wood flew like tiny daggers and missiles, raining down on them. Even though Joshua was already braced from holding McTavish, he instinctively hunched, wincing as debris shredded the thin panes on his back.

An eerie silence fell as if all the air had been sucked from the garden, leaving only the tell-tale smell of gunpowder. Joshua's head swam... that egg-like stench, the boom... Under attack! His arm reached behind, for the bow and arrow which should be there...

"Joshua," Nemis said, although her voice sounded muffled. "McTavish!" He felt something grip his wrist. "You have to stop!"

Soft fingers stroked his cheek. He opened his eyes, expecting to see Aioffe, but Nemis crouched beside him instead. He blinked and looked around.

The Lodging had been flattened, and most of the outbuildings close by had lost their roofs. His hand dropped back to grasp McTavish's neck.

"Bothwell. Making sure he got his target," he panted. "Bastard. He didn't bank on the king's proclivities though."

Nemis crawled over to Darnley. "That blast would have killed you too, if you'd stayed on the roof." She felt over the body, plucked out the dagger and plopped it on the grass.

Joshua stared at Aioffe's knife. The implications of Bothwell's plan clashing with McTavish's murderous plot hardly sinking in as he thought about his wife. Was she ever going to be safe?

Nemis wasted no time, ordering him out of his daze before wrenching the remaining clothes off Darnley. "Secure McTavish tight, and let's be gone before the hullabaloo starts!"

She was right - half of Edinburgh would rush to see what had happened. Joshua grabbed the vampire's errant arm and pulled it back at a deliberately awkward angle. The joint popped and he tucked the limb into the netting. "Make sure the bones stay displaced," he muttered Aioffe's instructions to himself. He remembered how Aioffe had been bound in her cape and left in the casket in St Paul's, and figured McTavish knew something about how to subdue supernatural beings. The technique of hog tying seemed like it might work on a vampire as well, so he pulled the rope out and trussed the body up tight.

He finished a few minutes later, by which time Nemis had propped a naked Darnley against a tree. She diligently rubbed her fingers over his numerous stab wounds, whispering under her breath. Under her touch and spell, the cuts disappeared, leaving his body strangely mottled with milky white marks between the purple-red syphilis lesions.

"At least it looks more like a natural death now," she said. "Rather than being stabbed, which screams foul play."

"There's nothing natural about being blown up either, but we haven't time to dismember him as if he'd been caught in the blast."

Joshua threw a last quick glance around the orchard as he bundled the trussed up vampire over his shoulder. Nelson had been thrown clear across the garden and lay, neck broken, in the middle of a rather fetching flowerbed of bluebells. Joshua felt a moment's pity, wondering if the valet had been a pawn, mesmerised by McTavish to lure the King outside with the promise of sexual favours and leaving the Queen alone in the Lodging. He wasn't sure why Darnley had been stabbed, if he was the intended victim at all. The attack had been frenzied, so perhaps McTavish was enraged at Mary's disappearance?

Either way, he doubted the pair's deaths would be much mourned.

"Ready?" Joshua called over to Nemis. She looked around, tears filling her eyes. "He killed a King, but not a Queen." Her shoulders dropped with relief. She stood, hands easing her knees as they straightened, then her eyes narrowed. Bending down, she picked up Aioffe's knife. "Did he mean to implicate her, do you think?"

"We'll find out. Rage makes a man do vile things. Perhaps that's what happened here. Uffer can make him talk."

His skin itched, as if he were being watched, but a quick glance around suggested it was simply his nerves. He heard shouts in the distance, men calling for each other and women wailing their worry. They had to get away though, before the area swarmed with witnesses. He held out an arm and she nodded. "Let's find the children," he said. "Come, I can bear two burdens for a short flight."

"Stay low though, in case he revives and you have to drop him to knock him senseless again."

"I planned on dropping him from a very great height if that were to happen," Joshua said, and smiled. "I'm fairly sure vampires don't bounce, but I'm willing to experiment."

Chapter 55

AMBUSH

Naturae

Henry snarled, "What do you want?"

Sat up in her transport, Illania's cherubic cheeks flushed as she pouted theatrically. "Why, is that any way to greet your mother-in-law?" A thin eyebrow rose on her forehead. "I'm sure I've told you before, Henry, I won't tolerate rudeness from your kind."

Aioffe took a pace towards the Queen, but Henry caught her arm then edged himself in front of her. "Answer the question."

He felt the brush of Aioffe's skirt as she stepped around him and stood at his side while he glared. Dammit, why had he locked all the soldiers in the High Hall? Henry withdrew the curved throwing blade from its holster.

"Queen Illania," Aioffe said. "What a surprise to see you here."

"One might say the same."

Aioffe lifted her hand to the sky, filled with sharpened spears. "Is all this necessary, though?"

"One never knows," Illania replied, "what kind of welcome to expect, from a vampire." She beckoned with her finger and attendants rushed over. "I am distinctly underwhelmed this time, however. Not even a pair of guards on your marvellous castle!" She tutted and waved her troops to descend.

Henry and Aioffe shared a panicked look while the servants helped Illania out of the tub. His heart sank. All that time wasted, trying to make peace with himself over killing her in the name of duty, and now Illania would no doubt revel in informing Aioffe of her destiny. The only good thing was the rest of his fae didn't know Aioffe was here, save Thane. Hopefully, he could simply claim the glory of restoring the vines himself.

Illania waddled towards them, a snide smile on her face. "I'm glad you didn't bother with a show of strength again, Henry. We are family, after all. Now, where's my daughter, the Queen?" She sniffed.

He waited until all her soldiers were on the ground before he said, "Otherwise occupied." Then he grunted, "And she is not yet queen."

At that moment, Caesaria's howl of frustration echoed from across the forest. Illania froze, her lips rubbing together as she ruminated silently.

Henry could hear Aioffe's heartbeat next to him, pounding. "You did not bring me a sacrifice," he said. "However, as you can see, I have the matter in hand." His arm shot out and grabbed Aioffe. He knew his face must betray his conflict, but there was nothing to be done about it. She had to comply.

"You... you meant..." she said. Her skin paled and her fists balled.

"I'm sorry," Henry said. "Truly. If there was any other way."

"Foolish boy," Illania said, then cackled. "I would never expect you could take royal fae blood for the vinexplicitity."

Henry gaped. "I thought..."

Illania's blonde tresses bounced as she roared with laughter. "A vampire.... Sacrificing a fae queen? Oh no, that's too funny. You creatures have a hard enough time dispensing with the banrigh and humans. Why would you ever think you could win against a fae queen?"

Aioffe gasped, then kicked Henry, hard, in the shin. He had to admit, he deserved it. She ripped her arm away from his grasp, spinning away and snatching his throwing dagger with her other hand. He frowned and snarled at Illania, "Then what?"

"I told you, minor royalty will do." Illania shrugged. "Dear boy, a delivery is on its way..." She tipped her face towards the moon. "Any moment now..."

Henry's eyes narrowed. The night sky was clear and crisp. From this height, one could see for miles, but the darkness was empty save twinkling stars.

Aioffe huffed. "I cannot believe you, Henry Fitzroy." She blasphemed as she stomped away from him and past Illania. She peered over the railing, tucked the knife into her belt as her wings rose.

Illania tittered. "Don't leave on my account, my dear. This will be a triumph for fae-kind. Don't you see?"

Aioffe shot into the air without a backward glance. He had never seen anyone fly away so fast, understandably. Would she return? He doubted it now, and cursed to himself for having delayed so long. He rounded on Illania. "What have you done?"

Her eyes rose to the sky and she held up a finger. "There they are. Wait...." She shuffled back to her tub, attendants dashing over to help her in.

He scanned the treeline. Aioffe had entirely disappeared south, but in the distance to the north, four fae flew towards the citadel. Between them, like the hub of a wheel, a body dangled by its limbs. Henry stepped back, aghast, as they slowed, then swooped across the landing platform.

Illania's guards picked up their poles, ready to lift the chariot. The body bearers hovered before Illania to display their prize. Henry caught a glimpse of Lord Darnley's dead, white face.

"Don't leave him here!" She peered closer, then leaned out of the tub and poked the corpse. She sighed. "He's not meant to be that dead, but he'll do if we need more blood." She gritted her teeth and scowled. "I'll need Aioffe's powers of restoration."

She squawked, flapping her arms to shoo them away. "Take him straight to the Pupaetory, you dullards."

The guards whisked him back up, but, "Where is the other one?" Illania shouted.

"Nowhere in sight, your Highness," one called back. "We left them looking."

Mouth agape, Henry's first thought was relief. His second, what in heaven's name had happened in Scotland?

"Well, come on then!" Illania said, flicking her beady eyes at Henry. "She'll turn up, eventually. What are you waiting for? Go and get Caesaria. Bring a few fae with you. Since he's dead already, we'll need to inject some life into him first. Aioffe won't get far, and together, we can perform a royal resurrection of sorts."

His fists clenched as he floundered for what to say. How could he keep her here to give Aioffe a chance to escape?

Then, as she rearranged herself in the tub, four more fae soldiers fluttered towards the palace. Empty-handed. They exchanged looks of commiseration with Darnley's bearers as they passed, then set down at the edge of the platform, as far away from Illania as possible.

She glowered. "Where's Mary?"

The cohort bowed their heads, studying the wood and shuffling.

"Well?"

One of them shoved another forward. He glanced at Henry, desperation on his face, then lowered his head again.

Illania's fingers curled. "Where. Is. Mary?"

"We searched. Everywhere. But she wasn't to be found." The soldier shrugged, terror whitening his lips as he mouthed helplessly. "N... n... nor was the priest."

Illania screeched. "Fie!" Her fingers straightened and then tensed. Her eyes closed as the guard cried out. His limbs shot out from under him and he seemed to crumple at the middle. His scream was cut off as he dissolved into ash. Illania's arms moved, pointing her digits at the remaining messengers.

But he was too late to intervene. Illania leaned back in her tub as if pulling, her fingertips waggling as she drank the life from another messenger. Her face flushed puce before her arms dropped to her sides, leaving only piles of ash on the wood. She pulled in a breath, and her skin seemed to sparkle. Then, her arms rose and rotated towards Henry.

The doors behind him creaked. Thane and a cohort of his soldiers peered out with horror. Now he understood what Aioffe meant by how Illania took Lifeforce from her fae, the possibility of what she could do terrified him. "No!" Henry cried. He darted to the doorway. "Fetch Caesaria," he ordered, opening the doorway wide enough for Thane and a few guards to launch themselves into the air.

Then he slammed the doors closed, shutting his people away. "No more, Illania." He glared at her as she frowned at Thane's retreating wings. "Or your daughter will pay."

A furious Illania shrieked as she turned her head towards Henry. The shrill sound was unearthly, unnatural.

Henry stood firm, balanced on the balls of his feet and ready to dash straight for her. He was reasonably certain Thane understood his message. Besides, with his speed, he could rip off Illania's head before her guards even drew their swords. Being flightless, speed was about his only advantage.

For a heartbeat, they stared at each other.

He smelled Caesaria's approach, like a stagnant pool of water bursting its dam. Illania gasped as the Princess wriggled in the air, caught between six fae like a skewered eel. She was thrust beside Henry, wings clamped and wrists bound. Thane and his men kept a tight hold on the pole threaded through her captive elbows. Her feet were still fettered, and her hair hung about her snarling face in a shambles. Caesaria screeched, "Mother!"

Lightning fast, Henry's fingers flew up, unerringly finding the soft point between jaw and neck to grasp. She squeaked as he squeezed tight and dragged her head in front of his chest. Her wings beat against her restraints as he held her cheek to his jowl.

Illania's jawbone jutted forward.

"How much land is she worth?" Henry guessed. "More than Aioffe would have fetched?"

The Queen puffed through her nose, fury steaming off her red cheeks.

Then she turned to Henry, and said quite calmly, "We could have been neighbours, if not family." She commanded her bearers to lift her with a flap of her hand. "But for incompetence." Her eyes narrowed. "You really have no idea, do you?"

"I know family matters. She matters." He shook Caesaria, who yelped.

"I have another daughter."

"Mother!"

Caesaria's strangled utterance would not release Henry's pressure to her throat, not for anything. But the value of his leverage was made clear when Illania dismissed her daughter's distress with a waft of her hand.

"It's clear she has not achieved what she was supposed to." Her face darkened. "But I will have what we came for."

"You shall not take Naturae," Henry said in a loud voice which would carry to his soldiers behind the door.

"If I wanted Naturae, I'd have taken it years ago. Too small for what I need." She laughed, low and sinister. "If you weren't so young, you'd know."

"It is land you want, isn't it?"

"Oh, and far more."

"Europe is your realm. Why can't you settle there?"

Illania's lips drew back in a grimace and she bared her teeth. "Because of your kind. It takes time to grow an army." She arched an eyebrow at him and hissed. "Space to train. To fight back."

Hairs on the back of Henry's neck prickled a warning as Caesaria wrestled against his grip. Why would Illania need another army? She had platoons of mottled green-winged soldiers, more than adequate for repelling simple attacks. More than Naturae had. Besides, there had been peace between creatures since the Sation wars.

"Choose your side, vampire." She glanced at her daughter, then with a flick of her fingers, she bade her bearers rise to a hover. "For chaos and war will come. It's too late to stop it now. The signs were there years ago, for those who were looking. I've merely hastened matters along." Her eyes glinted. "If you want to keep Naturae's throne, you're either fae or vampire. You cannot be both."

She clapped her hands. "Now! Drop everything except your weapons. Find Aioffe!"

The golden tub, followed by the rest of her people, swarmed into the dawn sky. Henry's stomach dropped as he put the pieces together. Those lights in the night, Fairfax's fears, Nemis's visions, Naturae's vines prepared for transport in barrels... he should have listened. Should have seen the ill portends hidden in all the royal deaths. He frowned. There was more to come, and it took him a moment to play the game out in his mind.

He cursed when he saw how it might unfold, for him and for Naturae. Aioffe and Joshua, he realised, had been too distracted by the knight, when the match was really about king and queen.

And now, he had failed to keep Illania here, where she could cause the least harm, because he'd been afraid of what she could do to his fae, the pawns. Many more lives would be lost if there was a war between their kinds. Why had he not jumped and throttled her when he had the chance? His chest tightened; only one hope remained. Much as though it would cost him personally, any delay would cost far more.

"Fetch me a kestrel, now!" He ordered Thane, then thrust Caesaria back to the guards. "Lock her back up. She's a prisoner of war." He stormed into the High Hall, shouting, "Awake! Arm yourselves!"

CHAPTER 56

THE BANRIGH

Beesworth

Once Joshua, Nemis and a bundled-up McTavish left Edinburgh and reunited with Hope, Mark and Spenser on the way south, they journeyed through night into dawn, and all the next day. They stopped only to feed the horse, and once, when a kestrel was spotted by eagle eyed Hope, to send a quick message ahead. Their exhausted nag managed to drag the wagon right to the bottom of the Hanley House hillock before stumbling to its knees. Mark, sat on the front bench with Hope and Nemis, crowed, "I said he'd make it!" The horse nickered as if to say, 'I'm done.'

Wedged in a hollow between hay bales with McTavish and Spenser lying prone beside him, Joshua sent a prayer of gratitude up for their safe arrival. Thankfully, few travellers or robbers bothered with what appeared to be peasants on their way south, and their progress to Beesworth had been uneventful, if bumpy. A stubby branch tumbled from his fingers, then he rubbed his aching biceps. The stump had served its purpose well, held aloft as the cart rumbled the many miles south, ready to batter McTavish's wrapped head whenever he stirred. The silver net was now hardly visible through the congealing blood all over the vampire's skull, but, keeping him unconscious was the only way to ensure everyone's safety. Joshua clenched and opened his hand a few times to relieve the cramp, before he stood and peered over the top of his hidey-hole.

Uffer plodded down the hillock towards them, raising his arm in greeting.

"I'll find Lady Hanley," Nemis said, standing and stretching. She glanced into the hay hollow, eyes appraising her husband's inert form. "I hope she has some human food in the house." The provisions she'd packed for herself and Mark had been demolished long before they passed Newcastle hours earlier.

"Mark," Joshua said, as he nudged McTavish in the ribcage with his foot, pleased by the lack of a moan in response. "Are you able to settle the horse while we get *this* to the stables?"

Hope yawned. "Papa, I need to hunt."

"Can you wait until it's full nightfall? The sun has only just set, and people might still be about."

She pouted, her face drawn and pale from tiredness, but gathered her skirts to step down from the wagon.

Joshua sighed.

Uffer arrived, puffing as he jogged down the hillock. "We got your kestrel. I've readied a stall, and a bed for the Ambassador." He began to pull the bales off; a grim look fell over his face as he noticed the bloodied net. "The sooner we get answers, the sooner we'll all be safe."

Joshua glanced over McTavish's inert body, resisting the urge to boot him again. "If you can carry your father up, Mark, Uffer and I can manage him."

Joshua pulled the edges of the net from McTavish's face and swiftly tied on a blindfold. The vampire's skull had already begun to reassemble since its last clobber on the cart, but his arms and legs were re-tied around a sturdy chair in such a contorted way the bones couldn't knit back together. The pain must be excruciating, Joshua thought, recalling the state he'd been in after Lyrus attacked him. Both creature-kinds could heal, and quickly, but the agony of re-growth was bad as it would be for humans.

He waited patiently, sipping on a cup of rabbit until the vampire roused. Uffer sat next to him, improvised torture instruments jiggling in his hands.

"Blood...." McTavish whispered.

"No." Joshua wet his own lips with the last of the rabbit. "Not yet."

Might as well dangle a little hope, even if he had no intention of supplying it. Rather, once he had the confirmation he needed, McTavish would be the one supplying the blood - for Spenser.

McTavish's lips curled into a lopsided sneer. "She'll find me."

"Who will?" Joshua glanced at Uffer, who shrugged.

"She always does. She knew it was meant to happen... yesterday?"

"Day before. I don't know who you mean, but if you tell me, I'll see if there's some more blood available."

McTavish shook his head and gave a weak chuckle, which ended in a raspy cough.

"I don't see what's funny," Joshua said. "You've failed. Queen Mary lives. So does Aioffe."

The vampire snorted. "They won't for long."

"Let's start with why, shall we?" Joshua asked.

The vampire huffed from his nostrils. "What's the point?"

"Why attack Mary? Or Aioffe?"

"I can't expect someone like you to understand," McTavish sneered. "You're as much of a pawn as I am in the game."

"Make me understand, and I'll think about some blood." Joshua paced around the chair, checking the knots. "I've got nowhere else to be, and we can do this for all eternity. Imagine - the pain I'm sure you're feeling, and the hunger, lingering forever, while my friend and I wait for you to tell me what I want to know."

The vampire's head revolved towards the sound of Joshua's voice. "There's nothing you can do that's worse than what *she* does. She'll find us before long, and then this will all be over."

Joshua's fingers curled into fists. As he suspected, agony was something this creature could endure. There had to be another way to break him. He pointed to the blindfold.

Uffer stood, clinking the instruments together in one hand. With the other, he grabbed the vampire's grey hair and yanked it back.

A hiss left McTavish's lips.

"Eyes first?" Uffer said, evenly. "Because once an eyeball's out, there's no putting it back in. Not even a vampire can re-grow it."

"Fine by me," Joshua replied. It was a good job McTavish was still blindfolded; the shudder which ran through Joshua would have betrayed his revulsion at the prospect of popping out an eye.

Uffer's fingers crept down McTavish's pale face, inching inside the fabric wrap.

McTavish's lips pressed together. Joshua saw his limbs shake under the net.

Uffer replaced his fingers with just a hint of cold metal underneath the cloth. "Who will come?" He pressed the tip of Aioffe's knife on top of the cheekbone.

"No..." McTavish wrenched his head away from the silver touching his skin with a little gasp, and Uffer let him. His head swivelled and shook, trying to avoid imaginary claws seeking to pluck.

"Tell me why, then," Joshua said. He gripped the vampire's jaw and held it firm. Uffer pressed the blade to his cheek, inching it up towards the blindfold again.

"I don't know!" McTavish gasped. "I don't. I take who I'm told to."

Joshua believed him, but... "You're not making me understand, Father." Uffer edged the blade closer to the vampire's eyes.

"I want to help you," Joshua said. "I really do. I hate being on the outside looking in. Not seeing the full picture. But," he gave a dramatic sigh, "my friend here will take away your ability to see at all, unless you start talking."

He glanced at wriggling arms, yet still the vampire remained closed-mouthed. The rope and knots held fast, but he had the sense McTavish was afraid of what, or who, was coming. Certainly, he wasn't afraid of pain, or of what Joshua could do. "For years you have been killing queens for someone else, if you are to be believed. Haven't you ever wondered why?"

"Of course I have, you fool," McTavish said.

The door at the back of the barn creaked. The vampire started, wrestling against his bonds even harder in desperation to escape. Joshua's head whipped around as he inhaled. His heart beat faster when his nose caught a faint scent of fir and witch hazel.

McTavish's voice was shrill, "But in the scheme of things, I'm nothing. I'm no-one."

Aioffe and Nemis tiptoe'd towards them. His wife's face was flushed with exertion, but her expression brightened with relief as she scanned the trussed up captive.

Uffer glanced at Joshua, a twinkle in his eye, then said to McTavish, "If you're nothing, then no-one will miss you."

Aioffe said softly, "No-one would know what you have done either. I don't know why you are bothering to keep him alive. He's worthless. Just a miserable old vampire who no-one will miss."

McTavish stiffened, a hiss escaping from his lips.

"I suppose we are wasting time here." Joshua let go of McTavish's jaw. "Save your energy, my friend, this one won't say anything of value."

As Uffer withdrew Aioffe's dagger from the vampire's neck, he said, "If you're not going to tell us who's coming or why you killed them, say your final prayers, priest. Would you prefer I use a stake, or do you think he should suffer as he goes?"

Joshua took a deliberate step away, noticing Aioffe then looking confused. He inclined his head towards an array of bottles on a window ledge and mouthed 'need his blood' to her.

McTavish's lips clamped, his head turned from side to side as if he could see what was about to happen but didn't know where the fatal strike would come from.

"A stake is quickest, then we can go," Aioffe said, passing Joshua the pointed weapon from her satchel. "Unlike poison, there's less mess to clear up afterwards."

Joshua placed the point over McTavish's heart. "Still, I would have liked to have known how a vampire could have killed a queen without being discovered, if not the why." He injected a note of admiration into his voice. "It takes a great deal of patience, I'm sure, to bide your time, like you did with Queen Mary of England. In the name of making her death plausible, I presume."

He leaned in so McTavish would feel its tip ready to pierce despite his squirms. "But some deeds deserve ignominy. Mary's death was written off as natural. Nobody can claim the credit. No-one but us will ever know it was you, even though you may have some skill with poison."

"*Some* skill? Ha!" McTavish scoffed. He drew his chin back as if retreating from the stake on his chest. "No-one else but a master could have achieved what I did. My deeds are worthy of respect; my name should invoke terror."

The vampire's ego was his weakness, Joshua realised and retracted the stake. "One queen," he goaded, "that's all you managed to kill. Someone of your talent could have managed so many more..."

"She wasn't the first, nor the last." McTavish fell silent, his mouth twisting as if he wanted to elaborate but couldn't find the words.

"Such a shame no-one will hear of you then," Joshua said. "The priest who killed a queen, that's the sort of tale which should fall into legend. Like Julius Caesar's demise made Brutus's name, or Thomas Becket enshrined Henry II into history. Your name, your deeds... no-one will know."

McTavish's lip curled. "Release me!" Seized with a surge of energy, the vampire rocked his chest, wrenching against the chair and constraints.

His shout frightened Nemis, who shrank back against the stable wall. Joshua put his hand on the vampire's shoulder, stake against his heart, while Uffer clenched his instruments.

"Of course, I could always write down your deeds... if you wanted me to. For posterity," Joshua offered. "I cannot guarantee they would be read about, but at least someone would know."

McTavish seethed. "My name alone should bring fear into people's hearts. I have slain hundreds, but none so significant as the queens. Who else could kill a *banrigh* of witches, a Queen of England, and Mary de Guise? As each crown fell, it should have been known who mastered their demise."

Joshua tutted. "Quite the list... I'm not sure I believe a wretch like you capable."

The vampire wrenched against the chair, rocking it.

Aioffe's eyes flared. "This *banrigh*, the witch, what was her name?"

"Ha! Discovered the connection finally, and think you have all the answers?" He grunted towards Joshua.

"Mary Smythson?" Aioffe said, looking at her husband with wide eyes. "Did you kill her?"

Nothing could have prepared Joshua. He reeled away from McTavish, fingers clenched around the stake so hard, they turned white.

"By mistake."

Scorn soured Aioffe's voice, piercing Joshua's thudding heart. "Killing Tarl Smythson's mother, was 'by *mistake*'?"

"She was accused of witchcraft, so it was only a matter of time before she would meet her death anyway. Before the tide of public opinion came dragged her into a formal trial, I went to visit her at the forge. Just to see." His head dropped and he mumbled, "I only meant to drink of her, taste her magic. I didn't know she was the banrigh. But she resisted. Bitch. Blinded me with a spell."

Aioffe touched Joshua's arm and he felt the wisp of her calming warmth enter, soothing his panic and grief. She glanced at Nemis, who whispered, "Then how did she die?"

McTavish drew his lips back then snarled, "There was a set of knives on the mantle. I stabbed her to break the spell. Then, she ran out. Disappeared."

"My... mother?" Joshua stared at Aioffe.

She nodded. "The first of the..."

"Queens," Joshua finished. The less information about Nemis's powers McTavish knew, the better.

The vampire demanded their attention, eager to gloat. "Her body washed up on the shore, days later apparently. A witch should never have been buried on sacred ground, but I had already left to seek treatment, not knowing she died in part by my hand. By the time the Council ordered my return, still blinded, her grave had been filled. *Someone* had convinced the authorities her sins should be overlooked." McTavish's head revolved towards where Joshua stood. "*You* then dared to steal from the church to pay for it."

"A price he paid highly for," Aioffe said. Her fingers squeezed his arm, but all her love could not prevent the pain of memory returning.

Her touch brought back the pent-up rage instead. He lashed out, whacking the vampire around his head with a muscled forearm. McTavish's neck cracked and his skull kinked to the side at an unnatural angle. His body slumped as consciousness left.

Joshua fell to his knees, clutching his forehead. Grief and shame washed over him as if her death had just happened. He blinked wet eyes and swallowed the lump in his throat. He felt as if everyone was looking at him, failing to keep his emotions in check, as he stared at the floor. His mother... who had soothed his pains with her herbs, lulled him to sleep with her songs. How could she have been the queen of witches and he not know?

And yet, the more he remembered of her, the more it made sense. She was frequently away, returning ablaze with an energy he had put down to love for her family. On nights which had significance to the faith, she had always made excuses not to attend church. And, in a cupboard, she kept a wooden crown, inlaid with silver symbols, which he used to play Kings and Queens with as a boy.

"Uffer," Aioffe asked, while McTavish was still unconscious, "What can you remember of that time? My mother. It was just before I escaped, before the Great Hunt."

The old fae frowned. "I was in the Beneath, most of the time then. After the Sation War where I served as a soldier, as you know, I became the Lord Anaxis, Keeper of the Beneath. I wasn't part of the Hunt; my job was to deal with those who had failed to bring back information on your whereabouts." He hung his head, a more unsuitable, gentle person to be a torturer, no-one present could imagine. "You can see the irony when Lyrus docked my wings for subversion. 'Tis a wonder Mary Hanley has forgiven me."

Aioffe glanced at the still inert McTavish. "There must be something. A rumour, or anything you heard from the spies about what was happening on the other Orkney Islands."

He blinked as he thought. "There was talk of an... imbalance." He moistened his lips. "Of course, Queen Lana hadn't been to any Gatherings for centuries. The humans had stopped believing by then, since the Catholic church had taken grip. There were still witches, mind, who continued their rituals on the solstices. Powerful ones, which your mother knew well. They maintained the balance on the islands, between creatures. Their presence, and adherence to the old ways, kept the influence of the vampires in check." He shrugged. "But they ceased holding their meetings... yes, possibly around then."

Uffer's gaze slid to Nemis. "Ambassador Spenser would know more. He was frequently on Naturae, then away to Europe, then back again. Quite puffed up with importance, in those times, I must say." Then his eyes narrowed on McTavish, squirming as he roused. "If the witch's leader, the banrigh, had been killed, it would explain why. Any absence of authority and vampires fill the gap. They rise no matter how much we resist."

McTavish rasped, "Of course my kind would rise." His head righted itself. "We are superior to witches, for all their magic. We are far more orderly and live longer. Even blind, surviving the banrigh's attack and drinking of her blood made my name, in vampire circles. I was the one who lived. I was glorious, untouchable, but..."

He fell silent, until Uffer prodded him with the dagger. "You aren't untouchable now. Speak, or die for your sins. My friend here has plenty more punches and we have as long a life as you."

Bitterly, McTavish said, "Maybe you're right. Long lives leave a trail. You can change your name if you like, Tarl Smythson, or whatever you are called now. Hide what you were and what you did, but the consequences of your actions live on." His shoulders shrugged. "I embraced my name, in the hope of protection by virtue of my reputation. Perhaps that's how she came to find me. My mistress swept me up when the Church had written me off and all but forgotten what I had done. She restored the gift of my sight with her powers, before demanding payment. In service to her, I would kill people of significance, rather than the nameless many I had killed before as a crusader. She promised me eternal notoriety. That my deeds would enshrine Blind Bill's name in history. I would be immortal, in every sense."

CHAPTER 57

KNIFE EDGE

"Confess, priest, and I shall write of your deeds," Aioffe said. "Your name will be recorded then."

She sensed McTavish's edginess was being overtaken by eagerness as he moistened his lips, then said, "Do you swear to protect me from her?"

"I promise nothing else, but to tell your tale, Blind Bill. The next to die by your hand was Queen Mary of England?"

"Easy. She wanted a babe and would take any tonic to help bring her one." McTavish proudly smirked. "A simple matter of small doses over a number of months, and the 'canker' grew. My own special blend of toxin. Shame she had enough time to name her successor."

Joshua seethed. After exhaling loudly through his nose, he said, "Queen Elizabeth."

"An unwed, childless halfling, who sadly did not like priests. I had no choice but to strike at her on a religious, ceremonial occasion where my presence would not be noticed." McTavish half-smiled. "A fast acting poison, designed for maximum impact. It should have caused pandemonium," he crowed. "Then England would have thanked me for liberating them from such a queen, and the vampire council. The Catholic church would glorify me for ridding them of a heretic."

McTavish was enjoying boasting about his exploits a little too much, Aioffe thought. "Except she didn't drink it," she said scathingly. "At the coronation."

The killer's head drooped. "My mistress was most displeased."

Aioffe frowned. "But you didn't stop trying."

His lips rubbed together. "I received other orders. My next target - Mary of Guise"

"As a priest and healer, you were again granted access," Joshua said, stiffly.

McTavish nodded. "A swift and merciful end. Another crown fell, to bring her daughter back from France."

"Then why did you attack me?" Aioffe asked. "Was I on your list?"

He gave a lopsided shrug, his arms still trapped by the net and rope. "A twist of fate in my favour. When we met in York, while I awaited news of Queen Mary's demise from London, I knew who you were. After a century, you were still playing an insignificant, displaced fae, dabbling in the affairs of daemons and humans, but I'd heard of your rise and fall from your realm. I told my mistress I knew of your whereabouts, thinking it would be of interest. She suggested I could kill you, but, she would not order it."

He grimaced. "But I warned you I was coming. A tease I could not help but relish the writing of, to whet my anticipation of the day we would again meet. By the time I returned to York, perhaps unsurprisingly, you'd gone. I didn't worry; I knew I would find you at some point. I knew your smell and no-one escapes me when I mark them. I lost track of you, while I dealt with my next target, Mary de Guise. After I dispatched her, I went to London to try for Elizabeth again. In the bear pit where she was supposed to go, I saw you with him." McTavish jerked his head towards Joshua. "Knowing my mistress desired your demise but for some reason wouldn't order me to do it, I hoped your death might be sufficient to release me from the chains of my debt."

Joshua growled, "To whom? Who is your mistress?"

The vampire babbled on, lost in his own reminiscence. "I was determined to present you to her before she heard of my second failure with Elizabeth. I followed you, waited until you were alone in the records office to capture you. I only left for a few minutes to fetch a special potion I had brewed which would overcome your innate immortality. But again, in the chaos of the storm and fires, you disappeared." He shook his head. "I should have known it wouldn't be easy to kill a fae. Her wrath, when she learned of my error…. She will finish me when she learns of Mary of Scotland."

Aioffe glanced at her husband, flushed with gratitude once again that he had saved her from what was probably an agonising fate. "You tried to kill Queen Mary several times."

"And yet she still lives," Joshua said.

McTavish mumbled, "That queen surrounds herself with murderers. Witches. If I didn't get to her, one of them will before long."

"Bothwell protects her," Joshua said.

The vampire snorted. "He'll break her heart and spirit. She should wish for a painless death by my hands."

"The poison you gave her wasn't painless at all," Nemis said. "She nearly died at Jedburgh."

"Her poisoning, during her Progress, was your first attempt, wasn't it?" Aioffe said, thinking of the night when David Rizzio had been killed, when they thought Mary was the one in danger. "Being stabbed isn't painless either." She withdrew the throwing dagger and balanced it in her hand so Joshua could see it. "You gave Darnley a knife, which you stole?"

McTavish's lips curled, and she knew their theory was right. "Darnley was a fool. Everyone knew about the plot to kill Rizzio, even Mary. I gave him the opportunity, even the powder to use. All he had to do was end his wife and rule in her stead. And yes, I lent him my lucky knife, the same one I used on the witch queen, in case she smelled something in the wine."

"Lucky knife?" Aioffe said. "The throwing dagger you used on the banrigh?"

"I don't know how it came to be on the boat I voyaged upon after my first meeting with my mistress, but it seemed prophetic that it should be used on another queen, even though my preference is always to use more subtle means. But, in the event, Darnley must have been blinded by jealousy or cowardice. The Lords of Congregation killed Rizzio, as they had planned, yet he failed to seize the moment to be King when he should have."

McTavish gritted his teeth. "For all my powers of persuasion, something stopped him from following through on our deal."

"Is that why you stabbed him at Kirk o'Fields? For failing?" Joshua said.

The vampire nodded and Aioffe stiffened. This must have happened while she'd been on Naturae. "What happened to Mary?"

Joshua said, "She intended to spend the night with the King at the Old Provost's Lodgings. Then Darnley appeared in the garden with his valet."

McTavish growled. "The valet was supposed to keep him occupied while I administered the poison to her night-cap. She would have slipped away peacefully in her sleep and all blame would have fallen on the King. The miserable worm couldn't have cleared his name." He huffed through his nostrils.

"Instead, Bothwell took Mary back to Holyrood, and Darnley went philandering in the orchard. This," Joshua shook McTavish, "creature stabbed him with *your* knife, Aioffe, before we captured him."

The vampire half-heartedly bucked against the constraints. "Traitor. He deserved it. The others... I see now I was just her weapon. A pawn." All of a sudden, he deflated in the chair.

Nemis said, "By using Aioffe's dagger, you meant for her to be implicated in the King's death. A way of suggesting to your mistress Aioffe was to blame for your failure, yet again?"

"I was just furious, and it was the only blade I had to hand," McTavish said. He sounded weary, as if his confession had drained him of all enthusiasm for fight. "Mary is rarely unguarded, yet her husband, worthless dolt, no-one cared enough to post soldiers to protect his life."

Joshua finished off. "But neither of us knew, Bothwell had already planted explosives in the Lodgings, which went off while Darnley was still outside. He had already planned to kill the King and save Mary for himself."

McTavish snorted. "Never trust a witch." His limbs shuddered. "Or a fae. She always finds me."

His sudden contrition niggled Aioffe. "Who finds you?" Although she had a dreadful suspicion she knew already.

"My mistress." His lips pressed together, then he said sarcastically, "The fae queen."

Joshua frowned and glanced at Aioffe.

"The fat one," McTavish elaborated.

Aioffe's throat tightened. "Illania ordered the murders?" She needed to hear it even though she didn't want her supposition to be true. "She wanted my death?"

McTavish nodded slowly, just as Uffer shot forward with the knife. At the same time, Joshua dived at McTavish's chest with the stake.

Nemis screamed, "No!"

Joshua and Uffer froze. Aioffe's mouth dried as her mind whirled.

McTavish snarled, "Do what you will. I'd rather die than suffer at her hands again."

Joshua's eyes flicked towards Nemis as he placed his hand on the vampire's shoulder, heaving a breath in and out. "I have seen what she can do, and I understand." He replaced the stake at McTavish's throat, even though his hands shook. "I can give you a quick death now, or you can tell us the rest of what you know now and maybe... maybe there's some redemption in it."

Uffer added, "Accept that this is the end for you, vampire. Extermination - seems appropriate for your kind."

McTavish stilled, and for a moment, Aioffe considered he might be hoping for Joshua to push the stake through his neck instead. Uffer's look of disgust suggested he would far prefer to be looking at a pile of dust than wasting hours bleeding him dry.

Just then, Lady Hanley banged the door open. "Fae approach!" She waved a tiny scroll in her fingers. "Henry has warned us." Her lips pinched together with disapproval.

Aioffe's face paled as a shiver of fear prickled down her arms. Her eyes met Joshua's. "I flew as fast as I could, but Illania could arrive at any moment. She was on Naturae when I left."

Nemis dashed towards the bottles. "The blood!"

Joshua's bow and arrow appeared, slung over his back. He looked at Aioffe and clenched his jaw.

Across the stables, Nemis stumbled, her fingers flying to her head. "Argh...." She fell to the floor and stiffened. The bottles rolled away.

Aioffe laid a hand on Joshua's arm. "I know the why," she said.

"Where's Hope?" Lady Hanley asked as she scuttled over to Nemis. Her gaze swept around the room. "I thought she was in here with you."

Joshua looked at Aioffe with stricken eyes. "She wanted to go hunting..."

"Papa!"

Hope's distressed scream wafted through the open door.

Chapter 58

Hope Lost

Aioffe rushed to the doorway and looked out. Hope's face, as pale as the moon, turned towards her. "Mama!" She screamed. Her blood-red wings bounced behind her, shredded and limp as she pounded up the hillock towards the stable.

Behind her, a wall of silver-green fae shimmered in the night sky. "Hope!" Aioffe cried as she hurtled down the slope, shoving the throwing dagger into her belt as she took flight. Within moments, she swooped and grabbed Hope's arms. Her wings beat faster, pulsing as she pulled her child into her embrace and the sky.

Hope clung to her, sobbing, as Aioffe darted up, away from the wall of fae and towards Hanley House. As she flew, she pushed her alarm and the vision of Illania's soldier fae into Joshua's mind. She landed by the back door and thrust her daughter inside.

Hope's wide eyes brimmed with fear. "Mama?" She clutched Aioffe's arm. "They attacked me. Strange fae." She shivered. "I was only stalking a deer." Her face crumpled into tears. "I'm so glad you're back. Don't go again..."

She couldn't just leave her like this. Aioffe reached out and traced her fingers over Hope's face, over the butterfly-shaped mark on her cheek and along her jaw. As she wiped away her tears, she whispered. "You are our Hope and we will protect you, no matter what. Once your father and I have made it safe, we can be together." Although her heart clamoured with longing to stay, hold her daughter close until the danger passed, she could not. Instead, she smiled reassurance at her while she pushed as much healing energy into Hope's skin as she could. "Stay here."

Hope blinked up at her and nodded. She glanced over her shoulder, relief softening her face as her wings began to lace their shreds together. A flutter, then a gust of wind brushed a wisp of her hair over her cheek. Seven fae spies alighted on the paving slabs next to them as Aioffe tucked the strand behind Hope's ear with a caress. "I'm so sorry, my child, I will not be far. Watch from the highest window."

"Our Queen," one of the fae spies said. "What are your orders?"

"Guard Hope," Aioffe said. She turned back to her daughter. "Be strong, my heart. Protect Spenser and Mark. Lock yourselves in!"

In the stable, Joshua held a trashing McTavish down on the chair, preventing him from wriggling. From Aioffe's flashed vision just after she left them, time was short. Outside, fae had gathered and, much as though he wanted to follow his wife and child, other lives depended on him as well. Nemis, Uffer, Lady Hanley... he could not slay McTavish, but if the vampire somehow got free, he would be swift and merciless in killing his friends to heal himself. He had to protect them, or everything they had worked for would be for naught. He had to trust Aioffe. Fae did not kill fae, he reminded himself of the unbreakable rule.

Illania would not kill Aioffe. He was almost sure of it.

In the meantime, he must extract the vampire's blood before Illania struck or Spenser might never recover. "Uffer," he said. "Bring the bottles!"

He looked over his shoulder. Nemis was gripped in the throes of a vision, but Lady Hanley was there, soothing her brow as her body bowed and writhed. A piercing scream filled the room, and he knew, their little hideaway would now be found.

"Hurry," he ordered Uffer. The stake shook a little as he moved it up to the vein running just below McTavish's ear. The vampire jerked his head, hissing. Joshua re-positioned his hand so he could better grip the jaw. His fingers whitened with tension as he held it still, ready to pierce McTavish's neck.

Uffer appeared by his side. "Let me," he said in a grim tone. McTavish wrestled again but Uffer already had his blade against the pulsing vein. As the knife tip slid in, the old fae brought the bottle neck up. Blood spurted into the vessel, splattering down the sides. The smell of ancient vampire essence reminded Joshua of musty books and his mouth dried, leaving a mouldy taste. But, as soon as the sliced wound was untouched by the silver knife, the sides of the vampire's skin began to knit together before their eyes.

Joshua gripped tighter. "Be still and this will be over quickly."

Uffer drove the knife point in again, deeper, and held the wound open until the vessel was full. When he retracted the blade, the skin closed like a seam being sewn. "Is it enough?" Uffer asked.

Joshua shrugged. "There's no telling until we try."

A soft moan escaped from Nemis, lingering like the last note of a symphony in the air. He looked around again: her body had fallen limp. No rising or falling movement to her chest. Her skin looked pale and clammy.

"Stab him again and hold the blade in, to keep him still," Joshua ordered Uffer and dashed to Nemis's still side.

Lady Hanley shot him a look of sheer panic. "She's gone?"

He shook his head, his fingers interlaced with the witch's. He felt the warmth of her return in the tingle of their connection. "Take control," he whispered in Nemis's ear.

Her fingers tightened against his.

"What's happening?" Lady Hanley said. "This is worse than before... will she die?"

"No, but it could be the final vision, where Lifeforce is drained out of.... Whichever queen it is."

His heart pounded with the sudden realisation. "Aioffe!"

"It's me..." Nemis whispered. "Next to die is me."

CHAPTER 59

BLAME AND BATTLE

In the distance, the burring, buzzing noise rolled over the countryside around Beesworth. Aioffe scanned the skyline as the spies trooped into the kitchen with Hope. The door slammed behind them and she heard the bolts grind home. She shot past the rosebushes and into the air and up, over the roof.

As she glanced down, the hillock's sides rippled. The European fae army set down on the earth and took up a defensive stance. Their mottled green camouflage glinted in the moonlight as still beating wings revealed the silver armour. At the base of the mound, a sea of muddy brown blurred her vision - Illania's workers hovered at the treeline. Hanley House was surrounded by hundreds, ready to attack at a moment's notice.

Where was Illania?

Her head whipped around as Joshua pushed an image into it. Nemis, death-like on the stable floor; Uffer pinning McTavish down, dodging his snarling teeth with a knife sticking from his neck. And Illania's golden air-chariot, blocking the stable door!

She darted over the slate roof, then dived towards the stables, tucked away on the edge of the forest. She glanced back as she flew, praying that Hope and her protectors had escaped notice. There was no escape from the house but up, out through the attic windows, which wasn't much use when there was a whole fae army ready to fly as well. Worse, her slender daughter was not strong enough to carry Spenser or Mark with her, but perhaps, if it came to it, they would have help from the spies. Her eyes rose skywards, thinking if ever there was need of Joshua's God, it was now.

But she could not rely on such an unproven belief. She clenched her fists; Illania had to be made to see sense. Too many dear lives were at stake to trust anything but her own family now.

"Illania!" She shouted as she neared.

Half in, half out of the door, the Queen's head revolved to face Aioffe.

"What do you want?" Aioffe said as she alighted a few yards from the stable.

Illania's lips twisted into a macabre grin. "Why you, of course." Her pudgy hands gestured for the bearers to reverse her out of the stable door-way. "And I see your handsome Princeling has something of mine and an extra gift for me as well."

"Why do you need me? Take your pet vampire assassin and be gone."

The tub advanced towards her, Illania with a deceptive, too benign smile on her face. "I'll go when I have what I came for."

Aioffe took a step back. If all Illania wanted was her, she would willingly go if she knew her family would be safe. But, it couldn't be that easy. Besides, there were the kills she'd ordered to discuss. And Hope, her priority. What could Illania possibly want with her? Her wings rose, and she balanced on the balls of her feet in readiness. "Why did you attack my daughter if you came for me?"

"Oh!" Illania chortled, as if cornering a girl was inconsequential. "She's grown into quite the fae, I see. Very... unusual. Something about her scent is familiar." Her fingers closed and the bearers halted a few feet away from

Aioffe. "Do thank her for me. My fae and I were in need of replenishment, and she had such a fine deer in her grasp."

"They didn't need to attack her for it."

"She was quite... protective, shall we say, of her prize."

"That's no excuse. Her wings were shredded! She was terrified. You can't just take what you want, especially not from a child!"

Illania laughed. "Oh, but I can. I take what I want. She'll recover, children do. Builds character."

Aioffe's fists clenched. Her gaze flicked behind Illania, to where Joshua stood in the doorway, bow at the ready. His head tipped to one side as he looked down the shaft, hands perfectly steady as he aimed the arrow straight at the back of Illania's head. With only her four escorts in the clearing, the queen might never again be as vulnerable, but her troops surrounded Hanley House. All the souls hiding there and in the stables would be overwhelmed if Illania suffered or had left them with orders to attack if anything happened. She breathed in and out as she listened to the low throb of their wings, but heard no sounds of fighting.

"Take what you want, like taking thrones?" Aioffe said, playing for time while she tried to think of a way out of this conundrum. "Because apparently you don't have enough of those already."

"My dear, one can never have too many."

"How on earth do you expect to rule them?" Aioffe retorted. "The English, the Scots - humans. They will never accept a fae as their Queen. What about the Treaty?"

"I thought you more astute than that. I'm simply hastening things along to their natural conclusion. Once it becomes known a vampire, a priest no less, has killed all those catholic queens, the humans will turn on the Church. Then they'll revert to the old ways. Our ways. We shall be gods once again."

She didn't care at all about McTavish, Aioffe realised. How ironic that Illania did, after all, plan to make his name known, but the vampire was simply a scapegoat. Expendable, and useless as a pawn to barter her way out of this.

"You are low in faith with humanity, then." Aioffe closed her eyes, sending a single word - escape - through her mind to Joshua while she bought him time.

When she opened them, Illania stared at her, smug and filled with self importance. "Faith does not matter. The humans will believe what their superiors tell them to. The power they see before their eyes."

Aioffe said, "You're mistaken if you think that will ever happen. The Catholic church may defy the protestant revolution, but the humans, even now, still believe in Christianity as a theology. Or Islam. Religions centred around a man, a human, with divine influence and purpose. Now, even the gods of other faiths do not walk on this plane. The nature of belief is in something intangible, the effect of an invisible hand. You, a creature with wings, cannot hope to rule over them being so visibly different. You can't rule if they fear you; there's too many of them. That's why we creatures need the Treaty - to prevent chaos and terror spreading among the humans."

Illania pouted. "The Treaty is dead. There's no need to hide ourselves any longer. The vampires have been breaking it for centuries. As soon as they started hunting down creaturekind, putting them on trial for their so called 'sins', the agreement became meaningless. Change - another war between creatures - it's inevitable." Illania pushed herself upright in the tub and leaned forward. "Then comes the age of the fae."

Aioffe's wings fluttered. "You mean to go to war... with the vampires."

"Oh, the battle has already begun." Illania bared her teeth. "Across Europe, then England, and now Scotland. The humans have spoken. Rejected the Catholic church. Like floundering fools, the vampire council wastes its time rounding up the witches and daemons, blackening their name to assert their weakened authority. I did not start this battle. The persecution. They did. Soon, leaderless, the witches will be eliminated as a threat, but not before the humans will rebel against anyone who is different. Taking the daemons out too. And in the meantime, faekind will build up its army, ready to strike when the hysteria peaks and the vampires are at their weakest. The humans will see us as saviours. Your mother saw this coming, as soon as the banrigh fell. I thought you would have, too."

Aioffe gasped. "How did my mother know the banrigh?" Her eyes landed on Joshua at the stable door, pale yet still taking aim with a steady hand. Behind him, Lady Hanley shuffled through the door frame, her arm around Nemis.

Illania placed the tips of her fingers together as if imparting wisdom to an idiot. "Lana had used royal witch blood to cure her vines before. They had an arrangement. When the banrigh died, I told her it was the perfect opportunity for her to take better control of her realm. Spread her wings, so to speak. I thought she would have mentioned it to you."

"She was in no shape to do anything. You know that. Spenser must have told you. Nor did she wish to upset a delicate balance between creatures."

Illania wrinkled her nose. "Spenser did mention she was weak. I had higher hopes for you though."

At the mention of Spenser, Aioffe's blood coursed through her. Illania had, she was sure, drained her own Ambassador to cause upset, or was there something more to it? Had Spenser known, or found out about, her plot to hasten war along? She looked up; Nemis crept her way down the stable wall. She had to give her more time... why wasn't Joshua swooping her away? She dug her toes into the earth, trying as subtly as she could to pull what little Lifeforce there into herself. "I am not my mother. Naturae, the world, is different now."

Illania's bow-shaped lips curled. "But you..." she glared at Aioffe and pointed her finger. "Let a vampire, a young vampire of all people, run your realm instead." She sighed and shook her head. "I offered you assistance before, but you refused. Then, when you disappeared, I tried to give Henry a chance. I really did because he didn't seem quite like all the others. He needed a queen, so I gave him one. Still he refused my offer. He'll serve his purpose though, before it ends, and you must return to Naturae. Cure and bless your vines. Take your place again as Naturae's rightful queen."

"Being a queen these days seems to be a death sentence. I had no desire to rule then, and still don't now."

Illania sighed. "One doesn't simply decide to give up being queen. On ruling. It's in your blood, your Lifeforce. It's your duty to faekind. Your vines need you, Aioffe. Why resist? You have your heir now. There's nothing stopping you reclaiming your birthright. I won't stand in your way. We could be allies. Neighbours."

"You were never my ally, and for all your machinations, we will never be neighbours. I will not go back."

The Queen shrugged. "If it is your wish not to return, alternatives are in place. Caesaria will come into her powers when you die and rule in your stead." Her fingers began to wriggle and twitch as her gaze fell on Aioffe's half buried feet. "Or, give me your powers. Renounce them and your throne, and I will restore Naturae's vines myself."

From the corner of her eye, Aioffe saw Joshua re-take his aim. "No!" she cried, more for his benefit than hers. "Fae do not kill fae."

"If I wanted to kill you, then we would not be having this discussion." Illania's fingers gripped the edge of her tub. "To cure the Naturae's vines, for the fae to have a future, requires sacrifice. Royal blood or a banrigh's - and there isn't one. An alternative source has been delivered already." Her lips twisted together in a tight, smug smile.

"What are you talking about?"

"Lord Darnley awaits us on Naturae. The proverbial royal lamb."

"But he's dead? Your assassin stabbed him to death."

Illania wet her lips. "A minor inconvenience, which I'm sure your powers can overcome. I know you have risen a human from the dead before, and Darnley didn't lose too much blood. Either return and fix him, or I'll take your essence and do it myself."

Aioffe's back stiffened. The only person she had truly managed to bring back from the dead was Joshua; her last attempt at bringing a man back to life, turning him into a fae for Illania had been disastrous. "Don't you remember? Resurrection cannot be done without love."

"And yet, you have another option which I had not foreseen... have you learned nothing today? A living se'er witch, for example? Her sacrifice might suffice." Illania grinned. "Your Princeling seemed to be in possession of one." She wafted her hands in the air, indicating she knew full well that Joshua was stood behind with an arrow pointed at her. "He guards her, along with the worthless priest. I'm surprised you haven't staked him already, I wouldn't have minded."

Aioffe glanced across to them. Lady Hanley hunched in the shadows of the stable roof, Nemis wavering like a stem of grass beside her. Joshua dropped his bow and looked straight at Aioffe. He reached for Nemis's hand.

"Or," Illania's eyes darkened and she pointed to Hanley House, "You have a daughter..."

"You cannot have them," Aioffe said. "I...." She lowered her gaze; she must not betray her love either, for in his veins flowed banrigh blood. "Take..."

From the stables, the sound of wood cracking silenced her tongue.

Then Uffer screamed.

CHAPTER 60

DOME AND DOOM

At the scream, Joshua darted back into the stable, although he hated leaving Nemis vulnerable with only Aioffe and Lady Hanley to defend her. He trusted Aioffe could keep Illania occupied, and he knew the speed McTavish could move. Only his strength could contain him, should the vampire decide to taste witch blood again. His skin chilled as he brought forward his inner armour, feeling it wrap around himself as he slapped his bow over his shoulder and bade it disappear.

Uffer screeched again, his fingers scrabbling at McTavish's head buried on his neck. The old fae's movements were jerky as he staggered under the weight of the attack, but the vampire clung on like the leech he was.

"No!" Joshua cried as he grabbed McTavish's shoulders and wrenched him off.

Blood dripped from the killer's chin, his eyes shifting wildly from side to side. The vampire's arms swung out as Joshua threw him to the ground. His broken arms had healed, and fresh fae essence fuelled the rain of blows.

Joshua drove him to the earth with the force of his wings, pinning his legs down with his feet and capturing grasping hands under his forearms. The memory of holding him thus swept over him... and he would not make the same mistake as he had over a century ago.

"Finish it, fae!" McTavish hissed.

"For you would rather not suffer at the hands of your mistress?" Joshua panted out. The temptation was great, however, but... had they got enough blood from him?

Uffer stumbled to his feet, then lurched to the shattered chair. Untangling the silver blanket, he staggered across the stable and threw it over McTavish's face. The vampire screamed as the metal touched his bare skin and wrestled against Joshua with renewed vigour.

"I tried to get another bottle of blood," Uffer huffed. "He seemed..." then stomped his foot onto the vampire's nose. After drawing in a shuddered breath while McTavish stilled, Uffer shook his head. "He surprised me."

"Get the rope." Joshua panted as he weighed up the risks and decided. "No... the stake. Enough of this."

"Call your proxy murderer off!" Aioffe shouted to Illania. "I'll come. I'll do it. Just leave them alone."

Illania's plump lips stretched into a grimace until dimples formed on her cheeks. "As you said, there is no resurrection without love." Then her eyes narrowed. "And it is clear you have no love for my proposed sacrifice, so another one must be secured." She flung her arm towards Nemis. "Seize her!"

"No!" Aioffe surged forward, flying towards Illania.

But the bearer fae shot across the clearing and converged on Nemis and Lady Hanley.

Aioffe landed on the lip of the tub and grabbed Illania by the throat. "Order them to stand down." She stared into Illania's dark eyes. "Now."

As they traded glares, it seemed as if the air vibrated with a pulsing buzz. Illania's arms flapped, trying to knock Aioffe's hands away as she squeezed harder.

"Call the guards off. Now!" Aioffe said, entirely focused on keeping her tenuous balance and grip. Her feet braced on the rim, wings beating to keep her stable. "I have agreed with your terms."

She felt the brush of Illania's fingers land on her thigh, then a pulling sensation. Her head span... all the earthy Lifeforce she had ingested, all her strength, seemed to fade. In its place, a growing ache spread through her joints, her limbs. It was as if her insides, her very essence was being dragged out through the fat fingers gripping her leg. Her wings dropped and she felt as if she were falling...

"Aioffe!"

She heard the voice, but it sounded terribly far away... She had to resist! This pulling sensation, she knew very well what was going on and yet her strength had left her. Why had she gotten so close to Illania?

Cool hands gripped her shoulders, then yanked. In her weakness, she released her grasp on Illania's throat and collapsed back into the embrace of.... Henry!

"Fae do not kill fae," he said, his voice sonorous in her ear. "Isn't that the saying?" From the edge of her hazy vision, she saw four fae soldiers unhook him from a harness and retreat. His head whipped to Illania. "But vampires..." His fangs glinted, so white they shone silver in the moonlight. He shoved Aioffe off the tub, replacing his hands where hers had been around Illania's neck.

"Oh!" The Queen squawked.

Aioffe tumbled to the ground. How... why was Henry here?

With the last of her energy, head spinning, she pushed herself up and glanced around. The air was filled with fae - Naturae fae! The buzz of their wings, the shine of their armour, overwhelmed her. Tired but familiar faces peered down, disbelief turning to joy. They huddled closer, as if they dared not approach, but, despite their exhaustion, wisps of Lifeforce trickled towards her. She sprawled, gazing up at them, and a smile spread over her face as their freely given energy seeped into her being.

"Now, Henry..." Illania said, her voice squeaky and breathless.

"You would turn vampire against fae?" He snarled. "In the name of war?"

"Well..."

"Kill Aioffe, her family, from the shadows? Then what? Blame me, or use me as the reason why there should be a discord between our kinds? Overthrow my lands to unite the fae against vampires?"

Aioffe started. Chess playing Henry had seen the nuance, the next step in Illania's plan, which she had not. Queen takes king.... Or king takes queen? Or queens...

Nemis! Her eyes flared as her gaze flew to the stables. The four bearers encircled Nemis and Lady Hanley, pining them against the wall with stubby swords. With her shoulders drawn back and a haughty look on her face, Mary glared at them as she held Nemis upright.

Joshua stepped away from the pile of dust and dropped the stake. Before relief could make him complacent, he grabbed the bottles of blood and flew to the doorway, Uffer close on his heels.

Outside, the sky was teeming with wings. He could hardly see through them to spot Aioffe... her gown a dark red shadow on the ground, but, through the haze of fae, he snatched a glimpse of her face, glittering as if starlight had settled on her skin. His gaze scanned the swarm, relief soaring through him as he recognised the armour he had forged.

A black form almost covered Illania's golden tub, its occupant obscured. Through the buzz, he caught Henry's voice shouting: "You dared even to order an attack on my sister."

With Aioffe empowered, Henry pinning Illania down, and the Naturae army poised to strike, Joshua calculated he had enough time. His heartbeat thudded, pulsing, racing in his ears, yet his mind was clear. Here, in the now, he knew what to do. He glanced along the stable wall, his breath caught as he searched for Nemis.

She was surrounded.

Without even thinking further, he reached behind his back for an arrow as his magical bow formed again in his other hand. Four bearer fae... a second later, three. Before they could react, two. The last one turned, looking for him, spear raised.

None.

As their bodies dissolved into wisps of grey, catching on the breeze from all the wings of the Naturae fae, he raced over to Nemis; Uffer not far behind him. "Get to Hope and Spenser!" Joshua said, then caught sight of the mound ahead. Their route to the house. His face fell.

Hundreds of fae stood in lines which circled the steep sides, wings up and alert. Most stared at the mass of Naturae fae swarming over the forest. Some held weapons, spears and swords, while others bounced on the balls of their feet in readiness to spring to the air once signalled by their mistress.

But the Europeans were so tightly packed, there was no way Nemis could sneak through the formation and up the hill. Joshua supposed he should feel grateful the armies hadn't attacked each other yet, but all it would take was a command. He glanced back: Illania was otherwise occupied. By Henry.

Uffer held onto Nemis's other arm. "This way," he said, pointing to a narrow path winding away from the stables and hillock.

Joshua's mind raced as his jaw dropped.

"The tunnel is ready?" Lady Hanley whispered, and Uffer nodded.

"You didn't think I just chopped wood all day, did you?" Uffer said with a wink. "Leads all the way to the pantry."

"Go then!" Joshua replied as reached for another arrow. "Before you are noticed."

The three shuffled along the wall as Joshua's wings rose.

"Henry!" Aioffe shouted. She pounced onto his back and tried to pull him from Illania's neck.

He wrenched his shoulders back, nearly tipping her off but she clung on. "She deserves to die," he snarled. His thumbs slid up to Illania's ears, rocking her head back and exposing the tender flesh with a pulsing vein. His eyes fixated upon the vessel. Although the fae's hands gripped Henry's thighs, whatever Lifeforce she pulled from him seemed not to matter.

Aioffe ordered, "Stop!"

Like an animal disturbed mid-hunt, his head twitched at the intrusion. Eyes blazing red with rage, his strength undiminished, he turned back to his prey.

A crack as the pressure of his grasp broke her neck.

Still, Illania's fingers pulsed as she pulled. Henry's jaw clenched as with one hand he grabbed her hair and twisted her skull around until it was almost backwards. Illania shrieked, thumping, kicking her legs against the tub like a drum beat. Such was the battle of fae strength and vampire determination to subdue, Henry's crown jostled from his hair and fell into the mud.

"You cannot kill an immortal," Aioffe said, horrified at how much pain Illania was able to bear and yet live. She was reminded of her brother, Lyrus, who had survived buried and broken for years.

Joshua alighted next to the tub and lowered his bow. "You can break every bone but she will still live. Drain every ounce of blood, but it won't work."

"Then I'll tear her head off and her heart out."

"Let go, Henry." Aioffe said, firm and calm, as she slid off his back and stood by the side of the transport with her husband. She lifted her arm and gestured to the armies in the sky and on the mound. "For the sake of Naturae, please, don't do this."

"It is for Naturae that I do this." Henry lowered his head and tore into Illania's neck. The stars disappeared and the night sky around them darkened, as if swallowing his deed.

Illania's shriek died in the air as he exposed her flesh. The wound, like McTavish's, began to close as soon as he stopped biting; the vampiric Lifeforce she had just pulled from Henry countering his attack. He bit again, tearing into her neck like a rabid dog. Droplets of blood splattered over the chariot, peppering its gleaming sides.

"Stop!" She grabbed his hair and yanked.

To her surprise, his head lifted easily. He looked at Joshua, then Aioffe. His eyes were now entirely pitch black as he stared at them both. "I'm sorry."

Something in his tone made Aioffe break eye contact and glance down at Illania - just as his hands wrenched her blonde-haired head clean away from her bloodied, shredded neck.

Aioffe gasped.

The head dropped, rolling down the side of the tub and the crown of the European Queen knocked off. Still pouting, Illania's skull landed with a bounce, then tumbled until it came to a rest, face down. A final spurt of blood spouted from her neck, then her body withered and greyed. As the queen's corporeal form dissolved into shimmering pieces, Henry collapsed, all arms and legs, into the tub. Specks of royal Lifeforce rose between his limbs, flashed brilliantly in the night, like the tail of a shooting star, and died.

"No..." Aioffe said, softly. "What have you done..."

Henry stared up at her. "I did what was needed." His eyes flicked and returned to their usual darkness with flashes of white to the sides. In a flash, he twisted in the tub to perch on Illania's seat. He looked incongruous and uncomfortable, long legs jammed up to his chest. Shocked even, as his shaking fingers drifted up to his face. He frowned, realising the absence of his crown, then used his cuff to smear blood across his pale cheeks. Pale-faced, he stared up at the stars with a vacant expression. "The stars foretold it. Fairfax was right."

"But..." Aioffe floundered, lost for words. She glanced over her shoulder, towards the mound. The European fae there must not have seen what happened, because Naturae's people had formed a tight, fluttering dome over the clearing and stables, shielding and guarding. Now, the same barrier prevented her from seeing their reaction to the death of their Queen.

Her face crumpled. It wasn't that she was sad about Illania's death. Rather, that she didn't know what would happen next. "Her daughters," she said in a quiet voice, then swallowed. "They'll come into their powers now."

A shadow crossed Henry's face. "Naturae. Before Caesaria can wreak havoc upon it. At least I won't have to marry her."

Aioffe glanced up at their army. "How many fae did you leave there?"

"Thane, a few elders who couldn't fly this far, and a cohort of guards. Everyone else wanted to come. To you, their true Queen."

Her ears picked up the rustles and whispers from the mound. A cry of "Accingo, accingo" ordered them to make ready their weapons… somehow, they must have sensed their ruler had gone.

A flash of resignation crossed Henry's face, and for a moment she was torn. She lifted her gaze and met hundreds of eyes. Watching, waiting for her to command them to strike.

Dread blazed through her, shooting to her stomach and swirling like molten steel. Battle between fae-kind could not happen. Especially not if Illania was right about a war between creatures.

Aioffe gestured for the swarm to descend. The worker and soldiers glanced around, searching for a place to land, but the nearby grassy hill was covered in the Europeans. "Go to the forest," she called.

Heads shook a refusal. If anything, the Naturae dome packed tighter.

She grabbed Illania's crown with one hand and Joshua's with her other. They flew up to the centre. "Fae of Naturae," Aioffe said. "I am heartened to see you. That you would put yourselves in harm's way for me, for us, means more than we can express. But," she pointed beyond, "let us not start a new chapter with a fight."

The sides of the dome rippled as the fae's heads turned to assess the threat behind them. Through the holes this created, Aioffe and Joshua saw the Europeans had flown into a wall formation, weapons pointed towards their lesser number.

Immediately, the Naturae fae began to holster their tiny arrows to the miniature bows set on their arms, others withdrew shining swords. Even the workers brandished a weapon of some kind, an axe or spear.

Aioffe pulled Joshua towards the edge of the curvature and hovered. "Let us pass," she said in a stern but respectful tone.

"We know you are at our backs," Joshua added. "Trust us."

Their fae parted. Hand in hand with Joshua, Aioffe flew between the wall and dome until they were midway between both sides. She addressed them all: "Thus dawns a fresh start. Change is scary, I know, but I ask you all to have faith. Faeth together. Trust that we can end this night without further bloodshed or loss."

The last thing she wanted to do was wear Illania's crown, so instead she held it in front of her, offering it to the Europeans to make that choice.

The mottled green wall brandished their weapons and advanced, determination on their faces, but Aioffe noticed some seemed uncertain. Hesitant. Fearful?

She threaded the crown, dangling like a bracelet, up her arm, and nestled it in the crook of her elbow. Then she lifted her hands. Summoning her energy, her fingers curled like claws as she wove them through the air. Ribbons of Lifeforce circled around her, threading through the crown, her digits, wrapping her with magic and power. Their presence emboldened her. She thought about the love and loyalty of her husband, family, and fae until, visible to others, her whole body glittered.

Aioffe's jaw set and she glared at those who carried the commander's insignia. "There is no need for us to be at odds with each other. We are all fae. But know this: I will defend this, my given realm and people."

Her fingers plunged, shooting the Lifeforce down into the vegetation beneath. The Europeans, nervous of her powers, shrank back as ivy tendrils shot from tree to sky. Aioffe wriggled her digits, making the creepers dance in the air for a few moments, while she sent her husband the image of what she intended to do.

Joshua winked, then she sent a pair of stems shooting around Joshua's legs to illustrate her point. Although his wings kept him airborne, it was clear that the bindings could, if she so chose, entirely disable him. Hundreds of other leafy ropes wavered beneath the feet of the lowest flying Europeans.

He grinned at her, then glanced at the Naturae fae. "Lay down your arms and set the example."

The swarm fluttered across to the trees and gradually dropped to perch on the branches. Their bows and spears still loosely aimed skywards, but, in the absence of any other leader directing them, uncertainty and a survival instinct overcame their aggression. After a few moments, the European army retreated and followed suit.

As they settled themselves on the mound, a few glared warily at the sky, but most simply hung their heads. Although she doubted they much mourned their autocratic and terrifying leader, their near retaliation had been understandable. Before the Europeans could reconsider revenge, Aioffe looked down for Henry, with every intention of handing back the reins of command and finishing the dance with him.

But he had disappeared. Only his golden crown band on the ground evidenced he had ever been there.

Chapter 61

TWO FALLEN CROWNS

"Where did Henry go?"

Joshua met Aioffe's eyes and shrugged. "Shall I find him?"

Henry could run fast, but there was a chance his scent could be followed. He glanced around, spotting the four harness-bearing fae nearby. He must have used his own legs, not flown.

She shook her head. "Hope, Spenser and Nemis need us more. Everything hath a time."

With a flick of her fingers, the ivy bindings fell from him, and immediately he flew over to cup her face. As he caressed her cheeks, she chewed her lip and stared into his eyes. He saw the fear in hers, the reluctance, and his heart ached for what he knew she would feel was right to do, even if it wasn't what she wanted. "Whatever you decide to do next, I will be by your side. Forever, my love."

She glanced away, to the Naturae fae beneath.

"It doesn't have to be permanent," he added. "We'll find a solution which works for us all."

She spoke quickly. "They deserve a queen who wants to rule, or a king. Maybe Henry makes his way back to Naturae already. Before what we now know, I promised I would return and try to cure the vines, but perhaps he has, after all, chosen Caesaria, now she will be fully a Queen in her own right. Before, Thane and he thought they could broker some sort of arrangement with the fae and I." She looked up at him. "Sharing the throne. But I don't see Henry actually wanting to, despite what he said. His ambitious heart could never settle to it. He just doesn't believe in power-sharing, not truly."

"He needs to choose."

"He should choose love, like we did."

"Like they have," Joshua said, sweeping his hand down to the faces staring at her.

She sighed, but with a small smile. "A Queen is not always so beloved. I am grateful to be so fortunate."

They landed by the side of the blood-streaked chariot. Aioffe's hair seemed to bristle at the sight. "What's done is done," he said as he swept a lock behind her ear. "We have now to deal with the consequences. I'll check on everyone in the house, but I'm sure your people will want to see you."

"Our people," she said. "For all Illania's meddling, perhaps she was right about needing to be unified. Take this," she passed him Illania's crown. "Until we know what to do with it, or who should wear it, as a symbol, it should be kept safe."

He nodded. "We should keep Henry's crown safe as well," he said, as he flew up to Hanley House.

Nemis's hand shook as she held Aioffe's dagger over Spenser's bare chest. "A direct infusion, Bothwell said."

Hope scrubbed the tears from her cheeks with the back of her hand. Her other hand trembled, but not so much it spilled the blood from the bottle. "Kill or cure," she whispered.

Nemis kissed Spenser's cold, still lips, then made an incision between his ribs, over his heart. The flesh parted easily under the blade, but nothing of his essence gushed out as it should have. Hope leaned over and poured McTavish's thick, dark blood directly into the wound.

As it ran over the skin, seeping into the tissue, they both held their breaths.

"Is it deep enough?" Hope's voice wavered, for the liquid was not being absorbed, only dripping off Spenser's chest.

Nemis answered by re-inserting the blade deeper, cutting the muscles between the bones. She hesitated, instinctively worrying about penetrating the slow beating heart of her husband. "More," she urged Hope.

A dribble directly over the organ did nothing.

Nemis's own heartbeat pounded so quickly, all she could hear for a moment was her own blood rushing through her ears. "Please," she whimpered, unable to drag her gaze away from the unchanged, inert body on the bed.

Hope blinked away tears of frustration so she could see where to pour the last few drops into his chest. Nemis forced herself to breathe, and try not to think about the fact that they had no other blood. No other cures. And her love had not responded to this last, maddening and unproven attempt to rouse him. She wasn't sure she had the courage to live the rest of her natural life without Spenser, without any other hope for his reanimation.

But he did not rouse. His heart simply.... stopped beating. Her breath caught as she stared at his chest, not rising. Not filling with even the shallowest of breaths.

Then the pool of vampire blood was rejected and began to seep out of his gaping wound. She could only stare in horror as it dribbled down his ribcage, onto the sheets.

"Cut your finger and touch his heart," Joshua said from the doorway. "Let him feel your love."

"Me?" Nemis said. "But... I...It's too late."

"If he died, he would dissolve into ash. How is this any different from massaging a babe's chest when born? Sometimes you have to push to get the heart started. You need to be more direct. I think that's what Bothwell meant. There is magic in your touch, your blood."

"What harm can it do?" Hope said.

"But my visions could transfer to him in my blood, or be rejected like McTavish's... I..." She looked at him. Fear clenched her chest. "I could not wish them upon anyone, especially not him."

Joshua crossed the room to her. "When our blood accidentally mingled when Hope was born, I received a sense of your power. It enriched my life, just as you enrich Spenser's." He picked up her hand and took the knife from it.

"But you are part witch, it seems. Maybe you should do this. He is fae."

"I am part witch, part fae, part human. It's irrelevant - he loves only you. It should be you. As long as you, his most beloved, try," he said with conviction. He sliced a thin cut on the pad of her index finger. "What is life without loving? You are what brings meaning to Spenser. Blood alone will not bring him back to us, just as Lifeforce alone did not change me. Use your vision. Show him the picture of the life you led together, and can again."

She smiled at his certainty and poked her dripping finger into the wound on Spenser. Her lips pressed together as she closed her eyes. She recalled to her mind those memories which meant the most to her - from knowing he would come and save her from the Beneath, despite having only glimpsed him when she arrived on Naturae, to his beaming face as she birthed their children. The tender moments when he held her close, and the exciting ones when he carried her high into the sky and flew over the waves towards the sun. She filled her own heart with the happiest of memories, the simplest of times, when all they had to do was love each other and their family.

"It's not enough, Nemis."

Joshua's voice cut through her reminiscence. "It's all I can remember... all I can think about." The vice of fear gripped her again.

"Is it the past?"

She nodded, not daring to open her eyes.

"Imagine the future," Hope said.

"Your future, se'er witch. Illania is dead. He has nothing to fear from her anymore." Joshua comforted her with a warm hand on her shoulder. "Queen Mary lives, and so do you and Aioffe. Control it. Control your vision."

Nemis swallowed, then brought to mind an image of them both, grown older together, sat side by side in front of a fire. Outside, warm evening sunlight bathed a garden bursting with flowers. In the picture, she reaches for Mark, taller and filled out as a handsome man. Hope, Aioffe and Joshua enter, beaming and full of good cheer.

Oh, how she wished for this to be their future! The impression in her mind was so realistic, it felt as if she were inside, living a vision again, but a brighter one. A vision which she would never want to leave, but perhaps this one, like her others, could also be a certainty in her future.

Her face screwed as the memory of the strange star lights intruded, and briefly, she saw the first queen - Joshua's mother, the banrigh. Felt the chill of the water and the pain in her chest. Joshua's fingers gripping her shoulder helped her to focus and her mind cleared. Predicting the death of the queen's had led them to this terrible point, where all that she held dear were endangered. Not all the crowns had fallen, after all. The future had been changed, and could again. And, perhaps the final prediction, where she met her own demise, could be avoided now McTavish the killer and Illania, Spenser's terrifying Queen, had both died.

She shoved the past aside and forced herself to think of just one moment she longed to have, if the stars could grant her just one more cycle. Because Spenser loved the Yule season, she imagined them all sitting down to a meal, laughter and joy filling the cosy room as much as the smell of roasted meat. She could almost feel the love surrounding them, as she turned to look at her handsome husband, lifting his goblet and toasting the future...

Nemis gasped as the tip of her finger tingled and her eyes flashed open. "Heartbeat!"

Relief coursed through her as she watched his skin begin to pink. "Since when did you get so wise, Joshua?"

"Must be the banrigh in me," he joked. "Knowing my history a little has helped me control my present. Perhaps my mother taught me more than I knew."

The tingle intensified and she gripped Spenser's hand. "That's it, my love, take what you need of me," she said, happiness bubbling from her although she could feel herself weakening. "I give it freely to you, just please, come back to us."

Her head reeled as she realised this moment was similar to her deadly visions. She did feel like her insides were being wrenched out, first by the possibility of losing Spenser entirely when the cure failed, and then now, as he drained Lifeforce from her. What she hadn't foreseen was that she would be so willing to sacrifice everything she had, and was, to save him.

"He's healing!" Hope said. "The wound closes."

Through lowered eyelids, Nemis saw Joshua grin. "Vampire blood and love. Tis a strange world we live in."

Spenser groaned. Joshua grabbed Nemis's wrist and pulled out her finger. Her head lolled against him as Spenser's flesh knitted together. She had a vague sense of being lifted, then laid down.

Joshua's voice sounded muffled. "She needs him as much as he needs her now."

The warm body next to her compelled her to wrap her arms around it and draw herself into its embrace. Finally, she could rest and sleep a dreamless sleep.

CHAPTER 62

SPENSER

As dawn's light brightened into day, Aioffe bade farewell to the swarm with Joshua stood by her side. While Spenser and Nemis recovered with Hope, Mark and Mary stood watch over them, the couple's night-time hours had been spent in the forest, thanking the fae for their support. Uffer, whom everyone had thought Outcast and thus dead, had been greeted with affection. When talking to the fae, Aioffe had been careful not to promise a solution to the problems the realm faced, only that she would see what was possible. It was a half-hearted vow at best, but grabbed at and repeated by hopeful hearts.

"I'll catch you up soon," Aioffe called. Her larger wings made that promise plausible, at least. The urgent departure was rooted in a mutual concern for Thane with a newly empowered Caesaria, who may or may not still be captive there. No-one knew what to expect upon their return to Naturae, but at least its shores were safer than England's for a people so obviously different. The threat of discovery jeopardised their existence; hiding armour clad fae in a forest so close to a town was impossible.

The fae ascended in one huge cloud of wings, Naturae and Europeans combined. Aioffe called out goodbyes, but her promise to arrive within hours stuck in her throat. As soon as the horde flew above the clouds, she collapsed against her husband. "Why did I say I would go back?"

"Because it's what they needed to hear."

"And what is right for Naturae, however much I do not wish to rule."

"One step at a time, my love," he said, taking her hand.

They walked up the winding path towards the house, the toll of their emotional reunion dragged their footsteps.

When they reached the back door, they paused for a moment, looking out over the rolling landscape. In the distance, grey smoke twirled from chimneys as Beesworth awoke and readied itself for the day ahead. Aioffe sighed, then said, "She invaded our last true sanctuary. Hope's birthplace. Our one constant. A haven, of sorts. I don't think I will ever feel safe here again, though."

He replied, "Illania, and all she has ordered done, proves nowhere is really safe. Hanley House, Beesworth, was a place of rest and recovery for our family, but no more. The illusion of safety is what we mourn, really. We know this as adults and parents, but when you strip it from a child, it hits you all over again." He turned to the door, then paused. "We can live anywhere in this realm, undetected, if that's what you want. But, Naturae is, whether you rule or not, our home. We promised to return, at least for a little while. We also promised Mary she could return, and Hope should at least see the island."

Aioffe's lips tightened as she knocked. "I'd rather know what to expect before we bring Hope. Her safety is the most important thing right now. War looms between creatures, and as heir, she cannot get caught in its crossfire. Who knows what revenge Caesaria might take."

The bolts slid back and Uffer welcomed them into the kitchen. His frown told them he had heard their conversation, perhaps shared their concern. Sat around the table were Spenser, Nemis and Hope, all equally tense of face. Aioffe brightened as she darted past the fireplace to hug her long-time friend and confidante.

"I chose a side," Spenser said, his voice muffled by her hair. "Chose a family."

"And it nearly cost you your life," she replied. As she pulled away from the embrace, she glanced at Nemis. Her friend's wan skin and weary expression lifted a fraction as they exchanged smiles.

Joshua pulled out a chair for Aioffe. "Was that why she drained you?"

Spenser nodded. "As you know, I was supposed to attend Mary Queen of Scots's wedding ceremony and the banquet after, but, just after you and Joshua left, a kestrel found me. Illania sent a missive: to attend her presence immediately. Her tone was conciliatory, although, I thought it strange, that she would dare to come so close to such a heavily guarded royal event. I went to her anyway, in the woodland outside Holyrood, just as dawn broke. When I asked why she had summoned me, on today of all days, she laughed at first, claiming I was and always would be hers to command. She ordered me to capture Darnley and bring him to her straight after the marriage to Mary, then return to bed the Queen. Because of my passing resemblance to him, she thought no-one would notice the switch."

Aioffe snorted. "She thinks so little of humans."

Nemis gasped. "The audacity."

Spenser's lips curled up as if it was funny, but his voice was serious. "My love, you're aware I have never told her who you are, but she knew I had a family. A wife. But, she never wanted to know details, and I wouldn't have told her, even under threat of torture." He snorted, as if his experience was inconsequential. "More peculiar was that, if I was to go along with her scheme to replace Darnley, Mary would surely see I have wings! I thought Illania joked initially, but my protestations were irrelevant to her. She insisted I would not be tied to Mary for long. I told her she was mad if she thought the Queen would fall for such a sham in the first place." He shrugged. "And, while I was to play at being king in Darnley's stead - a pawn in situ on the Scottish throne to hold off the Catholics - Illania would cure the vines on Naturae with his blood and double her army."

He sighed, "So I accused her of meddling in human and Naturae's affairs, and refused her bidding. She took affront, told me my memory clearly suffered with age, and that I had dallied with humans for too long and forgotten who my allegiance should be with – those who pupaeted me centuries ago." He turned to look at Nemis, "Then, when she mentioned pupaetion, and the problems Henry was having with the Naturae vines, I remembered Lana curing them."

His hands shook as he reached for his wife. He looked at Aioffe with eyes filled with pain. "I was the one who told Illania that your mother used the Queen of the Witches, the banrigh's, blood on the vines."

"My mother," Joshua said. "And McTavish's first victim."

"I did not know the banrigh had a family," Spenser said. "When word reached Naturae of her death, Queen Lana was distraught. All hope, should the vines suffer vinexplicity again, was lost. Illania tried to take advantage of Lana's distress and her distraction. She negotiated to bring you, Aioffe, up herself, but the price to raise you was more than Lana could bear to give up. I should have known Illania wouldn't give up on wanting land to settle on, but over the century, she didn't mention it again to me. Then you escaped, and Lana's mind spiralled and Naturae suffered."

Aioffe said, "So Illania knew banrigh blood was special, even if we didn't."

Spenser's eyes met Nemis's. "A banrigh is chosen by a binding of all the realm's witches. It is not a birth-right, a bloodline or who is the most powerful. Most often, it is a se'er witch, whose visions are proven. The choosing ceremony infuses the banrigh's blood, marking it with magic, but I think it's the power to foresee which makes the blood special for fae, as it isn't a trait we share. I feared if I failed to do Illania's bidding, she would demand another - similar and proven - se'er witch as sacrifice to try and cure the vines and make her daughter queen."

Nemis clutched his hand. "So, to protect me, you were supposed to catch Darnley, then pretend to be a king?"

"Destroy the treaty, or my family, yes. But, when I voiced my concerns about breaking the Treaty, she laughed even louder. Claimed it was already broken, and that crowns were tumbling all over Europe and Naturae's realm." He pressed his lips together briefly. "Her confidence unnerved me. I knew the visions about Queen's dying. She knew of the prophecy too, so why wasn't she more concerned for her own safely? Being in such close proximity to so many people – there could only be one reason why Illania was not hiding away, heavily guarded."

Joshua said, "You knew before any of us - we were hunting the wrong killer."

Spenser clutched Nemis's fingers and drew in a shuddering breath. "Not the wrong killer, for McTavish certainly was her hand, but on her instruction. In the madness of her proposed plan, I realised her desperation and the lengths she was prepared to go to in order to achieve her goal. Her glee at ignoring the Treaty showed me: she was the one taking aim at the Queens, to upset the balance of power. The mistress behind the murders."

Uffer said, "McTavish even called her Mistress."

Drawing himself up and rolling his shoulders back, Spenser pinched the bridge of his nose. "I knew full well how she could exert her influence to make others do her bidding, and I had long understood her hatred for vampires. Henry, I supposed, always sensed there was something more to her visit, for all his attempts to keep order. And McTavish probably didn't realise he was just her weapon, a means to get what she wanted. A scapegoat, like Henry would have been, in time. I hadn't comprehended, until then, how far she had already gone to bring about another war. All those times she told me about the witch trials across Europe, the Spanish Inquisition. I should have realised the glee in her voice was more than her twisted sense of superiority."

He pushed his chair back and held his head in his hands. "I wanted to warn you all, and quickly. But, when I tried to leave, pretending I agreed to her demands, she suddenly held me in her thrall. Demanded I swear allegiance to her, as family. I did. I said I would do what she wanted, and tried to insist I was remaining loyal to those I loved, but she must have known I meant you, my truest family."

His voice broke and became hoarse. "As soon as she started to drain me, she would have known I was lying. Her vengeance at my betrayal was... brutal." He hung his head. "And I left you in danger. Let you down."

Aioffe jumped to her feet. "Of course you didn't!"

"Never!" Joshua insisted. "How could you have known?"

Spenser bit his lip, holding in his tears. "I should never have met her. Should have flown away when she proposed her ludicrous plan."

Nemis clasped his chest. "You protected your family, that's what matters. She didn't, in the end, know what or who I was, thanks to you keeping our lives separate all these years." She nuzzled her head into him. "I used to hate it, but now I understand why."

"She also died not knowing Joshua carries banrigh blood," Aioffe said. She glanced at her husband, then back at Spenser. "Does Caesaria know the proven cure for the vines?"

Spenser replied, "When Lana used the banrigh's blood, Caesaria was no more than a child, but it's possible Illania told her."

"She knew about a royal sacrifice," Aioffe said. "Henry did."

"We should go, now," Joshua said. "Perhaps my blood is the solution."

Aioffe walked around the table, to Hope. "Part of it, maybe." She laid her hands on her daughter's hair and kissed the top of her head. Her eyes met Joshua's and she said, "We should go."

Hope growled, "You are NOT leaving me alone again. You promised."

Aioffe looked stricken. "But you will be safer..."

"What could be safer than with you and Papa?" Hope stood, pulling her head away from her mother's hands. "Where you go, I go."

Joshua stepped closer. "It will be dangerous, potentially, but..." He reassured Aioffe with a touch to her shoulder. "Fae and faith are stronger when bound together. Pack your bag, Hope. We fly to Naturae," he said, then looked at Uffer. "If you and Lady Hanley want to come, we'll catch up to our fae and send some back to carry you."

The old fae's head hung. "I think, perhaps... I'll have to discuss it with Mary, when she returns with Mark." He lifted his eyes just enough to look sideways at Aioffe. A flush rose on his cheeks. "We're quite settled here, now, you know. We rub along nicely together, and you'll need to keep abreast of what's happening in England. With Henry, too. Perchance Thomas Fairfax will know where he went."

She smiled, pleased the pair had found companionship for their autumn years, and grateful of his offer to maintain the spy network from Beesworth.

Aioffe turned to Spenser and Nemis. "I cannot ask you to put yourselves, your family, in harm's way again. You're always welcome on Naturae. If you want, we'll send enough fae to bear you and Mark so the journey will be faster. Or, a kestrel message with what we find, if you prefer to travel by horse and ship."

Nemis shared a look with Spenser, then said, "A banrigh is chosen. I should go to Bothwell and explain what we have learned. Perhaps there is a way still to avert war, although he seemed to think the age of the witch was coming." She shook her head. "Fae, witch, vampire... if the Treaty doesn't stand, then...."

Spenser said, "I will stay with my family, but, I shall tell you what I know of Caesaria before you leave."

"Thank you," Aioffe said. She passed Hope Henry's crown and said, "Pack this somewhere safe." Her daughter nodded then disappeared to fetch the bags.

Aioffe stood and embraced Nemis. "This isn't goodbye, just... farewell for now."

"It's a promise," she replied. "And if Joshua's blood doesn't work, then a banrigh must be chosen."

Joshua said, "A crown which fell, resurrected." He looked straight at Nemis. "Be sure the witches choose wisely."

CHAPTER 63

RETURN TO NATURAE

"This mist tingles," Hope said. She stretched her arms wide and wriggled her fingers as they flew through the silver shimmer. Her face shone with glee, making her appear far younger than her teenage years. For a girl who had been forced to grow up too quickly, Hope's joy reminded Aioffe of her own wondrous childhood discoveries. She turned her face aside so her daughter wouldn't see her sadness. Hope's innocence was already coloured by the dangers and hardship of the world, and this homecoming was unlikely to stain it brighter.

"It tastes of summer yet feels like snow falling on hot skin," Hope giggled.

Aioffe forced a laugh, but her voice caught. "Yes, I suppose it does." Every time she approached Naturae, emotion shrouded her perception of the veil. Anticipation, a dread of what lay ahead, made her experience of the blanket cling to her skin like slimy mud coats rocks on a riverbank.

Flying next to her, Joshua stared ahead, his jaw clamped shut. Enduring rather than enjoying. Maybe he dared not breathe in the magic while his black wings beat in long strokes through the fog. His armour and bow glinted as the mist thinned and hazy sunlight filtered through.

Aioffe glanced back. Behind them, she saw specks, dark grey shadows as the first of Naturae and European fae entered the mist. The figures slowed, as if the cloud delayed them whilst it decided whether to permit them entry to Naturae's shores.

"Wait," Aioffe said. "Let them catch up." The trio hovered above the sea, watching as the fae fluttered in dribs and drabs towards them. Exhaustion paled their faces, many bobbed towards them unsteadily in the sky. During the long journey, the hardier Europeans had flown alongside the Naturae fae, brown and green stubby wings blurring together. The flight had been largely silent for they did not share a common tongue, and flying was such an effort with stubby wings.

It took several minutes for the majority of the army and workers to amass, during which time Aioffe snuck glances over her shoulder to the shoreline. Her heart hammered a steady beat in her chest, but her stomach knotted tighter now they were actually here. The dock, where many a time, she had welcomed and said goodbye to those friends who sailed here, lay silent and low. There was no sign of The Wanderer, no news from Fairfax. She thought of Spenser, Nemis and Mark - family now left behind in England. And Henry, where had he gone? An ally if not quite a friend, or was he an enemy?

Her hand wandered up to straighten the slim steel hairband around her head, which Uffer had presented her with when they said goodbye. He said she ought to have something to keep her hair from flying about in the wind, but she knew he meant it to be a crown. Without Henry's support, Thane's concept of co-ruling was impossible. She sighed, looking sideways across the sky to her husband. The burden was hers and Joshua's to bear, come what may. She cast her gaze across the treetops, past the hulk of stone, to the citadel in the distance and sighed. There was, at least, a certain simplicity, a familiarity in reigning over only fae, on fae land, but it was not too late to turn back. Find a quiet corner of the Highlands and hide. Indecision plagued her mind, and, as if he sensed it, Joshua flew closer.

"All is quiet at home, it would appear," he said, taking her hand. "Although, the castle could use some creepers to soften its edges. Onward?"

The thrum of wings behind them intensified in volume, swelling her heart with courage. "Onward, yes."

They descended on the outskirts of the dwelling trees surrounding the palace. Unspoken, the fae remained clumped together behind them and did not disperse to their homes. As one, the column walked towards the central clearing, listening intently for any sign of life. Once they reached the gather space at the base of the huge supporting trees, Aioffe and Joshua paused. Lining the edges, piled against trunks or haphazardly leaning against each other, were hundreds of Illania's vine barrels. They had been stripped of their bushy travel camouflage, exposing weedy, brown stalks. No cocoons hung from the branches, no leaves to nourish the plant, and the exposed roots were withered.

Aioffe's fingers twitched as if she had sufficient Blessings to impart upon them, yet her heart was heavy with sadness. These unhealthy vines were close to death. Was this the dreaded vinexplicity? If so, it had spread beyond Naturae's vines. She chewed her lip as she looked down the narrow path to the Pupaetory. How much worse was it there? Could Joshua's blood really cure such devastation? She didn't set much store in restoring Darnley to life, or was it that her stomach turned at the prospect?

Joshua set his jaw, his lips pinched together as he met Aioffe's silent stare. He waved his arm at the swarm of fae, who had begun to mutter among themselves at the sight of the vines. He said, "Present, before future."

She nodded, then gave the signal to fly up. First the Naturae fae, then, unevenly and hesitant, the Europeans took to the air. Their audible ripple of anger followed Joshua, Aioffe and Hope as they flew to the landing platform. But, like a stream of ants, they filed behind them as they walked through the Atrium doors.

Aioffe glanced at her daughter, whose eyes were wide with wonder, looking around the ancient structure. Sunlight streamed through the glass ceiling, illuminating the dust blown up by their entry. The grey ash lingered, dancing on the puffs of their breath in a macabre fashion, then drifted down. The fragments landed on once shiny chest plates, arm braces and helmets. Aioffe's heart sank. There had been no debris when she left Naturae, and no reason for armour to be lying around in the Atrium.

She passed the central trunk, glancing down empty corridors leading to the chambers. There seemed little point in going to the castle, not now she had seen the remains of Caesaria's guards in the old citadel.

She stood, hesitant outside the double doors to the High Hall. "Let me," Joshua said. "Hope, stay back." He glared at her until she nodded. Then, he withdrew his bow, pushed himself in front of Aioffe and leaned on the doors. Shielded by his back, his black wings blocked her view as he stepped forward. "Caesaria!" He shouted as he took aim.

Aioffe couldn't wait. She flew up, over his head and shot to the rafters. With her hands outstretched, she looked down.

From the throne at the far end, Caesaria stared dully at her. On the long table before her, Thane was stretched out. His arms and legs were bound, and a gag stuffed in his mouth. He did not move, but Aioffe heaved a sigh of relief that he was not dust. Without her gaze shifting, Caesaria's long, spindly finger curled a wisp of Thane's Lifeforce out, which she wafted towards her long nose and inhaled.

"Stop it," Aioffe cried. "You do not have to become your mother."

Hearing the sound of boots, Aioffe glanced back to the door. European fae streamed past Joshua, towards Caesaria. She lifted an eyebrow. "What was it Henry called it? Time to dance."

Caesaria's fae ran to a defensive position in front of the dais. Line upon line then turned to point their spears.... Towards the Naturae fae.

"Lower your weapons," Joshua ordered.

Aioffe said, "Caesaria, there is no reason for our people to be divided."

"Oh, I think there is every reason," she sneered and pointed at the Naturae fae, who were still pouring through the double doors. "Those fae kept me locked up. My fae," she gestured towards her own kind, "will show them the proper way to be respectful to a Queen."

Aioffe flew lower, to a hover in the gap between the armies. As she landed, she said, "Your mother died trying to cause division between creatures. Here, we are all fae. Now you are Queen, will you make the same mistake?"

Caesaria tipped her head back and exclaimed, "Ha! My mother was a fool, wasting too much time on politics when she should have taken the power." An evil smile crept up Caesaria's cheeks as her hands rose. "There is a perfectly usable base right here, all along."

Joshua's arrow hit one of her arms, slicing through the forearm and embedding its tip in her waist. Caesaria shrieked, her arm pinned. Aioffe caught the flash of black wings as he flew to the other side of the High Hall and released again. With a whoosh, another dart hit her other arm. She snarled, and tried to lift her hands again. But all Joshua had achieved was to slow her down.

Her hands twisted around, fingers waggling like a spider righting its spindly legs. The digits then curled to pull.

Aioffe gasped as the nearest group of European fae began to grey and wilt. "No!"

Before she could reach her with a dive, Caesaria's fingers straightened. Jagged spears of green energy tore from her fingertips, wildly jerking without aim or control. "You dare to deny me!"

Lightning bolts seared her skin as Aioffe collided with Caesaria. Momentum pushed them both to the floor. The pair rolled and wrestled as the green energy spikes continued to splutter from Caesaria's fingers. Aioffe screamed, caught in the crossfire, but there was no living plant matter nearby for her to pull from or to create restraints with. A smell of singed flesh rose above the throne.

Shouts to attack came from the back of the room just as Joshua landed on the dais. He tried to capture Caesaria's flailing wrists, but she kept wriggling, bolts sparking even as he held her elbows down. The air was suddenly filled with wings and blades, swirling and slashing, as the Naturae fae tried to reach their Queen as well. The Europeans defended Caesaria by flying up into the wall formation and linking arms to create a barrier down the middle of the High Hall.

Their barricade was solid, flexing to the sides of the Hall, but inflexible. By preventing the fae from reaching Aioffe and Joshua, the Europeans also limited their means to defend themselves with their swords, because their arms were entwined.

Worse, Caesaria had weakened those brave souls first to rush to her aid, a group who ended up in the centre of the mottled green and silver wall. Trained by Henry to notice such weakness in a defensive line, the Naturae soldiers coalesced their miniature arrow-fire on the wings of those she had half drained. Wings punctured and shredded, they tumbled from the air, leaving a hole big enough to push through.

On the dais, Joshua and Aioffe pinned Caesaria down, one on each side of her. The strength she had gained from draining her fae was immense. They both wrestled to subdue her. "Fae do not kill fae," Aioffe said, closing her hands over Caesaria's still firing fingers. Her own fingers blackened, absorbing the energy, and she bit her lip to stop from screaming.

"Our Queen!" A voice called behind her. She looked over her shoulder. Ten or so of her fae hovered in the air, puffing from the exertion of having pushed through the barrier. Hope was with them, her eyes wide and dart-ing around in confusion. Like children wanting to be lifted, the workers stretched out their arms towards her. They opened their hands in a gesture she so often used when performing a Blessing Ceremony. "Take. Take what you need!"

Aioffe's fingers twitched with yearning, and she glanced at Joshua. He blinked, then flapped his wings. Within a second, he had sprung his torso up; his left hand remained, holding Caesaria down. In perfect synchronisation, Aioffe jerked off and rolled, just as he replaced her by landing fully on Caesaria's chest. With a swift movement, he pinned her right hand down.

Aioffe reached up to catch the strands of freely given Lifeforce with her fingers. She heard Hope exclaim, "Mama! The lights, I see the pretty lights now!"

Warmth, loyalty and love from the ribbons flowed through her veins, boosting her heartbeat and reviving her flagging energy.

She twisted back around, and, glimpsing her own fingers - curled, blackened and scorched by vile negativity - was reminded of a spider. No, this was not the way, Aioffe thought, as her hands healed to their normal colour. She had to show Hope the right example. Lifeforce was for creation, not destruction.

As she exhaled, her fingers straightened, splayed then spat the Lifeforce back towards Caesaria as one huge, concentrated pulse. A beam of purest white shot from her fingertips, hitting the black-haired Queen's head with a web of energy. Caesaria screamed as if it burned, but the Lifeforce merely fizzled as it spread over her mouth, sticking like a mask over her contorted face.

Joshua jerked away, his wings pulling his chest up as the web expanded. The white strands grew, reaching down Caesaria's body and wrapping itself around her arms and legs like a cocoon.

When she was entirely encased, Aioffe's hands dropped. She slumped, gasping. She held little hope this cocoon would have the healing, transformational effects of others she had spun before. The effort to bind Caesaria, without the emotional imperative of love, had been greater and hastier than when she had cocooned Joshua, and lacking the love she had infused his bindings with. She ran her hands over the hardening case, thinking the prison had only been made possible because of the Lifeforce given by her own people. Gratitude overcame her, and she blinked back tears. That they still believed in her, after all this time away, humbled her.

She glanced up - fae were still fighting fae all over the High Hall.

Joshua's hand took hers as they stared at the two peoples. "I thought they were coming around," he said, sadly.

"It takes more than a flight together to overcome centuries of difference," she replied.

"Then we shall win them over, one at a time," Hope said. She set down beside her parents and beamed at them both. "Fae and faith are stronger when bound together. Isn't that what you said, Papa?"

"It is, my sweet, it is," he replied.

Aioffe smiled then darted to the window. Reaching outside with one arm, she pulled a creeper from its home around the nearest tree. Concentrating, she closed her eyes and bade it to grow. The vine slid in, creaking as it stretched and extended. Aioffe controlled it with her hand, snaking the binding, splitting it so the new growth crept around the airborne fae. She lassoed both Naturae and European in pairs, or clumps of a few. Then, as they realised they were bound too closely to fight each other, she gradually lowered them to the floor. Having all seen her do this with Joshua only the day before, they put up little resistance, knowing it could be met with tighter bonds if Aioffe so chose.

Once the armies were both landed and began examining their wounds, Aioffe addressed them. "Naturae can be home to you all, if you so wish it. The condition of living here, together as one faenation, is that you abide by our rules. Primarily, fae do not kill fae." Her hand gracefully swept over the inert cocoon on the floor. With sorrow and a little regret, she admitted, "Queen Caesaria still lives." She glared at the swarm. "But, she will never be released from these bonds on these shores. She will be returned to Europe and released. We will find her sister, Tamara, who no doubt has also come into her powers and taken her mother's realms. Perhaps then, she will learn how to co-exist, co-rule even with her sister. Never here though, she will never threaten anyone on these shores again. I - we - promise you all, to never treat you in such a cruel way. Fae do not kill fae is the rule of faeth which Illania, and Caesaria, chose to ignore when it suited them. They did not look for another way, as we have on Naturae. They took. We give. But, if there are those among you who wish to return with her to Tamara in the realm in Europe, you are free to do so, or you may stay here and become part of our family of fae. You chose to do what is right for you, for your future."

She gazed along rows of anxious faces.

A lone voice called out from the back, "There is no future without more fae."

They had all seen the barrels. They all knew the risk of staying in a barren tribe. Dissenters murmured between themselves, in all the languages the combined populous spoke and from every corner and trunk of the High Hall. They whispered of vines, of vinexplicitity, and of isolation, in voices tinged with fear.

Aioffe glanced at Joshua and took Hope's hand. "A war is coming," she said, in a firm voice which did not waver although her insides knotted. "Yet we know, fae-kind must be united if we are to prevent, or prevail. My mother knew of a cure for the vines, which we will try. And if it fails, we will try again. And again, until we find a solution. It is our destiny as fae to rise to any challenge. Together, we have restored our home and secured the future before." She pointed at a few of the females around the room - both soldier and worker from Naturae. "We call them The Alices, in remembrance that with sacrifice, belief, blessings and love, we can create wonder for ourselves."

She turned and approached the table. Thane remained stretched out, utterly still. She could hear his heart beating. The pallor of his skin, his wasted body, told her he had suffered, was depleted, but he could be saved. It would take time, but Spenser had and so would her Advisor and friend.

The crowd fell silent, silent enough to hear the sadness in her voice. "If Thane were here with us now, he would tell you co-operation and belief is the key to restoration. Until he recovers to tell you himself, all I ask is that you believe...."

She lifted her head, trying to meet as many eyes as possible as she swept her gaze over the Hall.

"I believe in you, Mama," Hope said.

Joshua stepped forward. "And I."

An Alice laid down her spear. "I believe."

Another, and another, stepped towards the dais. "I believe, Queen Aioffe."

She felt a flush rise to her cheeks as more and more of her Naturae fae joined the call. Still bound to their European counterparts, their movement dragged them as well. Some bent to allow the loose bonds to flex as one by one the fae approached.

Finally, Aioffe heard "Credo," called out. It seemed to spark something in the Europeans, because the chamber echoed with "Credo, credo."

Soon, the Latin's two syllables replaced the three of 'I believe', then became a rhythm, then a stomp. With a whip of her fingers, the ivy creepers fell to the ground, releasing the faenation. The High Hall's rafters were soon filled with fingers snapping, hands clapping as the unity spread.

"Credo, credo... I believe."

Joshua leant towards Aioffe and whispered, "I never stopped believing in you. Welcome home, my love," then he kissed her.

Hope rolled her eyes, but, wisely, said nothing. Henry's golden crown dangled from her fingers.

Historical Notes

When writing the Naturae series, I have a method. I look first to history and for certain times during which there were rapid changes in a very condensed time frame. Whilst researching this book, I came to realise that there was an unusually high number of significant, royal deaths during the period of 1558 - 1560, and then, with the return of Mary Queen of Scots, suspicious deaths which could only be viewed as murder. This led to my investigations and imagination catching fire, and Destiny Arising is the result.

Artistic license.

Writing historical fantasy is a tricky - especially when I twist the events of the time to suit story purposes, so please forgive my liberal use of artistic license and timescales in my interpretation of the facts. I try to bring to life the times and circumstance of history for my readers, but this is a work of fantasy fiction, so sometimes truth and fact are blurred by the 'what if's' of the fantastical. I love to know what's real in fiction and what isn't so, below, I have detailed a little of the actual history.

England underwent a dramatic transformation during the short, brutal reign of the Catholic Queen Mary I. She did her utmost to revoke the many legal measures her brother, Edward, had brought forward to spread the Protestant word. She died firmly believing her failure to produce a child was because she had not managed to rid England of enough heretics.

Although the time-scales are condensed in this fictionalised account, over the first decade of Elizabeth's rule, there were numerous challenges to her throne, and many attempts on her life. England and Scotland remained divided over the matter of religion. Belief in portends and that witches existed was widespread. The years of 1560-61 in particular, many calamities occurred, including the strange death of Elizabeth's (probable) lover's wife, the fire at St Paul's cathedral and plague. These events, although blamed on papists and magic, undoubtedly rocked her people's faith in Elizabeth's ability as a woman to rule, not to mention she was the child of the unpopular Anne Boleyn.

John Knox's 'First Blast of the Trumpet Against the Monstrous Regiment of Women' pamphlet of 1558 detailing why women should not rule, was a popular, if much debated, piece of vitriol dressed up as an academic paper. Knox later claimed Mary de Guise should have listened to him and that her death was divine judgement. Elizabeth, a protestant like him, was so disgusted, he was refused entry to England and all those who had assisted him with publishing the work also exiled.

A reality check: Death by natural causes or murder?

The death of Queen Mary I was almost certainly of natural causes. Modern day reflections upon her passing suggest that she had a cancer, probably of the womb. Her first 'pregnancy' was most likely a phantom one caused by her desperation to have an heir, and her second was most likely a tumour.

Queen Elizabeth I was subject to many attempts upon her life, all of them foiled successfully but increasing her paranoia about her safety. It is true that she did not, as expected, drink from the chalice during her coronation.

Speculation surrounds Amy Robsart's death however, despite the inquest ruling that she had fallen down the stairs. Her marriage to the Queen's favourite was probably a love match turned sour, quickly becoming distant. The Dudley's lived separate lives for much of their marriage, although Elizabeth may have had a hand in that. Her death posed a significant problem for Elizabeth because it forced the point that she had to marry for love (as Dudley brought no particular advantages to her rule) or for political reasons. She chose to remain single, in part, because she saw how her sister Mary had wrestled with the problem of a man being viewed as her senior after marrying Philip of Spain. It's probable she was also frightened by the very real risk of dying during childbirth.

For the sake of the storyline, I took liberties with the date of the deaths of Mary de Guise and Amy Robsart (Lord Dudley's wife) and brought them forward in time for dramatic effect. They did both die in 1560, only later in the year.

Obviously, Mary de Guise, ruling in her daughter's name, was not made into a vampire, as far as I know! She died after a short illness, the final prompt for Mary's return as a widow from France.

The accounts of David Rizzio's death, Mary Queen of Scotland's subsequent escape from Edinburgh, her severe illness (poison was rumoured) and Lord Darnley's sensational death are drawn from various sources, including contemporary accounts by Elizabeth's ambassador and others in Mary Queen of Scots's court. I have tried to remain true as true to the facts in these chapters - because sometimes fact really is as peculiar as fiction. The following events are reasonably well documented: Mary's severe emesis, blindness and coma while on Progress at Jedburgh, and the rubbing of her arms treatment given (probably not by Bothwell, but we don't know); the wedding Mary attended, after which she was supposed to spend the night with her husband but disappeared off with Bothwell instead; the explosion of the Old Provost's Lodgings and the discovery of Darnley and his valet's bodies in the orchard.

Who really killed Darnley and his page remains a mystery much debated through the centuries. Bothwell, already angling to marry Mary was later tried and acquitted for the crime. Certainly, there is a substantial amount of evidence he co-ordinated the explosion, or at least, was aware of it being planned. Why Darnley was not in the house at the time, the middle of the night, remains unsolved.

Pendle Witch Trials

The sequencing of the Assize where Nemis is tried was loosely based upon the account of a witch trial as written by the Lancaster Assizes clerk, Thomas Potts. Originally when I drafted this book, I intended the trial to be held at Lancaster, where the majority of the twelve Pendle Witches were tried around 1612, but for the sake of the story it seemed unnecessary to move the family there so I kept it in York. I have used the same judges names - Sir James Altham and Sir Edward Bromley - as tried Jennet Preston about whom Pott's wrote, although, at the time I have placed Nemis's trial they would have been far too young to have presided.

Being only 9 at the time of her arrest, 14 year old Jennet was tried at York, charged with the murder by witchcraft of a local landowner, Thomas Lister of Westby Hall. Having seen her grandmother bickering with her neighbours and proclaiming to use magic her whole life, is it any wonder she confessed? She was subsequently and unsurprisingly found guilty. The girl was hung at Knavesmire, York, a few days after the trial ended. Most English witches were hung, while on the continent of Europe and in Scotland they were burned at the stake.

The Pendle witches tale is a sorry one, where a family feud descended into hysteria as the two matriarchs tried out 'bad witch' each other in an attempt to prove who was the more powerful. There appears little regret for their actions in the confessions and statements, which leads me to believe it was a matter of pride that they would become famous for their actions. Some might say serial killers today exhibit the same quest for infamy.

As you might expect, modern beliefs would find the 'evidence' more than circumspect, and I am grateful we live in more enlightened times. In the course of writing this book, I have attempted to expose the hysteria and have Henry and Nemis debunk the ludicrous, hysterical beliefs of the time. Thomas Pott's record stands as testimony to what was a 'given' at the time. At no point was the actual existence of witches questioned. They existed, everyone knew it for a fact. What these women were tried for was the harm they did through the application of witchcraft. Many so-called witches, were in essence, tried for being peculiar, unfathomable women.

If you wish to read Thomas Potts's account of the trial called *The Wonderfull Discoverie of Witches in the Countie of Lancaster*, which has informed much of what we know about the trials, it is freely available in the public domain from https://www.gutenberg.org/ebooks/18253

Witch Pricking

Nemis's experience of being 'pricked' is based upon accounts of witch tests performed at the time, from the walking and fasting to the pricking, and even the tricks with retractable knives the examiner would use to condemn. Don't forget, they got paid to do the job well - more confirmed witches, the more likely they would get used again the next time. This eventually turned into a lucrative business opportunity in the early 17th century.

Married Catholic Priests?

The Reverend in York's Holy Infinity Church I have used the name and example set by William Gippes to highlight the lengths which the clergy were forced to go to in order to keep their jobs. The real Gippes was one of the many clergymen who were allowed to marry under Edward's rule, but in December 1553, after the 'old' religion was re-invoked, Mary I repealed the law by Royal Proclamation. To keep his job and support his family, Gippes divorced, did public penance and was the first to be reinstated, being instituted to the church at Salcott Virley on 15th July 1554. Over a quarter of parishes in England at the time suddenly had vacancies because of priests refusing to give up their wives.

Violence in Elizabethan Times

I'm aware that some readers may be concerned by the bear-baiting chapter, and I apologise for the gruesome nature of the so-called sport. I included it because it was necessary as a plot point and, without much doubt, one of the most popular Elizabethan pastimes. Those were the days before football became a national obsession, but baiting had a similar level of popular endorsement and financial investment (not to mention the gambling!). More popular than the theatre, Queen Elizabeth was such a fan, she ordered new, bigger bear and cock baiting rings built so even more of her subjects could enjoy the entertainment. With modern sensibilities, most people would view it as barbaric. Like slavery, habitual animal cruelty is a shame we would prefer to overlook in a sanitised view of our past.

DEAR READER

This book would not have been possible without the constant support of my husband, family and team of beta and advance readers. Thank you so much for diligently pointing out every plot hole, typo and inconsistency, and your constant suport of my work – especially Beba Andric, Clare Meadows, Natalie Horman and Avril Mason. You ladies ROCK!

I always wanted to write a murder mystery thriller, although until I did, I hadn't realised how tricky it was to account for people's movement. It's also such fun writing baddies, and, now you know 'whodunnit', why not check out **Blind Bill** – a Fable from Naturae novella which is his 'confession'. Download your copy at www.books2read.com/blindbill

If you would like to discover more about the places in the York chapters, I have written an article about them on my website https://escapeintoatale.com/short-stories-and-articles/

I hope you have enjoyed Destiny Arising and the build-up to a war between creaturekind – more adventures will follow in the next book!

A Polite Request:

I am an independently published author and as such, reviews are critical to successfully getting my stories seen by readers like you. It would mean the world to me if you could leave a review on your favourite bookish websites about this book so that others can find it!

If you have enjoyed this book, why not visit my website to find out more about the Naturae Book series?

www.escapeintoatale.com/naturaeseries

You can also subscribe to the Escape into a Tale newsletter to receive free short stories, articles, book recommendations and news about other books by Jan Foster. To subscribe, visit https://getbooks.escapeintoatale.com/subscribe

BLIND BILL

 There is a dead body under that oak tree. I propped him there as blood still seeped from his wounds. I killed my first man at the age of 20, but it took another 321 years for me to commit regicide. This prattling youth, a King in name only, is my fourth.

Soon, everyone will know my name: Blind Bill.

I see you, but I doubt you'll see me coming.

Delve into the terrifying mind of a medieval killer in this enthralling historical fantasy horror story, set in the Tudor world of Naturae. A quick escape into a chilling magical past, weaving horrifying history with fantasy in a thrilling fable of villainy and murder!

OTHER BOOKS BY THE AUTHOR

The Naturae Series by Jan Foster

Risking Destiny

Discover a villain's creation in this Viking Age tragic romance Prequel.

www.books2read.com/riskingdestiny

Destiny Awaiting

The enemies to lovers Prequel. Escape to Agincourt, wherein averting a war between their races and their countries, Aioffe and Tarl's battles of the heart are destined to fight with faith and hope itself.

www.books2read.com/destinyawaiting

Disrupting Destiny

Book 1 –Tudor reformation tears a country and fae lovers apart. Can a
secret destiny bring them together?
   www.books2read.com/disruptingdestiny

Anarchic Destiny

Book 2 – A forgotten heir, a queendom in crisis... chaos will reign as
Bloody Mary makes her move for power.
   www.books2read.com/anarchicdestiny

Destiny Arising

Book 3 – Five crowns will fall in a deadly prediction. Can Aioffe catch the
killer of queens before she's next to die?
   www.books2read.com/destinyarising

<u>Fables from Naturae</u>

Historical Fantasy short stories featuring characters you love from the
Naturae Series in pacy adventures in a magical past.
   Myth, Mist and Madness
   www.books2read.com/mythmistmadness
   Blind Bill
   www.books2read.com/blindbill
   A Rose in Midwinter
   www.books2read.com/arim
   As Above, So Below
   www.books2read.com/asabove

Rebels and Resistance Series by J.H. Foster

Gripping WW2 historical suspense novels – parallel stories to share

The Rebellious Maus and the Pogrom – A YA Prequel Novella to Sewing Resistance set in 1930's Germany

A young Hannah and Kat decide to ignore their guardian's advice and go shopping. Can they escape danger when a Pogrom leads to a riot and will Hannah risk everything to impress a handsome saviour?

BUY NOW www.books2read.com/rmatp

or **READ FOR FREE by subscribing to my mailing list with a historical focus – www.escapeintoatale.com/rebels**

Sewing Resistance – Seamstress. Spy. Survivor?

As Nazi forces tighten their grip on Paris, two women are drawn into the heart of the Resistance. Bound by friendship, a silent son, and driven by survival, they risk everything in a dangerous fight for freedom. *Sewing Resistance* is an unforgettable tale of love, loyalty, and courage under fire.

BUY NOW www.books2read.com/sewingresistance

Boy, Resisting – Silenced. Steadfast. Saviour?

A middle-grade, illustrated novel **co-authored with James Warwood**

Silence was supposed to keep me — and my secrets — safe. So I accidentally became a spy...

BUY NOW www.books2read.com/boyresisting

Find out more about works authored by Jan Foster/J.H. Foster at **www.escapeintoatale.com/books**

Join the Escape Into A Tale Newsletter and receive a free gift of a book and much more!

www.escapeintoatale.com/subscribe

www.ingramcontent.com/pod-product-compliance
Lightning Source LLC
Chambersburg PA
CBHW061609210726
48287CB00001B/62